I0598134

NIGHT
MOVES

Also by DJ Steele

DECLARED DEAD

Dead Ringer (eBook short)

NIGHT
MOVES

A Novel

DJ Steele

SWITCHBACK
PRESS

NIGHT MOVES. Copyright ©2021 by DJ Steele. All rights reserved. No part of this book may be used or reproduced in any manner whatsoever without written permission of the publisher/copyright owner except in the case of brief quotations embodied in critical articles and reviews. For information, please contact Switchback Press, info@switchbackpress.com.

NIGHT MOVES is a work of fiction. Names, characters, places, and incidents are products of the author's imagination or are used fictitiously. Any resemblance to actual events, locales, or persons, living or dead, is coincidental.

Edited by Chuck Barrett
Cover by Chuck Barrett

FIRST EDITION

ISBN: 978-0-9985193-6-4 (Print)
ISBN: 978-0-9985193-7-1 (Digital eBook)
Library of Congress Control Number: 2020949054

Steele, DJ.
          NIGHT MOVES / DJ Steele
          FICTION: Thriller/Suspense/Mystery

Published by Switchback Press
www.switchbackpress.com

For Kates

NIGHT MOVES

"Workin' on mysteries without any clues,
workin' on our night moves."

—Bob Seger and The Silver Bullet Band

CHAPTER 1

Washington, D.C.

There are no undoes in life.

That bit of wisdom cost her 150 dollars.

This waiting game allowed her too much time to contemplate what had compelled her to take over a business she knew nothing about—from a man she hardly knew. Her thoughts told her it was guilt.

But why should she feel guilty? She didn't pull the trigger.

Julia Bagal fought hard to convince herself that she was not responsible for Fly's death, but that stain of guilt was still there. No, she didn't pull the trigger. However, in her mind, she should have reacted faster. She should have seen it coming.

Her mistake.

She took in a deep breath and slowly let it escape through her nose. The knot in her stomach tightened. She sucked in another breath with too much force causing her to cough.

"You okay?" asked the woman passenger.

She nodded, fist covering her mouth until the cough subsided. She took a swig of water from her Hydro Flask. The cool liquid soothed her throat. After a few more sips she returned the flask to the cupholder in the console.

The two women were sitting in her RAV4 parked across the street from a cheap run-down two-story strip motel where all the doors faced the parking lot. Weeds muscled through cracks in the aging concrete lot. The seedy motel didn't look like a place where people *slept* when they paid for a room. A forgotten section of town where abandoned buildings fronted both sides of the street. Several buildings covered with faded graffiti and profanities. Kids called it street art, she viewed it as vandalism.

Within an hour, the fall morning sun was hidden behind dark clouds. Julia checked and rechecked the address. She scanned the riffraff walking the streets. This was a good place to get mugged, she thought. Her hand pressed the car's lock button, again for the third time.

"How much longer we gonna sit here waitin' for 'em to leave?" quipped Laquita in her distinctive southern drawl.

Hiring the woman in the passenger's seat was probably a mistake. Before the ink was dry on the contract to purchase the former owner's business, Laquita showed up inquiring about a job. She claimed she had worked for Fly, even though Julia never found any records to prove it. The woman asserted that Fly paid her under the table to keep things simple. Julia was wary their personalities might clash. Laquita reminded her of an annoying coworker from her last job. She was hesitant but didn't challenge Laquita's assertion that she had investigative experience. If anything the woman told her had even a hint of truth, she could use her help. She decided to give her a week to see if Laquita was a good fit for her new business.

Julia was working on getting her license to be a private detective. Her Master's in accounting did nothing to prepare her for this daunting career change. Online classes for criminal law took time. She needed to eat. She considered this case just like her first case, on-the-job training. And more often than not, trial and error.

Her first case was to follow a recycling truck. The client,

an elderly woman, was convinced the truck hauled the recycle cargo to the local landfill and not to a recycle plant. After following the *Think Green* recycle truck all day, Julia was certain she had spent more on gas than the fifty dollars the old woman paid her. That was three weeks ago.

Julia shot Laquita a hard stare. Annoyed, Julia said, "I thought you knew how this worked. You have done stake outs before, right?"

The dark-skinned woman appeared amused. "Lotsa times And hookers are on the clock."

"I saw her when she opened the door. She didn't look like a hooker."

"Uh-huh." Laquita slurped her fountain drink. "And how we know that's her husband up there? That wife never gave ya no picture of him. Kinda strange not to have a picture of your man, don't ya think? All ya got was her husband would be meetin' some woman at this dumpy motel."

She ignored Laquita, raised the high-end camera she acquired as part of the transaction when she took over the business. The camera had more functions than she could wrap her head around, but the zoom on the lens made it appear like she was standing next to the motel door.

She wasn't an idiot. When she asked the client during their meeting for a photograph of her husband, the woman got emotional.

"I found a text she sent him," the wife's voice broke. She dabbed her eyes with a tissue. Her head hung low. "I don't mean to cry. It's just that I don't deserve this. Please, just get photos of my husband entering and leaving the room with her."

It was the substantial amount of money the wife placed on

her desk that stopped Julia from pushing for more information. She knew the location and time, after all. What else did she need?

"I did tell you she paid me a big deposit and I really need the money."

"I reckon you right 'bout needin' the money, 'specially after you followed that damn recycle truck all over town for fifty bucks. We ain't exactly solvent right now."

Another mistake was sharing with Laquita how much the old woman had paid her. She was frustrated. She vented. Laquita laughed so hard she fell out of her chair. In her embarrassment, Julia almost fired her that day.

"I got 'bout ten mo minutes and then I'm gonna pee in my pants." Laquita squirmed in her seat.

Julia lowered the camera to her lap. "Why'd you buy that giant Coke when you knew we were gonna be sitting in the car for God knows how long? You're the one who was supposed to have experience with this sort of surveillance."

"Wow. You got a burr up your ass or somethin'?"

Julia chided, "I assumed we'd be waiting awhile. That's why I don't keep drinking water. You, on the other hand, act like these assignments only take a few minutes. What's the longest time you've waited to get the information you needed?"

"Alrighty, Miss College Degree." Laquita put her drink in the console holder and faced her. "I don't git why we gotta stay here. We got photos of 'em. You got photos of the husband when he got outta his car and photos of that woman when she opened the door and let him in."

"The client instructed me to get photos of them leaving together. Maybe catch them kissing good-bye or giving each other a hug. I told you why I needed to hire you, you were the one who claimed to have previous experience. At least that's what you told me."

She had a feeling Laquita was not going to work out. She should have found out what she meant when she told her she was paid under the table. Desperation makes people do stupid things and Julia felt pretty stupid right now.

"What did that wife who hired you look like?" Laquita squirmed again in her seat.

"What?"

"That wife. Was she fat? Ugly? Old?"

A visual image of the client flashed in Julia's mind. "Maybe around my age. Late twenties. An attractive woman."

"How was she dressed? Uptown? Like 'em Amish people? Or on her last dime?"

Julia didn't think how the wife was dressed had any significance. The young woman's outfit was a tailored navy-blue blazer with a matching skirt. Low heels. Professional business attire. A client who could afford to pay.

"You know Laquita, maybe it'd be better if we just don't talk right now. Besides, I need to be ready to snap photos of them together when they come out if I want to get paid. And if I don't get paid, I can't pay you."

She hoped that would shut Laquita up. Her mind was made up, this would be their last assignment together. Right now, she wanted that ass-hole cheater to come out with the woman so she could wrap up this job and end the misery of being trapped in her car with Laquita. Her stomach growled.

Julia raised the camera and pointed it toward the door the husband had entered. She focused the lens on the large window. The curtain was pulled tight. She scanned the other rooms. Fifty-five minutes did seem like a long time for him to be in the room with this woman.

But, what did she know about two people in a mad passionate relationship? Her love life at this point in time lacked the unbridled sexual passion she could only dream about. There was one man she met who made her heart race whenever she was near him, but the timing and conflicts from both their lives interfered.

Practical Julia.

She hated practical Julia.

The camera caused a cramp in her back. She started to lower it to her lap. Then stopped. A movement caught her eye. It was the room next door.

A tall woman had moved the curtain back just enough to see outside. Julia focused the lens. The woman gave a furtive glance at the parking lot. Julia was guessing the woman heard something and was searching for the source.

Laquita kept crossing and uncrossing her legs.

"I'm gonna find a place to pee before I wet myself." Laquita was now holding her crotch.

"No," protested Julia. "What if they come out of the room and see you?"

"See what? A Black woman in this part of town?" Laquita burst out laughing. "You fer real? A white woman sittin' in a parked car with a camera glued to her face is what sticks out like a neon freaking sign."

Laquita pulled the handle and pushed the car door with her shoulder.

"Stop," Julia demanded, grabbing Laquita's arm with a shake. "It's him."

Laquita quickly closed the car door.

The husband stepped out and slowly closed the motel

door. Facing the door, he paused a moment, then turned and looked in their direction.

Julia and Laquita both held their breath and slid down in their seats. Julia had parked across the street where she had an unobstructed view of the motel room. Good choice for long distance photos, bad choice to avoid being spotted. Even though he had sunglasses on, she knew he was staring at her. She could feel it.

"Shit," mumbled Julia, "I think he might have seen us."

"You think we been made?" Laquita kept her head lowered.

"I don't know for sure."

"He's now moving toward the stairs. Maybe we got lucky."

Laquita had slipped so far down in her seat, she was almost under the dashboard. Julia was amazed the tall Black woman could bend her legs like a pretzel.

"What should I do? What the hell do you do when a subject spots you?" Julia needed advice. *Speak Laquita.*

The silence in the car lasted a mere second, but Julia panicked. "Dammit, what should I do?"

"Crank the car and ease away," Laquita lowered her voice. "Act like ya don't know he spotted us."

"That's your best advice?"

"You got a better idea?"

The husband zipped his leather jacket, shoved his hands in his pockets. The ball cap brim pulled so low the sunglasses weren't necessary. He continued down the walkway toward the stairs. Funny. She didn't remember the limp when he arrived and walked upstairs to the motel room.

In her peripheral, Julia studied the motel door as she eased the car away from the curb. No sign of the woman.

Things weren't working out with her new business venture.

Her mind sorted through what she had to do. Convince the client she had enough proof her husband was cheating and collect the rest of her fee.

That wasn't the biggest issue on her mind.

She knew now, she had to fire Laquita.

CHAPTER 2

The vibration on her nightstand buzzed in her ears. Julia fumbled for the phone and pulled it in front of her, screen displaying the incoming call from an unknown number. She moaned. Exhausted from a restless night, her eyelids sagged. Squinting, she read the time on her phone, 7:15 a.m.

During the night, she'd had another one of her recurring nightmares. Always the same. She was a small child. Running. Flames leaping toward the sky. When she tried to yell, her voice was gone.

Luckily, the nightmares that invaded her dreams weren't that frequent anymore.

Her phone vibrated again on her wooden nightstand. This time she didn't bother to see who was calling. She held down the power button and turned it off.

They could talk later, after she got to work.

She sat on the edge of the bed and stretched her arms upward until she let out a loud yawn. She stood and started shuffling to the kitchen when she remembered her gun. Her sleeplessness was making her careless. Earlier when she woke from the nightmare, she slipped her gun under the pillow next to her in bed.

She retrieved the gun and put it back in the nightstand drawer.

What she needed was caffeine to reboot her foggy brain. Yesterday had been a long trying day and her nightmare last night had interrupted her sleep.

She made a cup of coffee and sat at the kitchen table while she drained the hot liquid from her mug. She fought the urge to crawl back in bed. The problem with being self-employed, you don't work, you don't get paid. She rubbed her eyes and yawned again.

One cup of coffee wasn't going to cut it. She decided to get dressed and stop by *The Brew House* on the way to the office. Their coffee was much better than what she made at home.

It was important to be alert today and not find another excuse to do what she knew was inevitable.

Yesterday she had planned to tell Laquita she wouldn't be able to keep her employed when they got back to the office. But every time she thought about it, she chickened out. Knowing she should fire her was one thing. Breaking the news face-to-face was another. She decided one more day wouldn't hurt.

She and Laquita were shaken by what had happened at the motel during the stakeout. Laquita had been right. It was a mistake not to get a photo of the cheating husband when the wife hired her. The simple contract she had the wife sign was a boilerplate the previous owner had used. Nothing more than something he found on the Internet.

The client's name was Kat Lejeune. Kat told Julia not to call her, she would call Julia when her husband wasn't around. While Julia was packing up to leave the office at six last night, her phone rang.

Kat was not happy to learn there were no photos of her husband leaving with the woman. Julia slumped in her chair, certain the wife would want her to continue surveillance on the husband.

A pause.

Then Kat asked for the photos she had taken and agreed

to pay the remainder of the fee. She informed Kat that she needed the money first before she released the photos. She wasn't going to be duped out of her fee. They agreed to meet today in her office at five. She'd have the photos printed by the time they met.

The morning without interruptions at the office was a welcome relief. Julia was able to get a lot of work done. How the deceased owner managed to keep the business afloat baffled her. She asked the bakery owner below her office if she'd known the previous owner of the investigative business she had bought.

The woman appeared confused by the name Fly. It took a moment before she said she knew him by Mr. Nightingale. According to her he was a nice man who kept to himself. The only other thing she added was that he traveled a lot.

Julia had only known him for two weeks before he died. Fly's real name was Brailsford Troup Nightingale Jr. He had worked with her grandmother when they were with the Central Intelligence Agency. Her grandmother, Elke, was a field officer and Fly worked in the CIA's analytic arm of the agency. Both long since retired. If spooks really did retire.

He was nicknamed Fly because he could find out things without people realizing he was listening—like a fly on the wall. Julia was with Fly at the D.C. park helping Elke uncover a Russian mole when things went awry. That was the day Fly was gunned down. The Russian wielded a gun. Julia had a shot but hesitated. Fly died. Julia promised herself never to hesitate again when she had a clean shot.

After going through Fly's business files, she discovered that organization wasn't his strong suit. There was no rhyme or reason to his filing system. He offered services ranging from marital infidelity, tracing missing persons, to criminal cases.

She spent most of the morning color coding folders according to type of service and alphabetizing them. Next she tried to create a website to help advertise her new business.

Shifting in the faux leather chair, she felt an odd sense of comfort sitting behind the desk in what used to be Fly's office. It was Julia's company now. She was a business owner. And the office had potential. The best part were the aromas radiating up from the bakery located directly below.

The walls of the office were painted a drab olive and lined with bookshelves full of legal books, photography books and an assortment of travel books. A shelf with old cameras from different eras decorated the top shelf. On the side wall near the door was a dented metal three-drawer file cabinet.

When she cleaned out the office, the cameras and books stayed. Seemed appropriate for a detective agency. Fly had very few personal items. A precaution he no doubt learned from his CIA days. There was no sign on the door or website to advertise the business. She wasn't sure how Fly got his clients. Maybe by word of mouth, but they damn sure weren't beating her door down.

Julia didn't realize how late Laquita was for work until her stomach reminded her. The mounting headache and irritability let her know she needed to eat. Low blood sugar—her curse. She opened her lower desk drawer and scanned the assortment of snacks. Trail mix, granola bars, almonds and something yucky which had turned into a science experiment that she subsequently tossed in the garbage can. She saw nothing she wanted right now. In the small fridge in the corner of the office, she found leftovers from the other night. Food would improve her mood.

She had only taken a few bites of the leftover pasta dish when the door to the office swung open. It bounced against the file cabinet as Laquita stormed in. "Holy shit Julia. Why didn' you answer my calls this mornin'?"

"You're the one who called me at 7:15? It showed as an unknown number. I have your phone number listed. How come it didn't show up?"

"I lost my phone and had to get a new one." Laquita paused a moment, then added, "My friend, Max heard there'd been a double murder at the motel we staked out yesterday. I like to had a heart attack."

Julia had planned to say, "You're fired, things are not working out," yet her curiosity kicked in. "A double murder isn't that uncommon in D.C., Laquita. And that motel is in a part of town that's a breeding ground for crime. Besides, why would you need to call me so early this morning?" Julia's eyes bored into Laquita demanding an explanation.

"Ya know, I thought 'bout quittin' when Max told me, but…" Laquita shook her head. "I knew you done gone and bit off mor'n you could chew. Fly woulda wanted me to help ya out."

Julia arched back in her chair and countered, "Excuse me. You help me?" Julia crossed her arms and gave Laquita a withering look. "I might have taken on more than I realized at first with this business, but I *will* figure it out."

Now was the time to tell the woman in front of her she was terminated.

She started to speak but wasn't fast enough.

"That husband and woman are dead," Laquita spouted.

"Wait." It took her a second to process what she heard.

"What?"

"We're screwed."

The muscles in her back contracted. Julia sat rigid as her brain tried to analyze the situation. This didn't make sense.

"We saw him enter the hotel room. We saw him leave." Saying out loud what had happened seemed to be the best way to understand what Laquita told her.

"Where did this double homicide happen? Maybe, your friend is confused about what he heard. We know what we saw."

"When he told me it was at that motel where we were doing our surveillance, I asked Max if he knew the room number and that's when I 'bout shit myself."

"Why would your friend Max think you'd be interested in this crime?" Julia's voice became staccato.

Laquita began twirling strands of hair with her fingers with one hand and let the other hand rest on her hip. "Said he saw us parked on the street yesterday. That's his territory."

"His territory?"

"Omigod girl. Whatya been doin' all your life? Didn't your parents never let ya outside?"

"My parents died in a car accident when I was very young. And I did not lead a sheltered life." If only Laquita knew, how unsheltered her life had been. Her grandmother who raised her traveled a lot with her job. Julia never knew where that woman was most of the time. It was not a *Leave It to Beaver* kind of life.

Laquita began to chew on her bottom lip. "Let's just say my friend ain't exactly an upstandin' citizen, if ya know what I mean."

Julia let the things Laquita said roll around in her head. *Is she making this up? What's her angle?*

She picked up her cell phone from her desk.

Before her thumbs could begin to type, Laquita dropped her hands on the desk and leaned toward her. "What? Ya don't believe me?" she snapped. "I could'a just lit outta town when I heard 'bout them murders. I'm probably a damn fool." Laquita straightened. She added in a calm voice, "I already checked the internet. Ain't nothin' on it."

Julia stared a beat at the screen on her phone and then put it in her purse.

"Okay, Laquita. For argument sake, let's just say your criminal friend is right. I don't think he is, but like I said, that is a high crime area." Julia swiveled the chair staring out the window behind her. With her back to Laquita she continued, "We have to make sure what this guy told you is correct."

Julia stood, grabbed a sweater hanging on the back of her chair and faced Laquita. "We need to go see for ourselves. We've got plenty of time before I meet with Kat Lejeune to collect the rest of the payment."

"We can't go back there," Laquita protested. "Cops will be swarmin' all over that place."

"We'll just drive by and if that is indeed a crime scene, then the area will be taped off." Julia headed out the office door and started down the hall. She stopped, threw a quick glance over her shoulder. "You coming or not?"

Laquita placed both hands on her curvy hips.

"You one crazy white girl. Ya know that?"

Laquita ran to catch up to her.

CHAPTER 3

The heavy clunk of boots on the hardwood floor startled the elderly man who was dozing in the chair by the window. He grabbed his walking cane and pointed it toward the man in the cowboy boots.

"Don't you knock anymore?" the old man bellowed.

"I did."

"Damn good thing, cause people should knock before they scare the bejesus out of an ol' man."

"Might be a good idea to lock your door."

"Might be a good idea to mind your own damn business."

"Yep." The man smiled. "Good to see you Dad."

Mike Shockley was never sure what mood his father might be in when he visited. The old man had good days and bad days. Lately, it seemed mostly bad. His health had deteriorated in the past five years.

"Have you eaten today, Dad?"

The old man snapped, "I eat every day."

Bad day.

This visit wasn't going to be easy. Shockley checked the kitchen. No visible mess. Meaning the old man had not eaten.

"I'm hungry." Shockley tried to sound convincing even though he had eaten a cold piece of leftover pizza before he left his townhouse. "How 'bout we go grab a bite at Kozmo's down the street?"

"Hell no. Last time you took me there, they put pickles on my sandwich."

Shockley remembered. He tried to remove the pickles from his dad's sandwich, but that just made things worse. His dad came from the *no excuses* generation. You tell somebody something then it sure as hell better get done the way you told them. Or just don't do it at all. That was why his dad didn't want to pull off the damn pickles from his sandwich. He told the waiter no pickles and that was that. Take back the sandwich and do it right. Something so trivial as pickles could set the man off.

"I'll make sure there're no pickles on your sandwich."

His father grumbled some incoherent sounds as he pushed his 6'2" frame up from the chair with the help of his cane. The old man had lost a lot of his bulk, but still had strong forearms. Walking was slow. He had been shot in the leg during his service in Vietnam and then had a knee replacement a year ago. Age was catching up with his father.

He remembered his father's decline had already started when his mother died five years ago. Or maybe that's when the old man just gave up trying. After the funeral, the stalwart man refused to leave the grave of his mother. Shockley went back to the grave site that evening and found his father crumpled over the fresh mound of dirt sobbing like a child. That sight impacted him. He had never seen his old man cry. Another generational thing. Men don't cry. Just women and pussies. When he tried to pull his father up, the howls of misery worsened. The grief from that loss had devastated this strong man. Shockley went back to his car and waited. He leaned his back against the car. He could hear his mother's dying words, "Take care of your dad." She knew.

The house was his mother's idea. She wanted to downsize from the Texas ranch he grew up on. Besides, her elderly mother lived in the D.C. suburbs and she longed to be near her mom. And near him.

There were plenty of fights about moving. In the end, his mother won. When she found this home, it was love at first sight. The historic home was in need of updating. He spent weekends, when he had them off, knocking down walls and helping rebuild new ones.

His mother loved having family around. She always used her southern cooking to bribe him to visit. Now the home was as cold as the inside of a medieval castle. After the funeral, he waited to give his father time to grieve. Then two months later, he made the mistake of trying to pack away some of his mother's personal items—clothes, toiletries, and the knitted afghan she would wrap around her frail dying body to keep warm. His father got upset and ordered him to leave.

It was too soon.

Five years later, it still seemed too soon. His father refused to move on. The old man longed to join her in what he called Heaven. His father and he might look alike, but they did not have the same beliefs. Shockley was a light switch kind of guy. Life was the *on* switch. Death was the *off*. End of story. As much as he wanted to believe when his aunt told him God needed another angel, meaning his mother, he couldn't buy into it. His mother suffered too much.

Kozmo's Cafe was jammed with office workers and commuters. At this time of day, the atmosphere was utter chaos. It took more time for his father to put on his shoes and walk to Shockley's car parked in front of the garage door than the drive to Kozmo's. At least that was the way he felt.

"Seat yourself," a short girl with bright blue hair at the

register instructed.

They found a table in the corner of the plain cafe. The tables and chairs probably came from Ikea. Nothing fancy. Just fast service and food.

Within a few minutes, a gangly young man dressed in jeans and a tucked in t-shirt took their order. Shockley wanted to make sure the waiter knew the importance of not putting pickles on his father's sandwich. He grabbed the waiter's arm before he could dart off.

"What does this man *not* want on his sandwich?" Shockley kept a firm grip on the man's arm while he answered.

"No pickles, I got it. He told me like 3 times," replied the high school looking waiter.

"Actually, he told you 5 times, so no pickles, got it?" Shockley grinned and arched his eyebrows.

The waiter gave a sharp nod, pivoted on his heels and walked as quickly as he could back to the kitchen.

His father let out a chuckle. "You should have shown him your gun, sonny."

"Next time, Dad."

Across the small table, Shockley noticed his father still showed no signs of losing his thick mop of silver hair. People always told him he favored his father. He did have his father's hair only his was more dark-brown than gray. Lately though, he noticed graying at the temples and in his usual five o'clock shadow.

His father interrupted his reflective thoughts, "You need to shave."

Shockley's long fingers stroked his stubble. "Women like it."

"So, you got yourself a girlfriend?"

"No, I don't." Shockley knew where this was going.

"Then I suspect it ain't working. A real woman likes a man with a smooth face."

Real woman. His father was referring to his late mother. She always hated facial hair.

Still rubbing his stubble, he nodded. "Maybe so."

"It's time for you to find a nice girl, like your mom. You're gettin' on up there. I was married and had two kids by the time I was your age."

"You might be right, Dad. I'm thirty-five and over-the-hill," he said sarcastically.

"Yeah, and still a smart-ass."

His father was right about that. He was a smart-ass. The teacher had taught him well.

Growing up on a ranch in Texas, his father made sure his only son could handle anything thrown at him. Taught him to ride a horse almost before he could walk. Chores started when the rooster crowed. No excuses. He helped brand, feed and move cattle from pasture to pasture, fix fences, haul manure, bale hay and everything else that goes with ranching. Coyotes on a cattle ranch were a ruthless adversary. They were creatures of instinct and opportunity making them an incessant problem for ranchers. At ten years old, he hunted coyotes with a lightweight bolt action Ruger. His accuracy impressed his father. And the man was not one to hand out praise without merit.

Not an easy life by any stretch.

They didn't own a TV. No cell phones and the car was used only for emergencies or church. His father had done three tours in Vietnam. To help heal from the trauma of the Vietnam war, the old man lived his life in the past. His mother once told him his father was never quite the same when he returned from the war. Shockley only knew the *after Vietnam* man.

As a teenager he asked his father what it was like in Vietnam. The question was never answered. The guerrilla war was not won. The world had changed by the time his father came home. There was massive unemployment, a half-assed GI Bill and communities that did not seem to care about veterans.

"Heard from your sister?" his father asked.

"No. She's busy with the twins."

"Don't take much time to peck out hello on that damn phone," the old man hissed.

Shockley did not want to go down this road. Again. Trying to have a civil conversation with the old man was like trying to stand in a tornado and not get blown away.

"I've been thinking, Dad," Shockley's voice steady.

"You think too much," his father interrupted.

He pretended not to hear and continued, "I could move in with you. Help you out for a while."

"Once you jump off a bridge, son, you can't change your mind."

He knew his father was still bitter that at seventeen Shockley could not get far enough away from the ranch despite the old man's pleas to stay.

Shockley folded his arms tightly across his chest. He finally broke the edgy silence, "Mom hated the ranch. She was going to leave you if you didn't sell. Me leaving didn't make you move."

More edgy silence.

The high school looking waiter brought lunch to their table. In a boastful tone he said, "No pickles on your sandwich, sir."

"Good," snapped his old man. "Now my son won't have to

shoot you."

The waiter's eyes froze open for a second while he tried to understand what he just heard.

"He's joking." Shockley grinned. "I'm a cop."

The waiter headed back to the kitchen mumbling, "Not funny, man. Not funny."

"Dad, you could get us in trouble. You need to be careful what you say."

Shockley felt the vibration inside the pocket of his jacket. He slipped his hand inside, retrieved his phone, and placed it against his ear. "Shockley."

"Detective," the dispatcher said. "Got a signal 7 for you. Ready to copy?"

Shockley grabbed a pad and pen from his jacket and took notes. After the call ended, he started to say something to his dad.

His dad spoke first, "I know the drill, Mike. We need to leave."

CHAPTER 4

Shockley enjoyed watching his father's mood change when he activated the lights and siren on his unmarked car. The old man relished a little excitement even if it was just speeding down the road to take him home.

In his father's driveway, Shockley slammed the car in park and started to jump out to help his dad to the front door.

A rough hand gripped Shockley's arm. "You go do what you gotta do, son. I can manage." The old man opened the car door, used his cane to steady himself and stepped out. He looked back at Shockley making sure he had his attention. "Be careful, son. You hear me? This world just ain't no good anymore." His father had a worried look on his face.

Driving toward the crime scene, he pondered his father's words, *This world just ain't no good anymore.* In his line of work, there were days he would agree with what the old man said. One crime came to mind. A husband had beaten his wife unconscious and then poured drain cleaner down her throat. The husband's body was found lying in a pool of blood on the floor in the kitchen. He had put a bullet in his own head. The wife survived. She was only 19 years old. He clinched his jaw tightly. Yep, that night he felt the world was just no good.

He was glad he got a coffee to go. This could be a long day. Double homicide at the Willow Oaks Motel. Probably gang related. That part of town was known for drugs and prostitution.

He slowed his approach to the motel and observed the

crime scene perimeter had been cordoned off. The street patrol officer was doing a good job holding back the onlookers on the sidewalk opposite the motel.

"Shit," he hissed when he saw the white van. How she got here before any other news team was a mystery. Susan Porter was a crime journalist for the local news. He was sure she was part hound dog. Porter could sniff out a story before it was a story.

One of the patrol officers had his hands up blocking her and her cameraman from getting closer. Porter was good at her job, but she could be a cop's worst nightmare. The department had a hell of a good media relations officer to fend questions, but she wasn't here yet. Porter's problem was she was not a patient woman. Even at five feet, her penetrating steel blue eyes could send shivers down a cop's spine. Oh hell, she could send shivers down any man's spine. She usually disagreed with the boundaries of the crime scene.

He noticed her tight green dress emphasized her curves. She had her platinum hair pulled back in a high ponytail. And to give her two more inches in height, heels. He was amazed by her ability to navigate a crime scene in heels.

She had turned her attention from the officer to a small group of people on the sidewalk. Smart. She was hoping someone saw something. He hoped the First Officer had already rounded up potential witnesses and isolated them from the onlookers. Witnesses were hard to find in this part of town. Prostitutes, drug addicts and others with questionable credibility didn't want to step forward to help with a criminal investigation.

Maybe they'd get lucky today.

Shockley parked his department issued low-end import

behind a squad car, turned off the ignition and sat for a minute. A habit he acquired after being shot at when he went to investigate a domestic disturbance. Back then he was a rookie beat cop. Lucky for him, the husband was drunk when he fired. Back at the station, he learned the husband had been a sniper in the Army. After that near miss, he approached every crime scene like it was an ambush, even if he was not the first to arrive.

Shockley carefully surveyed the motel upstairs and down, the parking lot and the small crowd which had grown to eight. He took a slow draw from his coffee mug. A mobile crime lab emblazoned with Crime Investigation Division was parked near the outside staircase.

Standing in a huddle near the crime lab van was Terrance Bone, Amber Bull and a stocky man he didn't know. Bone was a patrol officer with over 27 years' experience under his belt. He was good at his job and knew how to keep the primary crime scene intact. Bull lived up to her last name, meaning she would not put up with *bull* from anybody. She was a seasoned crime scene investigator. Her short gray hair and narrow eyes emphasized her serious face. All business. What she lacked in personality, she more than made up for in processing a homicide scene. Bull had unshakable self-confidence and was the best in her line of work. Shockley had a great deal of respect for the middle-aged woman. She was a by-the-book CSI gal. Typically, when things went wrong with an investigation, it started at the crime scene. Bull made sure that didn't happen.

He took another swig of coffee, grabbed his jacket lying on the back seat and opened the car door. He took off his windbreaker, tossed it in the back seat and replaced it with his suit jacket. Jeans and a suit jacket would have to do. He leaned inside his car to retrieve his coffee cup. Shockley strode across the motel parking lot, lifted up the tape and ducked under.

"Nice of you to show up to the rodeo, Cowboy," said Terrance Bone. Bone had nicknamed Shockley *Cowboy* because he always wore cowboy boots. Otherwise, Shockley usually looked like a tall slim businessman with his well-pressed dress shirt, slacks and suit coat. The cowboy boots were part of his attire because he grew up wearing them on the ranch. And once he broke in a good pair of boots, he never wore anything else. They came in handy once when he had to get a knife-wielding criminal's attention.

"Glad I could help out, T-Bone," Shockley replied with a grin and raised eyebrow.

"What's with the jeans, Cowboy? You think it's sloppy-dress Friday?"

Shockley first met T-Bone almost six years ago at another crime scene. His first impression of the African American police officer was that he must have played football in a previous life due to his broad shoulders, barrel chest and thick neck. When he shook the man's hand, he was convinced T-Bone played ball. "Looks like they sent me a cowboy to solve a murder," was T-Bone's introduction to him. "Plan on chasing the perp in those fancy boots?"

"Nah." Shockley glanced down at his boots. "I don't like to run. I just use them for bustin' balls, Officer Bone."

T-Bone bellowed out a loud raw laugh. "Just call me T-Bone, Cowboy."

That was the beginning of their friendship.

From then on, Shockley knew T-Bone had his back.

T-Bone held a camera down by his side. Bull was wearing a white jumpsuit, which T-Bone called a bunny suit, surgical gloves, hairnet, and a mask dangling around her neck. The stocky man stood next to Bull. He was maybe 5'5", had dark leathery skin and greased back hair. The stocky man was in desperate need of a bath. Bull seemed unfazed. She was used to bad smells, he figured.

"Alright kids knock it off," Bull scolded. "This is a double homicide. I have done my initial walk-through, taken temperature of bodies and made sure the crime scene is secure."

"What, no foreplay?" Shockley teased.

Bull would have kicked another man's ass for saying that to her, but she liked Shockley. "Fill the cowboy in, Terrance."

T-Bone reached in his breast pocket, pulled out a small memo pad and flipped it open.

"The manager here called it in." T-Bone nodded toward the stocky man. "Said housekeeping found two bodies on the floor when she opened the door to room 205 for cleaning. The woman speaks no English and was interrogated by Officer Perez. The manager called 9-1-1 at 11:30 am to report two probable dead. Female and male inside room 205. The manager claimed he never went inside. Scared the shit out of him. When I arrived at 11:40 am, I entered room 205 and confirmed both victims were dead. The thermostat was set at 60 degrees. Felt like I was in a meat locker. Room was clear. I noted the room looked like a war zone. I called Metro and requested you and Bull. Bull arrived at 12:10 pm. She did a walk-through and made sure the crime scene was secure."

Shockley turned to the man standing next to Bull. "You the manager?"

"Yeah."

"The victims in room 205, did they check in together?"

"Nah. Some woman, named Miss Smith paid for the room."

"Cash, I assume?"

"Yeah. Most people pay cash. Don't trust credit cards."

"And what time did Miss Smith check in?"

"Noon yesterday. I remembered cause my favorite show comes on TV."

"What time did the man show up?"

"Don't know. None of my business who they have in their room." The manager crossed his arms.

"Is the woman who booked the room the one lying on the floor dead?" asked Shockley.

"Hell, I seen enough police shows to know you don't touch nothin'. I mean when I heard Yolando screaming like some freak, I ran up there and saw them two dead bodies on the floor with blood all over the damn place. I called 9-1-1 right then and there." The manager tucked his thumbs in his front jean pockets. "You know this is gonna hurt my business."

"Yolando?"

The manager said, "She's legal. Cleans rooms."

"That was at exactly 11:30?"

"I dunno. Shit I was shaking. Nothin' like this has ever happened here."

"Did you see anybody enter or leave the room?"

"Hell no. I give my customers privacy. I was in my office, like I said, watchin' TV."

"T-Bone, was there only this one car in the parking lot?" Shockley asked as he pointed at the car.

"Yeah. It was here when we pulled in. Otherwise, the place was a ghost town. Seems everybody heard the ruckus and vanished. I got Pete running the plate."

Shockley eyed the sky. "Those are nimbostratus clouds. Might rain. Go ahead and dust the car for prints. Don't want to take any chances."

"Bull, let's take the manager up and see if he can I.D. the dead woman," instructed Shockley.

The manager backed away from Bull and shook his head causing his greasy hair to stick to his face. "You gotta be joking. I ain't goin' back up there and look at that bloody face. I don't even remember what that woman who checked in looked like. After a while they all look alike."

T-Bone edged over toward the manager. He rested his oversized hand on his sidearm. In a low firm voice, he said, "I'm sure you wanna cooperate with the police otherwise we'll have to investigate what really goes on in this shit hole."

The manager wiped a strand of hair from his face. "You don't have to threaten me. I always cooperate with you guys."

Bull picked up her bag and headed toward the stairs followed by T-Bone, the manager and Shockley.

"Mike," a female voice yelled from across the street. It was the reporter, Susan Porter. "Mike Shockley. Can I have a moment of your time? Just a couple of questions."

Shockley knew the score. Unless he nipped this in the bud, Susan would pester another police officer until she got something."

"Bull, you and T-Bone go on up and I'll be there in a few minutes," Shockley instructed the group.

T-Bone shot a look toward Shockley and replied, "Yeah, Cowboy, go take your coffee break with that reporter and we'll work this case."

"Want to change places, T-Bone?"

"Not a chance. That woman has superpowers, and I ain't gonna let her melt me down." T-Bone chuckled as he, Bull and the manager headed up the stairs.

Shockley lumbered out toward the street to meet Porter. She had melted him down once. He wasn't going to let that happen again.

"Susan, good to see—"

A blast wave drove him forward onto the reporter.

His ears filled with the sound of a deafening explosion.

CHAPTER 5

L ack of conversation while driving to Willow Oaks Motel put Julia on edge. Yesterday she would have welcomed the silence. Today it gnawed at her.

Laquita's long intertwined fingers sat in her lap like she was silently praying. Maybe she was. Yesterday, when the husband they were surveilling appeared to spot them, Laquita crumpled like a rag doll on the floorboard of the car. Now Laquita believed her friend was right. The husband and the woman were dead. Murdered. In a motel room they were paid to watch.

Julia drove as fast as traffic would let her on the busy city streets. In less than fifteen minutes they'd be there and then she'd know if Laquita's friend was right. Her fingers wrapped tighter around the steering wheel. Bumper to bumper traffic didn't lighten the mood in the car either. Even with the windows shut, she smelled exhaust fumes.

Yesterday's events didn't add up. The nagging dread of what might be the truth caused her muscles to tense, her jaw clenched. Laquita's friend must be wrong or maybe.... *Don't think it.*

The voice from the GPS punctured the quietness.

Turn right in half a mile.

It wouldn't be long before they reached the cheap run-down motel. From the corner of her eye, Julia scanned Laquita's face. Her mid-length afro was pushed back with a wide multi-colored headband. Large gold hoop earrings dangled against her shoulders. There was a jagged scar on Laquita's forehead near her hairline. An injury that had never been stitched, leaving a lasting reminder.

Scars.

Her own past carried them. Not physical scars. Emotional. Her parents weren't killed in a car accident like she told Laquita. They were murdered. Her grandmother should have told her the truth. Elke was a trained liar. Then again, when she lied to Laquita about how her parents had died, it seemed too natural. Her therapist said to heal emotionally she had to forgive Elke. And herself.

Her anger with Elke started when she learned the truth about her past from her grandfather in Germany. A bomb was planted in Elke's home because she had information the Russians didn't want in the hands of the CIA. On that tragic day, Elke had taken her to the park while her parents waited at her grandmother's home. After her parents died in the explosion, Elke took her to Germany and had new identities made for them. She was a child. Elke brainwashed her. Julia forgot her birth name among so many other things. Elke continued to interfere in her life even when she became an adult. She resented Elke not believing she could take care of herself.

Perhaps she should never have bought the investigative business, but it was too late to think about that now. She wasn't going to give up. Not yet. She had to prove to Elke she had made the right decision buying the business.

Think.

What facts did she know?

She and Laquita both saw the husband enter the motel

room. And leave the motel room. Unless there was another person already in that room. Was it possible they were set up and the wife was somehow involved? Her legs stiffened as she accelerated through the yellow light.

Growing up she was taught not to trust people. She didn't know Laquita. Who was she? Maybe Laquita was part of this scam. She should have fired her yesterday. Damn

The woman in the passenger seat was probably close to her age. Late twenties. It was difficult to tell. Her ebony skin was smooth except for the scar on her forehead. Laquita was taller than she was. Maybe 5' 8".

Before they left the office, she read the words imprinted on Laquita's navy t-shirt. *I need a coffee the size of my butt.* That would be a big cup of coffee. Laquita was not a catwalk model. She probably never owned size 0 jeans. The woman had curves. Breasts large enough to catch a man's attention, high cheekbones, and full lips coated in clear lip gloss.

In 200 feet turn left.

Laquita stared at the GPS display tracking their position. They were getting close. They passed an abandoned car with the back windshield blown out. Soon they would be in a part of town you did not want to be in after dark. Or any time for that matter.

"Laquita," Julia's voice strained. "If there really are police at the motel, I'll slow down and we'll act curious."

"Do what?" Laquita raised her sunglasses to her forehead and shot a look like Julia had lost her mind. "We don't wanna stare. We gotta look innocent."

"We are innocent," Julia declared, her voice stiff. "But if we act like a crime scene is not interesting, we look guilty. People are morbidly curious sometimes, they look."

Laquita tilted her head toward Julia. "Sounds to me like you might know somethin' 'bout cops and crime scenes."

Julia's throat tightened.

"I watch TV." She feigned a smile. If Laquita only knew. Cops and crime scenes were part of her past. She had witnessed too many people die. All within close proximity to her. That bit of knowledge could scare her new hire into quitting. Maybe it wouldn't be a bad idea to share her past.

The GPS did not get a chance to tell her their destination was up ahead before Julia's smile quickly faded. The tension inside the car increased.

The motel parking lot was a hive of activity. There were police cruisers lit up like Christmas with whirling red, white, and blue lights. A white van parked on the side of the lot had the back doors wide open. Gawkers had gathered across the street on the sidewalk.

"Omigod," blurted Laquita. She pushed her sunglasses tight against her face and slithered down in the seat.

"Dammit Laquita. Sit up. You look like a criminal who just returned to the crime scene." Sweat began to dampen Julia's forehead.

"Hell girl, you and me are already sweatin' like sinners in church," Laquita's high-pitched voice hurled back.

"Sit up," ordered Julia.

Laquita straightened while admitting, "Cops make me nervous. I don't trust 'em. Ya watch the news, then ya know they shoot us Blacks."

Police made Julia nervous too. She had had her share of experiences with them. Once they hauled her into the station for questioning. There had been a murder at her previous employment. This was another part of town. There were lots of law enforcement agencies in the D.C. area. The odds that the officers she had been involved with would be at this location were slim to none. Julia forced her trembling hands to steer the car toward the commotion in front of them.

"The police are not going to shoot you. Quit being a drama queen," Julia said with a reassuring smile. *Why did I bring her?*

Your destination is 600 yards ahead on left.

Laquita reached over and twisted the volume knob on the car's dashboard to off.

"That woman telling us directions was gittin' on my last nerve," Laquita's voice unsteady.

Julia felt the same way. If Laquita hadn't turned the volume off, she was going to.

In the motel lot Julia spotted a tall slim man wearing jeans and a suit jacket, probably not much older than her. He was resting one hand on his hip and holding a drink in the other. Standing next to the slim man was a large Black police officer with a camera in his hand and a woman in a white jumpsuit, surgical gloves and a mask dangling around her neck. A short stocky man was pointing toward the upstairs. The side stairs to the upper level were marked off with yellow crime scene tape. Across the street a young woman holding an iPad followed by a man with a camera resting on his shoulder were being held back by an officer who was built like a sumo-wrestler.

Julia's pulse quickened. *Was there crime scene tape on Room 205?* It had to be another room. In this part of town, crime was on the news every night. Her eyes searched toward the upstairs of the motel as the car edged closer. She wasn't close enough to see which room the short stocky man was pointing toward. Traffic was at a crawl.

"We gotta turn around," Laquita said.

Suddenly, the brake lights flashed from the vehicle in front. Julia observed the sumo-wrestler officer blocking the road. A police car pulled into the middle of the street blocking traffic from entering. All traffic was being turned around. They were closing off the street.

She was almost to the exact spot she parked yesterday where she had an unobstructed view of room 205. Only now a white van with Channel 7 posted on the side was blocking her view. If only they had gotten here a few minutes earlier. *Should I ask the officer directing vehicles to turn around what was going on?*

Julia pulled up as close to the officer as he would allow and hung her head out the window.

"Excuse me officer, I was wondering if it was possible…." Her words froze in her throat. *Shit.* Laquita's friend was right.

"Miss, I need you to turn around now. This street is closed to all traffic," the officer said as he leaned toward her car window.

"Yes sir. I'm sorry. I was just in a hurry to get across town."

Julia sat back against the car seat and slouched. They wouldn't be able to see if it was indeed room 205 where the crime had been committed. At least not till the evening news. That didn't matter. She saw what she needed to see. The car the husband got out of yesterday was still in the parking lot. A wave of dread swept over her.

Julia needed to hurry back to her office. She had a lot of questions for Kat Lejeune.

Laquita read her mind. "What time ya meetin' that wife?

You think she had her husband murdered?"

Julia searched for the appropriate response. "I don't know what to think. If she did, then why would she have us at the scene of the crime?"

"Maybe to frame us."

"Frame us for what? I don't think that makes sense."

"What if that man we saw yesterday was the killer?" Laquita put her hands between her knees. "What if he seen us and now he's gonna track us down and kill us?"

Julia's mind was preoccupied with trying to sort out what had happened as she began a slow U-turn to head back in the direction she came. "Let's keep our heads, Laquita. We need to check the news stations and social media."

Laquita's head bobbed. Her hand rubbed the scar on the side of her forehead.

"Right now, I think we don't have enough information," Julia's voice faltered.

She wondered the same thing as Laquita. The man leaving the motel room might have been the murderer. There were too many questions and not enough answers. They could be potential witnesses. She needed to figure out their next move. When she sorted it out, they could go to the police and tell them what they knew.

A loud explosion caused the car to jolt and shake like there had been an earthquake. Julia slammed on the brake pedal. Her knuckles turned white from the stranglehold on the steering wheel trying to keep the car straight. A good thing she wasn't moving fast and Laquita had her seatbelt on. In the rear-view mirror she could see people running in all directions away from the motel. Plumes of white smoke billowed into the sky.

A look passed between her and Laquita. Neither one could speak. Laquita clutched her big pocketbook tight against her chest.

Julia pulled around a car in front of her and pressed the accelerator to the floor.

What the hell was going on?

Kat Lejeune had a lot of explaining to do.

She couldn't get back to the office fast enough.

CHAPTER 6

Fairmont Chateau
Lake Louise, Canada

Gingerly lifting his muscular arm draped across her hip, she slid out from under the warmth of the duvet. He stirred slightly. At the foot of the four-poster bed, she bent down and picked up the plush bathrobe lying on the floor and covered her naked body.

The man's hand patted her side of the bed. "Come back to bed," the man urged in a groggy voice. He slung the cover back. His deep-set eyes full of intensity zeroed in on her face.

Her eyes slowly roamed his body. The passing years had deepened the lines on his handsome face. He was slim with broad shoulders. Solid. Pectorals defined from days spent in a gym.

"No time. I have to get back to D.C.," she responded with a coy smile. "I have things I need to check on."

"You're the best lover I've ever had," he said as his lips twisted into a smile. "Come back to bed."

"You need to work on your lying skills, Alec. Women spies are not easily deceived, you know."

She tied the robe and padded toward the bathroom.

The suite was one of the finest in the hotel Fairmont Chateau, a suite that featured a spacious living area along with a secluded bedroom and a luxurious ensuite bath. The suite had stunning views of Lake Louise, the Victoria Glacier and the surrounding mountain range from its private balcony. It was an ideal accommodation to decompress and recover from her gunshot wound. That was what she told him.

"Did I tell you too many secrets during our passionate love-making?" the man teased.

"No," she answered, deadpan. "We both know if you did, it would not be good for your health." Standing in the bathroom doorway she kept her back to his prying eyes as the robe slithered down her body. She brushed her pearl white hair back allowing it to drape down the middle of her back.

Her fifty-year-old lover was twelve years younger. He had the same weakness as most spies she used to get information from—sex. Alec was a Russian spy who lived in Berlin when she first met him. He knew Elke had once worked for the CIA in her younger years. Now, Elke worked for herself.

When she contacted Alec about spending a weekend with him in Canada, Elke pretended she missed him and needed time to recoup. Alec did not hesitate to accept her invitation. He arranged for them to stay at the Fairmont Chateau. Elke knew the spy wanted information on what she knew surrounding a plot against the United States and its leaders. That was okay. She had her own agenda.

Two trained liars.

One, old school.

But the playbook on how to manipulate sources had remained the same.

The coded message she received this morning was unsettling. Elke needed to get back to D.C. ASAP. She had expected to extract more information from the spy, but now, time was of the essence. Alec was good at answering her questions with something unrelated. Perhaps her expertise in counterintelligence was slipping. There was a time she could read people and determine their motivation and vulnerabilities with relative ease. She had once been the CIA's best covert officer. Until her cover was blown on an assignment that resulted in the death of innocent people.

Time had not healed those wounds. That was the problem with an eidetic memory. Those murders were still fresh in her mind. What happened to her three decades ago still seemed like yesterday.

It started when she had discovered there was a mole in the CIA. An agency she had once trusted. Since that day, Elke never allowed herself to trust anybody. Or any agency. She learned that in the subterranean world of clandestine operatives officers would eventually be betrayed. Now, she was a lone wolf with loyalty to none. When she needed more intel, she relied on the Bridge Club.

The Bridge Club was a group of disgruntled retired CIA spies living around the world. They used old Cold War tactics to collect and disseminate information. Their intimate knowledge of the agencies they had worked for and their willingness to skirt the edges of legality made them not just dangerous, but lethal. The old spies knew the true threat to the United States was, as it had always been, Russia. U.S. spy agencies had become distracted. They were focused on terrorism, the Middle East, al-Qaida, North Korea and ISIS. Whereas *Illegals*, unregistered Russian assets, never lost their focus on America.

The President was foolish to think his task force, headed up by Speaker of the House, Alan Wagner and the FBI, could unearth the Russian asset. The Russians were already a step ahead. They had anticipated failure. That was why the attempt on the President and Vice President's life was made to look like the assassin was a jihadist inspired by the Islamic State. Sowing chaos. Stroking fear of immigrants and minorities.

A nuisance to the Russians was the Bridge Club. Especially Elke. A nuisance they wanted to eliminate.

The CIA had trained her. Now she worked outside their rules. Unlike the Bridge Club, she didn't skirt the edges of legality, she disregarded the law if it got in the way of her mission. The CIA knew she often broke the law, yet the agency chose to look the other way. In the past, Elke had provided them with valuable information, a relationship they didn't want to jeopardize.

In the shower, the warm water cascaded over her body and loosened the tension in her muscles. Her body relaxed for a minute. The message she received earlier indicated her granddaughter might be in danger. That message triggered those maternal instincts to protect Julia.

She wished she had brought her cigars. It was stupid to promise her granddaughter she'd give up smoking. Smoking was not what was going to kill her. She turned off the water and stepped out of the over-sized marble enclosed shower onto the tile floor. She heard voices coming from the bedroom.

Is Alec on the phone?

No.

She heard two voices, Alec and a female. The woman's voice was coolly authoritative.

Elke inwardly shuddered.

She thought for a moment about what to do.

"Elke dear. Do not keep us waiting much longer," the

woman raised her voice to make sure Elke heard.

She slipped the robe on, took the weapon hidden in her make-up case and put it in the robe pocket. She caught a glimpse of herself in the bathroom mirror. Her deep blue eyes now framed with sagging eyelids. Despite having a personal trainer and a facelift five years ago, time was catching up with her. Her hand pushed under her robe till her fingers brushed over the scar, a physical reminder of how close she came to death.

She clipped her long thick silver hair up in a bun, tightened the tie on the robe and walked out of the bathroom.

The woman did not look familiar. She stood near the bed with a pistol trained on Alec.

"You do not look surprised." The woman's cold gaze was piercing. Her voice professional. "I finally get to meet the infamous Elke?"

Elke studied the woman assassin. It was odd how different an assassin looked compared to TV shows. Her clothes were more befitting of a college student. A rose-colored pullover sweater and skinny jeans tucked into brown ankle boots. Not the all black ninja outfits assassins wore in a Hollywood film. A beige beanie pulled back at an angle on her head revealing short black bangs highlighting her ivory skin. Her face free of make-up. She could be young. It was getting harder to tell the age of people the older Elke got. They all looked young these days. The assassin had an assertive posture. Confident.

"Did you think we'd leave you alone Elke?" the assassin taunted.

"You should. I'm no longer a threat to your country." Elke replied. Her eyes bored into the woman. "You look very familiar."

The dark eyed assassin smiled. "You are too old to know me. This is a different time. Technology has changed the spy game."

"I no longer work for the CIA," Elke said as she sized up the woman pointing the pistol at Alec.

"We know." The assassin motioned toward a chair on the far side of the room with her pistol. "Sit down Elke. You look tired."

Elke walked across the room, sat in the chair, and folded her hands on her lap. "Could you put the gun down so we can work this out?"

"Shut up," the assassin barked, "I don't want to shoot you."

"Then you're not going to kill me?" Elke mocked.

"Don't play dumb, bitch," the assassin's tone hardened as she became agitated. "You know why I'm here, Elke. We need to know what information you have shared with the American spy agencies."

Elke noticed Alec shifting in the bed. He was nervous. This was not good.

Alec's chest heaved up and down.

"You are a traitor to your country, Alec. I will find pleasure in pulling the trigger to end your life," the assassin voice edgy with contempt.

"Now I remember," Elke's voice rising as she stood.

The assassin swung the pistol toward Elke. "Sit back down. Now. Or you will be the first to die."

"I do know you," Elke said as she eased back into the chair, turning slightly and crossing her legs, hoping the assassin didn't notice her hand had slipped inside the robe pocket. Her slender finger eased back the hammer of the gun. Alec's face rigid with fear.

"That is a lie. You say that to distract me. Who do you think I am? What is my name?"

"I speak the truth. It's like looking in a mirror. You are me, from many years ago."

"We are nothing alike," the assassin replied with a sharp laugh.

"You are right. I'm not an assassin. My expertise is… well, ask Alec. He can give you the details."

The assassin's dark eyes narrowed and hardened.

"But do you know how we are alike?" Elke quizzing, taunting.

"Do not speak anymore," shouted the assassin. She aimed the pistol toward Elke's head.

Elke continued despite the woman's warning, "We've both been betrayed by the agency we worked for."

"Shut up. Mother Russia does not betray those loyal to her."

"Your agency identified Alec as a double agent working for the CIA." Elke's palm inside the robe pocket cradled the grip on the revolver, the metal trigger snug against her finger. She eased the slack out of the trigger. "You said I didn't look surprised. That's because a mole in your agency warned Alec."

The assassin spun toward Alec.

Shots cracked the air.

CHAPTER 7

Two Weeks Earlier

Alan Wagner, Speaker of the House, sat on a couch directly across from the President in the West Wing of the White House. The Commander in Chief had entrusted him to form a task force to expose the *deep-cover* Russian asset they believed to be a threat to national security.

"All roads lead to Moscow, Alan," the President told him.

Fear had run down his spine when the President confided that he personally believed the traitor was somebody the President knew. Wagner, unsure if the President was pointing a finger at him decided at the time to play along.

"What are your suspicions, Mr. President?" he asked, watching for telltale signs on the President's face.

"A confidential informant told the AG that the suicide bomber was a Muslim American who served in the Army doing tours in Afghanistan and Syria. He was given an honorable discharge five years ago. Somewhere along the way he was radicalized."

"I'm glad you didn't put sanctions on Russia following the attempt on your life." Wagner felt his heart rate slow allowing him to take a deep calming breath.

"Hell, I didn't put sanctions on Russia because of your arm-twisting," the President countered. "There's no way the attempt on my life and the vice president was carried out by a lone terrorist. We were attending the Vice President's wife's funeral for God sakes when the suicide bomber denoted his vest. The CIA believes the only way the bomber got that close to the funeral was because somebody was helping him. They suspect those Russian bastards have infiltrated our inner circle."

Wagner felt a sledgehammer pounding against his chest. He knew the FBI was going to bust through the door of the Oval Office at any moment.

The President continued, "I think not imposing sanctions was the right call without having any hard evidence the Russians were behind this. At the time, all we had was a dead Russian handler and a friend of yours telling you there was an agent of influence that might threaten our national security. Your friend believed the Russians were involved and, at the time, I wanted to believe it was ISIS. There are many who want to destroy our country, Alan, but I'm convinced somebody is working in influential areas of our government and feeding the Russians intelligence. We have to be cautious. That's why I wanted you, Alan, to be personally involved in the investigative task force. I need somebody I can trust."

Wagner leaned forward. A pent-up breath escaped his lips

"My God Alan. You look like you just saw a ghost. Are you okay?"

Swallowing hard, Wagner forced himself to keep eye contact. "Yes sir, I'm fine. It's just…well, unsettling to think there's a Russian mole that might be operating within one of our most trusted agencies." *I've got to get a grip. The President doesn't suspect anything so quit acting guilty.*

"Damn Alan, you know there are more spies in the U.S. capital than any other city in the world. At least a thousand. Moscow has ramped up their spying through misinformation warfare and cyber-attacks to undermine our country's strength.

We must find this bastard. We're in a new Cold War with Russia."

"You're right." Wagner was surprised at how close to the truth the President had come. Except for *the number* of SVR assets. There were many more.

Wagner added, "We'll catch him. He'll make a mistake and when he does, we'll unmask him."

"Good. But don't be too short-sighted and believe this Russian asset is a man. It could be a woman. A wife. A lover. Remember Anna Chapman."

Shit. I should've been more careful with my words.

How could he forget Anna Chapman? His past handler had reminded him. He'd met Anna at a rave party in London's Docklands. She was one of the best Russian operatives due in part to her sexy looks. It was a shame she was caught before she could develop ties in policy-making circles.

"Yes, I do remember when Anna Chapman was revealed as a spy. She got sloppy and the FBI arrested her in New York City in 2010. It's said she was ordered by her superiors in Russia to seduce NSA whistleblower Edward Snowden."

The President's eyes narrowed. "We cannot be too careful. You, Alan, are one of the most eligible bachelors on the hill. I heard Time magazine is thinking of featuring you on their cover next year."

Wagner was sure he knew what the President was implying about him being a bachelor. The President was warning him that the women he dated could be spies, just like Anna Chapman.

"I understand and share your concerns. These long workdays give me little time to date."

"Alan, I'm not asking you to be some goddamn monk,"

said the President with a placating smile. "You need to find time to date. You should have a personal life. Just be careful who you associate with."

Wagner nodded.

"Right now, I've got the Vice President barking up my ass. He's convinced the Russians had something to do with his wife's death. I don't believe it, but the V.P. is a war hawk who'd blame Moscow for anything including his wife's death. The sooner we nail this Russian spy, the better for all of us."

"Yes sir, I understand. You can count on me."

He had lied to the President that morning, knowing it was a lie that could cost him his life. His fear was not the Americans It was the Russians. They would never tolerate failure.

Alan Wagner, a tall, thick man with deep-set blue eyes enjoyed the power that came with being Speaker of the House. His role as speaker gave him the ability to cultivate and influence American politics, especially the President. After the assassination attempt, he convinced the President against the impulse of escalation of the situation.

Wagner had worked hard long hours to become the top dog on Capitol Hill. His colleagues were impressed with his work ethic and ambition. But many expressed skepticisms he'd be tough enough to succeed in the hugger-mugger world of politics. Once the gavel was passed to him as the new Speaker of the House, the same naysayer colleagues rushed to show support. Political hypocrisy was part of the game.

The FBI had compiled and grown a list of suspected Soviet intelligence assets. None thus far were connected to the White House. The public and media were supposed to be kept in the dark, yet the Russian cyber warriors were hard at work on social media planting false stories to stoke fears about immigration and minorities. What better way to keep the public from thinking about a Russian mole in government than to throw one distraction after another at them.

He went back to his office after that meeting believing he'd been foolish to have worried the President would have suspected him of being the traitor. Sitting behind his desk, he told himself everything would be alright.

But two hours later, he knew he was wrong.

Congressman Dan Quatterman, a man he despised had burst into his office. The towering man had an uncanny ability to find dirt on other lawmakers. That was why Wagner had made sure to include the Congressman in his private meetings with other lawmakers. Keep your enemies close he reminded himself. It was wise to feed the over-weight man's ego. Wagner might find the man useful in the future.

Quatterman dropped a bombshell when he informed Wagner that a freelance reporter named Charlotte Bollinger was investigating a possible mole in the government. Wagner didn't have to pretend to be rattled by the news. He was.

Wagner took a few deep breaths before asking, "What'd she tell you?"

"Not much. She's just starting to interview people. She's a cute redhead. Told me she had read some online conspiracy theory that the Russians had infiltrated our government. That got her to thinking maybe the suicide bomber who almost took out our President and Vice President was somehow connected. The whole thing sounded far-fetched to me, but she's damned determined. Maybe she can help our task force find out if there really is a spy in our government."

Wagner was confident he could steer the task force away from suspecting him, but a story-hungry reporter wanting to make a name for herself was cause for concern.

He felt his leg under the desk start bouncing.

"All this reporter will do is interfere in our investigation. Sounds like she's inexperienced and could be dangerous making baseless accusations built on some crazy online conspiracy theorist. False accusations could hurt our party and destroy careers " said Wagner.

"Yeah, you're right. I hadn't thought about that."

Wagner placed his hand on his bouncing leg to settle it down. He sat back in his chair and swiveled to face his picture window in order to think about what to say next. With his back to Quatterman he said, "We can't afford to screw up this investigation. You're my biggest confidant, Dan…and my friend." He was glad his back was to the man he despised.

"Thanks Alan. It means a lot to hear you say that. I came to you first with this information because I knew you'd know what to do. I mean she could be a problem. Maybe she'll uncover things that are none of her business."

Wagner had to restrain a smile when he turned his chair to face Quatterman. He knew now that Quatterman would play ball.

"Give me her name again and I'll handle it. I'll meet with her. If she doesn't back down, then I'll turn her name over to the FBI."

Quatterman pulled out a calling card from his jacket pocket and offered it to him.

Lowering his eyes Wagner read the simple calling card.

Charlotte Bollinger.
Freelance Writer.
CBfreelance@gmail.com

"Also, don't say a word to anybody about this, Dan. Just in case there is a traitor in our inner circle," warned Wagner.

"I'd never leak anything to a traitor," declared Quatterman.

That afternoon, he made the decision to contact somebody he knew. His old roommate from Miami University in Oxford, Ohio. They were both economic and political science majors. That was where the similarities ended. Max wasn't a rich kid like the majority of Wagner's fraternity brothers. He kept his gang tattoos hidden. Max was trying hard not to end up like most of his family.

In prison.

Or dead.

After graduation, Max moved to the D.C. area. Except for the few times Max had run-ins with the law, Wagner never heard from him. When Max had gotten in trouble, Wagner would pull a few strings to help him. He liked Max. But Max still had plenty of bad habits. Mainly the people he hung out with.

His old roommate had jumped at the chance to help him. Max told Wagner he knew a guy who knew a guy who could help.

A short time later, a meeting was set up with Wagner and the stranger in a park across town. Wagner had been instructed to take the bus. Alone and without his security detail.

He remembered waiting in the designated area, his hands gripping the manila envelope tight. The stranger was late. After thirty minutes, Wagner doubted the meeting would take place. He silently chastised himself for trusting Max. He crossed the street to the bus stop and waited for the next bus.

A man in a long overcoat wearing a black fedora and

smoking a cigarette walked toward him from across the street. The stranger's eyes cast down toward the pavement until he stopped in front of him.

"Leaving so soon, Mr. Wagner?" he asked.

Something about the stranger's voice made him tense. Wagner's eyes darted from side to side to check if anybody was within earshot.

The stranger had a biracial look, full lips, slightly flared nostrils and a scar above his right brow. He stood straight, over six feet tall and held an air of confidence, a man you didn't want to meet in the dark. When Wagner looked into the piercing black eyes, he realized the stranger was waiting for a reply.

"I didn't think you were going to show," he had replied, extending his hand.

The stranger kept his free hand deep in his coat pocket. He tossed his cigarette butt to the ground.

"You should learn to be more patient."

Wagner then raised the manila envelope and extended it to the stranger. "The reporter's name, address and contact information are in the envelope. The agreed upon first payment is in there too. After you finish the assignment, I'll pay the balance."

"What exactly is it you want me to do?" The coldness in the stranger's voice caused Wagner to step back.

Wagner's eyes lowered in an attempt to find courage. "Find out what the reporter knows about the investigation into a Washington mole. Then I want you to persuade her to leave the area. If she wants money, I'll pay."

"Consider it done," the man had told him.

"I need to be kept out of this," he warned the stranger.

The man tucked the envelope inside his coat. "I'll be in touch." He turned and left in the direction he had come.

Wagner noticed the man walked with a slight limp. Not noticeable at first, but upon closer inspection, definitely there.

He had been clear concerning what he needed the stranger to do. Or had he? He never asked how the stranger was going to get the reporter to tell him what she had uncovered. Or how he'd persuade her to leave town. He wanted to ask, but his mouth had gone dry and the words stuck in his throat.

On the way back to his office he felt something was off with the stranger. It went beyond the guy's creepy looks. He didn't doubt after meeting the man that he could get the reporter to tell him everything she knew and scare her into leaving town.

That would solve his problem. Yet there was a little voice inside his head that told him it wasn't going to be that easy.

✝ ✝ ✝

Raymond House
Present Day

It seemed surreal, like a bad nightmare that kept getting worse.

Now he knew he'd made a grave mistake.

The Speaker of the House paced around his office. How could he have been such an idiot? When he first learned of the reporter, he should have alerted his handler instead of trying to resolve the issue himself. What drove him to handle it himself was a remembrance of something that had happened not that long ago. That event shook his mind. His previous handler had been murdered when her cover was blown.

If the reporter had discovered he was the Russian mole the FBI was hunting, then he would face the same fate as that handler. The Russians had their own way of handling problems. They eliminated them.

As it turned out, his problem with the stranger had gotten bigger. And messier. A surge of nausea swept over him.

That reporter was never leaving town.

She was dead.

CHAPTER 8

The truth.

That's what Julia needed to know.

She was sure she'd get Kat Lejeune to tell her what was going on when they met in her office at 5:00. Even though she had plenty of time before the meeting, she kept a heavy foot on the gas pedal. She was still rattled by the explosion.

"All I can find out is what we already know," said Laquita. She was using her phone to search for information on the explosion at the motel.

"We'll get to the bottom of this soon enough," Julia said with faltering determination.

"I reckon." Laquita stared out the side window and continued, "What if Kat doesn' come by herself?"

"What do you mean? You think she'd bring somebody to harm us?"

"Don't know fer sure, but I ain't buyin' that story she fed ya."

Julia felt the same way. She was nervous. It wasn't right to involve Laquita in this problem.

"Not doing it," spat Laquita.

"I haven't told you what I'm thinking. What I thought was when it's time for Lejeune to come, you could go down and wait in the bakery. They don't close till seven. Watch and see who takes the elevator up around five. If you see an attractive Black woman and a man together then you can call me on my cell."

Laquita nodded a couple of times. "Not a bad idea, detective Julia."

She stopped short of inserting her office key in the lock.
The door was ajar.
She turned her head and pressed her index finger against her lips to signal Laquita. Either Laquita had not pulled the door shut when they left for the motel or somebody had broken in.

Julia lowered her backpack to the floor and nudged the door open. Standing by the threshold, her eyes scanned the office area. Laquita leaned too close from behind bumping Julia. "For God's sake, back up," Julia protested in a whisper over her shoulder.

The tall woman took a few steps back.

"I locked the door and shut it tight when we left," Laquita said defensively. "You 'member how you gave me a dirty look for slamming the door.'

Annoyed, Julia glared at Laquita as she pumped an open palm down toward the floor like she was dribbling an imaginary basketball. "Shhhh!"

After not detecting anyone lurking inside, she decided to enter her office. Leaving the door wide open, Julia and Laquita inched their way inside.

Julia's hand grabbed the baseball bat she kept propped against the wall next to the tall bookcase. The bat came with the purchase of the business. She almost got rid of it when she moved in. Now, she was glad she had it. Back in high school, she had taken several self-defense courses. That was the reason she kept the bat. She knew how to use it as a weapon. Most people would swing the bat at the head or body of the attacker, she would shatter their knees.

Both hands wrapped tight on the bat, she sidled cautiously around the office. Laquita shadowed her every move. She bent down and checked under her desk.

Clear.

She tiptoed to the closet. The door was shut. Her hand reached for the round knob. Laquita was so close she could feel her breath on her neck. She started to twist the knob then abruptly stopped.

Something felt off.

With hand gestures she communicated for Laquita to open the closet door. She would stand on the other side with the bat aimed and ready to strike. Julia and Laquita locked eyes. They exchanged nods.

A quick twist. Laquita yanked the door open. In unison, they let out a gasp. There was nobody hiding in the closet.

"Damn, Julia," Laquita said while patting her chest. "I thought fer sure that killer was hidin' in there."

Julia lowered the bat and pored over the office again.

Even though there was no visual evidence that anybody had been there, Julia sensed she'd missed something.

"Maybe I didn't yank the door hard enough to latch it when we left," confessed Laquita.

"Perhaps," replied Julia. "Maybe we're just getting paranoid."

No, she told herself. She vividly recalled feeling irritated when Laquita slammed the office door.

Julia walked over and inspected her desk. Nothing was out of place. She opened the desk drawers and searched.

"Good Lord Julia, think ya got 'nuff candy bars in there?"

"I get low blood sugar. They're granola bars," snipped Julia.

"I shoulda figgered ya had low blood sugar. That explains why ya was crabby when we got here."

"I'm not crabby," Julia snarled while unwrapping a granola bar.

Julia held one out to Laquita. "Want one?"

"Nah. 'Em things are full of carbs and sugar.'"

"You're health conscious?" Julia stared at Laquita's large butt.

"Reckon I am. You need to watch what ya eat."

Julia was on the edge of a reply when her eyes focused on the dented file cabinet. She headed over to the cabinet and tugged on the file drawer till it finally pulled opened.

It didn't look like any of the files were missing. But one folder was out of order. A green one was misplaced. It was in with the blue files. She had color coded them herself earlier that morning. *How did I mess up and put this file in the wrong section?*

Julia pulled the green file out in order to file it correctly. The name on the file caught her attention. Kat Lejeune. The client who hired her to get photos of her cheating husband.

"The intruder's color blind," Julia blurted out.

"Whaa?" Laquita tilted her head to one side.

Julia held the file up "This file should be in the green folder section. Somebody took the file out and put it in the wrong place. They were looking for my latest case. Kat Lejeune." Her MacBook was still on her desk. *Why didn't the intruder take it?* Probably because the thief didn't need to. The thief was looking for something specific.

She had to warn Lejeune. If she wasn't involved in the murders, then Lejeune's life could be at risk.

The intruder had left the office without a trace anybody

had ever been there. Except the file being in the wrong spot and the door not being latched, she would've never known anybody was in her office. The intruder had left in a hurry.

Earlier when they left to go to the motel, Laquita slammed the office door because the inside lock was turned and there was no quiet way to shut it. Unless you locked the door from the outside with the key. Since the intruder didn't have a key, he wouldn't be able to shut the door without them hearing the noise.

Shit. Fear tumbled into her thought causing her heart to race. They must have just missed the thief.

"We need to get out of here," Julia instructed Laquita. "Whoever did this is looking for something and I'm afraid we still have it."

Julia retrieved her backpack by the door in the hallway and tucked the file and laptop inside. Luckily, she had left the camera inside her backpack and not in her office. She worried the man they saw leaving the motel murder scene wanted the photos she had taken.

Wait. How would he know they took photos? How would he know where she worked? License plate, maybe. That wouldn't tell him her office location. It could only be one thing.

Laquita.

The woman was texting on her phone. "Laquita, we need to talk."

She typed a second more and then shoved the phone in her back-jean pocket.

"I thought ya said we need to get outta here," said Laquita.

"How would the man we saw leaving the murder scene know where I work?"

"I figger he musta got yo tag number or coulda followed

us."

"My tag number wouldn't have told him where I work. He would've had a hard time getting to his car in time to follow us. I took lots of turns to make sure nobody was tailing us."

"I dunno. Maybe he wasn't here. Ya said we were probably gitten' paranoid. Maybe ya put the file in the wrong spot."

"Your friend. He told you he saw us taking photos yesterday at the motel. Said it was his territory. You think the man we saw also saw your friend? He could've asked your friend if he knew you?"

Laquita's big brown eyes widened. "Oh my God," Laquita cried out.

"Call him. Call your friend now and find out,' urged Julia.

Laquita held the cell phone in her hand and thumbed a message.

"I'll text him. He gits back faster that way."

Laquita's slender fingers moved to the scar on her forehead. Her fingers nervously stroked the scar.

The phone vibrated. Laquita thumbed more messages. She stopped and slipped the phone in her back pocket. "We need to call the cops," Laquita said. She traipsed over to the window, pulled back the cheap blinds and looked out.

"What did he say? Did he talk to somebody about our surveillance in that area?"

Laquita turned and faced Julia. "We need to git goin'."

Julia was losing her patience. "Did your friend say we need to leave? Why? What does he know?"

"He don't know nothin'." The quiver in her voice gave her away.

"You're lying. He does know something. What the hell is it? Tell me now," demanded Julia.

"I ain't lying."

"Then why are you in such a hurry to leave and now all of a sudden you want to call the cops? You don't trust the cops. Remember?"

"Cuz, my friend's worried. That's all."

"About what?"

Laquita shook her head. "I just think that file being in the wrong place means somebody probably got in here. Okay? That makes me nervous." She turned and peeked through the slats of the blinds.

Julia took a step toward Laquita, reached and snatched the cell phone from Laquita's back jean pocket.

"Give it back," Laquita yelled as she twirled around.

Julia scanned the text messages on Laquita's phone. She read the last few texts between Laquita and a guy named Max.

> Max—*Keep away from that PI and her office.*
> Laquita—*What?*
> Max—*Could be trouble*
> Laquita—*???*
> Max—*That man you took photos of at motel...he knows*

CHAPTER 9

Shockley hated the smell.

Antiseptic from cleaners, blood, vomit, and even the scent from get well flowers. Pongs that triggered memories of the time his mother spent in hospitals.

An orderly sped down the hall pushing a gurney. The patient on the metal table moaned as he was wheeled past Shockley. At least a dozen people were injured from the blast at the motel. Two known dead. A police officer and the manager of the motel had died at the scene.

The hospital corridor was a bustle of activity. Shockley had already been checked out by a doctor. A few stitches above his eyebrow and a small bandage on one hand were the only visible signs of his injuries. Luckily, the blast had propelled him forward causing him to land on top of reporter Susan Porter, protecting her from the impact. Others were not so lucky.

Amber Bull was in surgery. As the crime scene investigator, she was leading the team toward the exterior stairwell located on the east side of the building. The room with the bomb was located at least forty feet from the top of the stairwell. That distance probably saved her life.

"Is she going to make it?" was what he kept asking the nurse who had obviously been in this position too many times before. "I'm an officer." He flashed his badge. "I need to know."

The nurse answered, "All I know at this time is that the doctors are doing everything possible. Her condition is serious.

We've notified her husband. He's on his way. You should go home and get some rest."

Rest? Is she kidding? His friends were just blown up. He needed to make sure they would pull through before he left. Then he would hunt down the son of a bitch who did this and make him pay.

Shockley headed to the Intensive Care Unit to see how T-Bone was doing. The same nurse who advised Shockley to go home was leading him down the hospital corridor.

"Here we are," the nurse said, her eyes weary from a long shift. "Use the antibacterial foam located near the patient's bed to disinfect your hands."

"Thanks."

The nurse quickly held her hand up blocking Shockley from entering. "No more than ten minutes, please. Mr. Bone needs to rest. He's been heavily sedated."

Shockley nodded. This would not be easy. The first time he saw his mother in ICU he was shaken. He never wanted to see anybody he loved that helpless and vulnerable again. Shockley lowered his head, closed his eyes for a second. He had to be strong. His friend needed him.

He pushed the heavy brown door open.

T-Bone's head was wrapped in bandages. His face swollen with deep yellow-purple bruises. The familiar mechanical cadence of beeps and buzzes from the machines in the room made his chest feel tight. His friend was attached to IVs, a heart monitor and there was an oxygen tank next to him. His neck stabilized in a cervical collar. A doctor with a stethoscope hanging around his neck and a nurse by his side were at the foot of the bed doing an exchange of incomprehensible medical terminology.

The doctor noticed Shockley and gestured to the hand sanitizer dispenser. He walked over and squirted some in his palm. He worked the foam around the bandage on top of his hand. His hand hurt more than he wanted to acknowledge.

"I'm Detective Shockley." He flashed his badge. "How is he?"

"Critical, but stable," the doctor replied while he walked toward Shockley.

"I'm Dr. Williams." Shockley had to look down at the short man. He had black hair, Mediterranean features and could easily pass as Italian.

"What'd you mean by critical, but stable?"

"Means he will get round-the-clock bedside monitoring by one of our critical care nurses. We'll know more later today." Dr. Williams studied Shockley then pointed at him. "You were at the explosion?"

"Yeah. T-Bone, I mean Officer Bone and I were investigating a double homicide at the motel when the bomb went off."

"You were lucky you weren't in the room where the bomb exploded."

"Is he awake? Can I talk to him?"

"He's been asking for you. Right now, it's important he rest."

"I won't stay long Doc."

"No, you won't," the doctor said with a slight grin across his face. The doctor wheeled toward the nurse standing next to the monitors. "That's nurse Becky over there. She puts her patient's welfare first. I wouldn't challenge her if I were you. When she says you need to leave, leave." The doctor patted Shockley's arm as he walked past him and out the door of the room.

Shockley hoped nurse Becky might give him more information on his friend's condition. "What do you think 'bout T-Bone's condition?"

The nurse took a minute before diverting her attention away from the monitors and looking at Shockley. Her brown hair pulled up and back with two oversized twists on top of her head reminded him of Nurse Ratched from the old movie, *One Flew over the Cuckoo's Nest*. He hoped it was just an appearance similarity and not a personality one.

She smiled. "There isn't much else I can say, except your friend here is a very stubborn patient."

She was right about that. T-Bone was a stubborn man. There was a time T-Bone didn't have enough money to buy his son the birthday present he wanted. T-Bone's ex-wife had taken him to the cleaners during the divorce. He gave her everything. All he wanted was joint custody of his son. Shockley tried to loan him the money. T-Bone refused. Said he'd figure it out. He did. T-Bone got a job bagging grocery to earn enough extra cash.

"That's the truth ma'am. T-Bone makes a mule seem reasonable."

They both laughed.

"Your nickname for your friend is clever," she said. She adjusted the blanket on T-Bone and continued, "Being stubborn can be a good quality at times." She paused a beat. "We will take very good care of your friend."

Shockley smiled at her. Becky was no Nurse Ratched.

"I'm going to step out and give you some privacy, detective. No more than ten minutes. Try to keep him calm."

Shockley thanked Becky. He relaxed a bit, T-Bone was in good hands.

He drew closer to the side of the bed and studied his friend. The large man's swollen eyes were closed. He pulled up a chair and put his hand on top of the bed's side rail.

"Sorry man. It should be me in that bed, not you," Shockley choked out.

He blinked back the wetness forming in his eyes. His friend's grotesque face and all the tubes and wires he was hooked up to made the large man look like Frankenstein. T-Bone was almost unrecognizable.

"Cowboy," a weak voice spoke. "That you?" T-Bone had opened his eyes, yet the slits looked closed.

"Yep, T-Bone. It's me." Shockley took a deep breath. "How ya doing buddy?"

"My head feels like it's gonna explode. Hurts like a sonofabitch."

"I'll tell them to give you more pain meds." Shockley started to remove his hand and go find the nurse when a large hand stopped him.

"No," T-Bone's voice was barely audible. The hand on Shockley's hand was surprisingly strong.

Shockley leaned his head closer to his friend's face. "What is it T-Bone?"

"Something's not right, Cowboy." T-Bone moaned.

"Don't talk. Just rest. We need you back on the force."

T-Bone kept his grip on Shockley as he continued, "Dead guy…tattoos."

"From a local gang," added Shockley. "Probably a prostitute messing with the wrong guy. Maybe a local gang getting revenge."

T-Bone moaned again. Shockley knew the massive amount of morphine his friend had been given was overtaking his mind. The big hand held on. T-Bone closed his eyes.

"The girl," he whispered. "Wrong...place."

"What do you mean T-Bone?"

Shockley leaned his ear close to the man's mouth to hear the struggling man speak.

"Girl...wrong," T-Bone faint voice muttered.

The big strong hand opened, releasing Shockley's arm.

T-Bone had drifted back to sleep.

Shockley knew his friend would hear his promise. "Don't worry big guy, I'll find this bastard if it's the last thing I ever do."

CHAPTER 10

Fairmont Chateau
Lake Louise, Canada

When the assassin in the hotel room at the Fairmont Chateau had spun toward Alec to fire her pistol, Elke was faster. She didn't want to kill the young assassin, yet she had no choice. Alec instructed Elke to get out of there as fast as possible. He'd have the room sanitized before housekeeping arrived.

"Thanks for saving my life," he said.

He stepped closer, pulled her against him and passionately kissed her. "I owe you."

Alec was right. He owed her and she usually collected.

She pulled back from his hold and studied him. A man with lonely eyes. It came with this line of work. When you can't trust people, it's hard to get close to them.

"The Russians will soon learn what happened. We need to get out of the country," she warned.

"Already made the call. The agency will handle this. My orders are to get you out." Alec's voice stiffened, "I'm sorry. My intel on when the assassin would arrive was wrong. After you told her what she wanted to know, she'd have killed you, too."

"Your Kremlin mole told you the assassin would not arrive until tomorrow. Obviously, your mole is—"

"Being provided contrived information to ferret out the

mole."

"Therefore, your inside informant is—"

"Probably dead."

"We must move fast," Elke said as she began to dress. "The Kremlin will learn soon their assassin failed."

† † †

Calgary International Airport
Calgary, Alberta, Canada

There were no nonstop flights from Calgary International Airport to Washington, D.C. Her lay-over in Toronto was now delayed more than forty-five minutes. Due to the flight delay, Elke learned she wouldn't arrive in D.C. till late in the evening. *Damn. I need to be in D.C. now, not in the evening. Airlines are so incompetent.* She found an area away from the swarm of people in the terminal to make the necessary call.

"Situation report," Elke demanded from the man on the other line.

"She and another woman were near the motel when there was an explosion." The man had been instructed not to use names on an unsecured line.

Elke knew who she was—Julia.

Elke clenched her teeth. The thought of something happening to her granddaughter made the otherwise strong woman shudder.

"Is she…," Elke could not finish the sentence.

"She's fine. We're searching for clues to find out if she's

being targeted."

"I don't care what it takes, protect her at all costs."

"Understood," the man answered.

"Any victims from explosion?"

"Our source heard from an off-the-record police officer that there were two inside the motel room when the bomb went off. They were already declared DOA. They think a hooker met a gang member for drugs, sex or both. Rumors are the hooker was the property of a rival gang. Their MO is explosives. This is a rough part of town. Lots of gang activity."

"Two dead. Anybody else?"

"One officer and a guy who worked at the motel."

"You sure she's safe?"

"Yes."

"Did you search her office?"

"Yes. We know who hired her."

"Foreign influence?"

"Probably not."

"My flight has been delayed. I want to be debriefed when I get back."

Elke clicked off. She glanced at her wristwatch and then at the crowd of people.

Nothing suspicious.

Yet.

The call heightened her angst over Julia's safety. She could never allow anything to happen to her granddaughter. The Russians had already taken her daughter. She'd be damned if they would harm her granddaughter. Anybody who tried would pay the price.

The man on the call was part of the Bridge Club. Elke knew him from her CIA days. He was forced to quit after a botched extraction of a high value al-Qaeda target in Afghanistan. The Russians captured the case officer and tortured him. Elke was a member of the off-the-books extraction team that helped locate and smuggle him to safety. She had a dark suspicion the CIA had been infiltrated by the then KGB. Her concerns were rejected by both the CIA and the government.

Elke knew Julia was still angry with her. After her granddaughter learned the truth regarding her parent's death and that Elke had worked with the CIA, she was hurt and confused. Elke tried to protect her, but things got out of control. The girl was stubborn and headstrong. Even when Julia was a small child, Elke knew she was going to be a lot like herself. She struggled to convince Julia not to buy the private detective business. The more she pushed, the more determined her granddaughter became.

Julia had made Elke promise to quit interfering in her life. Elke, with sincerity in her voice, agreed. It was another lie. That same day she made the promise to stay out of her granddaughter's life was the same day she called the Bridge Club and told them to keep eyes on her.

Elke needed a drink.

The Vin Room Restaurant in the airport terminal had an extensive list of over 80 wines. Her drink of choice was vodka, but the wine bar restaurant was closer to her departing gate.

A quick scan of the people inside the airport restaurant did not send up any red flags.

Even though she could drink most men under the table, she would be conservative and just order one glass of red wine. It was important to keep her wits. She could not miss her flight. And even though Alec said the agency would handle the Russians, one could never be too careful. After all, Alec was a double agent. His motivation to betray his country was purely financial. Spying was known as the *second oldest profession.* When money was the main motivator, you had to watch your back.

Information she had received from the Bridge Club was unexpected. Was it a coincidence that her granddaughter was doing surveillance where a double murder took place? Then an explosion at the same location? This couldn't be as straight cut as it appeared on the surface. It never was.

Elke sipped her wine while keeping a watchful eye on the activity around her. A sea of people scurried past on the way to their gates. Their faces a mixture of bored and frustrated. A young tyke dressed in a Batman outfit wailed as his mother dragged him along by his small hand. Beeping noises from a motorized vehicle passed, transporting an overweight elderly woman holding a cane in her hand. A man walked a dog wearing a vest with the words **Therapy Dog** sewn on top. Constant announcements from the airlines blared through the terminal speakers. Airports were basically the same all over the world.

A man in his early forties with mostly black hair wandered into the Vin Room and sidled up to the bar. He wasn't particularly fit. His friendly face made him look like the kind of guy people felt comfortable having a beer with. Elke studied him. An average Joe who blended in with the other customers in the restaurant. The man never looked in her direction. She finished her glass of wine and was ready to leave when the waiter approached with another glass of wine.

"I didn't order another glass," Elke said to the waiter dressed in black pants and a white shirt.

"This is from the gentleman at the bar." The waiter gestured toward the man who had just sat down.

Elke looked toward the man sitting on the bar stool. He smiled, stood and strolled over to her table.

"Mind if I join you?"

"Actually, I do," she replied curtly.

The man slid the chair out and sat down facing her.

"You know who I am?" he said.

Elke tucked her long silver hair back behind her ear. Her silence did not faze the stranger.

"The years have been kind to you," he said as his gaze passed over her. "You're a very attractive woman."

"You're not my type."

"Let's not play games Addy. This is a serious situation." Addy Bravo was another identity she often used.

"Serious for whom?"

"You, your country. Possibly your granddaughter."

"Why would this situation concern her?"

"Because she's *your* granddaughter." The man lowered his voice and leaned closer, "Intelligence agencies in Russia look for weaknesses to use against our field officers. Your granddaughter is your kryptonite."

"Careful when you talk about my granddaughter," she warned.

The man sitting directly across from her worked for the CIA. The same agency she had once pledged allegiance to. He was no different than the assassin she had killed. They both wanted something from her and would use whatever means they could to get it.

"I am no longer an officer for the CIA," she said in a cold, emotionless voice. "I have a flight to catch which I'm sure you know since you paid for my ticket. I have nothing for you."

"The Russians believe you have intel they want. They'll do whatever it takes to get it. You need to cooperate with us. Addy. We can protect you and your granddaughter."

"Bullshit." Anger flashed through her eyes. "Like you protected my daughter?"

"We didn't know there was a mole in our agency. It wasn't our fault. As soon as it happened, we suspected the agency had been infiltrated and made moves to uncover his identity."

Then he quickly added, "Which we did."

"Too damn late, she was already dead," Elke's tone hardened.

"That's the nature of this business. You've always known the risks."

"I knew the risks. What I failed to realize was in our line of business you can't trust anybody." She stood, pointed her finger at the man. "Not even the agency you work for."

The man folded his hands on the table and continued, "With your help we can nail this bastard. We knew before the Russian handler was murdered in the park, she told you something. That information might save our country from another attack. Did she give you any indication who the spy might be?"

"If I did know something, you'd already know it."

"We need you on this one, Addy."

"Listen to me carefully," her voice rising in intensity, finger shaking. "Tell your boss to pull off all the tails you have on me. Now. Or when I do have intel, he'll be the last to know."

The man leaned back, rubbed his chin and repeated himself, "We need you on this one, Addy."

Elke grabbed her bag and headed to her gate.

CHAPTER 11

I t had been one hell of a day.
     Julia was mad. Too mad to talk.

Laquita had told her friend Max too much.

Julia and Laquita faced each other in her office in what appeared to be a staring contest. She handed Laquita back her phone.

Laquita chewed on her bottom lip. Her finger rubbed the scar on her forehead. "I…I'm worried," Laquita stammered. "Max is a badass. The only way he told that killer anythin' was with a gun to his head."

She knew this wasn't the time to blame Laquita. They needed a plan. First, she had to calm herself down.

After an edgy silence she placed her hand on Laquita's arm and looked her straight in the eye. "He knows about us. Knows where we work and probably where you live. We need to get out of here. We'll take my car and go to the police. It's the only option we have right now."

Going to the police and handing over the photos should keep her and Laquita safe, but she couldn't be certain. It seemed the best course of action, however she couldn't shake the urge to call her grandmother and ask what to do.

No, she thought. *I made her promise to stay out of my life. If I drag her back in, then I'm admitting I can't figure things out for myself. I can do this without Elke's help.*

Laquita slung her large pocketbook over her shoulder, picked up the bat leaning against the bookcase and said,

"Damn right. Let's git the hell outta here."

After locking the office door, she and Laquita hurried down the hall to the elevator. Inside, Julia pushed the button for the main lobby.

"Phew!" she said watching the creaking doors slowly begin to close.

Without warning, a hand from the outside squeezed in and forced the elevator doors open. A man shoved his way inside and stood in front of Laquita and to Julia's right.

"Going down?" his voice sounded familiar.

Julia nodded. His index finger pressed the lobby button.

The man was tall. His unbuttoned coat revealed a paunch that tugged at his shirt. His hair was an unnatural jet-black color that did not match his weathered pockmarked face. He reminded Julia of several of her accounting professors at college. Nerdy.

When the elevator stopped and the doors pulled apart, the man moved aside and stood in front of Julia to let Laquita pass by him. Then, he shifted to allow Julia to step out. Julia gave a brisk smile and started out when the man's hand wrapped around her arm pulling her back.

Julia didn't like the serious glint in the man's eyes. Laquita was shaking her head and swinging the bat in small circles by her side like she was ready to strike. Julia's breathing accelerated.

"Julia," the man said.

Julia looked back to the man.

The man spoke low and fast, "You and your friend go to your place. You'll be safe there. Take the long route. We'll make sure you aren't followed." He let go of her arm and shoved a phone in her hand.

"Did you break into my office?" snapped Julia.

He didn't answer.

"Who are you?"

"Bridge Club. We'll be in touch."

He cut her off before she could respond, "And get rid of both your phones. You can be traced with them."

The man strode briskly past Laquita, through the bakery and out the door of the building.

"Who the hell was that weirdo?" asked Laquita, her hand wrapped firmly around the bat. "I was fixin' to use this bat on him."

Julia stared at her hand holding the phone the stranger gave her. She quickly made up her mind.

"Let me see your phone," demanded Julia.

"Huh?" Laquita looked at her strangely. "Don't ya have your own?"

"I need it now," Julia's voice was impatient. "Trust me on this one. I'll explain later."

Laquita pulled the phone out of her back-jean pocket and reluctantly handed it to Julia. "I ain't heard from Max, if that's what ya wanna know."

Julia scrolled on Laquita's phone till she found Max's contact information. She promptly entered the info in the phone the stranger gave her.

"We need to hurry." She pushed Laquita ahead.

From the corner of her eye, she spotted a trash receptacle by the bakery exit. She tucked the stranger's phone in her pocket and collected her phone. Right before walking out, she tossed Laquita's and her phone in the receptacle. Laquita was in front of her and didn't notice.

Outside she gestured to the left. "I'm parked down the

street in the parking garage."

The sidewalk was crowded with pedestrians. A gathering of clouds had blocked the sun causing a slight drop in the temperature. They both buttoned up their jackets in an attempt to fight off the chill created from the cloud cover. Julia had stepped up the pace. Her long legs were no match for Laquita's giraffe's stride.

Her car was parked on the second floor of the parking garage. Nervously, they searched for any sign of possible threats. There were only a few people moving inside the garage and none appeared interested in them.

Julia beeped the lock twice and they climbed in her car. She backed out of the parking space and headed out of the garage. At the main street, she turned right and accelerated.

"I 'spect we ain't goin' to no police department since you're goin' the wrong direction," quipped Laquita.

"Not yet," replied Julia.

"What'd that weirdo man say to you?"

"He told me we need to go back to my place for now."

"Then we'll call the cops?" Laquita asked sharply.

"I'll let you know when we get there." She glanced and saw the frown on Laquita's face.

"I want my phone back now." Laquita held out her hand.

Julia mumbled, "I threw your phone in the trash."

"What'd you say?"

"I said, I threw your phone in the trash can at the bakery."

"You shittin' me, right?"

"I threw mine away too, Laquita."

"That supposed to make me feel better?"

"I'm sorry, really I am." Julia stared straight ahead. "But our phones could have been used to track us."

"Is that what that crazy ol' fool told ya in the elevator?"

"I know that man." The light rain grew heavier splattering the windshield. Julia clicked up the speed on the windshield wipers.

"Uh-huh. You sure as hell didn't look like ya knew him. I'm a damn fool for trusting ya."

Julia drove through two red lights before making an abrupt turn. Laquita grabbed the handle on the roof before she was slung into Julia.

"Now, ya gonna try and kill me?"

"What I meant was I don't know him personally. I know the people he works with."

"Ya know," Laquita began, "I thought he looked like FBI."

"FBI?" said Julia. "No. What makes you think…. oh, forget it. He's not FBI." Julia sensed Laquita was excited at the prospect of the stranger being with the FBI.

"He's CIA." Julia deliberately left out the word *retired*. She was busy making sure nobody was following them.

"Omigod. That's it. That's why ya bought Fly's business ain't it? He told me he worked for 'em way back. I never believed him. Thought he just wanted to get in my pants. Then I heard he got himself killed at City Park. It made me think maybe he did work for the CIA. I stayed away from the office for a while. I liked Fly. He was good to me. When you took over the business, I never figgered you were with the CIA. I needed a job and I liked the work."

Julia pressed the gas pedal to the floor. The car lurched though the intersection.

Laquita braced herself with both hands against the dashboard. "Looks like God has other plans for me," she said under her breath.

† † †

"Did you find anything?" the woman asked.

"Her most recent client is a person called Kat Lejeune. Not much info in the file on her," said the man.

"She didn't see you, did she?"

"No. I almost got caught but got out in time."

"You gave her the warning?"

"Yes. And she took my advice and headed back to her home."

"See if the Club can find out who this Kat Lejeune really is."

"Think it's an alias?"

"If it's connected to her surveillance at the motel, probably."

"Besides tracking down Kat Lejeune, what do you want us to do regarding Julia?"

"Keep eyes on her and keep me updated. She's not to know I'm involved. I plan on paying a visit to an old acquaintance."

"Alright, I'll let you know what we find."

The line clicked off.

Elke knew the Bridge Club was good, but right now she needed to speed things up. She had to make sure Julia was safe.

CHAPTER 12

A dead reporter.

The phone call from the man he hired was not what Wagner had expected to hear. The hired man was supposed to find out what the journalist knew concerning a Washington mole, then persuade her to leave the area.

Not kill her.

When Congressman Quatterman came to his office two weeks ago and told him there was a reporter snooping around the Hill asking questions about the rumor of a spy in a government agency, Wagner panicked. What if the journalist had made the connection between him and the Russians?

His Russian handler would have taken care of the reporter, but Wagner didn't tell him. If he had told his handler, he would never feel safe.

The Kremlin had highly skilled assassins on their payroll. The journalist would die in an accident of some kind. But his problems wouldn't end there. He feared the Russian government might see him more as a liability than an asset or at the least, a high risk. Perhaps he would be gunned down in a drive-by shooting. Or poisoned. The former Russian spy, Alexander Litvinenko was poisoned by radioactive polonium-210 believed to have been administered in a cup of tea. The assassins had elaborate methods of killing in painful hard-to-trace ways.

That's why he believed he had to make the problem go

away by handling it himself. It could have worked, except he hired the wrong man.

Why on earth had Max given him the name of a contract killer? Did Max know the reputation of the man he recommended? What the hell did it matter now, he thought while pacing back and forth from the large picture window in his office to the middle of the room. An overwhelming sense of dread made him too nervous to sit.

Max had graduated with honors from college. Besides his economic degree, he had a political science degree. A degree that taught how laws were made. Instead, Max chose to break laws. He was a petty criminal who had spent plenty of time in jail. Once for breaking into a closed liquor store in the middle of the night. The next time was more serious, selling crack to an undercover cop. He claimed he'd been set up by a police informant.

Wagner grew tired of helping the man out. Max always blamed others for his problems. Nothing was ever his fault. Always scraped by to make a living. Wagner shook his head thinking about Max never living up to his potential. Finally, he needed to tell Max not to call him again. *Get your shit together, Max. You can do better* he remembered telling him. Wagner knew Max might jeopardize his career if he stayed involved with him.

Then, the tables turned. It was Wagner's turn to ask for a favor. He had figured Max was a better choice than going to his handler thinking the reporter might not really know anything. Or had she?

The assassin instructed him over the phone to meet him again at the park, tomorrow at noon. Then he would reveal what he had learned from the reporter. The murderer demanded more money. Why he made this demand, he didn't say.

Wagner wanted to tell the smug killer he had fucked up the job he hired him to do. He wanted to say that, but rational thinking helped him keep his mouth shut. His mind was whirling with thoughts of having another meeting with the killer. What if he didn't go? What if—

A soft rap on his office door startled him. His nerves already on edge.

Standing in the middle of his office, he wiped his damp forehead, hurried over to his desk and sat in his high-back leather chair.

"Yes," he cleared his throat and composed himself.

His assistant, Megan eased the door open and walked in holding a tall drink with a cup sleeve wrapped around it. She was dressed in a tailored gray pantsuit accented with a navy blouse underneath the jacket. The way those pants snugged her curvy body distracted him for a second.

Megan was the most competent assistant he had ever had. He and Megan were alike in many ways. They both were Type-A personalities and cared nothing about a work-life balance. It was a high price they both paid in their personal lives. Megan, on the other hand, did have a boyfriend. Wagner was surprised when he found out. Why, he wasn't sure since she was such a desirable young woman.

"You look tired, Mr. Wagner. Is everything okay?"

Wagner shuffled a stack of papers on his desk attempting to look like he had been busy working.

"Please, call me Alan in private, Megan. We know each other well enough to drop the formalities."

"Sorry, Mr.—I mean Alan. You're right." Her lips curled upward, and she added, "It's a hard habit for me to break."

He grinned and continued, "I'm working on which legislation reaches the floor for a vote." His gaze passed over her again.

Gripping the cup with both hands, she said, 'I knew you were busy. You haven't even gone to lunch. I bought you some coffee with an extra shot of expresso, just the way you like it." She walked around his desk and stood next to him.

He could smell the scent of her perfume. Suddenly his thoughts were consumed with how he wanted to grab her and press his lips against her voluminous lips. It had been too long since he'd been with a woman.

Megan leaned forward and handed him the hot drink. "Is there anything you need me to do?"

His hand wrapped around the hot cup sleeve, accidentally brushing against her hand. Wagner felt a surge of electricity shoot through his body.

If he were to act on his impulses right now it might complicate his already complicated life. He had enough problems. Besides, Megan would probably reject him. He was almost twice her age.

He longed to share his problems with somebody. His last lover always listened, never judged. This time was different. They work together. She had a boyfriend. Even if Megan was interested, how would she react if she ever found out he was a Russian spy? Would she hate him if she knew he was involved in a murder? No, those secrets were better left buried.

Wagner coughed to clear his throat. "Not right now." He was certain if Megan kept standing next to him, he would no longer be able to resist the temptation to pull her next to him. He lifted the cup and said, "Thanks for this. I need it."

Megan turned and walked around to the front of his desk.

He saw the troubled look on her face.

"I've been concerned about you, Mr.—Alan. The long hours you have been working. Do you even go home at night or are you sleeping on your couch?" She nodded toward his leather couch.

"Didn't realize you noticed. I try to make it home, but some days I just can't seem to catch up. Right now, I'm trying to find common ground within our party to get legislation passed. We've got to get our fiscal house in order."

"I know how hard you've worked to get support behind the agenda of the President. You're doing a great job as Speaker."

"Your kind words mean a lot. Washington likes nothing more than to see a person in power crash and burn and my position makes me a target."

"If there's a fight, Alan, I know you'll be the one left standing," she said in a soft voice.

Megan had a way of calming him. Right now, though, he wasn't sure he was concealing his interest in her. Changing the subject, he said, "Enough talk regarding this job. How are you doing?"

"I'm fine. Like you, burning too much midnight oil."

"I hope this job isn't preventing you from spending time with your boyfriend."

Megan didn't speak, making him regret his poor choice of words.

Wagner shrugged and added, "Forgive me for prying into your private life, Megan. It's none of my business."

"It's okay. We broke up over a month ago."

"Sorry to hear that," he said with as much sincerity as he could muster, all the while excited over the prospect of her being unattached.

"Honestly, I don't know how we got together in the first place. We didn't have anything in common. All he talked about was football. When I talked about my job, he got jealous. We finally broke up over pizza."

"Pizza? Seriously?"

"No. Not exactly. We hadn't been getting along for some time. He was insanely jealous. I admit I talked a lot about my job and how I enjoyed working for you. He never liked when I worked late. There were a lot of little things that led to our break-up. It just happened the night we stayed at my place and ordered pizza. When we sat down to eat, I told him the first time I had the Margherita pizza was when you ordered it for us. He never let me finish telling him we had worked through lunch. We got in a fight and I told him to get out. It was over. So, I kid that we broke up over pizza."

"I hope this wasn't my fault."

"It all turned out for the best. He left and I got to eat the whole pizza myself."

Wagner chuckled. "At least it had a good ending." They both erupted into laughter.

"All your talk about pizza is making me hungry," Wagner said. "How would you like to join me for dinner tonight? We can discuss some of the projects I'm working on."

"Yes. I would like that. What time?"

A loud ping from his cell phone averted his thoughts. It was an incoming text message. He quickly glanced at his cell phone screen and noticed it was from the contract killer. His stomach shifted uneasily as he read the text.

Change of plans. Meet at 1pm. Don't be late. Money in brown paper bag.

Wagner quickly flipped the phone over to prevent Megan

from reading the text. He couldn't be sure she didn't see it.

"Do you need to answer your phone?" Megan inquired.

"No, It's nothing urgent." Wagner heard the strain in his voice. "How does six sound?"

"Could we make it a little later, say around 7:30? I've got some errands to run first."

"7:30 it is."

Megan turned on her heels and walked out of his office.

Wagner's fingers curled up inside his fists. He was certain tomorrow would not be a good day. He needed one more favor from Max.

A gun.

CHAPTER 13

Julia and Laquita sat inside her parked car watching the rain bounce off the windshield. The torrential downpour battered the roof of the car like a drum roll. An occasional clap of thunder lit up the sky.

"Ya ain't gotta garage or carport so we don't git wet?" groaned Laquita. "Ya gotta be kiddin' me."

Julia had circled the block twice to make sure nobody had followed them from her office. She parked her car along the curb in front of her home to wait out the storm. Hopefully the rain would stop or at least ease up allowing them to make a dash to her front door.

What was Laquita's problem anyway? The D.C. area was expensive. She was lucky she could even afford a home. A home with a garage was…well, out of her price range. Besides most people in D.C. biked, walked or took the Metro.

Julia, aggravated with Laquita's smart ass attitude, snapped, "I suppose you have a garage?"

"Lord no. Why'd I need a garage? Ain't got no car."

A wave of regret surged through Julia. There were many things she didn't know about Laquita. Partly because there was too much happening right now. And partly because she didn't care enough to ask the woman about her private life.

Julia made a sympathetic face and said, "I'm sorry Laquita. I just assumed you had a car."

"No hard feelins." Laquita leaned forward and peered through the windshield toward the sky. "I just figgered ya had a garage."

A slow smile crept across Julia's face. *Touché.* She deserved that.

Staring out the windshield, Julia saw in the distance the sky slowly beginning to lighten. "Looks like the rain should taper off soon. We can make a dash for it or just wait a little longer."

"Seein' these are all the clothes I got, I vote we stay put," replied Laquita. "This rain is a regular frog wash."

They stared out the car windows even though the raindrops pelting the windows obscured any view of what was outside.

Julia said, "My grandmother always had sayings for life events. But you have a very colorful way of expressing yourself, are you from the South?"

Tilting her head toward Julia, her face got serious. Laquita answered in a slow southern drawl, "I'm from New York City." Julia's eyes and mouth froze in an expression of stunned disbelief. She added, "It took a whole lotta practice to git me a Suthern accent."

Laquita's stone expression morphed into a grin. Julia laughed at the joke realizing how stupid her question sounded.

"I'm from a podunk town in Alabama, called Masonville. In the south we call it a one-horse-town, if ya git what I mean. Lived there till I was sixteen. Then one night momma packed up us kids and we upped and left for Dee-Cee. Left most our things we didn' need, includin' my no-good daddy. We moved in with my Aunt Selma till momma saved nuff for us to have our own place.

Julia didn't want to pry into why a mother would pack up and leave suddenly in the middle of the night, but she imagined it was to escape a bad situation. Maybe that was when Laquita got the scar on her forehead.

"Does your mother still live in the D.C. area?"

"Uh-huh. Not fer from the airport," piped Laquita. "I git my colorful language from Big G. She came and stayed with us after momma got us a place.

"Big G?"

"Big G was what I called my granny. When I was itty bitty I hurd my daddy call her that. Then, I just started calling her Big G and it stuck. Her real name was Gracelyn. She was a big bone woman. Liked her food. Specially sweets. Big G had a sayin' 'bout everythin'. She'd say, 'We don't have a pot to piss in or a window to throw it out of.'"

"That's funny. You'll have to teach me a few of those sayings." Julia couldn't believe she was actually enjoying being stuck in the vehicle with Laquita.

"Big G took care of me and my two brothers cuz momma had to work two jobs. I spent mosta my time with Big G. When she died, momma moved us back in with my daddy. Didn't take her long to figger out why she left him in the first place."

Laquita shifted uncomfortably in her car seat, her fingers gently rubbed the scar on her forehead. She continued, "I didn' like Dee-Cee. I had to go to a school I despised. 'Em yankee kids were mean. Told me I talk funny. Cause of that, when I was at school, I kept my mouth shut. Then one day my teacher asked me a question. I tried to sound like 'em, but I didn'. All 'em kids laughed at me."

Julia narrowed her lips as the familiar feeling from high school began to surface. In middle and high school, everyone wanted to fit in and be liked by the popular kids. Julia was shy and lacked confidence. Those years were difficult.

Laquita said, "Guess you was a popular kid. Cheerleader

or somethin'."

Julia shook her head. "Cheerleaders don't become accountants. I was a science-math nerd long before there was a STEM program for girls. My legs in middle-school were too long and my feet too big. Boys called me Olive Oyl. In high school I never felt like I fit in. Because my grandmother was away a lot, I never could do much with my classmates."

"Now look at me and you," said Laquita. "Whose gonna believe I'm working with the CIA? I shoulda believed Fly when he told me he worked for 'em."

A rumble of loud thunder caused Julia to jump and Laquita's hand to fly up to her chest.

Damn. She should never have misled Laquita about the man in the elevator working for the CIA. He was probably a retired CIA officer. Most of the Bridge Club were retired CIA officers not ready to spend their days playing golf, fishing or whatever retired people do. It was only a matter of time before Julia had to explain her past to Laquita.

"About the CIA." Julia intertwined her fingers.

Laquita turned in the passenger seat giving Julia her full attention. Julia stayed silent contemplating how much she should tell Laquita. The woman had already jeopardized their safety when she told her friend Max that they were surveilling the motel.

Laquita said, "How 'bout ya tell me how ya know CIA folks. How long ya been workin' fer 'em?"

"It's complicated." Julia's face stiffened. She folded her arms across her chest.

"So, ya don't work for 'em?"

"It's complicated," repeated Julia.

"I got that," huffed Laquita as she crossed her arms. "We

got 'nuff trouble without ya lying to me. How 'bout ya don't piss on my leg and tell me it's rainin'."

At first, Julia giggled at Laquita's remark then she burst out laughing.

Laquita joined in.

The rain was now a drizzle lightly tapping on the windshield.

"You're right Laquita. I need to explain everything to you. It is complicated, but…" Julia held up her hand to keep Laquita from talking. "But I do owe you the truth. We are in this together and I think together we can help each other figure out why Kat Lejeune hired my firm. The rain has let up enough for us to head inside my place, have some hot chocolate and—."

Julia froze in mid-sentence when she realized her problem.

CHAPTER 14

"You havin' a stroke or somethin'?" Laquita asked Julia. "What is it?"

Julia stared out the window. Her mind scrambling to figure out what she should do.

"Kat Lejeune." She turned her head toward Laquita.

"I was supposed to meet her at the office today at five and give her the photos I took and collect the rest of the money she owes me."

"Now hold your horses. Don't you be gettin' stupid Julia. Max warned me to stay away. That CIA man or whatever he is told ya to git out of there. Just call her up and tell her somebody in your family died and ya gotta go to a funeral. That's like almost the truth."

"She's probably on her way to my office by now. I've got to find her phone number and call. She could be in danger."

"Sure, you do just that. And maybe while you're at it, you outta ask that crazy bitch why she framed us. I betcha she hired that murderer."

"Frame us for what? That's absurd. She hired me to get photos of her husband and the woman together."

Julia twisted to reach in the back seat for her backpack. She unzipped the bag and quickly searched through the files she had taken from her office. Kat Lejeune's file was not in her backpack. Her heart raced causing her chest to hurt.

"It's not here Laquita. I must have accidentally left it at the office."

What if the killer was waiting to see who might show up at her office? What if Kat Lejeune became his next victim?

"Why would ya leave the one file we need? You *really* don't work for the CIA, do ya?"

"Dammit Laquita, I didn't leave it on purpose," she said curtly. She punched the burn phone on and saw the time posted 4:40. Julia let her head drop against the steering wheel and said, "We have to go back. We've got to warn Kat Lejeune. She might be innocent in all of this." Julia put the key in the ignition and started the car.

"Don't I git a vote?" protested Laquita.

The clock in the car glowed 4:42.

Laquita placed her hand on Julia's hand preventing her from putting the car in drive. "It's too late Julia. We don't have nuff time to git back to the office."

Laquita was right. This time of day was rush hour traffic. The streets would be clogged with workers trying to get home or to the nearest bar. She turned off the ignition and sunk down in her seat feeling defeated and frustrated.

"What are you doing?" asked Julia.

Laquita had the backpack in her lap and was rummaging inside.

Laquita announced, "What have we here?" She fished out a folder. "This one was put in upside down." When she turned the folder around, the name Kat Lejeune was on the label.

"Oh my God. Let me have it." Julia snatched the folder out of Laquita's hand, opened it and found the contact number for Lejeune.

"Yeah, you can thank me later," scoffed Laquita.

Julia's hands were shaking as she thumbed the number. The time had ticked to 4:45. "Shit, it's busy." She waited a second and called again. Still busy.

"Come on Kat. Get off your damn phone. Pick up," Julia muttered out loud.

Was Lejeune already at her office? Less than fifteen minutes and it would be five o'clock. The phone was ringing. Kat was not answering. Maybe she didn't recognize the number and thought it was a spam call.

Julia was considering her options if Lejeune didn't answer when she heard the woman's voice.

"Hello?"

Julia took a second to catch her breath. She blinked, calmed herself and asked, "Is this Kat Lejeune?"

"It is. Who is this?"

Julia gave Laquita a thumbs up.

"This is Julia Bagal with the private investigative firm you hired."

Lejeune said, "I'm very sorry, but I'm still at work. I'm going to be at least twenty minutes late. I tried calling your number to let you know. It just kept going to voice mail."

"Sorry. I have a different phone. My other phone broke." She watched Laquita mouthing the word *funeral*. She looked out her side window to keep from being distracted by Laquita.

"I'm afraid I'll have to cancel our meeting and reschedule with you. I have a funeral to attend. Very unexpected." Julia was hoping the last part of her sentence would cause a reaction from her client. Would Kat tell her that her husband and the woman were dead?

"Oh. I'm very sorry to hear that. I understand." Lejeune paused and then continued, "But, if it's possible I really need to see those photos right away. Can you email them to me, and I will send you the money?"

It seemed strange the client didn't mention her husband had never come home. Even if his body had not been identified by the police, Lejeune would have said something. A wife would have notified the police or called her to find out what happened to her husband when he didn't show up last night.

"When was the last time you saw your husband, Mrs. Lejeune?"

"What? I don't see how that has anything to do with what I'm paying you to do. Did you or did you not get photos of my husband and the woman at the motel?"

"Yes, I got photos. One of a man I thought was your husband entering the motel room. Also, I have photos of the woman in room 205. Would you like to tell me what's going on?"

"I'll pay you double to send them to me," Lejeune's voice sounded desperate.

"Maybe I'll send these photos to the police and let them know you're involved?"

"Involved in what?" Lejeune asked in an angry, irritated tone of voice. "What are you talking about?"

"The murder of a man and woman at Willow Oaks Motel. Was the dead man your husband or is your husband the murderer?"

Lejeune clicked off.

"What'd she say?" asked Laquita.

"She hung up. She didn't sound like she knew what had happened. If not, then her husband came home. Or lied and told her he was away on a business trip. Who knows?"

What Julia did know was Kat Lejeune would now check out what she had told her. Hopefully she would go to the police and tell them what she knew.

There were too many possibilities of what might have happened at the Willow Oaks Motel. But she was certain, Kat Lejeune's story was full of holes.

CHAPTER 15

"Rain's let up," announced Julia. "Let's make a run for it."
She tucked the burn phone in her jacket pocket.
Laquita had tossed the backpack in the backseat after retrieving
Kat Lejeune's file. She couldn't easily reach it from the front
seat.

Stepping out of the car, she noticed Laquita was by the
front door holding her pocketbook with one hand and the bat
in the other hand. "Damn," she whispered under her breath.
The least Laquita could have done was get the backpack. She
opened the back door, stretched across the seat and retrieved
the bag.

After slamming the car door, she scanned up and down
the street making sure she didn't see any possible threats
before scurrying to her front door. "You could've helped me
get everything out of the car," she said aggravated.

"Ya hangry?" Laquita's eyes looked amused. She bent down
and petted a calico cat that had strayed onto the porch. "This
belong to you?"

"No. That's Albert, the neighbor's cat. He likes to visit."

She thought about what Laquita had said. It was time to
eat. For the past hour she felt tired and grumpy. Her blood
sugar had dropped.

"When I open the door, make sure Albert doesn't sneak
in," she cautioned Laquita.

Standing in the foyer, Laquita's head swung side to side

surveying the home. "Wow, Julia. This place looks a whole lot better on the inside than the outside."

Julia tossed her backpack on the couch and explained, "It's a historic home that I had renovated. I liked that it was an end-unit row house and had a porch."

"I love how white people buy ol' run down homes and call 'em historic. I live in an ol' run-down apartment. We call it a dump."

Laquita kicked off her shoes and in her socks skated across the hardwood floors in the living area to the kitchen. "Damn, you sure ain't payin' me enough. You got yourself a chef kitchen with 'em stainless steel appliances." She ran her hand along the smooth granite countertops. "You done good for yourself, Julia."

Julia wondered where Laquita lived. The woman had told her she didn't own a car. Maybe Laquita lived in the projects or for all she knew she could be living with her criminal friend, Max. They were two people from very different backgrounds.

She had always been critical of people who made bad choices and didn't try to better themselves. Now things were not as black and white as she thought. It was gray and grayer.

Julia had always been conservative in almost every aspect of her life. From her finances down to the men she dated. She kept detailed spreadsheets to budget her spending and lived as she once told her best friend, *within her means*. Then her life was turned upside down when she learned about her past and witnessed the deaths of people she cared about. Things that had once seemed important, no longer had meaning. Her therapist told her she had survivor's guilt.

"Why ya got a bunch of dead plants?' Laquita's rubbed a dry leaf between her fingers making it crumble into a flowerpot sitting on the kitchen windowsill.

"They're not dead. They're dormant. Dormancy is when plants go into hibernation, allowing them to survive the cold weather," she explained.

"Hell, I know the difference tween dormant and dead. And these here plants are dead as a door nail." Laquita picked up a pot and added, "You should just toss 'em out."

Julia quickly snatched the pot out of Laquita's hand and put the plant back on the windowsill. "My therapist told me plants would be helpful."

"You got a shrink?"

"She's a therapist." *Why'd I open my big mouth?*

"Did that shrink tell ya to git dead plants or ya just got a black thumb?"

Ignoring the question, Julia said, "The guest bedroom is upstairs. I use the room on the right for my office. You can stay in the guest bedroom on the left."

Laquita's eyed the top of the stairway and then faced Julia. "Maybe we oughta eat somethin' first. Then we can figger out how to git our money from that Lejeune woman."

Strange how Laquita said *our money* when she was the one who owned the business. They weren't partners. Laquita worked for her.

"I've got some left-over spaghetti. How does that sound?"

After supper, Julia cleared the table while Laquita slipped upstairs to use the bathroom. When Laquita came back downstairs a half-hour later, the dishes had already been rinsed and stacked in the dishwasher.

"Can I help ya clean up?" Laquita asked.

Julia sat down at her mid-century dining table and opened

her laptop. Her backpack was propped up against the table leg. Kat Lejeune's file, a pen and notepad were next to the computer. She had a glass of water for her and one for Laquita.

"Just sit down and let's review the timeline and what we know. I think this will help us decide our best course of action." Julia pushed the yellow notepad and the pen across the table to Laquita.

Laquita tapped the pen on the pad of paper in front of her several times before asking, "So, this is how the CIA figgers shit out? Cuz I was thinkin' it'd be a bit more high-tech."

Julia caught the words before they escaped from her mouth. This was how *she* figured things out. It wasn't exactly a spreadsheet, but data organization was how she rolled.

If she wanted Laquita to help her, she'd have to be careful what she said next. Laquita wanted to go to the police. At first Julia believed that was the best option, but now she wasn't sure. The man who worked for the Bridge Club warned her not to go to the authorities. The only reason the Club would be involved would be if the Russians were somehow involved. That didn't make sense at the moment. Julia knew she needed to be honest with the woman staring at her and waiting impatiently for an explanation.

She took a sip of water before beginning, "First off, we're safe in my house. And yes, this *is* how the CIA does it." There was a scrap of truth to what she said. She imagined the CIA analytical team sat around a table hashing out the evidence during their conferences. She'd seen a movie once where this had happened.

"Then ya do work for the CIA?"

"No." Julia slowly shook her head. "Remember what I told you in the car...."

"Yeah, yeah, it's complicated."

"I'm not employed by the CIA, but I do assist them from time to time." It surprised her how easily that lie slipped out of her mouth. Maybe Elke had taught her more than how to use a gun.

"Holy shit. That's freakin' awesome."

Awesome was not the word that came to Julia's mind.

CHAPTER 16

L aquita lifted the glass of water toward Julia and asked, "Got anything stronger than water?"

"I have some wine in the kitchen," replied Julia. "Want red or white?"

"Got any beer?"

"No. I don't care for it."

"Shoulda figgered you were a wine kinda person."

"Not sure what you mean by that. Do you want a glass of wine or not?"

"Maybe later. I wuz wanting me a beer."

"Maybe we'll hit the bars later."

"Really?"

"No," Julia said tightly. "We've got to figure out what's going on."

Laquita frowned and began tapping her pen on the tablet.

"Let's start at the beginning with what we know. You can take notes," Julia instructed.

At the top of the yellow pad, Laquita wrote in big letters, *NIGHT MOVES.*

"Huh?" said Julia as her finger tapped the words Laquita had written.

"Max's favorite song. Bob Seger sang it." Laquita broke out singing, "*Workin' on mysteries without any clues, workin' on our night moves.*"

"I believe that song is about a guy trying to put the moves on a girl," Julia said.

Laquita erupted in laughter. "Yeah, Max was always workin' on his *Night Moves*." She made quote gestures with her fingers.

Julia's lips softened and curled up. "Okay, let's work on our *Night Moves*' timeline and figure this mystery out." She opened the file labeled Kat Lejeune and pulled out a form that resembled a legal document.

"Number one," Julia said while scanning the document. "A woman, who used the name Kat Lejeune, contacted me at the office to do surveillance on her husband."

"Member, I done told ya somethin' was wrong since that bitch didn't have a picture of her man."

"Actually, you said it was kinda strange not wrong."

"Same thin'."

Julia rolled her eyes and continued, "I printed out the photos I took." Julia placed the first photo in the middle of the table allowing them both to view it.

She tapped the picture with her finger. "This is the man who got out of the car. I wished I had gotten his tag number. He kept his back to us, but even with the ball cap on, you can see his hair sticks out and is a dark color. We believed he was the husband at the time. Here are several more photos of him walking down the upstairs hallway toward room 205. His dark sunglasses and ball cap conceal most of his features, but I can zoom in on my laptop." She turned the computer to give Laquita a view of the screen.

Next, Julia placed another photo in the middle of the table. "Here's the picture of the woman who opened the door. The red-haired woman was tall, almost the same height as the man in the doorway and dressed in slacks with a matching blazer." Julia hit the spacebar on her laptop to bring up the picture on her screen. "Now look when I zoom in on the woman's face.

What do you notice?"

"That ya need a whole lot mor' practice with that camera. That picture's blurry and that man's blocking a lotta her."

Agitated, Julia said, "Just look at the photo and tell me what you see."

Laquita squinted, leaned toward the screen and studied the picture for a few beats. "Oh my God." Laquita arched back, her voice rising in intensity, "I git it. That woman ain't happy to see that dude."

"You're right. If they were lovers, she'd be smiling, not looking like that. But there's something else not right in this picture."

"What? Ya think that husband got a gun?"

"Stay with me." Julia held up her hand to slow Laquita's questions down.

"The woman's clothes are too conservative to be at this dump for drugs or sex or both. Her outfit is what you would wear in an office, not seduce a man. You asked me when we were doing surveillance what Kat Lejeune was wearing when she came to my office. Well, she was dressed in a very nice professional outfit. Conservative. The husband is probably conservative. Why would he meet a woman at this pay by the hour motel?"

Laquita quickly started writing.

"I don't git it." Laquita quit writing and stared at the picture of the woman and man standing in the motel doorway. "There's gotta be a reason she's there."

"Yes, there does, but I just don't have an answer. Max told you there were two dead bodies in that motel room. We saw a man leave, therefore we know there were at least three people in that room. Two men and a woman."

"Ya think that husband finds out she's with another man. Shows up, kills 'em both?"

"Or maybe the murderer was already in the room," suggested Julia.

"But we both saw the husband leave."

"I don't believe the man who drove up was the same man who left."

"How come?"

"The man we saw leave had a limp and wore a leather jacket. The man in this photo," she pointed with her finger. "Is the man we saw park and go up to the room. He didn't limp and he wasn't wearing a leather jacket. I was focused on the baseball cap. Both men were wearing it."

"That's right 'bout the jacket. I didn' notice a limp."

"Because it was a slight limp. I saw it through the camera lens."

Laquita started writing again.

Julia waited till Laquita finished writing before adding, "The woman who opened the door wasn't unhappy, she was scared."

"Lemme see that close up of her again."

Julia zoomed back in on the woman's face and turned the screen for Laquita to study.

"Oh my god. She does look scared. Then which of 'em is the husband?"

"I don't know. But Kat Lejeune sounded surprised when I mentioned the dead bodies. It would make sense that her husband wasn't the one murdered by Lejeune's reaction."

"Unless." Laquita looked directly at her. "That bitch ain't got no husband."

"I thought about that too. What we need to know is her

motivation for hiring us."

"Even if she used a fake name, we can trace her number," said Laquita.

"I planned on doing that, but first I need you to call Max and see what he knows. Every time we learn something, add it to our *Night Moves'* list." She closed the laptop and sat back while Laquita called Max.

After several tries Laquita said, "He ain't answerin'. Not even my texts."

"Maybe you should leave a message and identify yourself on the texts. He won't recognize the number from the burn phone. Hopefully he'll get in touch with you soon."

Meanwhile, Julia went into the living room and switched on the TV channel surfing for coverage of the murders and explosion. A news station reported the victims had not been identified and no arrests had been made. Flipping to the local news there was footage which showed a plume of smoke from the explosion and the street was cordoned off by police investigating the bombing.

A spokesman for the Washington Hospital Center said the survivors had been taken there for treatment, two with serious injuries. The detective in charge of the homicide had been treated and released. A picture flashed across the screen with his name typed at the bottom. *Detective Mike Shockley.* Julia thought she recognized him from the other day when they drove to the crime scene.

Laquita walked into the living room and asked, "Whatta ya watching?

"Just an update on the bombing at the motel. Still no information on the victims. Did you leave Max a message?"

"Yeah. I hope he's okay. Whatta ya think we should do?"

"Right now, I think we're safe staying here. Kat Lejeune or whoever she is, knows by now about the murders. If she's innocent, I'm sure she'll contact the police. We need Max to call us. I'm going to go online and see if I can trace the number Kat Lejeune gave me."

"Are we gonna tell the CIA what we figgered out?"

"They'll get in touch with us. I'm certain of that."

The man from the Club said they'd be in touch. Julia just hoped that person wasn't Elke.

CHAPTER 17

S he shouldn't be surprised at anything Laquita said, but this
caught her off guard.

Laquita was wearing the robe she loaned her while Laquita's
clothes were being washed. She had politely offered Laquita
a few of her oversized t-shirts for her to sleep in tonight.
Tomorrow they would go by Laquita's place and get some of
her things.

Laquita informed her that she slept in the *au naturel*. She
whined that PJs confined her.

"You should try it, it's liberatin'," Laquita said.

Julia wondered what the hell she was thinking by inviting
Laquita to spend the night at her place. Hopefully there
wouldn't be a fire and they'd have to run out into the street,
Laquita swinging her big naked butt for all the neighbors to
see.

Max had not called back.

The Bridge Club hadn't contacted them, and she was
unable to find any info on Kat Lejeune's phone number.

Depressed by what wasn't happening, she decided she'd
have to take what evidence they had to the authorities in the
morning.

Like it or not.

She was having trouble falling asleep.

Laquita had gone to bed over an hour ago saying she

was pooped. She was pooped too, yet her brain was still in overdrive. It wouldn't shut down. Her therapist had told her about things she could do to reduce her anxiety. Meditate, exercise, listen to music, and buy houseplants.

Another suggestion from the therapist was to quit watching the news. The woman didn't mention what to do when she was the news. The one-hour sessions cost $150. She wondered if it was even worth continuing to go, but she needed an outlet for her problems. The therapist had heard all about her life. Julia wasn't sure she believed everything she told her. Hell, it was hard to believe herself.

Now, once again, she was caught up in another—another what? Murder-for-hire plot? Russian hit? Drugs? What? What was she not seeing?

Julia slid her pistol under the pillow next to her. She told Laquita they were safe, but there were too many unexplained issues with this murder.

Double murder.

And according to the news, the killer had not been caught.

Over seven months ago, she and Derick Carver, an ex-paratrooper, helped unravel a plot to assassinate the President and Vice President of the United States. What if Laquita knew all this about her? What if Laquita knew who really got her former employer killed? She had only met Laquita a little over a week ago. She shouldn't trust her. Not yet anyway. Trust had to be earned.

Right now, she hoped Kat Lejeune, or whatever her name really was, wasn't in danger or worse. Dead.

The last time Julia looked at the time on her bedside clock it was a little after midnight. She had fallen asleep for what seemed like fifteen minutes when she was jarred awake by a sound.

Outside.

Meow. Meow. It was Albert.

Why don't they lock that damn cat up at night?

The next sound she thought she heard was concerning. It sounded like the front doorknob being jiggled. She forced her groggy mind to wake up. She sat up in bed and listened. Her bedroom was located in the front part of the house adjacent to the living area. In the back of the row house was the kitchen and dining area.

She hastily slid her hand under the pillow and wrapped her hand around the grip of the pistol. She stood beside her bed and stuffed the pillows under the covers to make it look like she was underneath sleeping. Padding softly, she positioned herself by the hinge side of the bedroom door. She held the gun with both hands against her chest keeping a tight grip.

A second seemed to last too long while she stood motionless, listening. The only sound she heard was her heart thumping against her chest.

It's him. The killer has found out where I live.

Light footfalls eased across the hardwood floors, then silence. She tried to keep a steady grip on the pistol. The quiet sound of footsteps began inching toward her bedroom.

She held her breath, afraid to make a sound. Tilting her head, she strained to listen.

The sound stopped just outside her door.

The doorknob turned and slowly pushed open. Did the pillows fool him? Or did he know it was a ruse?

The shadow softly crossed the threshold and entered her bedroom.

He stopped.

Could he hear her pounding heart?

The shadow moved closer to the bed. Julia took three steps toward the back of the target and aimed her gun.

"Stop. Drop your weapon. Put your hands in the air and slowly turn around." Julia's voice gruff from her parched mouth.

The shadow raised its arms and slowly turned.

"I see you have learned a thing or two from me," said the shadow.

Julia knew the voice.

She lowered her pistol and switched on the light. "Dammit, Elke, I could have shot you."

"I've missed you. Come give me a hug, honey," her grandmother held her arms open wide.

It didn't matter how angry she might get with this annoying woman, her bright blue eyes always melted her anger."

The two embraced. "How did you get a key to my front door. I no longer keep one hidden outside."

The older woman's seasoned face with pale lips surrounded by wrinkles from years of smoking, laughed. She opened her hand holding some small tools. "Lock-picking is a very useful skill," Elke said grinning. "One I should teach you some day."

"Is it impossible for you to call first and not break into my homes?" Julia remembered the last time her grandmother had broken into her home.

"I didn't break into your duplex." Elke put the tools in the pocket of her jacket. "You left a key outside in one of those fake rocks. I'm glad you don't do that anymore."

"A lot of good that did. You still got in." Julia walked over to her nightstand, pulled open the drawer and deposited her pistol inside. "You could have called. I'm sure if the Bridge

Club gave you lock picking tools, they'd give you the number to the burn phone they gave me."

"I knew if I called, you'd tell me to stay out of your business."

"Even though you knew what I'd say, you break into my house anyway," Julia said stiffly.

"This is a dangerous situation, Julia."

"It's always a dangerous situation when you're involved. And almost always illegal."

Elke frowned. "Why don't we go in the kitchen and have a glass of warm milk and talk?"

Julia was now certain the Russians were involved. Otherwise, Elke wouldn't be here. She let out an exasperated sigh and led Elke to her kitchen, but somehow, she was sure that the woman knew where it was located.

"I like your new place," said Elke walking through the living area to the kitchen. "It's much larger than that cramped duplex."

"Glad you approve," Julia said sarcastically.

In the kitchen, Elke sat down at the table and Julia heated up the milk. "Do you want chocolate in your milk?" Julia asked.

"No. Chocolate has caffeine. I won't sleep if I drink it."

The clock on the oven said 1:30. Julia rolled her eyes.

The electric kettle quickly heated the milk. She poured the milk into two mugs and handed one to Elke.

"I remember when I used to do this for you as a little girl before your bedtime," Elke reminded.

Julia remembered too, yet those times were far and few between Elke's extensive travels. She used to believe Elke traveled for work, which was technically correct, only now she knew that job was with the CIA and not as a traveling nurse.

"Alright, Elke, let's cut the bullshit and get to why you're in my kitchen at one thirty in the morning."

"You never were patient. Not even as a little girl." Elke held the mug up to her lips and blew on the hot liquid. She took a sip. "We have reason to believe…"

Julia interrupted, "We? As in the Bridge Club?"

"Yes. We have uncovered some chatter that's very disturbing. The Russians are planning something. We don't know what yet. The fact you were hired for surveillance and then there's a bombing at that motel could be a coincidence. Or.. "

"Or what?

"The Russians might be sending me a message."

Julia's mouth fell open in disbelief. "What message?"

Elke's face had a cool indifference as if they were merely talking about the weather and not a Russian plot or homicide.

"Honestly Julia I don't know."

Julia felt the blood drain from her face realizing that Elke might think the bombing was a message to remind her grandmother of how the Russians had murdered her mother and father. The fact Julia was working an assignment when the bombing took place was why her grandmother was here.

Again.

Her grandmother was drawing a nexus between Russian activity and what had happened at the motel.

Maybe this was Elke's lame attempt to get her to quit her new enterprise.

Elke heard it first. She pressed her finger against her lips and slipped out a pistol from her holster in the back of her slacks.

Albert was making noises.

Only this time he was hissing.

Elke, with her pistol drawn, switched off the lights in the kitchen. Julia knew somebody or something, maybe a dog, was on her porch. Albert didn't get upset unless he was startled or scared.

"Stay here while I check this out," ordered Elke.

Julia fumbled over to the backdoor in the dark to make sure it was latched, and the deadbolt engaged. Elke crouched into a crawl and moved cautiously toward the living area. Julia needed to get to her bedroom and retrieve her pistol from her nightstand. Her eyes slowly adjusted to the darkness as she stooped low and rounded the doorway heading to her bedroom.

Elke's silhouette was below the living room window. Julia entered her bedroom, hit the light switch with her finger cutting the lights off. She moved swiftly toward her bed smacking her shin on the iron frame, mumbling curse words under her breath. Using her hand to guide her around the bed to the nightstand, she pulled the drawer of the nightstand open. In her peripheral she caught movement outside her window. She retrieved her gun and took in a deep breath and let it out slow. She squatted and moved to the side of the window. Easing upward she kept a firm two-handed grip on the pistol. She sucked in another deep breath, let go of the pistol with one hand and pulled the blinds back. Nothing. No movement could be discerned from the moonless night.

Maybe her mind had played tricks on her. Albert had quit making any noise. Tiptoeing, she headed back into the living room to check on Elke. The front door was ajar, and a cool breeze was chilling the air in the room.

Elke was gone.

She rushed to the front door, kept to one side and peered

out. She anxiously searched the porch and down the street keeping a strong grip on her weapon. Albert was no longer on the porch. A streetlight located several houses down from hers was casting a dim light on the cars parked along the curb. Julia strained to try and catch sight of Elke.

Where was she? Julia wasn't sure if the goose pimples on her arms were from the coolness of the air or from fear. Or both.

"Elke?" she whispered. No answer.

Again. A little louder. "Elke?" Silence.

She raised her voice, "Elke, you out here?" Why would Elke leave the door open? Maybe the wind blew it open.

Waiting a few more seconds, she stepped back inside, shut and bolted the door, still holding her pistol. "Elke are you in here?" she kept her voice low trying not to wake Laquita.

No answer.

Her hands were clammy around the pistol grip. She alternately wiped each hand on her sleep shirt. A noise from the front doorknob caused her to instinctively whirl around. Her eyes fixed on the knob as it turned back and forth. With a two-handed grip on the pistol and arms extended she called out, her voice unsteady, "Elke, is that you?" She took a step back prepared for whoever was trying to get inside.

"It's me."

She heard the aggravation in Elke's voice as she hastily unlatched the front door. Elke hurried inside.

"Why'd you go outside?" Julia reached under the shade of the lamp on an end table by the couch and turned the switch several times to light up the living room. "You always told me not to chase the danger, let it come to you."

"This is a danger I need to deal with, not you," said Elke

cocking her head to one side as she headed to the bathroom.

Julia wanted to challenge Elke, tell her grandmother to get out of her life, but the adrenaline had drained from her body and her mind was too tired to start a fight. It was late. Instead she went to the linen closet and got sheets, a blanket and pillow. Elke didn't protest her getting the couch ready for her to sleep on. Matter of fact, Elke didn't even question why she couldn't sleep in the spare bedroom upstairs. Probably because Elke already knew Laquita was staying with her. Her grandmother didn't just have eyes in the back of her head, she had them everywhere, courtesy of the Bridge Club.

CHAPTER 18

M orning came too soon for Julia.
        It wasn't the sunlight streaming through the slats in her bedroom blinds that woke her. It was the annoying noise in her living room.

Drilling?

And hammering?

Somebody had shut her bedroom door. What was Elke doing? She turned the alarm clock and read 9:30 am. Right now, she didn't care if Elke had decided to remodel her home, she just wanted caffeine and lots of it.

The reflection in her mirror over her dresser told her she didn't get enough sleep last night. Her tousled hair was not the sexy look she saw on Cosmopolitan magazine, it was a Medusa-like mess. Dark circles beneath her bleary eyes made her look like she could audition for a part in the zombie apocalypse. Her grandmother had a saying for people who looked like this, *death warmed over*.

She yawned and stretched her arms above her head. Time for caffeine and check out what Elke was up to. Opening her bedroom door, she stepped into the living room. There was something hanging from a cut out in the wall next to the front door with multiple wires attached. *What the...?*

She blinked and ambled over to the door. A man's voice caught her off guard, "Good morning, Sunshine."

She balled her fist and spun toward the voice in a fighters

stance. "Whoa, cupcake," said the man holding up his hands. Julia dropped her arms and her mouth at the same time. It was Mr. Milk Dud. At least that was the nickname she gave him when she was a little girl. It was payback for all the nicknames he made up for her. He was shorter than she remembered. His brown eyes still intense and his tan face heavily lined. His thick hair was thinner now, mostly white. She was impressed he still appeared to be fit.

"What are you doing here Mr. Milk..." she stopped, realizing she never learned the man's real name. When she asked her grandmother the man's name, Elke would reply, *today it's Tom, yesterday it was Fred and tomorrow who knows.*

He was a spook from the same clandestine agency as her grandmother. At the time she was told he was a family friend who had memory problems. Now after learning about her past, she knew Mr. Milk Dud was, according to Elke, one of the best spooks in the business.

Was.

That was the key word. He was too old to be in the agency now.

The older man had a wide grin pasted across his face. "Didn't mean to startle you, sweet pea."

"I'm old enough now, you can call me Julia. What's your real name?"

"Adam. Adam West. My friend and I are installing a security system for you."

"A what?"

"No big deal, Sunshine. Elke and the Bridge Club thought it might be prudent to lock this baby down to keep you safe."

"I don't want a security system, Adam. Maybe you could take it out." She lowered her chin to her chest, looked down and felt conspicuous in her night shirt.

"Please excuse me, I need to get dressed." She started to turn but quickly stopped, giving instructions, "Don't do anything else till I'm out here to discuss this. Elke doesn't pay the bills. This is my place." Julia marched into her bedroom, shut the door and felt bad about how she must have sounded to Adam. *Adam West? Was that really his name?*

She slid on a pair of jeans and a long sleeve t-shirt, along with some slip-on canvas shoes. After running the brush through her hair, she pulled it tight into a ponytail. She brushed her teeth and still not satisfied with how she looked, added a little blush and lip gloss. It was stupid to care what this man thought about her appearance, but she did.

Now ready to handle this situation, she opened the bedroom door and saw Adam West and another older man along with Laquita sitting in her living room drinking coffee. They all came to attention when she walked in.

"My goodness, ain't this excitin' Julia?" Laquita said with a toothy smile.

Julia rubbed the back of her neck, turned and headed for the kitchen, Laquita close on her heels.

"I made a pot of coffee. That okay? Them men wanted some."

"Sure. I can use some myself." Pouring herself a cup of coffee, Julia asked, "Where's Elke?"

"Omigod, that woman is sure 'nuff the real deal. You one lucky girl to have a grandma who works for the CIA."

"She's no longer employed by them." Yeah, she was lucky alright. Julia didn't even know her real name till recently and that was told to her by her grandfather living in Germany. A man she never heard from growing up.

"I know Elke ain't on their payroll, she told me that. But she still helps 'em. That's what this whole Bridge Club thing's 'bout."

"Sounds like you two got real chummy while I was sleeping. Where is she now?"

"Left bout an hour ago. I 'spect to meet with 'em club members and figger out our next move."

"I need to talk to Adam." Julia took a long draw on her warm drink. "I checked my phone this morning. Max hasn't gotten back in touch with us. Why don't you go into my bedroom, get the phone and try to contact him again?"

"Adam's a nice man. That Marvin man is kinda weird, but smart. Grossed me out, him spittin' tobacco in that empty soda can. Remember they just wanna help, that's all." Laquita walked out of the kitchen.

She remembered Adam was a nice man and she believed they thought they were being helpful. The problem was Elke. The woman never considered how others felt about what she decided was best for them. Never consulted them. That was because Elke thought she was always right and knew what was in everyone's best interest. But Julia wasn't a little girl anymore. She resented Elke's continual intrusions in her life. Tired of Elke taking charge of her life without so much as a single word. Dammit, she was an adult and could take care of herself.

When she entered the living room both men's heads snapped up. She didn't recognize the man sitting next to Adam.

Adam looked younger than Marvin who had a truck driver belly on him.

"I want to thank you for your concern about my safety and I do appreciate it, but..." It was the man next to Adam who interrupted.

"I have known Elke for a very long time. She's stubborn and strong-willed, but this decision was not made by her. She just agreed." The man raised the soda can to his mouth and spit.

"Who? The Bridge Club?"

"Sorry for my bad manners, Julia." The man wiped his chin dribbling drool with the back of his hand and stood. "My name is Marvin. I don't work with the Bridge Club. I own a company few people can afford." Marvin sat back down. "I have been commissioned to install a high-tech security device for your home."

"Who hired you Marvin?"

Marvin leaned back on the couch. He appeared to be done talking.

Adam shifted on the couch, picked up his coffee mug and took a swig. "Julia, can we go into another room and discuss this?"

"No. I want to know who authorized a security system for my home," she demanded.

"Sorry Sunshine, but even that information is above the Bridge Club's pay grade."

"Bullshit. Was it Elke?"

"Not exactly. Elke wanted to move you to a safe location. But somebody, we really aren't sure who, authorized this security system and wants you to stay put for now. Elke finally agreed, but it took some convincing. She really wants to keep you safe Julia."

Julia looked at the men, not sure how she felt about having the system installed without her permission. Something inside her said maybe the security system wasn't such a bad idea with all that was going on. Flustered, she started to speak when

Laquita came in the room shaking her head.

"Still no answer from Max. I'm worried about him," Laquita said as she plopped down on the couch next to Marvin. She looked at the man and continued, "Marvin, tell Julia bout this fancy ass security system you puttin' in her house."

Marvin had given the sales pitch before. He spit in the can he was holding and began, "Don't worry about it spying on you. It's designed for you, the owner, to keep tabs on anybody who approaches your home."

"I think everybody is over-reacting with my involvement in whatever they think might be going on," Julia said.

Marvin continued, "I've installed a five-camera system that records 240 frames per second and includes night vision and motion detectors. Best of all, remote viewing software allows you to monitor all the cameras' views in real time from a PC, laptop or even your phone. All you need is an internet connection or cell service."

Julia knew this meant somebody other than her had access to this monitoring. She didn't like it.

"That could be a problem since our neighbor's cat likes to visit," Julia added.

"This system has thermal cameras that detect the body heat of humans and animals."

Adam must have sensed her discomfort with the security being installed in her home. "Julia, we need to figure out why you're being targeted or even if you are indeed being targeted. Why don't we start by looking at the photos you took at Willow Oaks Motel the other day? You did take photos, correct?"

Julia's gaze darted from Laquita to Marvin before locking eyes with Adam. She paused, feeling uncomfortable. Maybe she was reading too much into Adam's request for the photos. He did work for the Bridge Club. And the man on the elevator said they'd get in touch with her. If she gave him the photos, then what leverage would she have to be part of the investigation? Something didn't feel right about handing over the photos.

Julia firmly reminded Adam, "If this is a serious matter then should Marvin be privy to our discussion? I believe he's not a member of the Bridge Club."

"Don't worry Julia, I've known him," Adam nodded toward Marvin. "For almost as long as I've known your grandmother. We worked together for a long time at the agency. He knows the importance of what the Bridge Club does. The Club vetted him decades ago. He can be trusted. Marvin was known as *Einstein* in the analytical arm of the CIA. That's why he quit and decided to go into the private sector and get paid what he's worth with his high-tech company. We, the Bridge Club, like to use the old ways."

"Yeah and it's long past time for you to come into the technical age," Marvin said. "That's why I can't work with a bunch of paranoid ol' farts who are afraid to use modern technology unless their old ways don't work. Which they usually don't." Marvin stood. "Julia, I'm going to finish this up and get out of your hair. I'll show you how to operate the system before I leave. Whoever's paying to have this installed knows the *old ways* can't protect you." He lumbered over to the front door, reached into his work bag pulling out tools to finish installing the security panel.

"Let's continue this conversation in the kitchen," offered Adam.

"Actually Adam, right now I need to get in touch with my client about the photos. Unless you can share with me what the Bridge Club knows then I don't think we have anything else to discuss."

Marvin let out a chuckle. "Wow, Adam. That girl remind you of someone? Someone who handed you your ass thirty years ago. How does it feel to have her granddaughter do the same?"

CHAPTER 19

"Looks like my work here is done," Marvin declared to Julia as she entered the living room. "After I explain how the security system operates, I'll get out of your hair."

Julia's brow furrowed when she noticed the soda can that contained Marvin's tobacco spit on the floor by the door. She hoped he wouldn't knock it over.

Adam West left earlier after he figured out Julia was not going to hand over the photos. "Marvin, can this system monitor me while I'm inside my home?"

Marvin used a thumb to push his coke-bottled glasses up his bulbous nose lined with red broken capillaries The only hair on his head was a gray mustache in need of a trim. "It could, but it won't. If you hear a noise in the middle of the night, you can immediately put eyes on your house and check the perimeter without getting out of bed. Any breach of entry will send a signal to the police."

Marvin showed her how to use her iPad on the dining table to access a live web cam feed. It was impressive. She was able to see all around her home and a wide-angle view of the street and back yard.

When he finished explaining all the nuances of the system, he asked, "You got a gun?" He bent down and began putting all his tools in his large heavy-duty tool bag.

Julia's mouth expanded into a wide grin exposing her dimples as she rested her hands on the small of her back. She replied, "With this sophisticated security system, why would I even need a gun?" Marvin didn't know she kept a pistol in her nightstand drawer.

"Julia, I do this for a living. I always give the spiel that once my security system is installed you've got nothing to worry about, but…" Marvin looked up giving her his full attention.

"But what?"

"I know your grandma. I have a lot of respect for her. However, when Elke's involved, people have a bad habit of dying."

The grin on her face quickly faded.

Laquita must have heard Marvin and came out of the kitchen asking, "Who's gonna die?"

"Nobody," Julia quickly responded. "Marvin was just telling me how his security systems keep people safe."

Julia wasn't sure if Marvin was trying to keep her safe or scare her. Probably scare her into being careful. It worked.

Marvin picked up his bag, soda can and warned, "Keep this system activated at all times."

He opened the front door, turned, and zeroed in on Julia's face. "Remember what I told you."

"Thank you. I will," replied Julia walking over to the door and closing it behind him.

"What was y'all talkin' bout?"

"How to operate the security system."

"He's kinda weird. That spittin' and his yellow teeth were gross."

"Marvin's okay. I think he did a good job installing the system."

Julia turned the dead bolt.

"Let me show you how to activate and turn off the system,"

said Julia. "Remember the code is 1015."

"Them numbers yo birthday?" quizzed Laquita. "Lotta people use a date they won't forgit."

"Yes. No. I mean it's complicated." Julia was impressed how Laquita figured the numbers were of importance, like her birthday.

"Seems like a lotta thangs in your life are complicated," Laquita shot back.

Julia disregarded the comment. She was sure her birthday was not October 15th even though that was what her birth certificate read. She planned on confronting Elke about it but had never found the right time. Her therapist told her a lie was more comfortable than the fear of being hurt by the truth. Perhaps that was why she never found the right time.

"I still don't feel safe," declared Laquita. "Even if that alarm goes straight to the police, we could be dead 'fore they git here."

"Have you been able to get in touch with Max?" She wanted to change the subject.

"No. I tried right 'fore breakfast. I told him I was usin' a friend's phone. We shoulda heard from him by now. Mor'n that, we shoulda heard from that Kat Lejeune woman."

"Kat Lejeune isn't going to call back. If she was, she'd have done it by now. We have to assume she's involved." She paused a moment and then continued, "Or something has happened to her."

Laquita rubbed the scar on her forehead. Julia saw distress in her eyes. "We're in a hot mess. I spect that woman set us up."

"I kept thinking that might be the case, but what does she have to gain? How would the photos exonerate her from the crime if she hired somebody to kill her husband and that woman?"

"Maybe the killer ain't who we think. Maybe that dead woman's husband got wind of what wuz happenin' and killed 'em."

"My biggest issue with everything is there has been nothing in the news about the identity of the victims. If the dead woman was the killer's wife, then he'd have to report his wife missing and establish an alibi. Same for Kat Lejeune."

"I reckon." Laquita plopped down on the couch and pulled up her long legs in a cross-legged lotus position. "We could be barkin' up the wrong tree. Sure wish Elke or that Bridge Club would call."

Julia remembered the warning from Marvin. *When Elke's involved, people have a bad habit of dying.* It was true.

"I'm sorry, Laquita," Julia said.

Laquita's face appeared confused. "Fer what?"

"For involving you." Julia sat in a chair across from Laquita. She leaned forward and clasped her hands tight. "I can't figure how to get us out of this mess." People had already died from this assignment. She couldn't do anything about that. But she could keep Laquita from getting hurt.

Laquita sat still and silently studied her face. The silence made Julia more nervous than those big brown eyes staring at her. She unclasped her hands and pushed against the back of the chair. Did Laquita blame her for the situation they were in?

Laquita broke the silence, "My Big G liked to say, 'Can't never could'."

Julia tilted her head to the side. "Huh?"

"It means quit saying you can't do somethin'. You have to try or ya never succeed. We might not be good at figurin' this out right now, but if ya wanna be a detective then here's your chance."

Julia's back started to ache. She shifted uneasy in the chair and tried to keep her tone even when she spoke, "This might get...no, this will get dangerous."

Laquita smiled with her eyes. "Well then, if it's dangerous you gonna need help. Count me in."

"You don't have to stay and help me. You can walk away. Go to the police."

"Ya need me. And right now, I need to be needed at somethin'."

A look passed between them.

Julia appreciated Laquita's brutal honesty. The woman she wanted to fire just a few days ago was at this moment the only person she could count on. "If we try to help solve this, there are risks. Lots of risks."

"Ya know Julia, Fly took risks and got himself killed tryin' to do good. I ain't saying I'm not scared. I wanna help ya help the CIA. I wanna do somethin' worthwhile for once in my life."

Julia shook her head like Laquita wasn't understanding the seriousness of the situation. She had deliberately misled Laquita to believe they might work with the CIA. The Bridge Club was not with the CIA any longer and even though they might be good at doing things the old ways, this was a new world. Marvin said the old ways don't usually work in this technological age.

"Honestly, I don't know what's going on. I don't know if the CIA is involved. Maybe we just stumbled on a murder and it's as simple as that. Wrong place, wrong time."

Laquita retorted, "Ya know that ain't true, it ain't that simple."

Julia pressed her lips together. They had nothing to go on

except the photos which, at this point, proved nothing. "If we withhold evidence from the police we could get in trouble."

"You already said, we don't know what we got. It ain't like we're helpin' somebody get away with murder. That Kat Lejeune woman hired us to take photos. We did our job and left."

Julia rubbed her hands together feeling a surge of renewed enthusiasm. "You're right. If we could help solve this case it would be a feather in our cap, as Big G would say."

Laquita scrunched her face and jerked her head back. "Big G ain't never said that."

Julia tried to hide her disappointment. Maybe that was a saying Elke used to say. Like Big G, her grandmother had her own share of idioms.

"We need to find Max. Do you know where he lives?"

"Nope. He moves around a lot."

"How about his place of work?"

"It ain't a place you'd be welcome at."

"How come?"

"Unless you're a drug dealer or a hooker or some sleazy creep ya caint git in that place."

Julia eyes stretched wide as she stared with a smile toward Laquita. She had an idea. It was a long shot, but it just might work.

Laquita must have read her mind. "Whoa, sista. I know what ya thinkin'. I said I'd help. Not help git us killed."

"Max knows something. He might be able to lead us to the killer or, at the very least, help lead us in the right direction. Since he hasn't gotten back to you, we go to him." She felt a surge of excitement. If they were able to solve this murder, they'd get the credit. Not the police. Not Elke. But them.

"Ain't happenin'." Laquita crossed her arms and shook her head. "Count me out. It's a bad idea."

"Just hear me out."

Julia leaned close and hashed out her plan.

CHAPTER 20

Wagner was an early riser, but today he had trouble getting out of bed. Last night at dinner with Megan, they both drank too much wine. He sensed she was nervous going out with him even if he used the lame excuse it was a business dinner.

He rolled onto his side and stared at the metal revolver lying on his nightstand. He felt a new kind of fear. It wanted to overwhelm him. The truth was he was in over his head and he couldn't see a solution.

Last night, Max had given him the gun and said it was untraceable. The serial numbers had been removed.

It wasn't like he planned on going out and robbing a bank or murdering somebody. He needed the gun just in case the killer threatened him. It gave him leverage.

Problem was he didn't really know how to use the handgun. It was never part of his official training. Wagner recalled a crash course on firearms when he was recruited by the Russian Foreign Intelligence Service (SVR). The first time he fired a gun, he hated it. He didn't need a weapon to infiltrate a president's administration. It was his superior intellect and ability to influence powerful American policy makers that made him Russia's most valuable asset.

His training and education were to be an American politician. In a strange recant of procedure, the Kremlin felt his lack of knowledge of firearms might be helpful to deflect any possible suspicion of him being a Russian asset. Their instructions were to focus on politics, leave all the dirty work to his handlers.

Last night during dinner he attempted to talk about the legislative agenda he was working on, but his thoughts were consumed with his increasing desire for Megan. She had changed out of her gray pant suit and was wearing a flattering light blue dress and black stilettos.

Megan must have read his thoughts from her expressions. Her hand slid across the table and cupped his hand. The touch of her warm smooth skin sent a shudder throughout his body making him feel more confident in asking her to come home with him.

As soon as he said, "Megan, I...", his phone buzzed. He tried to ignore it, but Megan had already withdrawn her hand insisting he check his message. She gave him a furtive look he wasn't sure how to interpret.

He reluctantly pulled out his phone from his jacket pocket and read the text. The message was one he couldn't ignore. He politely told Megan he was sorry, but there was a family emergency that required his attention. Megan said she understood and tried to hide the disappointment on her face After dropping her off, he had the driver take him to his home

He had pushed his key in the front door lock and turned it when a hand from behind gripped his arm causing him to instinctively spin around.

Facing him stood Max wearing a dark hooded sweatshirt, blue jeans and white tennis shoes. Max, at 5'10" was shorter than him but more muscular. Wagner could see on his old college roommate's face that he had lost the fight not to follow in his family's footsteps. The hard life on the streets made the man look ten years older than his age.

"We need to hurry inside," urged Max.

Anger flashed through Wagner's eyes. "That asshole you had me hire is a murderer. Now he wants more money, or I could be his next victim."

It took a few minutes for Max to calm him down and convince him that if he'd pay what the killer demanded he'd be okay.

What did Max know? He's the one who found this maniac.

"You hesitate, you die," warned Max as he pulled a gun from a paper bag and handed it to Wagner.

Wagner thought maybe he should remind Max of what he just told him. *Pay the killer what he demands, and you'll be okay. What the hell did he mean by don't hesitate?* Instead of asking, Wagner nodded and asked what Max knew about the man he hired. Max told him he had talked to the guy a couple of times in person and a couple of times on the phone.

The talk on the street was the guy was unstable. Even local gangs stayed away from him. Not much else was known about the man. Max claimed he didn't know any of this before a friend of a friend recommended him.

After Max left his home last night, Wagner made sure all the doors and windows were locked. He never felt this lonely and scared in his entire life.

Rays of sunlight streaked through the plantation shutters covering the floor-to-ceiling windows, casting long shadows across the hardwood floor. Wagner raised up and sat on the edge of the bed planting his feet on the floor. He thought about his face-to-face meeting with the killer at noon today. Even though Max had given him an untraceable gun last night, he didn't feel any safer. He felt more vulnerable, more unsure of how to handle today's meeting with this lunatic.

His head collapsed into his hands and he agonized over his decision not to contact his handler and deal with the reporter himself. What was he thinking? He massaged his forehead hoping it would help let go of the mounting headache.

Wagner could still call his handler, confess he made a stupid mistake and how much he regretted it. No, he had crossed a line and there was no stepping back. He shuttered thinking what the Russians might do to him.

His hands dropped into his lap and he eyed the pistol on the nightstand. Except for last night, it had been a very long time since he held a gun. The small handgun could take a life with just the squeeze of the trigger. Max told him it was a semi-automatic, six inches long and weighed just twenty-five ounces. Easy to conceal. He picked up the handgun from the nightstand. The grip felt comfortable in the palm of his hand. The pistol had a full magazine and a round in the chamber. Max said all he had to do was aim, pull the slack out of the trigger and fire. He already knew that, but it was good to refresh his memory. The bullet would travel at supersonic speed, pierce through flesh, tissue and bone before exploding out of the body.

An intrusive thought entered his mind. If he got to the meeting before Razor arrived, he could hide, walk up behind him, point the barrel to his head and fire. Death would be instantaneous. The gun untraceable. All his problems, his fears, gone in a flash.

He thought of his past handler being murdered in the park. His handler's head exploded as a pink mist sprayed in the air. She collapsed on the park bench. Dead.

His hand started to tremble. Every second that ticked

by, Wagner felt his desperation mounting. Breathing became labored. Pulse pounded in his ears as beads of sweat rolled down his back.

Then without warning Wagner heard the buzzing of his phone on the nightstand. His eyes stared at the vibrating phone for several beats thinking he should answer but couldn't. He lowered the gun to the nightstand, composed himself before picking up the phone.

"Alan, are you okay?" Megan's voice sounded upset.

He took a deep breath.

"Um, yes. I'm afraid I overslept," Wagner struggled to keep his voice steady.

"I just didn't know if you'd be able to come in this morning because of your family emergency."

Wagner had forgotten the lie he used last night that allowed him time to get home and meet Max. "It's going to be okay. My Uncle had a heart attack, but they got him to the hospital in time."

"Would you like me to send flowers to the hospital?"

He needed to be careful with his lies. Megan always handled things like this for him. "No thanks Megan. I already took care of it. I'll be in the office in forty-five minutes or so."

CHAPTER 21

Shockley tried to relax as he waited outside the Chief of the D.C. Metropolitan Police Department. How many times had he been in this hot seat since he started the job?

Too many.

He shifted on the stiff chair not because the chair was long overdue for the trash heap, but because the hard surface reminded him of all the times he spent in the principal's office during his high school years.

The Chief's aide, Amy Long, wasn't one for pleasantries. Amy had instructed him to take a seat and the Chief would be with him shortly. Sitting behind the computer monitor on her desk, she kept her head low clicking away on the keyboard. Amy's desk was tidy. Unlike him, she didn't have post-it notes all over her desk and monitor. Her files were in a vertical desktop organizer.

The Chief, Hubert Nowakowski, had grown up in a Polish immigrant family on the south side of Chicago. Shockley attributed the man's Attila-the-Hun personality to him learning how to survive at an early age in a crime ridden neighborhood. The man was tough, no doubt about it. He had served in Afghanistan as a member of the Army Rangers before joining the Metropolitan Police Department. Nowakowski had over a decade of experience in the District's police department and had worked many of its highest-profile cases. He gained a reputation for results—making arrests, closing cases. Now the man, who criminals on the street feared, was confined to a chair.

A wheelchair.

Five years ago, Nowakowski was part of the Special Operations Unit, doing a yard-to-yard search for a suspect involved in a shooting. The suspect, hiding behind a trash can in a dirt alley, surprised Nowakowski and opened fire. He was shot multiple times in the legs and spinal cord. Trapped on the ground, the suspect kept firing and would have killed him if his K-9 police dog hadn't pounced on the suspect knocking him over. A picture of the K-9 dog, Bandit, sat on his desk as a reminder that the police dog gave his life to save him.

After ten long minutes, Amy stood and walked over to the secure door to the Chief's office.

"Chief Nowakowski will see you now," she announced as she punched in a number to release the lock to the Chief's office.

Even though there was a small sitting area in the large corner office, he never sat there. There was always a wooden desk between him and the Chief.

Shockley was about to speak but decided against it. He'd let the Chief go first.

Nowakowski started the meeting showing a softer side. "Damn Mike, you look like shit. How's your head and hand?"

Shockley lightly touched his hand and responded, "I'm fine, Wheels, thanks for asking." Wheels was the nickname Nowakowski got when he returned to work confined to a wheelchair. The Chief let Shockley call him Wheels when in private conversations. Otherwise it was Chief or Chief Nowakowski.

It wasn't Shockley's head or hand that was bothering him.

His mind was in loop mode rolling through the events from yesterday. He had a hunch he had missed something. What that was he just couldn't figure out.

The Chief leaned back in his wheelchair and folded his arms across his chest. "Mike, you wanna tell me how you fucked up a simple homicide investigation and now we've got ATF breathing down our neck?"

Shockley wondered why Wheels considered any homicide investigation simple. He should remind his boss that only sixty percent of cases were ever closed. Most of the time the trail would grow cold, not because of lack of effort but most of their victims had criminal records. Witnesses, when lucky enough to find, usually had questionable credibility.

The meeting with Wheels would be nothing short of an ass chewing. He deserved it. Yesterday at the crime scene, his team headed up the motel stairs to collect evidence from the double homicide without him. Maybe if he had been in front of Bull, she wouldn't be fighting for her life in the hospital right now.

The Chief continued. "What I wanna know is why you were headed across the street, while your team was going up to the crime scene."

He figured this was coming. "That pain-in-the-ass crime reporter, Susan Porter, was at the scene," he explained. "I wanted to keep her at bay. Try to stop her from becoming a problem with her questions."

"Donna is the department's media relation's officer. She's trained to deal with the media, not you."

"She hadn't gotten there yet."

"Let me get this straight. You think you're better at dealing with the media than Donna who has a Master's degree and fifteen years' experience in public relations or just maybe you think you're better at getting Porter in the sack?"

Shockley knew not to tell his boss he'd already gotten Porter in the sack. Wheels would think his actions yesterday were based on not having his head on straight if he knew that.

"Susan Porter was just doing her job yesterday. She can be overly zealous and I…" Shockley couldn't finish his sentence. Maybe his boss was right. Maybe he let Porter's tight green dress distract him. He hoped that wasn't the real reason he made the decision to talk to her.

"I wanna know why Terrance Bone and Amber Bull didn't detect a bomb during their initial inspection."

"I don't know. The people who might have answers are in the hospital. One fighting for her life."

Shockley realized his mistake pointing out what his boss already knew. Wheels would have up-to-date information about his officers.

Wheels jerked forward and pounded his fist too hard on his desk. The lamp on the edge of the desk bounced and toppled onto the hardwood floor.

"You've got 48 hours to give me something, Mike, or I'm pulling you off this case and your ass will be stuck behind a desk for the unforeseeable future. Do I make myself clear?"

"Loud and clear. I'll do my best."

"Your best? Just do your goddamn job. I don't want that fuckin' cop killer on the street another day." Wheels powerful voice was ear-splitting.

"Yes Chief." Shockley wanted to catch the suspect. He was struggling with guilt over his decision yesterday. He got up and headed back to his desk.

Shockley was sure his boss had just told him he was looking for an excuse, any excuse to strip him of his firearm and put him on administrative assignment. He couldn't let that happen. He had promised T-Bone he'd catch the perp responsible for this.

When he got back to his office, Raymond Hauser was leaning against the edge of his desk, his face buried in a folder full of papers.

Hauser still had the look of a rookie officer and was part of Shockley's team. The first time Shockley met the awkward officer, he noticed the Duty Belt's stiff leather not yet broken in and creaked every time Hauser moved. That day the young rookie looked like he belonged anywhere but in a homicide unit. Shockley had his doubts the kid would make it in the unit. That was three years ago. Even though Shockley was in his mid-thirties, the new hires looked younger and younger. Like kids.

Shockley sat heavily in his chair and said, "What we got?"

Hauser's smile quickly faded when he saw Shockley's face. "Jeez man. You look like shit. What'd the Chief say?"

"That I look like shit." Shockley flipped him the bird.

Shockley knew how he looked. He saw his face earlier in his bathroom mirror. His eyes bloodshot and a purple welt above his eyebrow. Sleep deprivation was something he was used to as murders seldom happened during daylight hours. Yet last night he never made it to his bed. When he got home, he slumped down in his favorite chair and replayed the day events. The last time he looked at the clock it was 4 A.M.

Hauser cleared his throat making his protruding Adam's apple slide up and down. In a low-pitched voice, he said, "ATF's forensics are running tests to confirm the accelerants used in the blast."

"Run me through what we *do* know."

"One of my buddies at ATF said off the record that a cellphone was used to detonate a homemade bomb. A cellphone's electrical current has enough to jolt a small detonator charge, which in turn can set off the main explosive. He said modifying a cellphone into a trigger is a piece of cake. DIYers rig up old phones and blow things up all the time."

"DIYers?"

"You know, sites like Pinterest, DudePins, YouTube for do-it-yourselfers."

"You're saying this suspect might have gone online and watched a step-by-step YouTube video on making this bomb?"

"Could have. Even for first timers, there are scores of easy-to-follow internet tutorials."

"Does your buddy believe this is an amateur or professional?"

"No way to know at this point."

"Killers make mistakes. There's gotta be a paper trail. A motive is what we need. You got any witnesses?" asked Shockley.

"A prostitute named Bambi claims she might remember something if we can get some drug charges dropped. We ran down her timeline and she was making love to a pole in a bar down the street when this went down. We did get one possible lead, but the guy has since disappeared."

"Got a name?"

Hauser shrugged. "Might be a nickname. Max. No last name. No address."

"I want you to get feet on the ground and track this Max down. Memories are going to fade fast and lips will get tight if we don't get moving on this."

Shockley leaned an elbow on his desk and began to stroke the stubble on his chin. "Why do you think the killer waited to blow up the bodies? They were already confirmed deceased by T-Bone."

"Maybe its gang related, and they wanted revenge against cops. Could be they waited till we arrived. It's the Dead Zone's MO."

"Doesn't add up. If the goal was to kill cops investigating a crime scene, then the bomb went off too soon."

"Yeah...right," said Hauser. "The suspect would've waited till the crime scene investigators were all in the motel room where the bomb was planted."

Hauser's face beamed as if he had the answer. "Maybe the DIYer miscalculated the time it would take for the officers to get upstairs."

"Maybe." Shockley studied the report on his desk. "Or perhaps the suspect panicked."

"What would make the suspect panic?"

Shockley kept his focus on the report in front of him and stroked his chin. "Somebody recognized him."

CHAPTER 22

Rayburn Office Building

Wagner sat in his office chair staring out the large picture window and breathing hard.

Even though he'd been sitting for twenty minutes, his pulse rate was up. He needed to settle down and collect himself before his ten o'clock meeting with Congressman Quatterman.

He'd almost cancelled the meeting with the lawmaker, but he needed to know if Quatterman knew anything more about the reporter. The meeting had to end by eleven o'clock to give himself enough time to get home, collect the cash and get the gun. Then he planned on taking a taxi to the park to meet a man whose name he didn't even know. Max said the man's street name was Razor. That name made the hair on the back of his neck stand up.

Dan Quatterman didn't need Megan to announce his arrival. His booming voice could be heard down the hall.

A light rap on the door before it opened. "Congressman Quatterman's here for your ten o'clock meeting," announced Megan.

Wagner never got to respond. The large man elbowed past Megan bumping her to the side of the doorway.

"Alan, sorry to hear about your Uncle."

With a flash of annoyance, Megan quickly bowed out shutting the door behind her.

"My uncle's fine. The doctors said there is minimum

damage to his heart muscles. He was lucky. Thank you for asking."

"Hell, I didn't even know you had any relatives. Shows how much we don't know about each other. We're just too damn busy running this country and keeping it safe."

Quatterman tugged his pants up over his fat abdomen. The man needed to lose weight.

Wagner nodded. He'd like to tell the egotistical blowhard he didn't have a clue how much he didn't know about him.

"Alan, before we talk about the legislative agenda, what's the scoop on the reporter?" Quatterman asked. He plopped into the chair on the other side of the desk facing Wagner.

Wagner studied the man's face trying to determine if Quatterman really didn't know the reporter had been murdered. He could be a man with ulterior motives. Wagner needed to be cautious in how he responded.

"I'm sorry Dan. I've been extremely busy and haven't had time to follow up with the FBI about the reporter's prying into the investigation of a possible Russian spy."

Quatterman folded his hands, letting them rest on his large stomach. "Well, I'm not sure what the Feds did to nix the reporter from snooping around, but I'm glad they got her to give up and let us get our job done around here."

"What do you mean they got her to give up?"

"Not sure, Alan. Just seems she vanished. Nobody's seen her lately."

Vanished? Wagner supposed Quatterman had not heard the news or made the connection about a woman and man being murdered and blown up at a motel.

Or maybe he had and was testing him.

Wagner leaned forward in his chair. "I'm sure the FBI

is capable of handling any reporter snooping around their investigation."

"Our country is under attack," barked Quatterman. "We need to find this Russian spy who infiltrated our government and take forceful countermeasures against the Soviets."

"Dan, we've got to tread lightly with any allegations against the Russians. The last thing we want to do is create an atmosphere of a McCarthyism witch-hunt. The FBI doesn't have any credible evidence that a foreign asset *has* infiltrated our government."

Wagner felt his face heat up. He had to stay calm and fake empathy toward Quatterman's fears. He continued, "I realize our government has been cautious about standing up to Moscow. Russia and U. S. nuclear weapons and nuclear submarines are close to parity. We must avoid escalation that would play into our enemies' hands."

Quatterman drew in a deep breath and slowly let it escape through closed lips in what sounded like a whistle.

"Alan, the President listens to you. I listen to you. But the Russian government wants to weaken the West. The FSB operates with impunity according to its own secret rules. Moscow's espionage operations are to cultivate well-placed contacts. Think of what it would mean to our country if the Russians had a spy with policy making access."

Wagner felt the bile rise to his throat. He felt sick to his stomach.

Is Quatterman checking his reaction to what he just said?

Does he suspect anything?

Did he talk to the reporter who might have suspected Wagner was the Russian mole?

Or was he just getting paranoid?

He scratched his nose and cast his eyes downward. If Quatterman noticed he was nervous and uncomfortable, he didn't comment about it.

"I agree, Dan. The Russians have long concentrated their efforts on obtaining intelligence about White House policy views with their spies befriending people who work in U.S. policy circles. I hope you followed my advice and didn't talk to the reporter."

Wagner made eye contact and kept talking, "For all we know, the reporter could have been part of Russian espionage to seduce members of Congress."

Quatterman sat up in the chair and said in a biting voice, "I'm sure our intelligence agencies will ferret out any Russian spies."

Wagner nodded, but noted Quatterman had not denied talking to the reporter. He needed to redirect the conversation.

"I sure hope they do. Dan. Like you said earlier, we need to keep this country running, so how about we get started on the legislative agenda now?"

The discussion on the legislative agenda was lasting longer than Wagner had hoped. He needed to speed it up.

During their meeting, he was plagued with unpleasant thoughts about a man who was known on the streets as Razor.

It was easy to let Quatterman monopolize the discussion about upcoming legislation and just nod. The man relished thinking he was in charge of any discussion. Wagner had long suspected Quatterman knew he'd never be the Speaker of the House and therefore lived out his dream of power through him.

His thoughts drifted to his upcoming meeting with Razor. It made his hands sweat. He removed them from where they were propped on his desk and wiped them on his pants.

"I hate to break our productive discussion Dan, but I've got to leave for another meeting in a few minutes."

"Sure, sure. I understand. We've really got a handle on how to proceed with our agenda."

He was grateful Quatterman didn't ask what meeting he was referring to.

"Yes. Thanks for working with me on this." He hoped Quatterman didn't see through his facade.

"Lately it's been hard getting hold of you," Quatterman stated. "How bout I get Megan to put me on your calendar for a follow-up next week unless you need to talk before then."

Wagner opened his leather-bound appointment book lying on his desk in front of him. After a brief scan, he asked, "How does next Wednesday sound?" He didn't want Quatterman bothering Megan with a lame attempt to flirt.

"I see you're still old fashioned like me and use a paper calendar." He gave a loud snort. "I'll have to check and get back with you. Just send me a reminder."

Wagner rose to let Quatterman know it was time for him to leave.

He nodded. "I'll have Megan send you a reminder."

It was 11:15. The pompous windbag Congressman liked to hear himself talk. He couldn't stand the man. Yet, Quatterman was the one who helped him secure the House speakership. Quid quo pro. As much as he found it distasteful, they were allies. Quatterman was no fool. At some point the savvy politician would call in the favor.

When Quatterman left his office, he buzzed his assistant and told her to send a message to Quatterman about next week's meeting and that he would be out of the office for a couple of hours. He'd be back late afternoon. Hopefully this would be the last time he had any contact with Razor.

"How did your meeting with the Congressman go?" inquired Megan.

"Well, it is Quatterman you know. But overall productive. I think we have a strategy to get the fence-sitting members on the Immigration Reform Act to jump to our side."

"Glad to hear that. If something comes up while you're out, do you want me to contact you on your cell?"

Wagner mulled this over, unsure of what to tell her. He wanted to tell Megan to call the cops if she couldn't get hold of him. That he was meeting with a crazed killer who scared him shitless. If only he could confide in her. No. He didn't want her involved in this. No matter what happened.

"Thanks Megan but I don't think there's anything that can't wait till I get back."

† † †

His historic row house was walking distance from the office. He had to be careful, make certain he eluded his security detail. Although he was grateful he had U.S. Capital Police protection, there were times they made what he needed to do difficult. He knew if Razor thought for a second he had somebody following him, the deal would be off.

Hurrying home, a crisp breeze blew strands of his blond hair across his face. He needed a haircut and ordinarily would have had Megan make him an appointment. Lately, his hair was the least of his worries.

Closer to his home, he began to experience a fluttering feeling brewing in his stomach. The mere thought of Razor blocked his airways. *Nerves*. He had to remember to take the gun with him. Just in case. Walking to and from work used to help him relax, not the case today.

He heard him before he spotted him.

"Mister Wagner," the familiar raspy rattled voice startled him.

"Sorry Jackson, I'm in a hurry."

Jackson's uncombable brown hair sprouted from beneath the grimy ball cap like a chia pet. His overgrown beard was curly and matted like his hair. Jackson smelled as bad as he looked sitting on what appeared to be a plastic garbage can lid. The old maroon sweater hung loose on his rail-thin body. His sweatpants had small holes where the fabric had worn. All his belongings were in a garbage bag next to him. Propped against his legs was a piece of cardboard with the words written, "Please spare a little change. God Bless." He used to have a shaggy mutt with him, but the dog got hit by a car. Now the only reminder of the dog was the dog's old water dish he used to collect money from strangers.

Wagner had walked countless times past the homeless never really noticing them. There were thousands of homeless people in Washington, D.C. and after a while they became invisible. Yet one day, for some unknown reason, he stopped and talked to Jackson. The homeless man didn't know how many days he'd been living on the streets. He was a man who felt lost. He wasn't angry and only blamed himself for his predicament.

The articulate man told him that in another life, he had

been a successful Wall Street executive. But the financial crisis of 2008 changed his life. His employer, Lehman Brothers, declared bankruptcy. At the height of the market he got married, had a son and bought a big house. But during the crisis he lost it all, wife, son and home. He began drinking and doing drugs in order to cope.

Wagner was fifteen steps past the homeless man when he reached in his suit coat for his wallet and pulled out a twenty. He didn't like giving him money because he knew what Jackson would spend it on, drugs. However, he was beginning to understand the need to escape a bad situation. If only for a moment. He spun around, rushed back to the homeless man and said, "Get a bite to eat."

"Thanks man. You're too good a man to be in politics," Jackson called out to him.

Yeah. Too good to be in politics but not too good to spy on this country or get somebody killed, he thought to himself. The chuckle that escaped his lips surprised him. He was actually smiling at the irony of the statement.

It was 11:30.

He had to quicken his pace.

CHAPTER 23

There were days Shockley wished he'd never moved off his family ranch.

Today wasn't one of them. He was determined to ferret out the killer who had put two good friends in the hospital, one still on life support.

Since Shockley was a homicide detective, he was always on call for a major case. Yesterday was a long day. Actually, the past couple of days had been long. He wasn't surprised that after his take-out supper last night, he was asleep by 10 and didn't stir till 6 this morning.

He came into the office early to write up his report on the Willow Oaks Motel case and catch up on his inbox of emails and voice messages. Catch up was never going to happen with the high murder rate in his district. He had a stack of hot cases he was working on as well as a few cold cases. In his unit, cases stayed with detectives until they were solved, or the detective left the squad.

Fellow detective Hauser walked in holding a large cup in one hand and a paper carry-out bag in the other hand. His sandy hair was long and bound in a low ponytail. His pale blue eyes and clean-shaven baby face made him appear young. Until he opened his mouth and spoke. His low husky voice announced, "Gotcha a smoked bacon and cheddar egg breakfast sandwich."

"Thanks. I need more than that bowl of cereal I ate this

morning."

Hauser pulled out the wrapped sandwich and dropped it on the desk in front of Shockley and sat in the chair next to the desk. He unwrapped his sandwich and took a bite. "Surprised we didn't have a murder during Big Mac rush hour," Hauser said.

Big Mac was the term Hauser used to refer to the timeframe when most murders occurred, between 10 pm and 3 am.

"Yeah, pretty sure I wouldn't have heard my phone last night. I was out like a light by ten." The smell radiating from his wrapped sandwich was too tempting. He unwrapped the paper from his sandwich and started eating. "Man, this is good," Shockley said as he took another bite. "Any leads on this Max guy?"

With a mouth full of food Hauser replied, "Nah. We tracked down a few local gang members, but they lawyered up fast and refused to answer our questions. Maybe we'll get some actionable evidence analysis from ATF."

"Anything on the Dead Zone gang?"

"All got alibis. Claim they don't know this Max guy."

"I want you to run down any arrests in the past year with suspects named Max. I'm pretty sure this Max has a rap sheet."

"Got it." Hauser swallowed the last bite of his food.

"Did you talk to Minty yesterday?" The thought just occurred to Shockley. The homeless woman stayed in that area.

"Minty?" Hauser choked on a slug of Coke.

He waited a few seconds to let Hauser quit coughing and added, "Minty hangs out in that neighborhood. Maybe she knows something."

"Shit man. I guarantee that bag lady didn't see anything seeing as she's blind. No pun intended."

Shockley rose, holstered his pistol and put on his suit jacket. He balled up his trash before tossing it in the receptacle by his desk.

"Ready?" he said to Hauser.

Hauser shrugged.

On the way out the building and all the way to Shockley's car Hauser grumbled about questioning Minty.

Shockley hoped Hauser was wrong. He needed *something* on this investigation. Anything. Because right now they didn't have squat.

It took an hour to locate the *blind bag lady* as Hauser called her. She was pushing an old baby carriage stuffed with all her possessions and tapping the edge of the sidewalk with her cane. Shockley pulled his unmarked car to the curb and they got out.

Hauser was a good cop. The kid worked hard and never took the stress of the job out on others. Hauser wanted this cop killer as bad as he did.

Minty had stopped moving down the sidewalk and stood still as if she knew he wanted to talk to her.

"Hey Minty," Shockley hollered. "How're things going?" He walked up to her. Hauser stood next to him.

The cheap dark sunglasses hid her eyes. She had a worn weathered face and an unruly mop of brown and gray hair. Her hunched body covered with a coat Shockley thought he had given her last winter. The woman's appearance let him know she had lived a hard life out in the elements.

Shockley met Minty five years ago sleeping in a park. He got social services to help her, but she always went back to the streets. Told him the places she stayed in had too many rules.

"I didn't hit that kid with my cane Officer Shockley." That's what she always called him.

"That's not what I'm here to talk about." Shockley gave a sideway glance, watching Hauser smirk and shake his head.

"I just want to know if you were around when the Willow Oaks Motel exploded."

"Maybe."

Shockley heard a whimper under a blanket in the baby buggy. "Got yourself a dog?"

"It's mine. I didn't steal it. I found it in an alley lookin' for somethin' to eat."

"I brought you some cigarettes." Shockley had stopped on the way and picked up a carton. He motioned for Hauser to hand them to her.

Hauser held out the carton of cigarettes. Minty snatched the carton with both hands. Shockley grinned at the surprised look on Hauser's face.

Minty smiled revealing missing teeth and the ones still intact stained from nicotine. "Yous that Officer who's been asking lotta questions," she said to Hauser.

"Yeah. I was trying to run down some leads on a case." He studied Minty's face with a puzzled expression.

"You didn't ask me no questions. Think an old blind woman can't see?"

"No offense ma'am, but you are blind. I do know you have good hearing." Hauser was trying to make up to the old woman.

"You know why I got good hearing, Officer Hauser?" Hauser's jaw dropped a bit, when she spoke his name.

"You think when I lost my sight more than ten years ago, God just zapped me with super hearing?" The old woman pulled back the blanket to stroke a small puppy not much bigger than the sewer rats in town. She continued, "Hell no. The only reason I can hear what you can't is cause I train for it. I got over fifty thousand hours of practice listenin'. I sense people round me, I hear you swallow your spit, recognize a person by their voice. I'm not distracted like you is by seeing things, causing all my attention to focus on what I hear and what I smell. What I feel. It don't come to you easy, you know. You gotta train every day to git good at it. I do see, Officer Hauser, but just in a different way."

"Can you tell us what you saw the day of the explosion?" Shockley asked.

"I can. He smokes. Got rough hands like you Officer Shockley and has a slight limp."

"Who are you talking about?" quizzed Hauser.

"The killer. Ain't that who yous after?"

CHAPTER 24

The door chimed.

She strolled inside holding a pink leash with a small furry dog attached on the other end. The store was bustling with customers and their dogs.

Her eyes moved swiftly around the store while keeping vigilance on who entered the door. To her right was a long glass counter with bakery treats that would satisfy any sweet tooth. She scanned the labels in front of the treats. Drooling muffins, Barkery Bites, Yummy Yum Biscuits, Yapper Baguette, and a dozen other amusing names. A sign on top of the counter stated all treats were natural and organic. And of course, homemade.

The other side of the store looked like a clothing store for four legged animals. There were display tables with dog mannequins dressed in outfits for all occasions. She almost ran into the round rack with a sign that said *Pup-cessories*. Attached to the rack were doggie sunglasses, custom pup purses, nail paw-lish, and clip-on pet highchairs.

She picked up her small furry dog and in a baby talk voice asked the dog what he wanted as she observed the other patrons. It was true. she thought. Many of the dog-owners looked like their four-legged friends. A woman with tight curly hair had a poodle on a leash. A man with a thick beard accompanied by a long-haired dog looked like they went to the same stylist. What was apparent from her observation was that these owners had an intense emotional bond with their dogs.

The back wall had a sign in large letters—*Doggie Spa*. She continued toward the back of the store noting store security cameras mounted high on the wall near the ceiling.

"May I help you?" said a shrill voice. The spindly man with large eyes and prominent cheekbones clasped his delicate long fingers in front of his chest. His long beak nose had clearly been broken in the past.

"I'm here to see Jimi C." She smiled and stroked the furry dog's head she held under her arm. The man reached to pet the dog, but the dog growled and snapped at him.

He quickly pulled his hand back.

"I'm sorry. My sweet Bella is getting aggressive. That's why I must see Jimi C. She's the dog whisperer, you know, and I'm very desperate."

"Yes, she's very good with dogs." The man's left eye twitched and he folded his arms tightly across his chest. "There's nobody like her. I'll have to check to see if she's available."

The woman nodded as the man spun and headed toward the back of the store. He disappeared into a room in the corner. The office. She put the dog down. After a quick glance toward the front door, she led the dog on the leash to the office door and opened it. The man standing in front of a desk turned and approached her rapidly waving his hands like a large bird trying to take flight.

"Excuse me. You need to wait outside," said the overly animated man.

Jimi C was sitting behind a modern oversized glass-top desk with her hand to her mouth. The look on Jimi C's face satisfied her. Jimi C removed her hand and said in a gravelly voice, "It's okay, Luca. Leave us alone."

The woman smiled.

Luca's shoulders dropped along with his hands. He shot a glance at Jimi C. She nodded. He put a hand on his hip, tilted his head to the side, and pranced around her and out of the office.

Jimi C's surprised look morphed into a frown.

"What? You have a dog now?" she asked.

"Good God no. Did you know you can rent pets? Quite convenient. Kinda like having grandchildren. You can spoil them, play with them and then send them home to their parents."

"Only, you never could send your granddaughter home after you spoiled her." Jimi C's tight face twisted into a sinister smile. "Not after her parents were murdered."

The stoic woman's facial expression did not change even though the words were meant to sting. Actually, the words did trigger images from long ago. She stayed calm on the outside, while what she wanted to do was pull her pistol out and shoot the smirk off Jimi C's face. The woman fought back her internal rage. Now wasn't the time. She couldn't allow Jimi C to bait her into losing control. The CIA had taught her to never let a situation get personal. Most of the time she followed that lesson.

The truth was Jimi C wasn't wrong about what she said.

Especially when she felt responsible.

Jimi C looked different than how she remembered. But of course, the surgeon made sure Jimi C no longer looked like she did when she knew her. Her face was made-up, her nose smaller and her short spiky platinum hair had pink highlights. The woman's chest had been enhanced.

"I need information," the woman said calmly.

"You promised you'd leave me alone." Jimi C pursed her lips to demonstrate her disapproval.

"Circumstances have changed."

"That wasn't part of the deal, Elke. You coming into my business puts my life in danger."

Elke dropped the leash and took a seat in a white leather chair against the wall of the office. The small dog began exploring the room. "You're probably right Jimi C, or do you still go by Marcus?"

"I had the operation many years ago. I did it because I never wanted to be discovered once I went into Witness Protection."

"Yet, look how easily I found you. You were always crazy about dogs." The dog walked over to a large potted plant that looked like a palm, hiked his leg and peed. "That's why I don't have pets," declared Elke.

"What do you want, Elke?" Jimi C demanded. "I no longer work for the Russians. I defected and was promised protection and a new life. Everything I know, I told your government. If the Russians find me, they'll kill me."

"It is hard to find people you can trust in our line of work."

"What? You trust me now?"

"Of course not, Marcus. I still see you as the low-life double agent who now calls himself Jimi C. I'm here because I need you to find out something for me."

"What's in it for me?"

Elke gave her a wry smile and tilted her head slightly. "We don't ever change, do we? Once a spy for profit, a traitor for life." She crossed her legs and folded her hands in her lap. "I want to know who was at my granddaughter's house the other night and if her life is in danger from Moscow."

Jimi C crossed her arms and locked eyes with Elke.

"How the fuck would I know that? I'm out. I no longer have connections," Jimi C said, raising her voice loud enough to cause the small dog to bark at her.

"We needn't play games, Marcus. That's for amateurs."

Jimi C unlocked eyes with Elke and rotated her head in the direction of the window. Slowly, she responded, "If I did happen to know somebody, why would I ever help you."

"To keep your dirty lie a secret. You help me and I won't tell the CIA you still work for the Russians."

"That's a lie." Jimi C jerked her head back toward Elke and straightened in her chair. "I'm in witness protection. I could contact the Marshal Service and say you've threatened me with lies."

"You won't. That might make them question your loyalty." Elke shook her head. "I need the information by tomorrow."

Jimi C pushed herself to her feet and snorted, "You were once considered the best operative at extracting information. But that was a long time ago. You went off the grid and let your obsession with revenge for your daughter's death consume you. It was you who got her killed."

Elke brushed her pants with a sweep of her hand. "This is another reason I don't like having a pet. The hair. It gets all over you." She stood and walked over to Jimi C's glass top desk and placed a sheet of paper on it. "Tomorrow, I expect the information. You can deliver it here."

She strolled to the office door and placed her hand on the doorknob.

"You forgot your damned dog," hollered Jimi C.

Without turning, Elke replied, "It's a present for you. The owner had an unfortunate accident. I think you might have known her."

"I thought you rented the dog."

"I said you *can* rent dogs. I didn't need to."

She waited a beat.

"Anastasiya Morozov."

She pulled the door open and heard Jimi C gasp.

Elke headed out of the store and made a call when outside.

"It's done. She'll cooperate."

"The Russians aren't going to like this."

"Then our plan is working. I have to go." She tossed her burn phone in the receptacle by the curb.

A black car with dark tinted windows screeched to a halt alongside her. Three large men in dark navy suits jumped out and surrounded her.

The smaller of the men said, "We need you to come with us."

"Sorry boys, but my ride will be here any minute. We'll have to have a foursome another time."

The men moved closer.

"Pretty sure you know that's not happening. We don't want any trouble. Just get in."

One of the larger men opened the back door.

"Looks like I haven't a choice."

She leaned over to climb inside when the tall man grabbed her arm and held out his hand. "Your weapon," he ordered.

CHAPTER 25

"You don't actually believe a blind lady would know the perp was at the scene of the crime, do you?" asked Hauser as soon as he got back in the car with Shockley.

"I think she's the best lead we got right now," said Shockley. Actually, she was their only lead at the moment.

Hauser shook his head, pulled the seat belt across his chest snapping it in the buckle. "Now let me see if I got this right. Moments before the explosion the blind lady walked up to a crowd of gawkers standing across the street from the motel and some guy who smelled like cigarettes…" He paused, turned his focus to Shockley and continued, "Almost knocks the blind lady down, snags her hand, and walks off in a hurry with some kinda limp. And from that she believes this guy is the perp. Come on Shockley, that's bullshit and you know it "

Shockley understood Hauser's frustration. He felt it. Right now, his ass was on the line to solve this case. Their potential witness was blind, but every hour that went by gave the perp more time to cover his tracks. He'd take any lead he could get.

"Sacha van Loo. Ever heard of him?"

"Nah. Should I?"

"Van Loo has been blind since birth. He's a cop in Belgium."

"Huh? Now you think Minty should join the force?"

Shockley grinned and added, "From the purr of an engine, he can discern whether the car is a Peugeot, a Honda or a Mercedes. When the police eavesdrop on a terrorism suspect making a phone call, Van Loo can identify the number instantly by listening to the tones. The guy can hear the sound of a voice echoing off a wall and determine whether a suspect is speaking from an airport lounge or a crowded restaurant. My point is that even though Minty and Van Loo have lost their vision, their disability allows them to pick up clues you and I might miss."

Hauser mumbled under his breath like he always did when he was frustrated. "You want me to check the local gas stations and convenience stores in the area to see if anybody knows of a suspect who buys cigarettes and walks with a limp?" He didn't give Shockley a chance to answer. "I could ask if any of them held hands with the guy."

Hauser let loose a deep grunt and leaned his head against the head rest. "What I'd like to know Shockley is how Minty knows you got rough hands? Sounds like you two got cozy."

"Probably the same way she knows your hands have never done a day of physical labor. Did you feel her hand brush against yours when you held out the cigarettes?"

"Damn, you're right. Creeped me out." Hauser looked out the front and side windows and asked, "Where we headed?"

"Back to the station after I make a stop. I want to check on something."

Shockley pulled the car to the curb across from Willow Oaks Motel and stopped. When he opened the door and got out, Hauser followed. Shockley walked over to the motel and ordered Hauser to stand in the spot where the reporter, Susan Porter stood right before the explosion. He walked toward Hauser and counted the seconds till he got to the spot when the explosion occurred. Fifteen seconds. Another twenty to thirty seconds and Bull and T-Bone would have been in the room with the bomb. And dead. Why detonate the explosive early if you wanted to kill cops? Why even blow up dead bodies unless you wanted to conceal evidence? If that was the case why not do it before the police arrive? At any rate this was a sick dangerous killer. He needed to catch this perp before he killed again.

"What'd you think, Shockley? Think the explosive was detonated by the guy in the crowd, like Minty suggested?"

"Don't know. Maybe." Shockley headed to his car with Hauser in step with him. "But there's a reason the guy in the crowd left before the bomb was detonated." He opened his car door and climbed inside. Hauser slid in the passenger side.

"Then your theory that the perp recognized somebody and detonated the bomb might be plausible," concluded Hauser.

"If this is our guy, I think he spotted somebody who could ID him and panicked. We need to find Max. See if he smokes and walks with a limp."

Due to heavy traffic, it took almost an hour to drive back to MPD headquarters. Shockley parked and got out. Hauser stayed inside the parked car to take a call on his cell phone. Shockley hoped Hauser was tracking down a possible lead.

A heavy-set man with balding brown hair walked in front of him, took his cigarette butt and flicked it to the ground. The man kept walking. A pet peeve of Shockley's was how people discarded cigarette butts. Just because butts are small, people think they can toss them anywhere without understanding they're not biodegradable. Already frustrated by the case, he needed to vent and here was his opportunity. Shockley yelled at the man, "Hey you! Yeah you. This isn't an outdoor ashtray." The man kept walking, pretending he didn't hear him. Shockley turned up the volume, "Don't be a piece of shit, pick up your butt before I chase you down and kick yours."

Hauser walked up and said, "Hey man. Careful. We're standing in front of headquarters." He bent down, picked the butt up and started to walk over to the waste receptacle by the entrance to the station when Shockley grabbed his arm.

"Keep it. Place it in an evidence bag," ordered Shockley.

Hauser's face contorted. "You want me to have DNA run on this? Shit. If it bothers you that much, I can chase that asshole down and make sure he won't do it again."

"We're going to use it to help find our killer."

"If you want the perp's DNA, then why not go back to the area where Minty said the perp was before the explosion and search for cigarette butts?"

"It rained. Those butts won't have DNA."

Hauser twisted his mouth to the side. "You think if we pretend we have evidence, somebody will get nervous and talk. Not sure we should do that."

"I'm short on time. Everybody you interviewed lawyered up. I want you to convince them we have evidence that puts them at the crime scene."

"How do we know they even smoke?"

"A lot of criminals smoke. The part of town we're searching, it's not hard to find a criminal. I want whoever calls himself Max and I want him yesterday. You start getting the word out. I want this perp to know we're coming for him."

Hauser mumbled and headed to the door of the station.

Shockley started to follow when his cell rang. "Hi, Detective Shockley. We have patrol headed to the scene of a shooting. Male victim. They are requesting you respond." He tensed when the dispatcher read the address.

"On my way," he replied.

Shockley shouted, 'C'mon Hauser, we've got a lead." He waved him to hurry back to his car.

Hauser stopped, turned and hustled over to Shockley's car. He hopped in.

Panting, Hauser slammed the car door and asked, "Where to?"

"Mason Street in front of the closed down auto-shop. Two blocks from Willow Oaks Motel. Possible homicide."

Shockley threw the car in gear, accelerated in a hard turn causing the tires to squeal. This was probably Max's territory. Maybe he was still in the area.

"Think it's our suspect, Max, or coincidence?"

"I don't believe in coincidences." Shockley felt a sense of urgency with the thought he could be responsible for another person's life. He pressed the gas pedal harder and activated his lights.

"Me either," replied Hauser.

CHAPTER 26

Her reflection in the bathroom mirror looked like a stranger. Julia's usual simple cosmetic routine consisted of mascara, blush and lip gloss. Heavy face paint, deep red lipstick and overdone hair gave her the look of an older woman ready to work the streets.

Earlier, Laquita had helped pick out clothes at the store that were provocative in the wrong way. Her short leopard pattern dress was a size too small. They argued about it in the store because she had to tug on the sides to keep the dress from riding up her thighs. Laquita told her to quit whining, she looked sexy. The four-inch spiked black heels raised her above Laquita's 5'8" height. The shoes had already started to hurt her cramped feet.

When she entered the living room, Laquita quipped, "Strut yo' stuff, gurl."

"I thought this was a good idea when I had it," said Julia. "Now I'm positive, it isn't."

"I'm beginnin' to like it," chuckled Laquita. "Time to see how good ya work a pole."

"Pole dancing? That's not happening." Julia tugged on her dress. "Think they'll believe I'm a hooker?"

"Hell no."

Not the response she expected. Laquita was the one who helped with her make-up and selected the outfit for her to wear.

"What's wrong? You picked this out at the store."

"Yeah, I did. But you walk like ya got hemorrhoids…or somethin' up your ass. You better practice walking fore we leave."

Julia had never owned a pair of stilettos and now she knew why. She walked across the room faster than her heels would allow, rolling her ankles several times. She had to catch her balance on a chair more than once to keep from falling. How on earth did women wear high heels all the time? They required balance. And more, demanded sacrifice in comfort.

"Slow down Julia. Take small sexy steps and lean back." Laquita stood and declared, "Watch me. Ya gotta believe ya got it and then flaunt it."

Laquita strolled across the room, head cocked to one side, shoulders back and chest pushed out. One arm rested on a hip and the other swung loosely as she swiveled her hips side-to-side, her large butt moving in rhythm.

"You want me to walk like that? You gotta be kidding?"

"It's called confidence. Look like ya belong. Drive 'em crazy. I guarantee 'em horny men will line up and tell ya where Max is at."

Julia slowed her pace, placed a hand on her hip, pulled her shoulders back and let one arm dangle by her side. It felt strange and unnatural to walk like this, yet she did feel sexy. She smiled.

"What'd you think? Better?"

Laquita's eyes blinked, she pulled in her lips and shook her head. A beat later she said, "Better. Just keep working on your night moves. You gonna need 'em gurl."

✝ ✝ ✝

She walked slowly down the alleyway flanked with old brick walls and littered with trash. The deeper she went into the alleyway the harder her heart pounded against her chest. Straight ahead she saw the sign on a windowless building, *Dark Alley Warehouse*, which she thought was a fitting name. When she looked up, the afternoon light was giving way to dark threatening clouds. Laquita was waiting in the car down the street. If Julia didn't check-in in thirty minutes, Laquita was to call the police on the pre-paid phone they got while out shopping.

Laquita told her she had gone to the Warehouse a few times with Max. She claimed Max had a business relationship with the owner. Laquita said he felt it was better if Laquita didn't know what he did for a living, especially since she worked at an investigative firm. Drug trafficking and prostitution were what happened inside this sleazy dump.

Her knees tried to buckle as she moved toward the steps leading to a red metal door that was covered more in rust than paint. A tall dark hulking man posted in front of the door leered at her like a wolf observing its prey. For a split second, she considered kicking off her heels, turning and running back to the car. If Max had a *business relationship* in this dump, then Laquita was right. Max was not an upstanding citizen, he was a criminal.

When Julia hatched her original plan, Laquita was coming with her. Laquita, who at first didn't like what she had planned, convinced her that since the people at the strip club would recognize her, it'd be better for her to wait in the car down the street. Max had made it clear she was never to come here unless he was with her. It made sense at the time, but the oversized doorman caused Julia to regret not forcing Laquita to come with her.

Julia approached the big man, flashing a private invitation on her smartphone. An invitation Laquita somehow knew how to find. The doorman was difficult to look at with his tattooed face and metal piercings. Silent, his eyes traveled from her spiked heels to her eyes. Her throat tightened. A Bluetooth device was stuck in his left ear. Seconds passed. A bead of sweat rolled down her back. She wasn't sure what to do if he refused to let her in. Did he see through her veil attempt to be a hooker? Should she offer a cash bribe or try flirting? Flirt first then bribe. She pushed out her left hip, planted her hand on it trying to look impatient. She over exaggerated chewing the wad of gum Laquita gave her.

The freakish man pressed his lips together and let an audible snort escape his nose. His large hand reached for the handle and he opened the door. She glanced back down the alley before entering.

It took a few seconds for her eyes to adjust to the dimly lit room. The crowd was thin since it was still early. The air reeked of cigarette smoke, cheap perfume and body odor.

The place was just as Laquita had described.

There was a round stage with a pole in the middle. A young woman in heels, fishnets attached to a lacy garter belt and nothing else was swinging on the pole. Her long hair flying in the air. Circling the round stage were shabby purple velvet couches. A few men were sitting next to the stage. One loud, obviously drunk man kept trying to stuff money in the dancer's garter belt.

A long bar lined one side of the room with a bartender serving drinks to men and women sitting on bar stools. Several girls were topless. She remembered Laquita's warning not to touch anything covered in fabric which included the velvet covered chairs by the stage and the curtains that hung-over doorways with signs proclaiming VIP. Laquita told her that the VIP rooms were where strippers and clients engaged in open sex acts.

Julia gagged when she noticed what looked like a condom on the floor by one of the curtains. She wished she were wearing a hazmat suit instead of this skimpy tight dress.

A skinny girl with long wavy red hair was performing a lap dance on a man sitting in a chair near the stage. The man sipped a beer while the girl with make-up that glowed under the black light arched her back grinding away on his lap.

After scoping out the place, she headed to the bar to question the bartender. He was average height with sandy blond hair long enough to tuck behind his ears. He was busy drying glasses and putting them away.

"Excuse me," Julia said while slipping onto the barstool.

"What you need?" he said.

His question was odd. Maybe he thought she wanted drugs.

"I'm looking for somebody. My friend told me he works here."

The bartender threw the drying towel over his shoulder and leaned on the bar allowing her to see his biceps bulging against his t-shirt sleeves. "A lot of people work here. You got a name?"

"Max."

The bartender's face did not reveal any recognition when she spoke the name. He straightened, pulled the towel off his shoulder and answered, "Never heard of him. You want a drink?"

"Nope. Never buy my own." She winked at him and started to slip off the stool when a server approached the bar and put several drinks on her tray.

"I was wondering if you might know somebody who works here. His name is Max," Julia asked the older woman who had bleach blonde hair with dark roots. The woman had on more make-up than clothes. She had winged eyeliner, bright blue eye shadow, thick false eyelashes and the same color deep red lipstick Julia was wearing. Julia worked hard not to stare at the woman's Dolly Parton size breasts.

"Max? Is that short for Maxine?" asked the server.

"No. Just Max."

"Sorry, can't help you honey," the server replied. She turned and strutted toward a table to deliver the ordered drinks.

Julia had a sinking feeling that her ploy to find Max wasn't going to work. After a quick assessment of the place, she decided to ask the dancer who was leaving the stage when the Dolly Parton server returned to the bar. She heard the woman tell the bartender she needed to go to the restroom. He barked back that she needed to wait till her break. Julia heard, "Fuck you." The woman's hand was by her side and out of sight of the bartender. She was waving a finger that seemed to say, follow me.

She decided to take the bait but waited a few moments and wandered around the club in the hope that it wouldn't be too obvious she was following Dolly into the bathroom.

A man sitting at a table across the room smiled and raised his glass as a signal for her to come over. This was the opportunity she needed. She smiled back at the older man and carefully waltzed over with one hand on her hip, the other swinging by her side.

She stood in front of the seated man and asked, "How 'bout a sip of that drink?" Her tongue wet her lips followed by a sly wink.

"How 'bout you join me, and I'll buy you whatever you want."

She held out her hand demanding he give her his drink to taste. "First I'll taste what you're drinking and then I'll let you know what I want. You don't want to let me get away. Do you?"

The man lips slightly parted as he straightened in the chair. He raised his glass toward her. She wrapped her hand around his hand holding the glass and pulled it next to her, leaned forward to distract him and tipped the glass over spilling the liquid on her dress.

"Shit," she yelled. "You spilled your drink all over me."

The man's confused expression was pleading. He said, "I'm really sorry, babe." He took napkins and tried to wipe her dress.

"Forget it." She snatched the napkins out of his hands. "I gotta go to the bathroom and try to get this shit off my dress before it's ruined." She didn't wait for a response, turned and made her way to the door that Dolly had disappeared into.

When she reached for the knob to the bathroom door, alarms sounded inside her head warning her not to go in. She threw a quick glance behind her, twisted the knob, pushed the door open and entered.

CHAPTER 27

When Wagner reached the steps to his row house, he was surprised how out of breath he was. Before he met with Razor he needed to calm down and appear confident. In control. That's why he needed to take the gun. It would give him the leverage and courage he might need.

Wagner headed up the steps to his front door and froze. He had an idea. Jackson. What if he paid Jackson to take the money to Razor? That could work. He was certain Jackson would do it for him, he always needed money. And why would Razor care, as long as he got the money?

A calmness settled over him. Then panic. What if Jackson left before he got back to him? The homeless man stayed in that area most days till evening. No need to get upset. If for some reason he wasn't there, he'd just stick to his original plan.

He unlocked the front door and stepped inside the marble foyer. The historic row house had been professionally decorated. The interior designer mingled modern decor with the historic interior.

Still not convinced Jackson would be where he saw him, Wagner darted past the living area to his bedroom, retrieved the brown paper bag from his top dresser drawer. He deposited the bag with the money inside his leather briefcase. Not only was this the end of his ordeal, he didn't have to meet a man who terrified him. Everything was going to be alright. Nobody would ever know who he really was and how he was involved in a murder.

His eyes caught sight of his nightstand and remained fixed as his brain tried to process what he saw. Or didn't see.

Maybe he had forgotten. Maybe he had put the gun inside the nightstand drawer and had not left it out. He rushed to check the nightstand drawer. It wasn't there. Where was the damn gun? In desperation he began tossing out the clothes in his dresser. Nothing. Did he absentmindedly put the gun in his briefcase? He checked. It wasn't there. He was distraught this morning. Maybe he took the gun and laid it down in the kitchen when he made breakfast. He grabbed the briefcase, hastened out of his bedroom toward the kitchen.

"Mr. Wagner, what's the rush?" said a deep throaty voice from the living room.

"What the…" Wagner spun toward the voice and was unable to finish his sentence. He wasn't sure he could remember to breathe.

Sitting in his leather chair was Razor wearing a long overcoat. One hand was resting on his leg holding a gun. His gun.

"Why don't you have a seat? You don't look so good." Razor motioned with the gun toward the leather couch. "Did you decorate this place, cause I gotta tell you it's like you got taste and money."

Wagner eased over to the couch and sat on the edge, put his briefcase by his feet and folded his hands in his lap. His bowels churned. "How did you get in here?"

"Not important." Razor began waving the gun. "What is important, is why would a Congressman have a pistol, loaded and ready to fire?" He lowered the gun. His eyes bored into Wagner's eyes.

How did this man, this killer know he was a Congressman? He had explicitly told Max not to tell him what he did for a living.

"Actually, a lot of House and Senate members own guns and are allowed to carry them to their offices," his voiced cracked.

He almost took the gun with him this morning. He now regretted that decision. He added, "Congress members get threats about controversial legislation. I keep it for protection in case somebody breaks in."

He regretted the words, *breaks in*. That's what Razor had done.

"Correct me if I'm wrong. You weren't planning on taking it with you to our meeting today?" Razor pretended to study the pistol.

"No, of course not. I have all the money you asked for." Wagner reached down and opened his briefcase. His hand grabbed the brown bag and opened it to reveal the stacks of money. "Just like you instructed, in a paper bag."

"Uh-huh. Just curious why a lawmaker has a semi-automatic gun that has the serial numbers removed. This was bought on the black market. Untraceable. Where would a Congressman get an illegal weapon like this?"

Razor knew. The man was playing with him. He had to think and think fast.

"A friend got it for me. He said I should have one. You know, for protection."

"Uh-huh." Razor stood, walked with a slow deliberate stride over to him and pushed the cold barrel of the pistol against Wagner's temple. "Your friend's name. What is it?"

Wagner's hands shot up. Sweat drenched his forehead. His mouth spasmed for a second. Finally, he forced his voice to vocalize, "Please. I did what you asked. I got you more money."

"His name."

"You don't know him."

Razor pressed the barrel harder against his temple.

"Try me."

Wagner hastily said, "Quatterman. Dan Quatterman. He's a Congressman." Why he said it was Dan Quatterman was he feared if Razor knew it was Max, he'd know why he had the weapon.

Razor lowered the gun allowing Wagner to finally let out a deep breath.

"We had a deal, Congressman. Now you go and get a gun and then lie to me about it."

"What do you mean?" Wagner had the sensation his throat was tightening making it difficult to talk.

"Why would a Congressman deal in black market guns unless he plans on committing a crime?"

Wagner wiped his forehead. "It's not like that at all. He… he just knows somebody who does it for him. Maybe he owes him a favor. You know there are Congressmen who break the law. I didn't want to know how he obtained the weapon. He insisted I needed it for protection. I'm not sure how to even shoot a gun."

Razor kept the gun dangling in his hand by his side. His eyes hardened, scaring Wagner even more.

Razor raised the gun with the barrel pointed directly at Wagner's chest. "How bout I show you how easy it is?"

"Oh my God. No. Please, don't. I can get you more money. Anything you want. Please don't do this."

The cold look in the killer's eyes told Wagner he was going to die.

As Razor squeezed the trigger, Wagner shut his eyes.

He heard the click, opened his eyes and with disbelief he was still alive ran his hands over his chest and arms.

"See how easy it is," declared Razor. "Just aim and squeeze."

"You're crazy," Wagner shouted furiously. "You know that?"

He expected the killer to respond with anger, yet the man just bounced his head from side to side. "Who knows what crazy means. I just don't let things bother me like you do."

Razor placed the weapon on the coffee table, held out his hand for the money. Wagner handed him the paper bag but kept hold of the end.

"I need to know what the reporter told you before she died," said Wagner. "That was our deal."

Razor smirked. "Whatta ya know. A Congressman with balls."

Wagner released the bag of money. Razor rolled up the bag and stuffed it inside his coat.

"She said the FBI is looking for a possible Russian spy in our government."

Wagner swallowed hard before he spoke, "Did she find out who it was?"

"That would be bad for business, wouldn't it, Congressman Wagner? I think that's why you and your crooked friends didn't want her to talk. Maybe get rid of her before she wrote about it. She was kinda attractive, but a screamer. I did you a favor when I shut her up for good. The stakes are higher now. Since her boyfriend came looking for her, I took care of him too."

"What? You murdered her boyfriend too? This isn't what I hired you to do. I never told you to kill that reporter or her boyfriend. Shit. If the police find out, I'll end up in prison."

"Looks like you're starting to understand the situation. You can't afford any loose ends."

"What kind of loose ends?" Wagner struggled to not sound scared, but his lips began to quiver.

"I figure by now the FBI's involved and maybe you already know all this. Can't have loose ends, can we? Half a million to tidy up this mess and when you find that Russian bastard, a million to eliminate the threat to your career. Not sure how you're connected in all this. Maybe you're the spy."

"That's ridiculous. If I was a spy for the Russians, I wouldn't have needed you. Now, would I?"

Razor bounced his head side to side again and said, "We'll talk again. Soon. Meanwhile, remember Congressman Wagner, I don't like loose ends."

A sinister smile swiped across his face. "And I hate Russians."

CHAPTER 28

The office was the same as last time she was here, except for the personal touches the new Director of the CIA seated behind his desk had added.

Rick Piagno had been Director of Central Intelligence for less than six months. Elke had known him a lot longer. Their paths had crossed during a covert operation more than thirty years ago.

"Good to see you Elke. I'm glad you accepted my offer to meet," said Piagno with a hint of a smile. The man still looked like she remembered. Except now he was a little soft around the middle and had dark circles that shadowed his eyes. Piagno was a good-looking man with thick gray hair showing no signs of letting go. She knew there was opposition to his appointment, but she considered it one of the better decisions by the presiding president.

After a few awkward seconds of silence, Piagno said, "Please have a seat." He stood and motioned with his hand. "Would you like something to drink?"

"Do you have vodka?"

"Anything you'd like," he responded.

"Vodka, water and …"

"No ice," he interrupted. "I do remember some things, unfortunately not as detailed as you do." He nodded to the tall man stationed by the door.

The man immediately left the room.

Elke walked to the side of the room and sat, sinking into the distressed brown leather chair.

"At times, my memory can be a curse. But you know my past."

"Yes, I do." The man's eyes filled with concern.

Piagno had begun his career serving as an officer in the United States Navy before being recruited by the CIA as a field officer. He had a Ph.D. in history from Harvard with a focus in Russian studies. He spent time abroad and became fluent in Russian. She admired the man who had been raised in a home without running water or electricity and worked hard to rank fifth in his class at Harvard.

He had a more hawkish view than his predecessors on Russia. He had denounced Russia for its role in the annexation of Crimea, support for Syrian President Bashar al-Assad and the meddling in U.S. politics. The current administration wanted to reach out to the Kremlin in hopes of avoiding a tit-for-tat escalation with the Russian president.

The door to the office opened and the tall man dressed in the dark suit entered, walked over and handed her the drink.

"Thank you." She arched back in the chair, took a sip, and nodded in approval. "This is good."

She took another sip, let it linger in her mouth and slowly swallowed. She tilted her head up toward the tall man's face and in a serious tone said, "You can leave the director and me alone now."

The tall man's jaw tightened, and she was sure he wanted to respond, but he was well trained. He remained silent.

Piagno appeared amused. He placed his hands on his desk and ordered, "Give us some time."

The tall man did not look back in her direction. He nodded

to the director, turned and walked out of the room.

As soon as the door closed, Piagno stated, "Still as spunky and arrogant as I remember."

"He took my weapon, under those circumstances it only seemed fair I take a dig while I had a chance."

"He was following protocol."

"You honestly think I'd shoot you?"

"Only if you felt it was necessary, Elke. I'm not a gambling man." He laughed. "Besides the CIA's not a law enforcement agency. You don't need a weapon."

Elke took another sip of vodka and placed the glass on the table beside the chair. "Perhaps. You were always by the books."

"And the law," he included.

"You're no longer a Boy Scout," she reminded the director recalling he had attained the rank of Eagle Scout in the BSA. "The law is subject to interpretation and can be very ineffective at times. I'm sure you will agree. Or have you forgotten?"

"I haven't forgotten."

"We both know how the CIA operates. The law works until it doesn't. Isn't that why I'm here?"

"We do understand how the agency has to work in order to be effective. Your service, even in an unacknowledged capacity, is a value to this agency." Piagno lowered his eyes, clasped his hands resting on his desk "You need to let me know when you're going to meet with a person in protective custody. I can't have you working behind my back," said Piagno.

"I hardly believe you didn't know of my meeting."

"It would be better to contact me instead of finding out after the fact. You need to be careful. For whatever reason, the Russians still view you as a threat."

"As they should. Thanks, by the way, for cleaning up that mess in Canada…and for safe passage back to the States."

Piagno leaned back in his chair. "I need your help."

"Apparently you're asking me to operate in a capacity you cannot. Outside the law. And I suppose if I fail, I never worked for you and if I succeed, the CIA takes the credit."

Elke knew how the process worked. She was naive when she first joined the agency swearing an oath of secrecy and always playing by the rules. Years later she became disillusioned by the agency's utter disregard for her well-being and her family.

She picked up the drink, tipped it up and drained the glass. After she placed the empty glass on the table she began, "I'm glad you have not forgotten. You and I understand Russia cannot be trusted."

"I believe Russia has ramped up its spying activities in this country."

"They are activating their sleepers," she said letting him know she already knew the game the Russians were up to.

"Yes. They have long concentrated on cultivating well-placed contacts."

Piagno picked up a photograph on his desk and handed it to her. It took a moment for her to recognize the man in the grainy photo. It gave her chills. He wore a hat and his face was turned sideways. The man had grown a thick beard covering the jagged scar on his neck. She knew the scar was there just like she knew about the skin graft on his left inner thigh.

"Do you know this man?"

"No. Who does he work for?"

"We believe he's working for the Russians. He's a person of interest in the attempted assassination plot on the President and Vice President. His name is Adrik Kuznetsov."

"Then bring him in for questioning. I don't know why you need me."

"Kuznetsov has disappeared."

"You think I can find him?"

"I know you can. We believe Kuznetsov can help us find the Russian spy who was supposed to meet his handler in the park on the day the handler was murdered. Why the Russian spy didn't show, we can only speculate."

"You know, Rick," she began, "I don't play games. You honestly think I can find a man who the CIA with all its resources can't?"

Piagno's dark eyes emphasized the hardened expression on his face. She remembered that look from a long time past.

He said, "Russia's president has transformed Russia into a giant spy state using Cold War techniques. Their tactics come straight from the KGB playbook."

"Disinformation, propaganda, and subversion used to weaken the West," she said.

"Yes. If Russia has eyes and influence inside our government, we need to find the traitor." The Director's eyes bored into hers, he steepled his fingers propped on his desk and continued, "I value human source intelligence. Looking a person in the eyes and figuring out what they know isn't something technology can do. We can't use satellites to see into the minds of humans. Hell, they can't even see inside my file cabinet. You and the Bridge Club have an extensive network of human intelligence. Randall Ottmeyer told me the Club still uses short wave radios and invisible ink?"

"Randall is still with the FBI? I thought he retired."

"Next month. He's got his last day down to the minute. The Bridge Club might want to consider recruiting him."

"I doubt it. Randall drank the Kool-Aid and I'm not sure he'd fit in with the Club. But stranger things have happened. Does the Vice President still believe the Russians are responsible for his wife's death?"

"He is, but the Russians deny everything. The President is cozying up to the Russians and wants to blame ISIS. And we lack proof to prove otherwise."

She shook her head. "The Russians are testing the waters. Their goal was not the assassination of our leaders, but to show they could. The Russian cyber warriors hacked and planted false stories to throw off our intelligence agencies. They know we don't want to accuse them of something we can't prove, thus the smokescreen of lies."

"We have to tread carefully, Elke. The President wants to avoid any escalation that might play into Russia's hands."

"To make sure we're on the same page let me see if I understand what you want from me. Unofficially I'm to find a man the CIA can't find and turn him over to you while the President pretends to reset relations with Russia?"

Piagno's face changed colors. He looked like his blood pressure had spiked. "Dammit Elke, this is serious. The people at the top are becoming paranoid. They're finger pointing in a fishing expedition that could destroy people's careers, their personal lives. What I need is hard evidence. Not speculation. Not finger pointing. You were in the park that day the handler was murdered."

She knew now where this was headed and Piagno was holding the winning hand. He was playing the guilt card. She hated this damn agency. She was the one who had talked with the Russian handler in the park right before the handler was murdered. The Bridge Club had tipped her off the Russian spy would not show for the meeting. She was sure she'd get info from the handler, then the whole thing blew up in her face. She had been set up.

"Bullshit. You blame me. Think I scared the Russian spy off?"

"I think you know more than you shared in the debrief."

He might have the upper hand, but she was tired of playing the game.

She kept her eyes locked on Piagno and said, "You're wasting your time. I have nothing more to add to the statement I gave."

Piagno shifted in his chair, wiggled his nose and combed his hair with his fingers. It was a habit he had when she irritated him.

"I need you to find this man and find out what he knows and who he works for. You and I knew during the Cold War we were closer to nuclear devastation than the American public realized. That war is still going on and we must win it."

"You suspect the danger has already unfolded inside our country?"

"I need you to exhaust all your contacts and make this a priority. We want him alive."

Elke crossed her legs. She gazed out the window behind Piagno. Ironic how the American public was going about their daily tasks unaware of what was happening in the director's office. Politics was always at the heart of the problem. And if they were successful in stopping the Russians, the President could claim credit. His approval rating would go up with American voters.

She said, "I want all surveillance on me stopped."

"Agreed."

"Does your boss know you're involving me?"

"As far as anybody's concerned, this conversation never happened."

CHAPTER 29

Dark Alley Warehouse

Julia feared she would breathe her last breath in this back room.

Dolly, the overly endowed waitress, had lured her into the bathroom and she fell for the ploy. Now she was sitting in a back room on a metal chair with her wrists tied behind her back. Her purse and phone had been taken and were on the table in front of her. The only person who could rescue her was waiting in a car down the street.

She frowned at the time on the wall clock across the room. Maybe it was slow. If not, she had twelve more minutes before Laquita would call the cops. In twelve minutes, she could be dead.

The man hiding in the bathroom had shoved a gun in her ribs and forced her into this dark windowless room. With no outside light, the room felt damp and cold. Two lights with metal covers dangled from the ceiling, leaving the corners of the room cloaked in darkness. Paint peeled from the yellow concrete walls. Even the floor was concrete. The only way out was the way she entered or through a back door guarded by a beefy guy with his arms intertwined across his oversized chest. Pistol holstered to his side. She wouldn't be leaving voluntarily out the back door.

Her mind began swimming with possibilities of what

might happen to her.

None of them good.

She did a quick assessment of her surroundings. The room was not large. At least what she could see of it. A long wooden table in front of her had five metal chairs tucked under it. In one corner was a small desk with scattered papers and file folders on top. The dark recesses without overhead lights were filled with stacks of crates and boxes. She was able to make out the words *Powdered Milk* on the crates and numbers. Vietnam was stamped under the numbers. Two hand trucks with oversized wheels were next to the crates. She figured the crates had more than powdered milk in them. Probably drugs.

Over in the far corner was an average built man, young, probably in his mid-twenties and sporting a man-bun. He was arguing with Dolly. Judging by what she could hear, he was angry about something. Dolly took a long drag on her cigarette and blew the smoke out the side of her mouth. She dropped the cigarette butt to the ground, crushing it with the toe of her stiletto. She said something to the man Julia couldn't quite hear. He shoved what looked like money in her hand and as she took it, he twisted her wrist and shoved her against the wall. The low hanging pendant light fixture washed a wave of light across the woman's face exposing fear in her big eyes. Still holding her wrist, he twisted harder making her scream.

Julia guessed nobody in the club could hear or maybe in this place they knew better than to interfere. He leaned close to the woman, whispered in her ear and then let go. Dolly shoved the money down her cleavage and beelined out of the room. Two men almost ran into Dolly as they entered from the club. They lurked in the shadows, making it difficult to distinguish their faces. One man she was sure was old because he was hunched forward and used a cane for support. The other much younger. Even without much light this man's silhouette was muscular.

The three men huddled on the side of the room. Man-Bun lit a cigarette. Man-Bun must be in charge, she thought, since he was doing all the talking. The younger guy nodded while his arms hung to his side. She strained to hear their conversation while keeping her eyes averted from the beefy guy guarding the door.

A sharp tingle raced up her spine. Max. Did Man-Bun just call the younger man Max? She was about to look in their direction when she noticed a dark crimson colored stain on the table in front of her. It took a full second for her brain to register what she was looking at and what it meant. Fear took control of her body as an audible gasp escaped her lips.

Man-Bun turned his face toward her and flicked his cigarette across the floor. With his face out of the shadows, she saw that he was older than she thought. His head too large for his small frame. One side of his face had a purple-red birthmark under his eye. She didn't like the aggressive way he moved in her direction.

"Guess you're one of my new girls?" His voice raspy and unpleasant.

She felt goosebumps rise on her arms. Her eyes found the clock, hoping enough time had passed for Laquita to have called the authorities.

He caught her looking at the clock. "You expectin' somebody?"

"Max." Maybe that was a good lie. She needed to stall long enough for the police to arrive.

"Really?" Man-Bun knitted his eyebrows and pulled his lips

up to his long nose. He turned toward the two men standing in the shadow. "Hey Max, looks like our new girl is waitin' on you. Why don't you come over and show her how things work round here?"

The younger man started toward her.

It was him.

Laquita had described him to a tee. Dark wavy hair and thick eyebrows accented his sunken eyes. He wasn't as young as she first thought. She had assumed he was Laquita's age. He looked much older. His face didn't match his muscle toned body.

Max stood next to Man-Bun and shook his head.

"I don't know her. She won't work out. I can tell she's too picky."

"How come she's asking for you Max? Is she a cop?"

He thinks I'm a cop? She rolled her eyes.

"I'm not a cop, jerk. I got stiffed by a client. I need money. That's why I wanted to talk to Max." This wasn't how she had planned this out in her head.

"Is that right Max?" said Man-Bun.

Max paused a moment. He snickered. "If she's a hooker, I'm Santa Claus."

Both men including the door guard belted out a laugh.

The cold room suddenly felt warm to her. She broke out in a cold sweat.

Man-Bun picked up her purse from the table, pulled it open and dumped the contents on the blood-stained wooden tabletop. Wallet, lipstick, and pepper spray scattered across the table.

He reached for her wallet, thumbed through it and pulled out her driver license. His gaze lingered on the license in his hand.

"Julia Bagal. This address ain't from around here."

She shuddered. Her dry mouth made it difficult to swallow He knew she was a fraud.

"You know something." He leaned close forcing her to turn her face sideways. "I think Julia Bagal ain't your real name, now is it?"

"So what?" snapped Julia. She wanted to tell the creep he was right. Her birth name wasn't Julia Bagal, but this wasn't the time for sharing her past.

He straightened, tossed the license on the table.

"Maybe you got a thing or two to hide. We all got things to hide in our lives," Man-Bun said nodding his head toward Max and then the guard at the door. "Ain't that right boys?"

A chorus replied, "Right boss."

"What don't make sense is how come a sweet thing like you is hanging out in a place like this?"

"I need a job." Her voice was strained. "That's why I came to find Max. A friend told me Max is good to his girls."

"Yeah. And who might that friend be?" Man-Bun's eyes narrowed.

Still five minutes till Laquita makes the call. *How long would it take the cops to get here?*

"I can't say."

Man-Bun smiled and reached in his coat jacket taking out a box. He opened it and showed her what was inside.

"You came to the right place. I'll make sure you get work."

Every muscle in her body knotted. She felt light-headed and sick to her stomach. She didn't want to believe her eyes.

A syringe and vial. This was how Man-Bun controlled his girls. He kept them addicted to whatever was in that vial.

Probably heroin, she theorized.

She shook her head fiercely while she twisted in the chair and tugged on the binding wrapped around her wrist. This wasn't going to happen. *Please God, don't let this happen.*

"Max, give my new girl a little brown sugar and then put her in my car." His slender fingers stroked her cheek as he smiled.

The older man with the cane moved out of the shadow and growled, "Stop right now, Caleb. She don't look like no stripper. Maybe she's a narc. You want 'em swarming this place searching for her?"

"Shut the fuck up ol' man. You're no longer the boss, I am."

"Jesus Caleb," said Max. "Your ol' man might be right."

Caleb shoved his finger in Max's chest, pulled a gun from the back of his pants and hissed, "Don't ever side with him! Got that?" Caleb threw the old man a look and continued, "You do it now or I'll shoot you and that bitch."

Max backed up, raised his hands and relented, "Okay man. Just put the gun down."

Caleb lowered the gun and pushed the box containing the needle into Max's chest. Max took the box and nodded.

Caleb stalked over by the door to the club, stopped, spit on the old man and left the room.

"Max, you don't have to do this. You know this isn't right." Julia's voice broke.

Max stayed silent, set the box on the table and threw the old man a quick look. He picked up the syringe and vial and faced her.

Two more minutes maybe seven with the time it takes the police to get to the club. If only she could do something. She kicked him as hard as she could in the shin. Max yelped and the guard by the door pulled his gun from his holster and stepped forward.

Max waved him off. "It's okay, Lopez. I got this."

He held the syringe in his hand like a pencil, with the needle pointed up. He inserted the needle into the rubber top of the vial and pulled the plunger, transferring the liquid to the syringe. Standing on the side of her, he told her to relax. It wouldn't hurt if she didn't move.

He reached and cupped her arm with his free hand.

"Laquita said you would listen," she could barely get the words out, her throat was dry.

"What?"

She heard a pop-pop sound from inside the club. Max, Lopez and the old man focused their attention on the club door.

The old man yelled, "Max. Get her the hell outta here."

Max tossed the syringe on the table, moved to the back of the chair and began to untie the bindings. Lopez raced over, picked up the syringe and smashed Max in the head with the butt of his gun. Max grunted and fell limp.

Terrified, she twisted violently in her chair, trying to get free. The binding on her wrists cutting into her bare skin. It was almost time for Laquita to call the cops. Not enough time to escape being drugged. She screamed as loud as she could, "Help, help…."

She saw it coming, closed her eyes. A flash of light, then darkness.

CHAPTER 30

Shockley and Hauser hurried toward the man spread in a supine position on the road next to a silver Toyota Corolla. A dark pool of blood congealed on the pavement next to the body.

Two responding uniformed patrolmen standing next to the victim raised hands to protest their presence. Shockley and Hauser held up their badges and identified themselves.

The older uniform he knew. The tall middle-aged African American's shirt revealed the man had packed on a few more pounds since last time he saw him. The man gnawing a toothpick said, "Sorry Detective, didn't recognize you at first. By the time we got here, the vic was on the ground not moving. I checked for a pulse. DRT. *Dead Right There.* One in the gut, another right between the eyes." The younger uniform looked like he was just a few months out of the academy. His clothes pressed and shoes shiny. The rookie's pale-skinned face was sprinkled with freckles and looked eager to please.

Shockley snapped on a pair of latex gloves, stepped next to the body and squatted, arms resting on his thighs. He studied the victim and noted the man had clutched his stomach when he was shot. Both hands covered in his own blood. His lifeless eyes wide open, back of his head missing. Gone. The second shot killed him instantly. He couldn't help but notice the victim was about his age. Early to mid-thirties.

Resting on his heels, Shockley directed his attention to

both patrolmen. "Were you aware of any persons or vehicles leaving the crime scene?"

"No sir," said Officer Carlass.

"Witnesses?"

"Light traffic. Nobody stopped. No witnesses observed and none have come forward. Our presence in this part of town is never welcomed."

"Who called it in?"

"Not sure."

"I'll check with dispatch," offered the rookie.

"Either of you touch the vehicle?"

Carlass shook his head before sarcastically saying. "Followed protocol. Been doing this a lot longer than you, detective."

"Then you're used to being asked these questions." Shockley caught Carlass roll his eyes at the rookie.

He stood and scanned the surrounding area thoroughly. A vacant commercial lot littered with piles of discarded tires on one side and across the street run down homes and trailers with overgrown yards littered with cars, shopping carts and other junk.

The police were often summoned to this area for prostitution, drug dealing, overdoses, and gun possession. Last week they arrested three men, one was seventy-five years old for running a chop shop down the street. The group had stolen a dozen cars and disassembled them for the purpose of selling parts.

"Hauser."

Hauser had his memo pad out taking notes. He was inspecting the inside of the dead man's car. "Yeah?"

"Get me a witness. Somebody somewhere saw or heard

something."

"Gotcha." Hauser took off at a clip toward a row of houses on the other side of the street.

"You." The young uniform gave Shockley his full attention. "Tape off this crime scene, have all traffic diverted from the area. I don't want a circus when the media arrives."

"Will do, detective. Sir." The young uniform hurried toward his patrol car.

Shockley bent down and checked the dead man's pockets for ID. The pant pockets contained no wallet, just a set of keys. Could have been a robbery. A drug deal gone sideways. Heroin flowed through this community like water rushing down a stream and out into its tributaries. Drugs, hard drugs, had no boundaries. He checked the man's arms for track marks. None. The man had several tattoos on his left arm. None were tats from local gangs. No wedding ring.

He said, "Looks like the vic was shot at point-blank range. The entrance wound to the head is surrounded by a wide zone of GSR–Gun Shot Residue—and seared blackened skin." Thinking aloud, he added, "Why'd the vic let the perp approach him?"

"Maybe this guy was set up in a drug rip. Robbing drug dealers is spreading like wildfire in this area," offered Officer Carlass.

"Officer Carlass, run the plates and tell me what you find."

Carlass moved the toothpick to the other side of his mouth and without a word stepped to the back of the weathered Corolla. The rookie was stringing the plastic tape around the perimeter of the crime area. Shockley seethed with anger knowing the people he wished could be at the crime scene were in the hospital. T-Bone's condition had improved, but

Bull was in a medically induced coma due to the swelling on her brain. Presently, he needed a crime scene investigator. A specialist that could uncover trace evidence he wouldn't be able to see with the naked eye.

He called in his request for CSI to be dispatched to the scene. He stressed urgency since this was an outside crime scene and evidence could deteriorate quickly, especially when he studied the clouds. Nimbus clouds. Rain on the horizon.

"Looks like the car's registered to a Chance Martin Stephens III," Carlass read from a small tablet in his hand. "Last known address is an apartment in Nashville, Tennessee."

"Thanks. If this was a drug rip, then we should know soon enough after we run a background check on Stephens. If he's involved in drugs, then he's probably got a rap sheet."

Shockley stood over the body and noted the white male's face was unshaven. Maybe he had traveled from Nashville. Long way to travel to buy or sell drugs. The victim could have been targeted for various reasons.

Hauser walked up with a stocky Hispanic woman beside him. "We've got a possible witness," he said.

The woman stood silent until she caught a glimpse of the corpse. One hand flew to her mouth and the other hand made the sign of the cross on her chest.

Shockley hooked the woman's arm and guided her to the other side of the car, out of sight of the dead man and the blood.

"Sorry," he said looking down at the woman who was maybe five feet tall. "Did you see what happened?"

The woman tilted her full face, blinked back tears, pointed in the direction of the body. Her hands began to wave like she was swatting flies as she began to rattle off Spanish. The woman kept the machine gun speech rate without realizing he didn't understand a word she was saying.

"Hauser," he hollered unaware the man was right behind him.

Hauser stepped around and broke into a conversation with the woman. Shockley was glad Hauser was fluent in Spanish.

"She says she saw another car pull up to the victim's car."

"Ask her if she saw the man in the other car."

Hauser rattled off a string of Spanish words that sounded like a series of vowels separated by RRRs. The woman replied, "Sí, sí," and nodded. As the woman communicated with Hauser, she used her hands, eyes and arms with an occasional shoulder shrug.

Hauser interpreted as the woman spoke. "She saw a dark car parked in front of the dead man's car. He was tall." The woman pointed to Shockley. "Tall like you. He wore a hat. He walked close to the other man." Hauser said something and she shook her head. "She did not see a gun. She had bread in the oven and left the window to check on it. A few minutes later, she heard a loud noise and ran to the window. The man had fallen to the ground. The tall man got in his car and left. She called 9-1-1 and told them to come fast. She did not leave the house to help the man because she was afraid the bad man would come back."

He now knew who called it in.

"Which house does she live in?"

Hauser pointed to a house down the street. The house was not close. And there were bars on the windows.

"Ask her if she has seen either the victim or the other man before."

As soon as Hauser asked, she shook her head and said,

"No." The woman said something to Hauser that caused the corners of his mouth to lift up into a smile.

"What is it?" asked Shockley. "What'd she say?"

"She wants to know if there's a reward for helping catch the bad man."

"Damn." Shockley shook his head. "Tell her if she sees the bad man again, give us a call."

Hauser thanked the woman and she started to leave when Shockley thought of a question for her. "Hey wait. Ask her if the bad man walked with a limp."

Hauser asked and the woman replied, "Sí, sí."

Shockley had a lead. Two witnesses identified the perp as having a limp which meant the crimes were probably connected somehow. The blind woman named Minty told him she believed the perp was among the crowd across the street from the motel when it exploded. She said the man had a limp. The Hispanic woman saw a man with a limp approach the man who was now deceased. What he needed was a background check on the victim. Who was this guy? This dead man might be able to connect them to the killer.

By the time the CSI unit arrived on site, the rookie patrolman had the area taped off with Day-Glo police tape. Shockley knew the CSI investigator, Asmita Patel. He was good, but he was no Amber Bull. The CSI crew was gathering physical evidence, taking photos of the body and making documentations in their notebooks.

Shockley heard Hauser call him. He was standing near Shockley's car. Shockley walked over and stood next to Hauser, "What ya got?"

"One of our guys got a hit on Max. Somebody told our guy that a guy called Max works at Dark Alley Warehouse."

"The strip joint? That's not far from here. You stay here and make sure all evidence is gathered and bagged. I'll check out the Warehouse."

"You're not going there alone are you? That joint doesn't lay out a welcome mat for cops. You're gonna need a search warrant and back-up," warned Hauser.

"I'm not there to arrest. Just talk. If I wait for a warrant, Max could slip away."

Shockley heard Hauser grumble as he left and headed toward his car.

CHAPTER 31

Dark Alley Warehouse

Shockley was sure the mountain of muscle guarding the door to the Warehouse club wouldn't let him inside without causing trouble. The imposing size of the bouncer and his tatted-up face made Shockley question his decision to visit the place without back-up.

Two women in front of him looked like they were regulars. They laughed as they sashayed toward the entrance, never looking in the direction of the bouncer. He scanned their skimpy outfits and figured they probably worked here.

Shockley trotted up to the women. "Hello ladies. I was wondering if either of you know a guy who works here named Max?"

The women stopped and faced him. "Is this person you call Max in some sort of trouble?" asked the older woman with the pink hair.

"It's important, I just wanna talk. That's all. Don't want any trouble."

Pink Hair placed a hand on her small hip and studied him. "You know, you're kinda cute, in a cowboy sorta way." She arched her eyebrows and shared a curious gaze with the other woman.

The woman next to her was younger by a decade. She had tattoo sleeves on both arms. The tattoo woman took a drag on her cigarette, blew the smoke out the side of her mouth and nodded to Pink Hair. She looked down. "I like them boots. If you wanna find this guy, maybe you're at the right place. But you got one big problem."

Shockley and the two women stole a look at the beefy bouncer.

"Yeah, Bruno don't look too friendly," remarked Shockley. "I'd be in your debt if you could help me out here."

The women shared a look and smiled.

"Honey, this is your lucky day," Pink Hair said. "We're the number one girls. Just stick with us."

They flanked Shockley's side, laced their arms through his and headed to the entrance of the club. At the door, the women shot Bruno a flirty smile. He nodded and let all three waltz in.

Once inside, Shockley said, "Thank you ladies."

"Anytime cowboy. Right now, we gotta clock in," said Tattoo Woman.

Pink Hair chimed in, "We'll see you later for a drink or a lap dance." She slapped his butt. "I've heard you never forget your first cowboy," she whispered in his ear before heading toward a back room.

He grinned.

Inside, the club was dark with pulsating lights and an old-fashioned disco ball. He knew there were plenty of things going on in here that were outside the law. The bartender's hard stare told him he needed to watch his back.

An anorexic stripper worked the pole with a small audience of three men and one woman. Sitting on a stool next to the bar was another young woman. She had long auburn hair, deep red lipstick and appeared nervous. One of her legs kept bouncing as she talked to the bartender and then to a waitress with the biggest boobs he'd ever seen.

When he first joined the force, he'd visited strip clubs with fellow cops after their shift was over. He soon realized he didn't care for them. Too many lonely men paying an exotic dancer to listen to their fantasies and problems at home.

The back wall had rooms with drapes for doors and VIP signs hung above them. A topless woman wearing spiked heels, a thong and a tattoo across her backside was escorting a short male with balding brown hair to one of the rooms. At the moment he didn't care what went on behind the drapes, he only wanted to find Max.

As the pole dancer left the platform, another dancer walked up to replace her.

"Howdy cowboy," the replacement said. It was Pink Hair.

"Hi," he responded.

"You find what you're looking for?"

"Not yet. I'm not sure who can help me in here."

"Well, if I were you, I'd ask Jimmy, the bartender. Probably won't tell you anything, but who knows. Today does seem to be your lucky day." She puckered her lips out and made a kissing sound. "See you later cowboy." The woman made her way onto the stage.

"Thanks." He started for the bar. The young auburn-haired woman walked to a table where a man had held up a glass to welcome her over. What distracted him from going to the bar was the three men who entered. Three Hispanic men.

The men were average height, muscular and gunned up. One of the men had a tattoo wrapped around his neck. He knew this man—Roberto Vazquez—a gang member he had arrested several years ago for drug possession and selling illegal weapons to a Mexican cartel. These guys weren't here for a lap dance. They were here for a different reason.

The stripper was wrong. This was *not* his lucky day.

Shockley didn't remember the names of all the perps he had arrested over the years, but Vazquez stood out. He had killed one of Vazquez's men during a raid. When he cuffed Vasquez, the man vowed the next time they met, he'd put a bullet in Shockley's head. Shockley was sure Vazquez was a man of his word, especially when he was the one responsible for interrupting his lucrative gun running business. Vazquez did a nickel for his crimes and had been paroled for about a year.

Shockley found a table on the far side of the stage. The stage helped obscure the view from the bar area. Vazquez and his thugs were making their way to the bar when the young auburn-haired woman shouted, "Shit".

Vazquez and his protection stopped and all three reached inside their jackets. Shockley instinctively reached beneath his jacket and gripped his pistol. He had his back-up weapon strapped to his ankle. Guns in a place like this made him nervous. He hoped the bartender was paying attention. His eyes locked on the three Hispanic men. With their hands still resting inside their jackets, one of the men said something to Vazquez. All three men burst out laughing. Vasquez let his hand drop to his side. Shockley relaxed the grip on his pistol.

He saw the auburn-haired woman head to the back through an entrance marked *Restrooms*. Vazquez and his men continued toward the bar. Vazquez slowed his stride and glanced across the room.

This was not the place for a shoot-out. Too many innocent by-standers and at this point he had no way of knowing whose side the bartender was on. Three against one. Maybe four if the bartender went the wrong way.

"Need a drink?" a raspy voice asked. He slid his weapon back in the holster and turned toward the voice. It was Tattoo Woman.

"No thanks. See those guys over there?" He nodded his head in their direction.

"Sure do. They look like trouble."

"I need to make sure they don't see me."

Tattoo Woman smiled and quickly stood in the line of sight between him and the three men. She pushed him against the back of the chair and straddled her legs over his. She arched her back twisting her head toward the pink-haired woman pole dancing. A nod and the two seemed to communicate what to do next. The pole dancer ripped off her top and threw it out to a customer near the stage. He hollered in delight.

The diversion worked. Vazquez watched the pole dancer for a few minutes before he and his men approached the bartender. With their backs to him, Tattoo Woman whispered, "Follow me." She took his hand and lead him to one of the velvet curtained rooms marked, VIP.

Inside the room, Shockley said, "Looks like I need to thank you again for your help."

"You're a cop, right?"

"That obvious, huh?" Shockley stood next to the curtain and eased it back to check on the Hispanic men at the bar. Vazquez didn't look happy. Neither did the bartender.

"When you asked about Max, Barbara and I knew you must be a cop. Max treats us good. But now things have changed."

"Whatta ya mean?" He kept his focus on the men at the bar.

"You not gonna arrest Max, are ya?"

Shockley let go of the curtain. "Is Max here? In the building?"

"You gotta promise me, you won't arrest him," the woman pleaded. "This used to be the place to work when the ol' man ran it. Now, his son Caleb has taken over. Max tries to protect us from him. Caleb gets girls hooked on drugs to keep 'em doing what he wants."

He moved within a few inches of the woman, looked down at her and said, "If you know where Max is then you need to tell me. Those guys out there are dangerous. Max could be in trouble. I can protect him."

Pop. Pop.

A woman screamed.

Tattoo Woman pressed her body against the far wall. Her hands flew up covering her mouth. Shockley drew his weapon and shoved her to the floor. He held up a hand to signal to stay down while his gun eased the velvet curtain back.

The bartender was sprawled across the bar, his hand still gripping a shotgun. The three Hispanic men had weapons drawn and aimed at a guy with a man bun and purple birthmark under his eye. The birthmark guy was speaking Spanish and holding up one hand. *What was in his other hand?*

Without warning the front door to the bar flung open. Three uniforms stormed in. "Police, hands up."

Vasquez jumped over the bar. His men ducked behind a table.

The room erupted in gunfire.

Shockley rushed out of the curtained room, dropped on one knee and fired several rounds toward the Hispanic men. He saw two officers crumple to the floor. One didn't move, the other moaned and grabbed his thigh. Another uniform turned a table over and took cover. Bystanders scattered and screamed, ducking under tables and crawling behind the stage. A young man trying to escape ran toward the front door, clutched his chest and collapsed to the floor.

Shockley hollered, "Everybody down."

Vasquez rose from behind the solid wood bar and fired Shockley returned fire. Bursts of gunfire sent splinters flying. Vasquez yelled something in Spanish to his men. A spray of bullets passed over Shockley's head and hit the stage behind him. He dropped and belly-crawled to the back side of the stage.

Behind the stage, he crouched and bolted to the other end where the wounded officer was lying. He reached for the downed officer. Three rounds hit nearby.

He couldn't get to the downed officer without exposing himself. The officer behind the table was pinned down. He was no help.

The wounded officer moaned.

Time was running out. He peeked around the stage and saw a target's head raise above the overturned table.

Shockley aimed and squeezed off a three-round burst.

He saw the man's head snap back.

One down, two to go.

Shockley crouched and maneuvered to the side of the stage closest to the bar.

Vasquez sent a barrage of lead in the direction of the officer behind the table.

Shockley took a deep breath, swung around and shot his pistol till he emptied the magazine trying to hit Vasquez.

He looked at his weapon, slide locked in the back position.

He ejected the spent magazine, reloaded a fresh one from

his belt and chambered a round.

Vasquez alternated his firepower between Shockley and the other officer.

Again, Shockley returned heavy fire, only this time striking the mirrored glass behind the bar causing shards to rain down on Vasquez.

He leapt to his feet and sprinted toward the bar, firing as he ran, sending more pieces of glass flying behind the bar.

He was a stride away when it happened.

His right foot slipped in a slick pool of blood from a patron lying face down on the floor. Before Shockley hit the floor, his hand struck against a chair knocking his pistol free. Lying on the floor without a weapon, he saw Vasquez ease around the corner of the bar.

Vasquez positioned himself for a kill shot.

Shockley pulled his knee to his chest, grabbed his ankle pistol, cocked it and tucked it next to him.

He wanted Vasquez closer.

Vasquez crouched, inching closer to him.

The officer kept Vasquez's man busy. Rounds whizzed through the air.

Just a little closer.

Vasquez had his finger on the trigger and pointed his weapon at him.

Shockley fired two rounds.

Vasquez staggered backwards.

Shockley fired again.

Vasquez's man yelled, "Bastardo!"

Shockley stood but before he could fire, the uniform shot Vasquez's man three times in the chest.

The gunfight was over in less than three minutes. A thick

haze of smoke hung in the air. The warehouse reeked of burnt gunpowder.

Blood was everywhere. Two officers down. Shockley hurried to the down officer not moving and checked vitals. DRT. Dead Right There.

Pink Hair ran to his side, squeezed his arm and asked, "You okay?"

He felt her hand tremble as the adrenaline raged through her body. Same thing was going on with him.

"Where does that back door lead?"

"To an office."

"Is there a back way out of the office?"

"Yeah."

A gunshot echoed from the direction of the office.

Then three more.

CHAPTER 32

Dulles International Airport

S he darted past several travelers on the moving walkway when she heard one of her two cell phones ring. Rummaging through her large purse strapped on her shoulder, she tried to locate the ringing phone.

She stumbled and lurched forward. A young man beside her quickly grabbed her arm and pulled her upright. Her fingers gripped the phone and drew it up to her ear while she thanked the man for his help. The young man shot her a quizzical look when the ringing continued inside her purse.

She had the wrong phone.

"Damn," she muttered as she reached back into her purse, retrieved the ringing phone and quickly swiped to answer the call. The young man's curious face was too much for her. "Two phones. One for my husband. The other for my lover," she said curtly, her steel blue eyes staring at him.

The young man's face flushed. As soon as they stepped off the moving walkway, he hurried ahead. With the phone snug against her ear she heard the caller ask, "What husband. What lover?"

She moved away from the assault of travelers, ignored the question and snapped, "This better be important. I've got ten minutes to get to my gate."

"Elke, Jimi C showed up. I told her you were tied up and

I would be the courier for the information you asked her to get. Jimi C said her sources tell her that Moscow isn't doing surveillance on Julia's home."

"Do you believe her?"

"She's Russian. Still passes information to the Kremlin. But she knows what you're capable of doing."

"Thanks," Elke replied to the man on the phone. "I want eyes on Julia at all times."

"Um," the caller said softly as if thinking out loud.

"What is it?" Elke responded annoyed.

"We found out that the FBI officially pulled Metro police off the Willow Oaks case."

"What?" Elke said. 'That means the FBI knows. It was only a matter of time. Have they paid Julia a visit?"

"Our informant at the FBI says they've been ordered to do surveillance only. No physical contact with your granddaughter. Any suspicious activity is to be reported immediately to Special Agent Black."

"Damn, I think Special Agent Asshole is fishing and using Julia as bait," shot back Elke. She never could hold back her disdain for the intelligence community.

"It's going to be difficult to keep eyes on Julia with FBI interference," cautioned the man.

"I want Julia moved out of town to one of our safe houses."

"And if she won't go or the FBI interferes?"

"Put all-hands-on-deck and make it happen. I'll be in London in a little over seven hours. I expect an update."

"I understand," said the man on the line.

"Is everything in place in London? I can't afford to miss this opportunity."

Elke scanned the travelers around her. A man she had seen

earlier when she checked her baggage walked by. He was dark skin, hair to match, wire rimmed glasses and early forties. Looked like he could be a Boy Scout leader, an ordinary dad with a brood of kids waiting on his return. Hopefully he wouldn't be on her flight.

"All assets are in place. Just be sure you make your bathroom break. They'll have eyes on you."

She knew Director Piagno wouldn't trust her to keep him in the loop. *Smart man*, she thought.

The line clicked off.

Elke glanced at her watch and hurried toward her gate.

✝ ✝ ✝

"I still have eyes on Grey Goose, Director. She's lining up to board the plane."

"You think she knows she's being followed?"

"No sir. We've been very cautious."

Director Piagno doubted Elke would believe he wouldn't have her tracked. All he needed from her was a location, they would handle the rest. The ex-spy still had many contacts and the CIA had benefited from her since she quit the agency and changed her identity. He was certain there was a spark of recognition of the man in the picture when she studied it in his office earlier. Maybe not. He still couldn't read her.

"You're certain she checked a bag?"

"Yes sir. Non-stop flight all the way to Heathrow International Airport."

"Once Grey Goose boards the plane, pull back. We'll let

our team in London handle it from there. I'll make sure there are field officers at baggage claim. Good work. If anything changes, I want to know immediately."

"Yes sir."

† † †

"Can I get you another drink?" asked the male flight attendant.

She liked flying business class which not only offered wine and champagne, a three-course meal, a seat that converted into a 6-foot flat bed, but also fast-tracked security to help speed passengers through the airport. That was important since the clock was ticking on finding the man DCI Piagno asked her to locate.

"A glass of Chardonnay would be nice," Elke answered smiling slightly with her eyes.

Not worrying about Julia's safety was like trying to swim against a rip current. The harder she fought it, the more helpless she felt. She almost didn't get on the plane. If anything happened to her granddaughter, she was sure she wouldn't survive the grief. The FBI was good at surveillance, but not so much in a gun fight. If they wanted to flush out the Russian asset, then they could use her, but never her grandchild. She would deal with Special Agent Black when she got back. Whether he knew it or not he had poked the mamma bear.

The only thing that pushed her to get on the plane was knowing this had to end once and for all. She needed to keep Julia safe and the only way to do it was to find Adrik.

When the Director of Central intelligence showed her the picture of the man he needed to locate, she pretended not to know for good reason. Even though she didn't tell him everything she knew or suspected, she was damn sure the Director shared even less with her.

The man was Adrik Ivanovich Kuznetsov. His dossier had "CONFIDENTIAL/SENSITIVE" stamped in red on the outside of the CIA folder. Details of the man's life and photos were classified. The file read that Kuznetsov was an Irish Russian whose father was Ivan Kuznetsov, a Russian social elite and his mother, Ciara Barrett, an Irish woman whose family owned a large sheep farm outside Dublin.

Most of the information contained in the dossier she already knew. Kuznetsov's mother divorced his father and moved to London where she passed away ten years ago. Adrik once worked as a businessman with ties to some of Russia's most powerful organized crime figures.

She barely recognized the photo of the sixty-one-year-old man. Adrik's thick hair and beard were now wiry and reddish gray. His green eyes ringed with dark circles longed for a good night's sleep. A heavily lined ruddy face revealed the story of a man who liked to push the envelope and live life on the edge of right and wrong.

A fact not in the file was that Kuznetsov had been hired as a contractor by the CIA to help develop informants in the Russian circle of influence. He worked with a CIA unit dealing with money laundering from foreign governments. Not until the Director of the CIA showed her the picture of Kuznetsov did she make the connection. That was why finding Kuznetsov was paramount. He was a man who could not be trusted. She knew this long before the CIA began surveilling him. The FBI

let him slip through their fingers in the United States and the
CIA was on the hook to find him.

After the tragic loss of her daughter and son-in-law, Elke
was battered with guilt. In the aftermath of the tragedy, she flew
to Wiesbaden, Germany where she had new identities created
for her and her granddaughter, Julia. She felt isolated, scared
and angry at what had happened. And for the first time in her
life, vulnerable and fragile. It was in this state of mind she met
Kuznetsov at a bar one evening. Most of the people in the bar
were with friends. She sat alone at the bar sipping vodka when
he approached. He was attractive, but not her type. When he
asked in German if he could buy her a drink, she replied in
German that she did not accept drinks from strangers. He sat
down heavily on a stool next to her and ordered a beer. During
the next hour they talked and eventually found a booth where
they could continue their conversation. She liked talking to
him and he seemed harmless enough. He shared with her that
several months prior his girlfriend, who had recently moved
to Germany from Russia, went missing. It was the intensity of
their grief that bonded them that evening.

It was not like her to say yes to a stranger's invitation to
travel to another country for the weekend. Perhaps it was the
profound sadness in his eyes or more likely a secret desire to
escape her own mounting pain and guilt and, above all, the
emptiness that caused her to go with a man she hardly knew.

She missed her daughter's face, her quick wit and mostly
her voice. This was not the order of how life should happen.
It should have been her daughter surrounded by her husband
and child mourning Elke's death. Perhaps she should have felt
comfort and gratitude that her granddaughter was alive, but
strangely it made things worse.

Sweet Maus, the nickname she gave her granddaughter. Every time she wanted to give up and die, she thought of Maus.

Adrik had rented a home on a small island called Inishmore, one of western Ireland's Aran Islands. After the ferry from Rossaveel deposited them on the island, she saw a freckled-face boy herding sheep. Kuznetsov had arranged for a pony trap to take them to the place they would stay. The treeless landscape had an endless maze of stone fences throughout the island, which was separated from the sea by steep cliffs.

The next day they hiked to a remote part of the island called Dún Dúchathair, The Black Fort. The fort was situated on the cliffs at Cill Éinne. As she stood by the edge of the cliffs and stared down at the water, wind blowing against her face, Kuznetsov's arm slid across her shoulders. "You're not thinking of jumping, are you my sweet Elke?" She turned and was mesmerized by his eyes the same shade of green as the water below the rugged cliffs.

"No. I couldn't even if I wanted to. I have two things that are too important to me," she responded.

"And what might those two things be?"

"A granddaughter to raise and now a man I hope to get to know better."

He smiled, lifted her chin upward and kissed her gently on the lips.

She did have two things she needed to do, but getting to know him better was not one of them. He was a distraction. Her other reason was personal.

Revenge.

On the ride to another clifftop to explore a 2,000-year-old Celtic fort called Dún Aonghasa they spotted a seal colony. It was on this tiny bleak island cloaked in mystery she was able to figure out what she needed to do.

After that long weekend they went their separate ways. Both promised to stay in touch yet knew they wouldn't. Kuznetsov and Elke needed the escape from reality, if only for a few days.

Several years later she learned from a friend he had been offered a contract with the CIA. It was during that time their paths crossed. She was convinced it was Kuznetsov who leaked info to the Bridge Club that the Russian asset had been tipped off and would not meet his handler in the park that fateful day.

Relaxing in her seat on the plane, she raised her glass of Chardonnay and took a long sip, letting it linger in her mouth before swallowing. Her eyelids were heavy, and she needed to rest. Because tomorrow she had to be mentally prepared to pull the trigger.

CHAPTER 33

Dark Alley Warehouse

Panicked patrons scrambled for the exit.

The short man that had been led to the curtained room earlier ran out in his underwear. The chesty woman sprung from behind the bar and bolted for the door, pushing people out of her way. Her heavy breasts slapping against her body. People were herding out like a stampede of wild horses.

Except the two women he met earlier. Both were trying to help the downed officer who had been shot in the leg.

"Keep pressure on it and keep talking to him," Shockley yelled over the pandemonium. "Help should arrive soon." Both women nodded. Brave women he thought. Probably seen more than most people.

He kept his gun trained on the door to the back room and cautiously advanced toward it. Shockley needed to check the back room where he heard the gunshots after the fire fight in the club ended.

"Careful cowboy," cautioned Tattoo Woman. "Caleb is dangerous."

Caleb must be the birthmark man he saw earlier. The man who disappeared when the cops barged in.

Shockley checked Vasquez's pulse. He needed to make sure the guy was dead. Vasquez had been hit by three rounds, but he knew, in a gunfight never assume anything.

He stepped over the dead man's body and stood next to the door leading to the back office. As soon as he touched the doorknob, he felt something hot hit his neck and splinter the doorframe. Before his brain could process what had happened, he swung around pointing his weapon toward the thump. The burly bouncer dropped in the front doorway. His eyes as wide with disbelief as Shockley felt his were.

For a second Shockley believed he had fired his weapon until he saw Pink Hair pointing a gun at the bouncer. Her hands shaking uncontrollably. Lowering the weapon, she looked at Shockley. He nodded at the stripper. He'd have to thank her later.

He tried to turn the knob, but the door was locked.

Only one thing to do.

He drove the heel of his boot into the door with a forceful kick.

When the door swung open, he knew he was too late.

More dead bodies. An old man was lying near the door, hand wrapped around a gun. The birthmark man was down on the other side of the room. A man almost the size of the front door bouncer was slumped in a sitting position next to the table.

He walked around the table and saw an overturned chair with something lying next to it. On closer inspection he decided it was leather bindings. Somebody had been strapped to the chair.

Who?

Maybe they escaped out the back door. He was a few steps from the back door when out of the corner of his eye he saw what looked like a driver's license on the table.

His hand was about to pick it up when he heard a voice

from behind, "You okay?"

Without turning he knew it was Hauser.

He snapped up the license and slipped it in his coat pocket. "Yeah. How come you're here?"

"Seriously? Half the force is here. What happened?"

Before he could answer, Hauser moved closer and pointed, "You've been hit."

Shockley touched his neck and felt the warm sticky blood. "Flesh wound. I'll live."

"Maybe from the flesh wound," Hauser said. "But Wheels is a different story. He wants you in his office ASAP. Didn't sound too happy with you going all cowboy on him."

Hauser moved toward the dead man with the birthmark. "Is this Max?"

"No. That guy's called Caleb. Max wasn't here."

"What you gonna tell Wheels?"

"Nothing. I gotta check something out before I meet with him."

"That's not a good idea. Wheels told me to personally make sure you get your sorry ass in his office."

"Not yet. I gotta run down a lead while it's hot and then I'll check in with the boss."

"Pretty sure this is another one of your bone-headed stupid ideas."

"You're probably right, but I owe it to Bull and T-Bone to find this cop killer. I need you to cover for me."

"This could cost you your badge. Worse, it could cost me my badge."

"Not if you didn't find me here. This one's all on me."

Shockley heard Hauser grumble as he walked out the exit door.

Sirens pierced the air as he stretched his stride down the back alley. He assumed the alleyway emptied onto the main street.

The truth was he didn't know if he had a lead or not. The driver's license was probably one of the girls who worked at the club. Yet the picture of the girl on the license didn't look like the type to work as a stripper in a sleazy joint. The name on the license was Julia Bagal.

Could the Dark Alley Warehouse be a front for human trafficking?

He needed to track down Ms. Bagal and get her to talk. Find out why her driver's license was left at the warehouse.

On the main street, he located his car without attracting attention and sped away from the swarm of police converging on the crime scene. He fished the driver license out of his coat pocket and read the address. She was local. But not from this part of town. He plugged the address into his GPS. Hopefully Julia Bagal was alive. Maybe she was a link to Max. Just the thought of Max slipping through his fingers made his blood boil. As he pressed the accelerator, he hoped this was the break in the case he needed.

Shockley parked behind a RAV4 in front of the row house that was Julia Bagal's address. At least according to the driver license he held in his hand. There was a light on which meant somebody might be home. This better lead to something, he told himself, or the fallout from today's events would probably end his career.

Walking up the sidewalk, he noticed a security camera mounted above the door. Not Home Depot quality either... better. Much better. Somebody doesn't feel safe in an otherwise safe looking neighborhood. When he pounded on the front door a large calico cat pounced on the porch, pranced over to him and rubbed against his pant leg. He shooed her away with his boot. The cat hissed and fled the porch.

Seconds passed. No answer. He pounded again. A faint sound of footsteps grew louder. Then stopped. Somebody inside was trying to determine whether to answer the door. After glancing up toward the camera, he pounded again. A little harder to show his impatience.

The door eased open. He kept a hand on his holster inside his jacket. Just in case.

"You can quit banging on my door."

The woman in the doorway wasn't who he expected to see. He expected Julia or even Max, but not the tall Black woman blocking his entry with a baseball bat propped on her shoulder.

"Excuse me, ma'am. I'm looking for Julia Bagal."

"Well, she ain't here," said the woman in a terse tone.

The woman's eyes were swollen from crying. He could see she held a death grip on the bat and looked like she was ready to use it.

"My name is Detective Shockley with Metro PD. I found Julia Bagal's driver's license at a crime scene. It's urgent I talk with her."

"Yeah. Where's your badge?"

He fished his hand under his jacket and pulled the badge out. After showing it to the woman, she studied him.

"Are you a friend of Miss Bagal?" he asked.

It happened fast. The large calico cat had snuck back on the porch, meowed and leaped between his legs and into the open doorway. He quickly reacted as the woman bent down, cussed the cat and tried to catch the furry animal.

Shockley shoved the door open and stepped inside,

knocking the woman aside. "Thank you for inviting me in," he said.

The woman raised the bat with both hands. "I didn' invite you in. Now git out fore I bash your head in."

He took several steps back and raised a warning hand. "Put the bat down. I just need to make sure Miss Bagal is safe." He'd been hit with a lot of things. Never a bat. He wasn't about to let this be the first time.

"She ain't here. I done told you that."

"Okay. Please just lower the bat so that I don't feel threatened. Can you do that for me?"

She lowered the bat. "Mister, you broke into my home and I feel threatened."

"This is your home?"

"I live with Julia."

"What's your name?"

"None of your damn business."

"Do I need to come back with a search warrant," he said hoping she'd take the bait.

"Laquita Morrison."

"And Julia isn't home?"

"You deaf? I done told you that twice."

"Then whose car is that parked out front?"

"It's my car."

"Your car?"

"That's right. Now git out fore I call the real police."

"Alright. I'm sorry to have bothered you." He started to turn toward the door, stopped and added, "I'll have to run the plates to verify that's your car."

The woman bit her upper lip and shifted uneasy before saying, "What I meant was its Julia's car, but she lets me drive it. We're real close."

"Could you explain, if Julia isn't home, why you'd have her car?"

The woman frowned. She rubbed a scar on her forehead. "Just give me her license. She'll call you when she gits home." Laquita held out her hand.

"I'm afraid I can't do that. If I file my report about finding Miss Bagel's driver's license at the scene of a crime, I'll be back with a search warrant. And Laquita, you could be charged with obstructing justice. If she's here, then you need to tell me."

Silence.

"When will Miss Bagal be back?"

More silence.

The woman was right. He didn't have the authority to be inside the house, much less search the place without a warrant. It wouldn't be hard to get a warrant, but all that took time.

Time he didn't have.

He handed the woman his card and opened the door to leave. "Call me if you happen to see Miss Bagal. I fear her life might be in danger."

Walking down the sidewalk toward his vehicle he remembered what Hauser told him once when they worked a case a few years back. One they never solved. *Seems like we're running on a damn treadmill headed nowhere.* Was Julia Bagal in the home hiding? Was she dead? The woman in the house knew something. He decided his best move would be to park around the corner and wait. And hope it didn't take too long for the woman to show her hand.

He was a few steps from his car when he heard, "Hey mister. Wait. Wait." The tall woman was holding the cat in one hand and waving him to come back with her other.

CHAPTER 34

Julia recalled going in and out of consciousness in the backseat of a car.

Sounds. Sirens. Voices.

A man arguing with Laquita. *How did she escape the club?* She had a vague recollection of what had happened. A man carrying her and then putting her in a car. Who was that man?

And why was she now in her bed at home. A searing pain roared through her head like waves crashing against rocks causing her vision to blur.

She heard a different voice. When she tried to move, a strong hand holding her down. She winced in agony as the pain rippled down her neck into her lower back. Where was she? She blinked several times forcing her eyes to focus.

A tall man leaned close and said something. A deep slow drawl. Different than the man's voice she heard earlier. She could smell a sharp pungent odor on his clothes.

Gunpowder residue.

A smell she remembered from her teen years when she'd go to the firing range to target practice with Elke.

She drew back from the intruder unsure of his intensions.

He gently placed something cold on her face. Her head hurt. She tried to think. What happened?

"You think she's got a concussion?" Laquita asked.

"Possible. We need to have her checked out," said the man.

His face slowly came into focus. Her brain struggled to

clear the soup of fog in order to make sense about what was happening.

"Julia, I think you might have a concussion. I need to take you to a hospital," the man stated.

"No." Her voice sounded like a whisper.

"I'm so sorry Julia. I shoulda never let ya go in there by yourself." Laquita whimpered.

Julia pushed her hands down on the mattress in an attempt to raise up. The cold pack fell to her lap. She grunted. The movement pulsed every nerve ending on fire. She collapsed on the bed, closed her eyes and bit her lip to keep from yelling out.

"Don't move. We need to get you checked out." The voice was warm. The man placed the cold pack in her hand. "You need to place this on your eye for twenty minutes every hour to keep the swelling down."

The man looked familiar, but she couldn't place him.

She pushed the man's callused hand away. Maybe he was a friend of Laquita's. She gingerly eased up and rested her back against the bed frame. "Would you get me water? My throat's dry."

"I'll git it for ya. This'n Detective Shockley. He's gonna help us. I already told him how Max carried you outta the club and brought ya to the car. You was just there trying to find Max."

Julia cradled her head with her hands. It was slowly coming back. "Tylenol too. I need something for my head."

She remembered.

The big man with the needle. He was going to inject her with drugs. What had he injected in her? She held her arm out and searched for the needle mark.

The stranger took her hand and held it. "You're okay.

Laquita said Max told her the old man shot and killed Lopez before he was able to inject you. But unfortunately, not before he knocked you out. I think you need to let a doctor examine you."

"Ugh, my head hurts. I don't want to go to the hospital. Please, just get me some Tylenol."

"I have a friend who's a doctor. I can give her a call."

The man had an accent similar to Laquita's southern drawl just not as pronounced or soft. He had thick brown hair with wisps of silver on the sides, deep brown eyes that hadn't had enough sleep, tanned skin and maybe mid to early thirties. She remembered his name and the face. The man she had seen on the news earlier during the coverage of the motel bombing.

"Thanks, but I really just want a glass of water and some Tylenol."

He arched an eyebrow and removed his hands. "Ok. Just don't be so stubborn and let me help you. You took quite a blow to the head."

"I'm not pigheaded," she snapped.

"Excuse me?" His eyes scanned her face searching for an explanation.

"What I mean is I'm easy going." She didn't like a stranger characterizing her when he didn't even know her.

Laquita had walked in with a glass of water. She said, "Gurl, you a lot of thangs, but easy goin' ain't one of 'em. Detective, she's stubborn as a mule. And if she don't eat, ya don't want to be around her."

The detective's face broke into a boyish grin exposing his dimpled unshaven face.

If her head didn't hurt like hell, she'd let both Laquita and the detective have it with both barrels. Right now, though, she needed to talk to Laquita.

Alone.

"Would you mind stepping out of the room Detective and letting Laquita help me change clothes." She was still wearing the too tight dress she had worn to the club.

"Of course. I'll wait in the living room."

After he shut the door, Laquita handed her the water and Tylenol. She popped three pills and gulped the water.

"You want me to help ya git up?"

"Yes, I do."

Laquita bent over Julia and started to wrap an arm under Julia's back when Julia reached out and clasped Laquita's shirt, yanking her so close their noses touched. Laquita's face morphed from startled surprise to fear.

"What in the hell have you told him?" she whispered in a harsh voice. "Remember, the Bridge Club told us not to go to the police."

"I ain't told him nothin'."

"Well, he knows about Max and what happened to me at the club."

"I had to tell him somethin'. He found your driver's license at the club and told me he needed to make sure you were ok. If I didn' let him, I could be charged with obstructin' justice."

"My license? That's how he found me? You didn't tell him about the surveillance we were doing?"

"Hell no."

Julia shot Laquita a questionable look.

"Cross my heart." Laquita used her finger and made an *X* on her chest. "Max told me ya almost died, and that the killer might track us down. He warned me to stay away from the cops too. Said they might try to connect him to 'em murders."

Julia let go of Laquita's shirt allowing her to back up.

A light rap on the door. "Are you ready? My doctor friend will wait for thirty minutes, then she has to go home," said Shockley through the door.

"A few more minutes Detective," replied Laquita. "Ya gotta go. Ya might have a concussion."

"A concussion? That's nothing. Your friend. Max almost shot me up with heroin."

"Max saved your life. He got in over his head. He didn' wanna hurt ya. That's why he's worried we ain't safe."

"Damn Laquita. Max is a criminal. What'd he tell you about the killer?"

"Said he didn' know the guy would kill that woman."

"What's the killer's name?"

"All he knows is his street name."

"What's his street name?"

"Razor."

"Sounds scary. Does he...."

Another soft knock on the door interrupted her. "You gals ready."

Julia warned, "Don't say a word to that detective. Not till I've had time to contact the Bridge Club. Understood?"

Laquita nodded.

Getting dressed was slow. She had the worst headache she'd ever had. Laquita had to hold her steady while she slipped on dark olive colored leggings and pulled a long sleeve white t-shirt over her head.

"That Detective out there," Laquita said as she motioned to the door. "Is a fine lookin' man. Lean as an alley cat. And he ain't married."

"Maybe you ought to ask him out then," Julia replied

sarcastically before heading to the bathroom.

Looking in the bathroom mirror she yelped "Oh my gosh."

Her eyes settled on the reflection in the mirror. A purple yellow welt surrounded a swollen left eye with broken blood vessels. There was dried blood on the side of her nose. Her face looked like a war zone and worse, felt like one.

Washing the blood off her face, she felt lucky her nose wasn't broken. Detective Shockley must think she looked awful.

She did.

Brushing her hair was painful. The bristles hurt against her tender scalp. She threw the brush in the sink and used her fingers to gently smooth out her hair and pulled it back into a ponytail.

Standing in the doorway, she could feel Detective Shockley's piercing eyes on her face. A surge of attraction made her body flush.

Laquita was right. He was fine looking.

What the hell was wrong with her? She almost died, looks like hell and she's having a schoolgirl crush.

Detective Shockley was holding one of her plants. "Looks like you don't have a green thumb."

"It's getting late," she said, her tone full of anger. "My head hurts like a son-of-a-bitch. Can we get this over with? After I see your doctor friend, then you bring me back."

Detective Shockley's mouth tightened. "I got some questions I need you to answer. We're going to have to go down to the station and file a police report. You're a witness to a murder."

She glanced at Laquita and back to him. "Laquita told you, didn't she?"

He hesitated. "We talked." His calm demeanor had left

him. "This is serious Julia. You could have died today."

"But I didn't."

"That was a stupid thing you did. It could get more dangerous."

Knowing she did something stupid was one thing, but to hear him say it was another. She knew Laquita had lied to her and had told him they were at the motel doing surveillance.

"But right now," he said, "I need to get you checked out by a doctor."

"I'll pass," she said with an irritated tone of voice.

Laquita picked up Julia's coat and held it out to her. "I think ya gotta go to the doctor Julia. Your face is a mess."

"Thanks, Laquita. Telling me that makes me feel sooo much better." she said, annoyed. She turned to Shockley. "If my symptoms don't go away, then I'll go. Besides, all they'll tell me to do is rest, which is impossible with Detective Shockley here wanting to haul my ass down to the police station."

"I'm sorry Miss Bagal, I don't have a choice. Can I see the photos you took while doing surveillance at Willow Oaks Motel?"

"If I refuse?"

Shockley's forehead furrowed and his lips parted in surprise. He strode toward her and stopped a few feet in front of her. She immediately took a step back.

His intense eye contact made her nervous and self-conscious.

"I'll get a search warrant and charge you with obstruction. You'll be compelled to turn over the photos." His tone softened. "Look, you want this killer caught as bad as I do, right? We have the resources to find him *and* keep you safe."

Julia was conflicted and overwhelmed about the situation.

Being safe was what brought her to this point in her life. She played it safe becoming an accountant. She played it safe with every guy she ever dated. Being safe had not turned out that great for her.

It was foolish to think she was a detective after only a few weeks of online training. She had helped Elke thwart a plot to kill the President and Vice President of the United States. But that was different. Elke and her friend, Derick were the true heroes in that.

She did have clues to help solve this case. Furthermore, she wanted to do this without Elke's help. Prove something to herself. Redeem herself.

Shit, I need more therapy.

She lowered her eyes to give it some thought. Her fingers curled tightly into her palms. Her eyes slowly raised till she was directly staring into the Detective's eyes. She fought to keep her voice strong,

"Sorry Detective Shockley. You'll have to get that search warrant."

CHAPTER 35

Heathrow Airport
London

"No visual on Grey Goose. I repeat, negative visual on Grey Goose." The man's voice rose in intensity, "Are you sure we've got the right baggage carousel?"

The man scanned the crowd and reached up with his right hand to touch his earpiece. He wanted to be sure he heard the next transmission.

"Copy that. Check the other carousels," a female voice crackled in his ear.

"We've got eyes on this whole area."

"It bloody well isn't working, now is it? Don't lose the rabbit. Grey Goose is too damn important."

The man quickly circled the area around the carousel while keeping sight of travelers exiting the airport. Two other field officers caught his eye and shook their heads indicating no luck locating Grey Goose. There were two unclaimed bags spinning on the carousel. He grabbed one and after reading the luggage tag tossed it back on the moving conveyor belt. The next bag he gathered from the carousel was problematic.

The field officer read the luggage tag attached to it.

Elke aka Grey Goose
007 Fake Street
Washington, D.C.

He dreaded his next transmission. "Inform the Director we have a problem. We've lost Grey Goose."

† † †

Inishmore, Aran Island, Ireland

The ploy worked better than she had anticipated. Her London connections and the Bridge Club had done a good job.

Elke was almost, perhaps 90% convinced Director Piagno believed Kuznetsov was hiding in England. He had been spotted in London two weeks prior and then disappeared. Intel had been leaked he was still in England, but where, they didn't know.

The Director knew she would go to London and she knew he'd try to track her. *Did he know her history with Kuznetsov?* Unless Kuznetsov told somebody in the CIA, then the answer was no.

At Heathrow airport, Elke went to the designated bathroom as instructed and was given a change of clothes, a brown short wig, and glasses. It took the young woman helping her all of two minutes to apply the makeup. The young woman known as Margaret was the granddaughter of a Bridge Club member who recently passed away. She was a special effects makeup artist who worked in the science fiction and horror genre. Margaret apologized that she didn't do a better job, but she wasn't used to changing a person's appearance like a NASCAR pit crew.

When Elke exited the bathroom steadying herself with a cane in one hand, a man standing behind a wheelchair was waiting. He wheeled her to another section of the airport where she hastily boarded a private jet headed to Dublin.

Checking baggage in D.C. to London was the Bridge Club's idea, which she thought was a clever ruse. The bathroom charade was her idea. The private jet was a favor owed.

It was a little over an hour till wheels down at the Shannon Airport, northwest of Limerick, Ireland, the closest airport to her destination capable of handling the private corporate jet aircraft. She changed out of her costume and back into her own clothes, washed her face and swept her silver hair up into a bun. Her vanity forced her to apply fresh makeup blush, mascara and lipstick. She hadn't seen Adrik Kuznetsov for many years but held the hidden desire that he'd still find her attractive. She momentarily hesitated when applying her lipstick, fixed her eyes on her reflection in the small washroom mirror.

Would she actually be able to do what might be necessary?"

✝ ✝ ✝

She was glad she was able to sleep on the overnight flight to London. It was going to be a long day. All her transportation had been arranged for her, courtesy of the Bridge Club.

There was no way she'd get behind the wheel of a car in a country where you drive on the opposite side of the narrow, twisting roads between high hedges. No room for error. A driver had been hired for her trip from the airport to Rossaveel. Right now, she wasn't sure she even needed to concern herself about what she was going to do with Adrik, because several times when her driver swerved to avoid a head on collision, she saw her whole life flash before her.

In a tight voice she asked the driver, "Can't you slow down?"

"I'm being paid to get you to your destination by a specific time in order to catch the ferry. If I miss that time by as much as five minutes, I bloody well won't get my bonus." He shot her a wink. The middle-aged driver had protruding ears, large like his nose. He had a slight English accent and unfortunately loved to hear himself talk.

She survived the car ride but wasn't sure she'd survive the boat trip across the rough seas to Inishmore. After disembarking the boat, she clutched her umbrella tight in her hand. The sky had filled with dark tumultuous clouds threatening rain. Gusting wind pushed against her as she strolled toward the main street to find transportation, whipping her hair loose causing strands to blow back and forth against her face. So much for fixing my hair on the plane, she thought.

S tanding by a wrought iron gate hinged to a stone fence, she paused. She needed a moment to collect herself.

The thatched roof cottage with whitewashed walls and a vibrant green door standing at the far end of the courtyard stirred memories. Plumes of smoke billowed from the chimney.

She recalled sitting on the couch with Adrik in front of a hypnotic fire and drinking too much vodka.

Two bikes leaned against the cottage wall near the front door. They could be the same ones she rode the last time she was here. Vines and weeds crept into the bike spokes telling her they hadn't been used in a very long time.

The blustery wind calmed without warning and the sun peeked out from dark ragged clouds. Irish weather, she mused, remembering the day a storm had blown in providing them with an excuse to stay inside all day. She felt engulfed in an emotion she didn't like

Her head dropped, breaking the spell this place had on her. Remembering things this vividly was hindering her from focusing on a potential threat. *This could be a trap.*

The pistol provided by the limo driver, as per Bridge Club orders, was stashed in her coat pocket. After drawing a deep breath, she steadied her nerves and hesitantly opened the iron latch. Unsure of what she might be walking into, she scanned the windows. No sign of him.

She strolled along the gravel path toward the green door, legs heavy like they were full of lead. There was a surreal feeling to be back here after all these years.

Knocking on the door, she recognized the voice calling out. Her heart skipped. Chest tightened. She felt her fingers grip the pistol inside her coat pocket. The safety off.

The door swung open.

"Elke," Adrik exclaimed. "How wonderful to see you." He instantly peered over her shoulder into the yard.

"You don't trust me?" she snapped.

His attention returned to her face. "No. Of course not," he answered with a slight twist of humor in his voice. "Yet, it isn't you I'm concerned about, it's others who might have followed you."

"As always, Adrik, I am very careful," she reminded him.

She squeezed her way past him and over the threshold into the main room of the cottage.

He didn't try to conceal that he was checking her out, but neither did she hide the fact she wanted to examine him.

Adrik no longer had a beard. His clean-shaven face exposed his sagging jowl. And the jagged scar on his neck. His hair was cropped and dyed black. Years made his eye lids droop along with rows of deep forehead creases. The one thing that had not changed was his strong build.

His green eyes sparkled as his gaze swept over her.

"May I take your coat?" he offered with his hands stretched out.

She stepped back out of his reach and replied, "We must talk first."

Dancing flames in the open stone fireplace crackled as the dry wood burned and filled the room with warmth. She removed her coat, folded it over her arm making sure the pistol was within reach.

"Would you like a drink? Vodka?"

"Yes. Vodka and water but no…"

"Ice. I remember," his low intimate voice placed her on edge.

She deliberately ambled past the couch and sat in a straight back chair next to the fireplace. The warmth of the fire felt good.

The 100-year-old single-story structure still had the feel of a bygone era even though it had been updated. Traditional stone floors complimented the rustic exposed wooden beams bolted across a low ceiling. The quaint cottage had a combination kitchen-living room anchored by the cozy open fireplace. There was one-bedroom downstairs and two loft-style bedrooms accessible by a ladder.

"Here you go," Adrik said holding the glass out to her. "You could sit on the couch. It's more comfortable." His eyes met hers.

She looked down. Her pulse quickened. His eyes still had a mesmerizing effect on her.

"I'm fine where I'm siting." She took the glass and placed it on the table next to her chair.

He sat on the couch end nearest her and leaned too close, their knees touching. "You look beautiful. Your blue sweater makes your eyes look like the ocean."

Had she worn the snug sweater and black slim pants for him? Perhaps.

"This isn't a social visit, Adrik. I need to know some things about the Russians."

He released a heavy sigh. "Haven't you already paid enough of a high price for the CIA?"

The warmth sprung from her neck to her face. "I don't need to be reminded about what happened to my daughter and son-in-law." Her lips curled into a snarl.

"I apologize for upsetting you. That was never my intent. You know that."

She gazed at the flames in the hearth and watched as the heat reduced the logs to ashes. That eventful day came rushing back to her.

An explosion. Her home engulfed in flames. The emotions were as raw as the day it happened.

Grief. Pain. Guilt.

Then uncaged rage.

Sickened from the memory, she closed her eyes.

The touch of his large hand on her knee startled her, bringing her back into the moment.

"You can't blame yourself Elke. You had no way of knowing the Russians had planted a bomb in your home. If you hadn't taken your granddaughter for a walk to the park, she'd have died too. It's time to let those demons go. You have done what you felt you needed to do. You left a trail of bodies as proof."

She felt the moisture collect in her eyes. "All those responsible for taking my daughter from me deserved to pay."

"And they have."

She picked up her drink, lowered her eyes with the rim of the glass almost touching her lips.

"Have they?"

He straightened, removing his hand from her leg. "What are you implying?"

"Who do you work for Adrik?"

The look on his face told her what she suspected. Adrik was a double agent.

He swirled the ice in his glass, raised it to his mouth and drained it. "I admit I've made mistakes."

Her hand slipped inside the coat pocket on her lap and gripped the pistol.

"That's your problem Adrik. You've made many mistakes, but you never learned from them."

He snorted. "You always did like to bust men's balls."

"There're men who have no balls."

An awkward silence hung in the air.

Finally, he spoke, his tone serious, "I tried to protect you."

"It was you who told the Bridge Club that the spy would

not show in the park."

"Yes. You shouldn't have gone."

"I didn't ask for your help."

"But now you want my help?" he asked.

"I want a deal with the SVR."

He tilted his head, a confused look unfurled across his face. "You no longer have anything of value for the intelligence agency. Except for those who grew old and died of natural causes, you have exposed and eliminated all the Russian assets on the list you memorized. Now there's only one left that Moscow must protect."

"They don't think I know who that might be?"

"At first there was suspicion, but no longer. I made sure of that."

"How would you know?"

"If you knew who the Russian asset was, he'd be apprehended by now. Or dead."

"Perhaps. There are benefits to allowing a spy to continue in his role."

Adrik laughed too hard and loud. "You don't know who it is, do you?"

She studied her watch. "Five minutes."

"Five minutes? Till what?"

"Till you tell me who it is that Moscow needs to protect."

She stood, removed the pistol from her coat pocket and pointed the barrel point blank at Adrik's center mass.

"You plan to shoot me?" Adrik didn't act surprised.

"I'm doing my job."

"And I was doing mine until the CIA grew suspicious."

"Let's not play games anymore. It was no accident that you ran into me at the bar in Wiesbaden. Who was your employer then?"

"CIA," Adrik replied.

"And now it's the Russians."

"They pay better."

"To end this, I need the name," she demanded.

"Even if I had a name, I couldn't tell you."

She held the pistol steady, her finger resting on the trigger guard.

"I was trained to never put my finger on the trigger unless I was ready to shoot."

"Come on Elke. I know you care about me the same way I care about you."

You are right about that, she thought.

She slowly moved her finger to the trigger.

"Wait," he said. "I don't have a name. You must believe me."

She lowered the pistol.

He continued, "I have only heard he has a lot of influence with the American government."

Without a word, Elke spun toward the door and walked out.

She had once again lost somebody she loved.

CHAPTER 36

Shockley eyed the morning sky through the windshield while waiting impatiently for the light to turn green. A well-defined mass of cumulus clouds moved over the sun, causing his mood to downshift. Not that he wasn't already in a bad mood. The gloomy weather and traffic just added to it.

He rubbed his jaw to help soothe the pain from TMJ. The dentist told him it was probably caused from a blow he took to the head a year ago. He didn't share with the dentist that the person delivering the punch was a petite older woman. That was a story he kept to himself. The jaw pain was always worse in the mornings.

He planned on getting to work early but slept through the alarm. He was irked he didn't get on the road early enough to avoid the morning commuters. He had already cut off several drivers as he sped toward the Metro Police Department.

The light turned green and he accelerated just as a car in front made an illegal U-turn causing him to slam on the brakes. Frustrated, he cursed out loud.

Distracted by the near miss collision, he almost didn't hear his phone buzz. Keeping one hand on the steering wheel, he retrieved his phone from inside his jacket with the other. It was Hauser. Hopefully Hauser had good news about the search warrant.

After leaving Julia Bagal's home late yesterday, he called Hauser, filled him in and tried to swear out a warrant, only to be told by the judge that he'd have to wait till morning. Hauser was to let him know the moment they had it.

"You got the warrant?" he asked Hauser.

"Well, not exactly."

"What the hell does that mean?" He didn't want to sound pissed but after his shitty day yesterday and being given the finger by Julia, he was pissed. The photos might give him a suspect.

"You don't need to bite my head off. I'll explain when you get here."

"Sorry." He paused. "I gotta see the photos Julia Bagal took at the motel before we have more victims." Shockley didn't want to feel responsible for another life taken. He needed to catch this perp.

"I do have something. Info on Chance Martin Stephens III."

"Who?"

"The guy gunned down yesterday. You know. Mason Street. Two blocks from Willow Oaks Motel." Hauser gave a weird laugh and asked, "You okay?"

"Yeah, I'm fine. Whatcha got?" Four hours sleep wasn't enough.

"No priors. Guy's clean. We had somebody notify his parents. Stephens lived in Nashville. They said his girlfriend was working in the D.C. area."

"You got a name and address on her?"

"Working on it. Parents claim they never met her. Girlfriend's name is Charlotte. They couldn't recall her last name. Stephens and his parents didn't have a close relationship."

"Do they at least know what she did for a living?"

"Said she was a freelance reporter. Maybe she's our Jane

Doe from the explosion."

"That doesn't add up. Two dead bodies at the motel and nobody has filed a missing person report for her. Whatcha got on the car parked at the motel?"

"Registered to Mateo Martinez. Small-time drug dealer."

"Then where's Jane Doe's car?"

"Authorities questioned Stephens' boss at a local restaurant Manager said she never met Stephen's girlfriend. They hadn't been dating long. Stephens told the manager his girlfriend didn't have a car and had an opportunity for a big story in D.C. He took some vacation days to drive her here. His girlfriend probably used public transportation after he left. The boss said he came to work upset the other day since he hadn't heard from Charlotte in a couple of days. He asked to take time off and drive to D.C. to check on her. That was the last time his boss heard from him."

"Must have been one hell of a story she was working to come all the way to D.C."

"Must have been," Hauser agreed.

"If the dead woman is Charlotte whoever, somebody out there must be looking for her."

"I already figured Jane Doe might not be local, therefore the APB has been extended statewide and to Nashville. Maybe you're right about a connection between Chance Martin Stephens and our Jane Doe. Jane Doe might just be this freelance reporter. Could have been doing a story on low life in the big city. Or trying to score some shit."

"Make sure the authorities search Stephens' residence. I want to know who Charlotte is. I'll be at the office in ten." He drained his mug.

Before Shockley clicked off, Hauser added, "Wheels wants

us in his office as soon as you get here."

With the fresh developments, Shockley had a feeling he might finally be getting somewhere with the case. The feeling lifted his mood. He hoped Wheels would give him more time to track down possible leads. He needed to know if Chance Stephens' death was somehow connected to the murders at the motel. To do that, they'd have to track down his girlfriend. And he couldn't wait to shove that search warrant in Julia Bagal's face.

Laquita was right. Julia was stubborn. And foolish not to share what she knew about the murders. This perp would want to eliminate anybody who could identify him.

The sound of an approaching ambulance had traffic veering to the curb. He was impatient to get to the office and find out what Wheels wanted. Hopefully the meeting wouldn't last long. Then he and Hauser could serve Julia Bagal. As soon as the ambulance passed, cars eased back into the road. *There are too many damn cars in the D.C. area. No wonder road rage has become such a problem.*

Instead of ten it turned into twenty minutes before he parked his car at the station. He rushed inside and walked down the hall toward his boss's office. When he passed Hauser's desk, the man stood and fell in beside him.

"Not sure what's going on," said Hauser. "Fifteen minutes before you got here, I saw several suits walk into the war room." That was the nickname Hauser had for Wheels' office. Wheels had been a Ranger in his previous life and his *military* management style made it difficult at times to work for him. Praise was rare and criticism plenty. No excuses for why you failed. Hauser didn't like Wheels, but Shockley understood the man. He had been raised by a father with the same military standards. They never asked more of a soldier than they'd do themselves. That had to be respected.

"Any idea who the suits might be?"

"Looked like fibbies."

"What would the FBI want?"

"Your guess is as good as mine."

"Got the search warrant?"

"It should be sitin' on Wheels' desk." Hauser popped the tab on a Red Bull and took a swallow. "How's the neck?"

Shockley touched the bandage he had put on his neck wound from the Warehouse club. "Not bad."

"Maybe next time you'll take back-up."

Shockley grunted. "Maybe."

The Chief's aide saw Shockley and Hauser coming and waited for them by the Chief's door. With a tight smile she said, "The Chief is ready for you."

He got an uneasy feeling when she pushed the door open. There were three men dressed in dark suits, white starched shirts and ties standing like mannequins with their arms hanging stiff by their sides.

The FBI always looked too serious. He wasn't sure they were even breathing. His brain scrambled to figure out what he had screwed up. He came up blank. Shockley had no idea why these agents were in his boss's office.

"Come in detectives," said Wheels.

Two of the men in suits could have been twins. Both men were tall, dark hair, dark skin, and stone-faced. The other man was not particularly fit, thinning white hair, round eyes with wire rimmed oval glasses perched on a hooked nose. He was older than the twin suits. Even at 5'5" the older man had an authoritative air about him. Someone with a high opinion of himself and maybe for good reason. Respected in the ranks and feared.

The older agent put out his hand to Shockley.

They shook and he said, "I'm Senior Special Agent Sid Black with the Federal Bureau of Investigation." He turned and gestured to the twins. "This is Special Agent Ken Farris and Special Agent Gary LaMay."

Shockley and Hauser nodded to acknowledge the silent twins.

Agent Black stepped over and promptly shook Hauser's hand.

"Have a seat Detectives," he said. It sounded more like an order than a polite request.

Shockley squared his shoulders and replied, "I'm fine." He wasn't going to sit if the agents stood. Hauser didn't move.

The smile evaporated from Agent Black's face.

Wheels said, "Detective Shockley, Detective Hauser take a seat."

Hauser didn't move until Shockley did. Shockley gave a hard-sideways glance at the three men in suits before taking a chair on the other side of the room. Hauser sat next to him.

Shockley had been told when he was in training to be a police officer to always trust your instincts and right now his instincts told him something was off. He was sure he was about to find out what.

Agent Black looked at Wheels and then turned his focus to Shockley.

"Your boss tells me you and Detective Hauser have done a good job working the Willow Oaks murder case." He paused as if he was waiting on a response from Shockley or Hauser.

Both remained silent.

Shockley knew when somebody starts a conversation with a meaningless compliment that the next thing out of their mouth wouldn't be liked. He hadn't made much progress on the investigation. Agent Black was setting him up.

Agent Black cleared his throat before continuing, "Let me cut to the chase detectives. The Bureau is officially assuming investigative jurisdiction on this case. We will need you to turn over all case work. You are not to discuss this case with anyone outside this room."

Shockley and Hauser exchanged puzzled glances.

"We still need to track down some leads, Special Agent Black," said Shockley. "Would you explain the FBI's interest in this investigation? Cause I've got quite a few more unsolved cases that you could take a look at."

Shockley didn't mind working with the FBI if they could nail this perp. However, what gnawed him was being told they were no longer on the case.

Wheels' face didn't reveal how he felt about the FBI taking over a case in which one of his own had died. A police officer they both knew.

Special Agent Black's face tightened. Obviously, the man wasn't happy with what he said. He didn't care. Right now, he was tired of being jerked around by some high-ranking FBI prick.

Agent Black reiterated, "Detective Shockley, you and your partner, Detective Hauser, are to give all your case work to the FBI. You won't have contact with anybody connected to this investigation. You won't contact Julia Bagal again. Special Agent Farris and Special Agent LaMay will stay and collect all your files on this case."

Shockley stiffened as he looked at his boss who offered

nothing.

"This is bullshit, Wheels," Shockley hissed. "We have a search warrant for Julia Bagal's home that could help us break this case."

"Not my call," replied Wheels. "I got a call from the mayor. Our jurisdiction has been trumped."

Shockley could feel the heat radiating off his face. It made no sense.

"The Mayor's on board with this?"

"The decision's been made. Our orders are to comply," said Wheels.

He stood and narrowed his eyes at Agent Black, "I promised a fellow officer, a good friend who's in the hospital that I'd find this perp. I intend on keeping my promise unless you can give me a damn good reason the FBI's taking over *my* investigation."

Agent Black puffed out his chest and declared, "I don't have to tell you anything detective. This is a sensitive situation that carries with it classified National Security concerns. You are to back off. And that means now."

CHAPTER 37

"What we gonna do?"

That was the question Laquita asked her yesterday after Detective Shockley left. Julia didn't have an answer yesterday and she still didn't have a clue what to do this morning.

She had a restless night trying to keep the cold pack on her eye for twenty minutes and then repeating it every hour. The cold pack was a bag of frozen peas wrapped in a dishcloth. Laquita claimed her mama said a sack of frozen peas was better than an ice pack.

It was only five in the morning, yet there was no sense trying to get back to sleep. Her mind was reeling ninety miles an hour with everything that had happened and all she had yet to do.

Was she still in danger?

She moaned when she rose out of bed and swung her legs out. Sitting on the edge of the bed with her feet on the hardwood floor, she took a minute. Her head still throbbed and now her teeth hurt. She needed more Tylenol and a hot shower.

In the bathroom, she examined her face in the mirror. What a day yesterday had been. She tensed staring at her bruised face, a reminder of what had happened to her.

She was angry. The person who was responsible deserved her wrath. The only problem was the person she was the angriest at was the person in the mirror. It was her fault she was almost injected with drugs and got knocked out.

She had screwed up. How naive could she be to follow the waitress from the strip joint into the bathroom? She remembered distinctly the alarm bells going off in her head, warning her something was off. Then why'd she do it?

Again, she misjudged a person.

Again, it cost her.

From now on, she'd trust no one.

There was still dried blood caked around the rim of her nose. She dampened a washcloth and gently wiped it off. The swelling wasn't as bad as she thought it would be. The bluish-yellow color circling her eye was more pronounced. Leaning closer to the mirror she gently touched her swollen face. She winced.

Her first shiner was a beaut.

Steaming hot water from the shower considerably eased the throbbing and ache in her head. She didn't want to get out, except the water temp was quickly getting cooler. Historic homes had amazing character along with outdated plumbing among other issues.

She toweled dried her hair, climbed into a pair of jeans and slipped on a cream-colored cashmere V-neck sweater. As she padded to the kitchen, she noticed Laquita's bedroom door was still closed.

After brewing a cup of tea, she sat at the kitchen table and let out a loud groan. It startled her. The sound reminded her of Elke. Even though Elke had a youthful appearance and the energy of a teenager, her grandmother was getting older.

She wrapped her hands around the warm cup, raised it to her nose and inhaled the sweet, floral aroma. After a few sips, she felt the caffeine start to kick in.

She struggled over what to do about the photos she had taken of a man who might have murdered two people at the Willow Oaks Motel. The photos could prove definitively that the man was guilty or at the very least place him at the murder scene.

Detective Shockley wanted them. He'd be back. She saw it in his eyes—determination. Then what would she do?

She was so damn certain when she went to the strip club she'd find Max and get him to tell her what he knew about the man they saw at the motel. Instead, Max came seriously close to injecting her with drugs. Laquita tried defending him, saying he saved her life. That was the way Laquita wanted to see it.

Laquita said Max told her that after she was knocked out, the old man with the cane shot the beefy man who had been guarding the back door before he was able to stick her with the needle. Then Max untied her hands and carried her out the exit door. He was headed down the alley with her unconscious in his arms when he spotted the parked car with Laquita standing next to it. As soon as Laquita recognized Max and her, she ran toward them. Laquita and Max put her in the backseat of her car. Max climbed in the passenger side.

She vaguely remembered hearing them argue and Laquita helping her out of the car and inside her home. Laquita said she let Max out of the car after they drove a few blocks from the club.

Julia lifted the cup to her lips, reflected a moment, then remembered the promise she made to herself. *Don't trust anybody.* That included Laquita. Max knew the killer and Laquita knew Max.

It still bothered her that Laquita showed up almost as soon as she purchased the detective agency, claiming to have worked for the previous owner. Why did he pay her on the side and not put her on the payroll?

Sitting at the kitchen table she analyzed the situation. Everybody had secrets. She should know, since her whole life had been one big secret. Or rather, one big lie.

Her birth name was Lisa Saitow. Her parents died in an explosion. Her grandmother worked for the CIA. Those three facts were hidden from her growing up. Even now, knowing the truth, she kept most of that to herself. Maybe some secrets were better left buried.

She wanted to live in the present, not the past.

What would Elke think about the mess she had gotten herself into? If her grandmother knew, she'd interfere—again— and tell her what to do. She didn't want to be told what to do.

Out of the corner of her eye, she spotted Laquita's purse on the counter next to the refrigerator.

"Secrets," she mumbled under her breath. A hunch told her Laquita had something to hide and maybe that something was in her over-sized purse.

She stood and slowly walked over to the purse on the counter. Concerned Laquita might catch her, she opened the refrigerator, took out a carton of eggs and placed it next to the purse. If she heard anything, she would start cooking. To make sure Laquita was still upstairs, she hurriedly tiptoed out of the kitchen, rounded the corner and glanced up the stairs to the bedroom. The door was still shut.

She scurried back and took a breath standing next to Laquita's purse on the counter. Her hands dove inside the purse and began rummaging around. Laquita was not a minimalist.

She was a hoarder.

In the purse were a pair of sunglasses, phone charger, water bottle, gum, lip balm, pink lipstick, Tide To-Go-Pen, assorted candy wrappers, and lots of old receipts. Beneath the mess, she found what looked like an expensive leather wallet.

What was it that Laquita had said when they did the stake-out at the Willow Oaks Motel? *Kinda strange not to have a picture of your man.*

Opening the wallet, she said, "Okay Laquita. Let's see who your man is."

The card slots held a Visa card, Starbucks gift card, a punch card for a sandwich shop she'd never heard of and a driver license. Even though Laquita didn't own a car, she probably had to have one for identification.

Laquita Morrison.

It was a good picture of her. Unlike the mug shot on Julia's license with her lazy eye making her look literally hungover.

Laquita was attractive with full lips, large brown eyes and high cheekbones. Her address was somewhere in the D.C. area. She had guessed right about Laquita's height, 5'8", although she did a double take on the weight. There's no way she weighed 135 pounds. Not even close. Maybe she'd gained weight since this license was issued.

Inside a fold she pulled out a creased yellowed picture of a very large Black woman with a small girl wearing a big toothy smile sitting on her lap. This must be her grandmother she called Big G. Julia felt sad recalling the story Laquita had told her about her childhood. She carefully eased the picture back in the fold. In another fold she found several receipts for bus fare and miscellaneous purchases. Tucked behind the receipts she slipped out a small photo booth picture. A smile curved her lips. Now she knew who Laquita's man was.

She froze. Footsteps on the staircase.

Quickly she put the picture back where she found it, closed the wallet shoving it in the purse and scooped up the carton of eggs.

Standing in the kitchen doorway, Laquita said accusingly, "What ya doing with my pocketbook?"

Julia's tongue didn't want to work. She struggled to figure out what to say.

"Good morning." She tried to keep her voice normal, but she sounded out of breath.

Holding the carton of eggs, she couldn't think of a good lie. "I was going to make breakfast." Julia sounded as convincing as a teenager lying to the teacher about the dog eating their homework.

"I like 'em scrambled," said Laquita followed by a loud yawn.

Julia felt a rush of relief until Laquita followed up, "Ya gotta work on your detective skills."

"What do you mean?" Julia frowned.

"I think we both know what I mean." Laquita strolled over to the refrigerator and opened the door. "You got some bacon we can fry up?"

"Yes, of course. It's not what you think."

Bending over with her head in the refrigerator Laquita responded, "Another thin' is ya gotta work on tellin' fibs."

Before Julia could shoot back a rebuttal, Laquita added, "Don't fret 'bout it. I done the same thin'."

"What?" cried Julia. She marched over to the refrigerator, grabbed Laquita's arm and yanked her up. "You snooped through my purse?"

"Don't have a conniption fit. We even. Tat for tits."

"It's tit for tat. And I'm sorry. I had no right to look in your purse. When did you go through mine?"

"When ya was knocked out. I didn' steal nothin'. Laquita gave Julia a reassuring smile.

"Good to know," Julia responded with dripping sarcasm.

"Hows 'bout you?"

"No. I don't steal." Julia pivoted and headed toward the oven.

Laquita reached in the refrigerator, took out a pack of bacon and closed the door. "Your face ain't that bad."

Julia cracked an egg in a bowl and without looking up, shot back, "I think somebody else needs to work on their fibbing skills."

As Julia cleared the dishes, Laquita said, "That was mighty good. Almost as good as my Big G's cookin'."

"Thanks. We've gotta come up with something before Detective Shockley returns with a search warrant." Julia had no idea what to do.

Laquita wiped her mouth and offered, "How 'bout Elke?"

"We're not involving her." Julia stood and began to clear the table. Standing, she asked, "Did Max tell you how he knows the man called Razor?"

"No."

Laquita answered too fast. Julia put the plates back on the table and accused, "You're lying. What'd he tell you?"

"Said somebody gave him that name. He met Razor maybe one time. Max got a friend who needed somebody to convince a person to do the right thin'. He didn' know the guy wuz crazy."

"Who's the friend?"

"For Christ Sakes, Julia. I ain't lying. I didn' ask. I was scared, okay? It ain't like I'm CIA."

Without thinking, Julia put her hand on Laquita's arm. *CIA.* The word echoed in her mind like canyon voices.

The Bridge Club might be able to help them.

Julia knew her next move better be the right one.

CHAPTER 38

Let it go? That was the best advice Wheels could give him regarding the FBI taking over his case?

Shockley clenched the steering wheel and took in a deep breath. Anger boiled inside him making it difficult to think clearly. The red light caught him by surprise. His foot slammed the brakes. The tires squealed against the pavement. The car rocked to a stop. A long hard breath escaped his lips. When the light changed, the tires squealed again when he accelerated fast heading to the one place he felt he needed to go. The clouds had cleared, and the chilly morning low was slowly rising as the sun's rays warmed the concrete, asphalt and other man-made materials in the urban city.

Fueling his irritation were all the long hours working this case and then getting booted off without a good explanation. *National Security.* How could the explosion at the motel and the photos Julia Bagal took be considered National Security? What was the connection? At least now he had to assume she played him. His chest tightened. Let it go, he kept telling himself.

National Security, my ass.

He pulled his car to the curb in front of Harley's liquor store. A six pack might make his visit more tolerable. He wasn't sure it was a good idea, but he was headed to his father's place. He had been ordered to take the afternoon off.

Right now, he knew he needed to get his bitter anger under control. Maybe his ol' man could offer up some advice. His father never talked about the war, but he once overheard him and another veteran talk about losing a battle buddy to suicide and the recurring nightmares that plagued most of them. His mom told him later the man had almost died of a drug overdose and it was his father who helped him get better. The veteran stayed and worked on the ranch for almost a year.

Ken, the owner of the liquor store, was behind the counter ringing up a sale. He gave Shockley a chin up. "Nice to see you again, Detective."

"You too, Ken," he replied. Ken was average height, slim, and always greeted his customers with a smile. He looked to be in his late forties.

Ken bought the store a little over two years ago from the previous owner who got tired of being robbed.

Ken got robbed.

Once.

The robber pulled a weapon on Ken. What the robber didn't know was Ken had been a navy seal. Ken ducked, grabbed his 9mm SIG from under the counter surprising the robber. The robber made a fatal mistake when Ken ordered him to drop his weapon. The story aired on TV and Ken hadn't been robbed since.

Shockley pulled a six pack of cold beer from the reach-in refrigerator and was walking up to the counter when something caught his eye. He grabbed a bag without stopping. At the counter he laid his purchase down in front of Ken.

"Huh," snorted Ken. "Beer and Cheetos. Bad day at work, huh Detective?"

"Had better," replied Shockley with a weak grin.

Shockley wondered if Ken remembered his name. All Ken ever called him was Detective. Not that he came in the store that often. He'd seen too many men on the force ruin their professional and personal lives with the bottle. It was one of the many casualties of the profession.

In his father's driveway entrance, Shockley debated if this was a mistake. He and his father had a rocky relationship ever since he moved to D.C. He might be in one of his moods and right now Shockley didn't want to deal with it. He eased the car to a stop in front of the garage and turned off the engine. With the beer in one hand and the Cheetos in the other, he made his way to the front door.

He stood outside the front door. *Do I really want to do this?* A fleeting thought of knocking before entering didn't register. He was thinking about what he'd tell his ol' man, if anything at all. It was his problem, but he didn't know how to digest it.

On the way over he wanted to let it roll off his back and not think of the investigation he had been ordered to surrender to the FBI. But there were too many things blocking him from accepting it. He'd made a promise to T-Bone to catch the bastard who had killed a fellow officer and critically wounded Amber Bull, a damn good crime scene investigator and friend. He had checked on her condition yesterday. No improvement. Still hooked to a respirator. The doctors were unsure if she'd be able to walk again.

Shockley turned the knob and pushed the door open. It didn't matter how many times he'd told his father to lock the door, he never did. He claimed he locked up at night, but he'd be damn if he'd lock his door during the day. Anybody who came in uninvited would wish they hadn't. The ol' man was still a tough talker Still acted like he lived back in Texas on the ranch. D.C. was different. Doors should always be locked.

Night and day.

The sound made him recoil. The unmistakable cocking sound of a double-action pump.

"It's me, dad," he hollered. "Put the gun down. Okay."

He heard grumbling and then, "Nobody comes in my house without knocking."

"Sorry dad."

In the den his father was sitting in his recliner. The shotgun was propped against the wall near his chair.

"How come you didn't knock?" His father scowled at him.

"I usually do knock and you never hear a damn thing. How come you heard me this time?"

"My hearing is just fine. You ain't exactly twinkle toes."

His father was bad about turning down his hearing aids when he napped. Obviously, he was awake this afternoon.

"Whatya got there?" his father asked eyeing the beer and Cheetos.

"I stopped by Harley's on the way over and got ..."

"I ain't blind either. Are you gonna give me a beer or what?" his dad said gruffly.

He thought maybe he'd leave the beer and Cheetos and make an excuse to get the hell out of there when his father softened, "Sit a spell son and let's pop a cold one."

His father was good at reading people, especially him.

Shockley handed him a beer and the bag of Cheetos before sliding into the chair across from him. They both twisted off the tops of the bottles and each man took a long slug.

"Good beer," his father said.

"Yup," Shockley added.

"Aren't you going to eat the Cheetos I got you?" he asked, still unsure how much to tell his father. He felt his gut churn.

"Later."

A few seconds ticked by in silence. Both of them nursing their beer.

"You look plumb tuckered out, son. What's on your mind?"

It was times like this he was glad to have his ol' man close by. He needed somebody to vent to and his father was all he had. His father was attentive the whole time he recapped the Willow Oaks murder case and how the FBI showed up and ordered him to cease and desist his investigation.

Telling his father what was going on brought a sense of relief.

The beer helped too.

He left out some specifics that could impede the investigation but said enough to let his father know how he felt. Being able to unload all the things bothering him about the case allowed the tightness in his chest to loosen.

He knew his father wouldn't respond till he had given it some thought but surprised him and spoke up without hesitation.

"Son, the Army had a saying. If you're in a fight and things are going well…it's probably an ambush. Sounds to me like you got too close to the truth about what was going on." He raised a finger. "I'm just speculating here, but I reckon that young lady is your key to why the FBI is involved."

"That's what I thought, but I'm not sure how she's connected." Shockley raked his hand through his thick hair pondering his lingering suspicion. "I've been struggling to look at this from every angle, but I keep coming up empty."

"FBI might think she's a spy or…perhaps she's the bait for a bigger fish," the old man offered.

Shockley almost choked on the swallow of beer in his

throat. "Damn, I think that's it, dad."

"Which one? The spy thing or the bait?"

He stood, patted his father on the shoulder and said, "Thanks for helping me figure this one out."

Before he turned around his father grabbed his arm and cautioned, "Watch your back."

"I will, dad."

At the front door, Shockley twisted the lock on the doorknob. He wished his ol' man would keep the door locked.

Walking to his car, Shockley punched in Hauser's number and listened to it ring as he climbed in the car.

Hauser picked up on the fourth ring. "Did you give the FBI all the files?" asked Shockley.

"I did exactly as you told me," replied Hauser. "The FBI has everything they need."

"Good. I don't like them taking over this case, but if they catch the perp, we win."

"Yeah, with the resources these guys have, the case could be solved in the time it took me to run the 5K."

Shockley forced a chuckle. "Just leaving my father's place."

"How is the old man?" asked Hauser.

"Cantankerous as usual. Took him a six-pack and Cheetos."

"Cheetos? You really need to take him some healthy greasy food next time."

"I'll be sure to remember that. Headed back home for some long overdue rest. Check in tomorrow."

Shockley had the feeling he was being watched even though he had scanned the street before he entered and left his father's house. The FBI might tap his phone. That was why he and Hauser used a cryptic conversation letting them know they'd meet later.

He turned the ignition, put the car in reverse and eased out of his father's driveway. Checking his watch, he saw he didn't have much time.

†††

Wiley's Kitchen of Ill Repute was the best place in town for greasy food. He knew to meet Hauser here in 25 minutes. That was how long Hauser would bullshit he could run a 5K.

He spotted Hauser in a back booth. The skinny kid kept his head low not wanting to draw attention. On the table in front of him was an oversized drink and a basket of the best salty fries in town.

"I'd have ordered for you but not sure what you'd want," Hauser said in his husky voice.

Shockley raised his hand and flagged Naomi, the waitress, who always waited on them. Naomi with her shirt unbuttoned one too many buttons for her large breasts, waltzed over and let her eyes drift up and down his body before asking, "Hey hon, whatcha havin'?"

"What's the pie today?"

"Apple. Made it myself." Naomi smiled exposing the gap between the center of her two front teeth.

"I'll take a slice and add some ice cream on top."

Naomi's face lit up. She liked when he ordered her pies. "Anything for you babe," she replied with a wink before sauntering back to the kitchen.

"Looks like she's got the hots for you," Hauser said after

she walked away.

"What's not to like," joked Shockley. "We don't have a lot of time. Whatcha got?"

"You think we're doing the right thing? If the Feds find out we didn't give them all the files, we could end up doing time."

"I'll take responsibility. If you want out, I understand. I have no idea what we're getting into." Shockley kept his eyes on Hauser trying to read what he might be thinking.

Hauser screwed up his face. "A little late not to involve me. When I held back files, I became an accessory for not cooperating with the FBI."

"Sorry man."

"No, you're not," scoffed Hauser. "You needed me, and you involved me in your personal vendetta against the perp who put T-Bone and Bull in the hospital." Hauser's round eyes narrowed.

They exchanged a silent stare. Even though he didn't like what Hauser said, he knew it was probably true. The kid never whitewashed how he felt. He respected Hauser for that.

"You think I should let it go? Let the Feds catch this perp, because you know they don't give a shit about that. They have another agenda."

"Mike, you couldn't let it go if you tried. It's not in your nature, man. You already left the reservation. Now, you've got two, maybe three days to figure this out before the shit hits the fan."

CHAPTER 39

Julia rapped her knuckles on the car window causing the older man inside to jump. She wasn't sure if he was asleep or had his head down reading the book lying in his lap.

He quickly lowered the driver's window, took a good look at her face and asked, "What the hell happened to you? Are you okay?" his baritone voice reverberated in her ears.

She wasn't surprised by the question. Even with make-up, she couldn't completely mask the bluish-yellow color bruising around her eye.

"Don't worry about it, I'm fine."

She wrapped her arms around herself but was unable to stop shaking. The morning sun had not been out long enough to take the bite out of the crisp air. Was she shivering from the chilly air or nerves? Probably both.

She bent forward toward the open window and continued, "But, I do need the Bridge Club's help."

Leaves on the street rustled and swirled with a crisp burst of wind. She wondered if the man would invite her to get in the car to escape the cold.

She managed to force a smile at the man with hair so thin she could see his mottled scalp. His emotionless face let her know there would be no offer to sit in his car.

"Have the Feds tried to contact you?" he asked.

"The FBI?"

"The guys down the street. Can't miss 'em."

She raised her head and stretched to search the street. There were several cars parked along the curb. Nothing looked suspicious. She was going to tell him she didn't see anybody when he directed her to look in the opposite direction.

Her eyes froze wide. Two men sitting in a dark Suburban were parked down the street. What unnerved her most was they locked eyes with her instead of looking away.

"What are they doing here?" she asked.

"Same thing I'm doing," he replied with a trace of sarcasm that crept into his voice.

"They have no right to surveil me. I'm going to talk to them." Her nostrils flared. She knew with certainty that with the involvement of the FBI, the Bridge Club wasn't trying to solve a murder. The Feds and the ex-CIA operatives wanted to find a murderer who posed a threat to America. That had to be it.

The older man startled her when he reached out the car window wrapping his large hand around her arm.

"Not a good idea, Julia. We're working on getting you to a safe house."

She snatched her arm free and snarled, "I'm not interested in going to a safe house. With you and the FBI keeping tabs on me, I think I'm safe."

"Elke doesn't think so."

"Elke doesn't make my decisions. Besides, I need the Club to check on something for me. Otherwise I'll go to the police with it."

The older man hunched as he intertwined his fingers that rested on the book in his lap. He slowly let his hooded eyes meet hers.

She stood impatiently waiting for his response. None came.

Julia was certain her face betrayed her thoughts. Her entire life she had been accused of wearing her emotions on her sleeve. Surely, he could tell she wasn't kidding. If they refused to help, she would have no other option than go to the police and let them have the photos.

Every time she thought she had a good idea it turned out not to be just a bad idea, but a disastrous one. This once, she thought, if she could actually find the killer then any lingering doubts about her buying the investigative business would be gone. She wanted Elke to admit she was wrong in telling her it was a mistake buying the business.

She began shifting from one foot to the other, impatient for his response.

Then, after a few moments, he spoke, "What do you want?"

A rush of relief paused her feet as she leaned toward the open window. "I have photos of a man leaving the Willow Oaks Motel. I want you to find out who he is and give that information only to me, nobody else. I'll work with the Bridge Club to solve this case, but I have to have assurance that I will be kept in the loop. If you don't get back to me within 24 hours, I'll send copies to the police."

"Do you have the photos on you?"

"Yes. I have them inside my coat. Do we have a deal?"

"There are too many eyes on us here. Keep the photos. Do you still have the burner phone we gave you?"

She nodded.

"Somebody will contact you soon. Go back inside your home and don't leave till you hear from us," he instructed.

Her nose began to run from the cool air. She pulled her coat tight with one hand and wiped her runny nose on her sleeve.

She straightened, watched him pull his seatbelt across his chest and start the car. The silver Honda Accord jerked into the street and drove past her home to the intersection and made a sharp right turn. It looked like he was on his phone, but she wasn't sure.

She checked the FBI agents who now had binoculars stuck to their face. Hurrying across the street she knew the FBI wasn't here because they cared about her safety. They were doing surveillance on her to see if she would lead them to the Russian.

Julia saw Laquita standing watch in the front window of her home. As Julia climbed the front porch steps, Laquita promptly swung the door open.

"Well? How'd it go? They gonna help?" Laquita's excitement was a welcome relief. It made her feel like she had made a good decision.

She sniffed and replied, "Yes, I think so."

Laquita grabbed Julia's arm and began hopping up and down. "We're gonna be awesome detectives. This calls for a celebration. Got any vodka?"

"Sure."

"Where's it at?"

"In the cabinet above the refrigerator."

Laquita marched into the kitchen, humming to herself.

Julia took off her coat and dropped the envelope of photos on the dining room table. A wave of exhaustion washed over her. She headed to the living room and threw herself on the couch. She could hear the sound of Laquita chopping something.

Five minutes later, Laquita appeared with a glass in each hand.

"Fixed us a nutritional drink to celebrate. Had to improvise."

"Bloody Mary?"

"Yup." She handed a glass to Julia and sat in the chair next to the couch.

"Here's to us bein' detectives and solvin' this case." Laquita lifted her glass.

"I'll drink to that." Julia smiled as they clinked their glasses together.

"How come ya didn't give 'em the photos?" asked Laquita.

"I will. They'll call and then we can arrange to hand them over."

Laquita didn't ask why they needed to wait. And she didn't volunteer that the FBI was parked down the street.

Laquita picked up the remote on the coffee table and clicked on the T.V. She kept the volume low as she flipped through the channels.

She stopped on a news channel flashing *Breaking News*.

Julia straightened when she recognized the crime scene investigator from the Willow Oaks Motel.

"Laquita, turn it up. That woman." Her finger wagging at the image on the T.V. "She's the reporter we saw at the motel right before the explosion."

Laquita thumbed the volume louder. They sat listening intently to the newscast.

The reporter's name was Susan Porter. The blast had injured her face above her right eye. The woman had a butterfly stitch on it. Julia thought she looked prettier on T.V. than when she saw her from the car that eventful day. The shapely reporter was standing in front of the Metropolitan Police Station holding a microphone to her face.

"The top story tonight is Channel 7 news has learned from a source who is not authorized to comment publicly that the Metro Police Department has been pulled off the Willow Oaks Motel explosion investigation and has turned all evidence over to the FBI. Our request to interview Detective Mike Shockley, the leading homicide detective on the case has been denied. The FBI director said any information they have at this time cannot be released because it would jeopardize the ongoing investigation."

Laquita muted the sound, faced Julia and asked, "What does that mean?"

Julia shook her head, not sure herself what it meant. The police being pulled off the case left her feeling unsettled.

"I don't know what's going on." She paused. The tension that had left her earlier had returned. "But now we know that going to the police isn't an option." Why had the FBI pulled the police off the case? Just yesterday, Detective Shockley was at her home claiming he could help keep them safe. Did he know this then?

Unsure of what to say, Julia kept quiet. This might be a whole lot messier than she was willing to admit. She and Laquita weren't really detectives. Not by a long shot. Maybe at this juncture she should just walk outside and turn all the photos over to the FBI and bow out.

Her hesitation was her distrust of the agencies—FBI, CIA and police. Her grandmother had planted that seed long ago. Should she call Elke and ask for help? That was a lot of pride to swallow.

"We wait," Laquita said.

"What?"

"I can tell you f_xin' to throw in the towel. Our one big case. Our chance to make a name for ourselves."

"We might be in over our heads."

"Ain't no *might be* Julia. We way in over our heads. We're smack dab in the middle of somethin' big and the way I see it, if we give 'em what we got then we're out. We gotta wait on the Bridge Club to call us. I believe there's a reason this happen to us and we can't give up."

"Sure, there's a reason this happened to us and that reason is Kat Lejeune or whatever her name really is. I wish we knew her real identity. Why ask us to do surveillance on her husband at Willow Oaks Motel? This isn't about a jealous wife."

"She ain't his wife."

"How would you know that?"

"Remember she never showed ya a picture of him."

"Yeah, you're right. I got distracted by all the cash she plopped down in front of me. She had an ulterior motive when she hired us to do this assignment."

"Not us. You. She gotta know ya somehow," said Laquita

"I'd never seen her before she came to my office."

"Then somebody done told her about ya or coulda been she hurd about ya from somebody."

"I don't know. I'll give the Bridge Club thirty more minutes and…."

The cell phone buzzed.

CHAPTER 40

Shockley brushed off the guilt after Hauser reminded him that by not turning all the information over to the FBI might land them in jail. He was well aware of 18 U.S.C. Section 1001 that had convicted many people who intentionally misled FBI officials.

Hauser was right when he told him he couldn't let it go. His earlier conversation with his father only strengthened his resolve to stay on the case, even unofficially. It felt wrong to turn a blind eye on this investigation.

Wiley's Kitchen was quiet. He and Hauser were the only patrons. Even though the place was a dive, it had a certain charm with its historic past. The two-story brick exterior had the appearance of a historic bank when in reality it had been a brothel. Forty years ago, the city council wanted to tear the building down but, as the legend goes, one of the regular customers bought it and converted it into a restaurant. The business had been in the family ever since. The current owner, Sid Mulvaney said his grandfather, Wiley, who bought the place, did it to help people in the neighborhood. Mulvaney kept the tradition of helping those in need, especially the homeless. Nobody was ever turned away because they couldn't pay.

Rust colored concrete walls were plastered with photographs of the building in its heyday and current photographs of Mulvaney hugging some of his customers— regulars, famous and even infamous. From Shockley's seat he had a view of the entrance to the restaurant. It was a habit. Never sit with his back to the door. He began to fidget on the padded vinyl booth seat that had long lost its springy comfort. Patrons would say the seats had more duct tape holding them together than honest men in Congress. He figured Mulvaney spent his money on better things, like feeding the homeless.

While Shockley ate his pie, he watched Hauser, amazed at how the skinny kid could down a Philly cheesesteak sandwich dripping with grease, a generous helping of salty fries and a brownie large enough to be considered a cake, and then wash it down with his oversized drink. "How do you eat all that crap and not die of a heart attack?"

"Least this way I die on my own terms instead of some scum bag shooting me in the back."

"Good point," replied Shockley as he reached across the table and snagged a few left-over fries off Hauser's plate.

Hauser wiped the grease running down the side of his mouth with his fingers. Then he slid his plate with the remaining fries over to Shockley. He reached down beside him and retrieved a manila envelope off the bench seat.

"Ready?" Hauser leaned across the table. "Cause after this we're gonna be in the eye of a shit storm."

Hauser was usually upbeat even during times when the department was facing layoffs, which was happening more often these days due to budget cuts. What Shockley was asking Hauser to do was putting the young detective in a bad position.

Shockley gave a curt nod.

Hauser moved the empty plates on the table to the side and pushed the envelope across to Shockley. Shockley unlashed the clasp, opened the envelope and emptied the contents out in front of him.

Hauser lowered his voice, "That's the file we held back. The one on Chance Martin Stephens III's case."

While Shockley studied the photos one by one in front of him, Hauser read him in on the case.

"What we know from the plates on the vehicle outside Willow Oaks Motel is it's registered to Mateo Martinez. At that time, we speculated it was narcotics activity or prostitution since one of the victims was a female and Willow Oaks caters to this type of business. The explosion fits the MO of the Dead Zone. Martinez was in a rival gang. We didn't have much to go on until now."

Shockley stopped scanning the incident report of the accident and looked up. "Until now? You found a witness?"

"Remember Bambi?"

"The stripper who claimed to have information about the murders."

"Right. We screwed up not interviewing Bambi."

"I thought she was at work when all this went down."

"She was. You and I don't believe in coincidences. I think somehow Bambi knew something."

Shockley scratched his stubbled chin and said, "I'll bite. What's the coincidence?"

"Bambi was found this morning in her apartment. DOA. Severe blunt-force trauma to the head. Didn't appear to be a break-in."

"Son of a bitch! She did know something. You thinking what I'm thinking?"

"Yup," answered Hauser as he raised a hand to signal Naomi. "The perp coulda been one of her customers. When he found out she wanted to cut a deal with the cops, he got rid of her."

"Is the FBI aware of the connection?"

"Not sure. Bambi was never in the report since we believed she was a dead end. No pun intended."

"I think we need to pay Bambi's boss a visit. See what he knows."

Naomi strolled over. Shockley got a coffee to go and Hauser ordered a Coke.

Extra-large.

† † †

Outside Wiley's Kitchen, Shockley told Hauser to leave his car and they'd ride together to Club Sepia. It was the stripper joint where Bambi worked. Or used to work.

Club Sepia made the Dark Alley Warehouse look uptown. Shockley had never been inside, but the reputation of the Club was well known. It was a corner building with faded facade and weeds that grew through the cracked cement walk around the side of the structure. It looked abandoned and this was considered the roughest part of town. A half-lit flashing neon sign was the only indication the place was open for business. Hauser told him the bartender, also the owner, had an attitude when it came to his girls. The customers were hardhat guys not thugs like he found in Dark Alley. According to Hauser it was a rather friendly bar and even offered Karaoke night on Thursdays.

Soon as he buckled up, he felt the phone inside his jacket buzz. He slipped the phone out, swiped and not recognizing the number cautiously answered, "Shockley."

It took a couple of seconds to recognize the voice, but once he did his mouth fell open. "T-bone is that you?"

A grin crept across his face as the man on the other line talked. T-bone was out of intensive care. He needed to talk to him. Right now.

"Be there in twenty, bro. Good to hear your voice." Shockley clicked off and placed the phone on the console. "That was T-bone. He's out of the woods. Says he needs to talk ASAP now that his head isn't groggy from all the drugs."

Hauser unlatched his seatbelt and said, "I'll catch up to you later after I check out our lead at Club Sepia."

"Sounds like a plan," responded an upbeat Shockley after hearing his friend's voice.

Standing outside the car, Hauser leaned in holding his giant Coke.

"Tell T-Bone it's good to know he's gonna be okay." Hauser slammed the door and walked in the direction of his car.

CHAPTER 41

Wagner hadn't slept for the past couple of nights.
The man he hired was out of control and the body count was mounting. He had been clear with his instructions to Razor about the reporter. Murder wasn't part of the deal.

The last conversation he had with Razor haunted him. *Remember Congressman Wagner, I don't like loose lips and I hate Russians.*

He wasn't a Russian citizen. His parents were. Both were born in Russia, recruited as a couple by the KGB and trained in Moscow, then sent to a way station in the Netherlands. After passing as Americans they were sent to the United States as part of the *Illegals* program, a Russian network of sleeper spies. They lived a low-keyed life in an Ohio suburb after he was born. It was between his Junior and Senior year of college, while doing a work study program abroad he was indoctrinated. He learned his parents' sole purpose was to provide what Russia needed—an asset who could influence powerful U.S. policy makers.

He exceeded all expectations.

The biggest threat to his career was Razor. The blood thirsty maniac had murdered the reporter, another man in the room with her, a police officer killed from the explosion at the motel and now, the reporter's boyfriend.

The hitman seemed to have a *to do* list and the Congressman was afraid he might end up on it. In addition to his killing spree, Razor was now demanding more money for jobs Wagner didn't sanction. He had never felt this much hatred for another human being as he did toward Razor.

What the hell had he done? What would the Kremlin think if they found out? He could easily go to the FBI and turn himself in. Seek protection in exchange for information. Yet he couldn't. Power was addictive. As Speaker of the House he had a lot of power. He couldn't walk away from what he had worked so hard to achieve. Razor had caused him enough anguish. All he had accomplished was not going to be taken away by a stupid lapse in judgment. He'd messed up, but he was smart, and he would come up with a plan.

He needed more caffeine to wake up his sleep-deprived body. He glanced at his wristwatch. Time to get to work. There was a street vendor he liked to stop by on the way to his office where he could get a coffee and an orange Danish to go.

Before he walked into his office, Megan questioned if he was feeling alright. He stopped in front of her desk and told her the truth, he hadn't been sleeping much, then he lied about working long hours trying to put together some ideas to pitch to his colleagues on how to increase competitiveness and growth in the country.

She offered an empathetic smile, her brown eyes wide open, full of warmth. He couldn't help but stare into her eyes and got lost for a second. Ever since their dinner date his attraction toward her had ignited a passion he couldn't quell. Not that he tried to. Or wanted to.

"Megan, I apologize again for leaving during our dinner the other night." He purposely left out the word *date* after *dinner.* He didn't want to scare her off. "I would like to make it up to you."

"That would be nice," she said in a guarded tone.

He stared into her eyes trying to identify the tone of her response. She appeared uneasy, drumming her pen on her desk.

He was silent trying to figure out what to say next.

Suddenly he believed he'd made a mistake assuming she'd be excited to go out with him again. He didn't need this now. Not with all he had on his plate.

Megan broke eye contact, her mouth grimaced. "I've been trying to find a way to tell you something Alan."

He cringed. They hadn't really dated. She didn't even know him. Not really, and yet she sounded like she was breaking up with him.

"I wasn't snooping, I swear."

Snooping. What did she find? He stared at her, not sure how to respond.

"I went in your office, to tidy up and throw away your coffee cup that you always leave on your desk when I saw a note. It just caught my eye and I read it. I regret it now. And I should have asked you about it before…"

"What note?"

"Charlotte at Willow Oaks Motel, room 205".

He struggled to maintain composure. He was conflicted. He was angry but he also had amorous feelings toward Megan. His anger wasn't at her for cleaning off his desk, it was at himself for leaving that note in plain sight. "Did you think I was meeting a woman at that dump?" His biting tone surprised Megan. The stress of his situation had reached a tipping point.

"No. I mean, I'm sorry. I was curious that's all and just didn't understand. That's the place where those people were murdered."

A wave of panic jolted through his body. His composure slipped. "That information came from the FBI, Megan." He cursed himself silently, pissed, but mostly afraid. "I'm working with them and that was about an informant who might be able to help us unravel a traitor in our government. It's a very sensitive matter."

"Oh my. I'm sorry, Alan, please forgive me," she begged.

He had stepped over the line and there was no going back. "I agreed to meet with her, this person named Charlotte, not her real name I'm sure, but at the last minute something came up and the FBI sent somebody else."

"Thank God." Her hand flew to her mouth. "You could have been killed. I'm sorry the other people lost their lives." Megan plucked a Kleenex out of a box on her desk and wiped her damp eyes.

He hated seeing her upset. Barking at her was the wrong thing to do. *Why had he been so careless to leave the note on his desk?*

Megan stood and hurried around her desk. "Alan, you spilled your coffee on your suit, let me help."

"No. It's okay." He used his free hand to halt her. "Have you told anybody about the note?"

"No, of course not. I just felt I should tell you. I'm truly sorry I read it."

"Megan, I'm sorry I snapped at you. I've been under a lot of stress lately. Work and now the possibility of a traitor among us. You can't tell anybody about that note or anything I just told you. If it were to get out, it could hinder the investigation. The FBI told me to keep everything confidential. I hope you understand."

"Yes, of course. I wouldn't want to interfere in the investigation."

He stared into her eyes. Her big beautiful brown eyes.

She didn't believe him.

Sitting behind his desk, Alan tried to sort out the predicament he was in. *Why me? Why me?* He kept thinking. Megan's confession complicated his dilemma. She seemed to be holding back something from him. What could it be? Maybe Megan had told a girlfriend what she found. Maybe she had overheard some of his conversations with his handler. If he were to tell Razor that she read the note, he would kill her too. Is that how he solved this problem? She seemed genuinely upset she had read the note. Maybe she thought he'd done something wrong and just wanted to help? One thing he was sure of, she knew more than she told him.

His breathing became shallow and rapid. He could feel the blood thumping against his temples.

Suddenly he was hot and began to sweat. His hands and legs started tingling. The room was spinning.

Something's wrong, something's wrong.

The Russians. Had they found out what he did? The coffee and food from the roadside vendor. Was it poisoned? The man who usually operated the food truck wasn't there. The woman told him he was sick and she was filling in. His worried thoughts accelerated in his mind. He tried to calm himself with several deep breaths. But he couldn't breathe, as if somebody was holding him underwater and wouldn't let him come up for air. His trembling hand tried to reach for the phone on his desk to call Megan, but his vision was blurred.

His heart pounded against his chest so hard he knew he

was going to die. *I've got to get help fast.* He didn't want to die in his office. Alone. He pushed himself up and felt the room spinning.

Oh my God, this is it.

He tried to steady himself with a hand on his desk. His chest tightened. His arm too weak to support his shaky legs caused him to falter, his hand swept across his desk knocking the lamp to the floor as he collapsed.

Lying on the floor, he could hear her voice. "Alan, are you okay?" It sounded hollow, like an echo.

Then.

"9-1-1, I have an emergency. Please hurry."

CHAPTER 42

Julia awoke with a start from a loud noise.

Her heart raced, skin damp.

Disoriented, she took in the room around her. It took a full second to realize she was safe in her home. She must have fallen asleep on the couch right after the phone call from the Bridge Club. For some reason, maybe because of the vivid dream, she still felt tired.

An aroma drifted from the kitchen. Laquita was cooking. Food might help perk her up.

Standing in the kitchen doorway, she saw Laquita stirring something in a pot on the stove. She smelled garlic.

"Sorry if I woke ya," Laquita said. "I dropped a pan on the floor."

"No problem. I needed to get up. How long was I asleep?"

"You were out like a light for 'bout two hours. We need to eat 'fore we head out, so ya don't git grumpy."

"Good idea. What are you making?"

"Spaghetti with meatballs and garlic bread. Found everythin' I needed. Ya hungry?"

"Starving. Smells delicious."

Julia rubbed her eyes gently with the heels of her palms as she tried to stifle a yawn. Her bruised eye still tender. She said, "I don't like waiting till dark to meet Lester from the Bridge Club."

Laquita broke the pasta in half and dropped it in a pot of

boiling water. She turned, propped a hand on one hip and said, "Ain't that how the CIA works? In the cloak of darkness?"

She laughed. "You've been watching way too many movies. Besides you and I aren't CIA operatives and the Bridge Club members are no longer employed by the CIA."

Laquita turned her attention to the stove. "Leastways, I wish Elke was here. That'd make me feel a whole lot better bout everythin'."

"We don't need Elke," snapped Julia.

Laquita stirred the noodles in the boiling water. "I 'spect Elke works with 'em CIA. Once a spy always a spy. It's in her blood."

Julia didn't doubt Elke was involved with the CIA. But Elke would never go back on their payroll. Elke was still bitter about what happened when she worked at the agency.

"How 'bout ya set the table, Julia. It's almost time to eat."

After supper, Julia went to her bedroom to get ready to meet Lester. The Bridge Club had instructed them to wait until after dark. Then she and Laquita were to leave by the back door and walk to the playground on the corner of D and 15th Streets. She had gone on runs to the playground area in the past and felt the best route would be to go down the side alley and head west to 15th Street. Turn north to the playground. It wouldn't take longer than fifteen minutes to get to their rendezvous spot.

She studied the photos she had taken during her surveillance at the hotel. *Who was he? Russian?* A chill bolted up her spine. There were so many things she wanted to forget when it came to Russians and regrets that chipped away at her confidence. Laquita being involved didn't help.

Laquita was smart but had never acquired many of the skills Julia had. Growing up she learned how to shoot moving targets and took self-defense classes. At the time she didn't appreciate what she was forced to learn. But tonight, she did.

She stuffed the photos in a manila envelope and eased it down in her backpack. Only ten more minutes before they needed to leave.

Her body fussed at her when she got dressed. The blow she took yesterday made more than just her head hurt. She slid on leggings, ankle boots, and a black cable knit pullover sweater. After slipping on her navy wool coat, she parted the mini blinds and swept the street to see if the FBI was still there. Not able to see anyone from her window, she opened her laptop and activated her home's outside cameras. They were still there. She hoped they were freezing.

The FBI's presence made her paranoid. Would they get suspicious when they didn't notice movement in her home? She set light timers to come on and off at irregular intervals throughout the house, giving the FBI the impression they were still in the house and moving from room to room. She instructed Laquita to turn the TV on in the living room.

She picked up the burner phone and a mag light then pocketed them in her coat. Hurriedly, she powered down the laptop and stuffed it in her backpack just in case the FBI figured out what was going on and broke into her home. She knew that was an irrational thought since the security cameras would catch them breaking in. Unless it was the FBI who had installed the security in the first place.

She strapped on her backpack and made sure her pistol was in her purse. It was there and it was loaded.

Earlier the Bridge Club said they would take Laquita and

her to a safe house where they could work the case with their assistance. She refused the offer and told them she would hand over the photos only if they worked with her from her home. Staying in her home gave her leverage if the Club decided to leave her out of the loop. The FBI was just down the street and she knew the Club wouldn't want her to involve them.

Slowly she headed to the kitchen door when Laquita beckoned, "You comin?"

"Yeah, yeah. Give me a minute."

Julia had lived by herself a long time. It was difficult having another person staying in her home. They were able to get Laquita more clothes from her apartment a couple of days ago. Laquita's apartment was an efficiency located in a sketchy part of town. There was no television or dining table. A beige couch full of vibrant cushions, a bed with a bohemian flair and a wall covered in framed photographs of happy memories. It was modest and tastefully decorated.

In the kitchen, she tugged the straps tight on her backpack and said, "Laquita, I've been thinking...."

Laquita quickly cut in, "I shoulda gone with ya to the Warehouse. I ain't makin' that mistake again. I'm goin'."

"Would you just hear me out? All I've got to do is walk to the park and give Lester these photos. In exchange he's agreed to give us info on the car parked at the motel."

Laquita shook her head. "Nope. I'm goin'. Sides, we're partners."

Julia knew it was pointless to keep arguing. "Suit yourself. You have the flashlight I gave you?"

"I got everythin' ya told me to git." She pointed. "TV's on like ya said. Now, we gotta go or we gonna be late."

Julia set the alarm system and they scurried out the back

door through her backyard to the side of the house. They crossed 17th Street SE and onto Kathryn Lane, which was nothing more than an alley that connected 17th Street SE and 15th Street SE. "Don't switch on your flashlight unless we absolutely need it," warned Julia. "We don't want neighbors seeing lights outside their homes, getting scared and calling the cops."

The light of day quickly drained away this time of year. Dark cloudless skies sparkled with an endless parade of stars. The high relative humidity made it feel colder than the actual temperature.

A light crisp wind nipped at her face as they walked down Kathryn Lane. Julia pulled her coat collar up and tilted her head upward to view a sliver of the moon, which looked like a sharp sickle glowing in the sky. In her present state of mind, the tiny crescent moon reminded her of the sickle on the flag of the old USSR.

Laquita was dressed in jeans and an over-sized pink sweatshirt. A wide multi-colored headband pulled over her ears. She saw short wisps of Laquita's breath and thought she heard her roommate's teeth chatter. She kept an eye on the surroundings and listened for footsteps behind them. She didn't hear any.

Kathryn Lane appeared deserted. She tensed walking down the unlit lane. At the midpoint of the lane she saw a streetlight shining on 16th Street. Her pace increased.

Stopping under the streetlight, they both scanned 16th Street in search of anything that might send up a red flag. The quiet street was lined with cars parked along the curb. She figured most people were home from work and in for the night.

This street, like the one she lived on, didn't have a lot of traffic. That was one of the reasons she picked this area. The neighborhood was a mix of Millennials with children, seniors and people wanting to escape the hustle and bustle of city life. It wasn't the country, but less hectic and safer than most parts of D.C.

She and Laquita kept pace side by side without any exchange of words as they crossed 16th Street and continued down the lane. Tall historic homes on both sides of the lane enveloped them in darkness. A short distance in front of them was the yellow-orange glow from another streetlight. Together they picked up their pace, anxious to get to the streetlight.

They were almost there when they saw a silhouette at the other end of the lane moving in their direction. Perhaps if there were other people around it wouldn't have been unsettling to her. Julia kept walking. Laquita stopped.

"It's okay," Julia said in a low cautious voice. "I see a dog on a leash. He's just out walking his dog."

"That ain't no dawg. Looks more like a bear," scoffed Laquita. "Sides, I hate dawgs."

As the man with the large dog got closer, Julia hesitated. They had cleared the homes and a tall fence was on one side of them. The streetlight revealed a perpendicular alley on the other side. Maybe they should cut through that alley, she thought and make their way to the street.

Just keep moving she said to herself. She hoped Laquita couldn't see her face. It would have given away her real thoughts.

The man wore a short jacket, was almost as wide as he was tall and wore a baseball cap. The dog seemed to be walking him instead of the other way around.

Unexpectedly the dog barked. The sound echoed down

the lane.

Julia yanked on Laquita's arm, pulled her to the right and hustled into the alley toward the houses that lined the street parallel to the lane. She could hear hard rapid breaths coming from Laquita.

"Shit," whispered Julia. "Dead end." All the homes had backyard fences preventing them from cutting between them to gain access to D street. They'd have to go back to the lane and continue to D street.

When they turned to head back, Laquita accidentally knocked over a metal garbage can. The loud clanking noise alerted a neighbor who turned on a floodlight.

"Hurry up," Julia said to Laquita. "We're behind schedule."

Back in the lane, underneath the streetlight, she eased the loaded pistol from her purse and shoved it in her outside coat pocket.

"Damn," piped Laquita. "You didn' tell me you were packin'."

"Just in case."

"Gurl, you are Elke's granddaughter," snickered Laquita.

Mark Miller was the man who taught her how to use a pistol. Elke had him do it as a favor to her. She secretly had a crush on Mark. Unfortunately, she was a teenager and he was much older and married.

"Just stay close, okay?"

Before Laquita could respond, the night air filled with the sound of wailing sirens.

"Oh crap," Laquita said. "Somebody called the cops on us."

CHAPTER 43

Shockley was frustrated that he was no closer to solving the case than when it happened.

In the hospital lot, he parked, took a swig of coffee and started to get out when he caught sight of four men wearing FBI windbreakers. They were exiting through the large sliding glass door entrance. He swiftly shut the car door and studied the men.

Only one looked familiar to him. The man with white hair and glasses appeared pissed. It was Special Agent Sid Black.

He waited till the Fed's black Suburban pulled out of the lot before he made his way into the hospital. The FBI must have left instructions for hospital staff to contact them as soon as T-Bone and Amber Bull were able to talk.

T-Bone's room was on the third floor. When he opened the door, T-Bone was asleep in the dim lit room, metal bed rails pulled up. The pungent smell of antiseptics filled his nostrils as he stepped inside. T-Bone's head was still bandaged, but alot of the swelling on his face had gone down and the cervical collar had been removed. An IV bag hung from a metal stand with a drip line hooked to his arm. Once again, the sound and smells made his mind relive the times visiting his cancer-stricken dying mother.

There were several *Get Well* flower arrangements and one with balloons attached to it filling the windowsill. His boots clunked on the concrete floor as he made his way around the hospital bed over to the windowsill. He glanced at his friend making sure he was still asleep before he plucked a card out of a plastic pick. It read, *Get Well Soon, Love Claudette & Eric*

A strong voice hissed, "You doing detective work or just being a nosy bastard?"

Shockley pivoted on his heels and saw T-Bone grinning.

"Hey, big man. Thought you were asleep." He quickly reattached the card in the plastic pick.

"Had to be for the Feds. They got mad when I pretended to be drugged." T-Bone grunted.

"One of them called Special Agent Black?"

"Sounds bout right, Cowboy. I think he's the one who got in my face and told me I better cooperate, or he'd have my badge. A real prick."

"That's him."

"Are you and the ex on the mends?" Shockley nodded toward the flowers. "Claudette, right?"

"Yeah. I'm sure she did it for my kid's benefit. Eric's a good boy. But there's no love lost between me and the ex. She fooled around with a guy at work and then to top it off took me to the cleaners in the divorce."

Shockley dragged a chair over to the hospital bed and sat down. "You said come ASAP. Got something to tell me?"

"I do. First, I wanna know if the FBI lied about you being pulled off the case and now they have taken over the investigation."

"That's not a lie."

"What did Wheels have to say?"

"Not much. It wasn't his call. Agent Black said it had to do with National Security."

T-Bone's eyes closed, his face grimaced as his large

chest heaved inward. He let out a weak, low moan before continuing, "We lost a good officer in that explosion. I knew Manny Hernandez for over eleven years. After my divorce I spent holidays at his home with his wife and four kids. A good officer died for only one reason. He wasn't standing where I was that day."

"Don't beat yourself up T-Bone. You almost died too."

"Yeah, but I didn't. I want the son-of-a-bitch to pay for doing this to Manny and Bull."

"The Feds will get him. Even if we aren't on the case." Shockley felt his words trail off. He had to be careful what he said.

"Agent Black said something about national security to me too. I just murmured and pretended I couldn't stay awake. I figured he was blowing smoke up my ass to get me to tell him what I saw that day. Never trusted the Feds."

"Honestly, I don't know what this is all about, but there's this girl who has a detective agency. She was there that day."

"Whatya mean she was there? What girl?"

"Her name's Julia Bagal. Appears she was hired to do surveillance on a man who was supposedly cheating on his wife. The man was meeting his lover at Willow Oaks Motel."

"I don't get it. If the FBI have the photos and an eyewitness to the crime, why harass me?"

Shockley let out a long drawn out sigh, crossed his arms and leaned back in the chair. "I don't know. I don't think they have the photos she took."

"Could be they already ID'd the perp and want him to lead them to a bigger catch," added T-Bone.

"I thought of that. I've been trying to sort this out and the more I learn the less sense any of it makes."

"There's something that doesn't add up about this case," said T-Bone.

"Like what?"

"I saw the two bodies in the motel room. One vic was a male, tattoos and definitely a gang banger. The woman was in the wrong place."

"What makes you think that?"

"She was dressed conservative. Navy pinstriped slacks and matching blazer."

"Not a hooker then, maybe someone looking to score some drugs?"

T-Bone looked up at the ceiling and appeared uncomfortable. "You know what my first thought was when I saw that young woman lying on the motel floor?"

"What?"

T-Bone looked back at him and said, "A reporter doing a piece on drugs in our city. A reporter trying to expose the problems nobody wants to believe are as bad as we know them to be."

Shockley leaned forward in the chair, rested his elbows on his knees and clenched his hands together. He could feel the hairs on the back of his neck standing up.

Now it was more than a hunch that Chance Martin Stephens III and the murdered woman at the motel were connected. Hauser had found out that Stephens had driven from Nashville to check on his missing girlfriend who was a freelance reporter. It looked like T-Bone had unwittingly ID'd the woman.

Shockley contemplated his next move. He had mixed feelings about involving T-Bone in what was proving to be as Hauser called it a *shit-storm*. T-Bone had already given him all the intel he had.

"Odd place to meet," said Shockley.

"Maybe a kidnapping," argued T-Bone. "Maybe that's why the Feds are involved. If this is a national security issue, then the Feds would want all hands on deck including using local resources. They're holding out on us."

"Probably right about that. The issue is Agent Black has made it clear they aren't gonna play ball."

"At the present time, I might be stuck in this bed, but my mind still works like a cop. My instincts tell me you're holding out on me too. I have a right to know what's going on," said T-Bone.

Shockley sat straight up. The man lying in the bed was a good friend and a damn good officer. There was no way in hell he'd jeopardize T-Bone's career.

"Agent Black will be back."

"So what?"

"If you know what I've got and don't tell them, then you could lose your job and worse, prison time," Shockley's voice was strained.

"I figured as much. You don't need to protect me. I'm a big boy."

"It's more than your job at stake."

"Hauser's in on this? I shoulda known. T-Bone grunted. "And this national security bullshit. You believe that?"

"It doesn't matter what I believe. I just want to get to the truth. Whatever that is."

T-Bone used the remote to raise his bed. The movement caused him to wince. "This girl. Julia Bagal. Are you sweet on her?"

The question came out of nowhere and caught him off

guard. He shifted his eyes from T-Bone's face to the covers on the bed. "Sweet on her? Nobody says that anymore." He felt his neck grow warm and his jaw tighten.

"Us old farts do. You don't need to answer me. I see it on your face."

"I don't even know her and she's stubborn as a mule."

"A quality you like in your women." T-Bone snorted a laugh.

Shockley raised an eyebrow, shook his head and grinned.

"Take care of yourself big guy," he said, rising to his feet. "I'll check on you later."

He ambled to the door.

T-Bone yelled, his voice hoarse, "Hey Cowboy."

Shockley stopped and faced his friend.

"You catch that son-of-a-bitch."

† † †

After identifying himself, Shockley inquired at the nurse's station which room Bull was in. She was still in ICU in a medically induced coma. When he asked about her prognosis, the nurse said it was guarded.

Her name tag said Trudy. She offered to walk him down to Bull's room. While he shortened his stride to match hers, he mentally prepared himself for what he was about to see.

When the door to the ICU room was pushed open, he attempted to hide his surprise. Bull rarely talked about her personal life. What he knew about her came from other officers. Sitting next to her bed with a book in his hand was a guy with long auburn hair tucked behind his large ears. He didn't appear to be a lot older than himself. His first impression would have been this was Bull's son, but he knew she didn't have children. He'd heard she'd married a younger man. *Cradle-robber* was what one officer called her but warned Shockley not to ever joke about it in front of Bull.

The man's light gray eyes were magnified by the thick lenses in his black framed glasses. It was obvious he hadn't slept in days.

Nurse Trudy quickly handed out introductions. "Carl, this is Detective Shockley."

The man stood, revealing he was much taller than Shockley first thought. Maybe 6'4" with rolled up sleeves that revealed several tattoos. Not a guy he pictured Bull would marry. The man shot his hand out and gave him an overly strong handshake. "I'm Amber's husband. Good to meet you."

"Likewise, Carl."

"Amber told me a great deal about you. She has a lot of respect for you."

Shockley found himself staring at Bull. Her head bandaged, a tube in her mouth hooked up to a ventilator, several monitors and a bag hung on an IV pole were at the head of the bed. There were multiple electrodes taped to her chest and several monitors around her bed. He felt his eyes moisten.

"You should talk to her," Carl said.

Surprised, Shockley responded, "What?"

"I know it's hard to see her like this Detective, but studies have found that even though she can't respond, you should act as if she can understand you."

"Alright. What should I say?"

"Tell her who you are and that you hope she gets better. Knowing Amber, tell her that she's had enough time goofing off. You need her back on the case."

Shockley snorted. Carl was alright, he thought.

He moved to the side of the bed and leaned close, his mouth next to her ear. His voice low and his words only for Bull. If she really could hear him, she was going to kick his ass when she got well.

† † †

Walking down the hall toward the hospital exit, Shockley got annoyed. First, no matter which way he turned he couldn't get enough cell signal to call Hauser and find out what he had learned about Bambi. Second, seeing his friends in the hospital drained him emotionally. Third, he had to admit T-Bone hit a nerve when he implied Shockley was sweet on a woman he didn't know. Yeah, Julia Bagal was cute behind her bruises and she had a nice body. However, she was a pain in his backside, but he did want to protect her. That was what he did for a living. Protect the public.

After exiting the elevator into the lobby, he looked out the glass door exit and knew he'd lost track of time. The sunlight had been replaced by darkness.

His phone vibrated in his hand. Hauser.

Anxious to hear what Hauser had learned about Bambi he swiped the phone and sprinted for the exit to get a better signal.

The message caused him to stop right outside the hospital door.

Another homicide.

CHAPTER 44

A chorus of police car sirens lashed the night air signaling to Julia something was wrong.

This wasn't a neighbor reporting them to the police. Too many sirens. Something serious had happened.

She and Laquita hurried down the lane toward where it intersected with 15th Street. At the intersection there were two-story homes on both sides of the lane blocking their street view.

Julia stayed low and eased along the home facing the street on the north side of the lane. A row of tall shrubs alongside the home's front yard provided cover to peer around.

In the distance she saw the reflection of blue and red lights dancing off homes and treetops. Quickly she sized up the situation to figure out their next move. She was too far away to see what had happened. One possibility of why there were so many police cars made her chest hurt.

"Laquita. Listen to me. We've got to get closer and find out what happened."

"Ya think somethin' happened to Lester?"

"There's only one way to find out."

Laquita rubbed the scar on her forehead.

Julia asked, "You okay?"

Laquita shook her head. "I got a bad feeling."

"Let's not jump to conclusions. You can stay here if you'd like and I'll check it out."

"I should go with ya. It's just all 'em police make me

nervous."

Only one of them needed to find out what had happened. She placed a hand on Laquita's arm.

"Partners work together. If you stay here, you can keep an eye out for anything suspicious. You still have the phone we got you the other day when we went to your apartment, right?"

"Yeah." Laquita reached around and got her phone out from her back-jean pocket. "I'll call you if I see anythin' that gives me the willies."

She looked up the street. "It's not that far. I'll be right back." Julia forced a smile.

She didn't allow herself to think the worst. Cautiously, she stepped out on the sidewalk and headed toward the parade of lights, her senses on full alert. Every step closer, she tried to determine if the commotion was at the location where they were supposed to meet Lester.

If this didn't involve Lester, he would have taken off when he heard the sirens.

Hurrying along the walkway, a bright red door to her right swung open before she passed by. A round man, barefoot and wearing an unwrapped bathrobe, stepped outside onto his concrete porch.

"Hey," the man yelled. "You know what's going on?" He seemed indifferent that his oversized beer belly and tighty-whities were on display. Not to mention it was cold outside.

"No," she said. "Hopefully nothing serious."

"Probably that ol' woman on the corner. She calls the cops every time the wind rattles her door."

"Maybe that's it, but that's a lot of sirens, don't you think?"

The round man mumbled something as he headed back inside and slammed his door.

She hoped Laquita's suspicion was wrong. If Lester was in trouble, they were in trouble.

The parked cars and trees on the street obstructed her view from the rendezvous spot. A crowd of curious gawkers had gathered on the sidewalk. Some of them wrapped in heavy robes, most in coats. She hustled along keeping vigilant of her surroundings.

She stopped when she heard one couple say, "Do you think something happened to Amy or Theodore? He does have a heart condition."

"Excuse me," she interrupted. "Which house do Amy and Theodore live in?"

The woman averted her eyes from Julia and said, "The recently remodeled blue Victorian home."

"Do you know the address?"

"No. Not their address." The older woman pointed. "It's the one just around the corner, across from the playground."

"Do you know them?" asked the woman.

Julia ignored her and continued toward the crime scene. She felt a rush of relief.

Maybe this wasn't about Lester after all.

† † †

Shockley hit the gas pedal and sped out of the hospital parking lot headed to the crime scene. What bothered him was the crime scene wasn't far from where Julia Bagal lived. If the homicide was connected to her in any way, he needed to get there fast. He activated his emergency lights and sirens.

He was more than twenty minutes out. This might be the break he needed to blow the case wide open.

Shockley thumbed the number on his cell while he kept his eyes trained on the traffic in front of him. He needed to catch up with Hauser who was already on the scene.

"Hauser," he began. "What's going on?"

"Thankfully the media hasn't arrived."

"What do we know?"

"Caucasian. Male. Mid-seventies. No ID. Took one to the right temple. The bullet exit shattered the driver's side window. Looks like the killer was next to the victim in the passenger seat."

"Witnesses?"

"A man who lives a couple houses down. He came outside to investigate, saw the blood and called 9-1-1."

"Did he see anybody leaving the scene?"

"No. Pretty shook up though. Says this is a friendly quiet neighborhood."

"Have the plates been run?"

"As we speak."

"I want eyes on the ground for Julia Bagal. Twenty-nine, long brown hair, blue eyes, thin, 5'6". She might be with another woman. Black, short hair, 5'8", full figure."

"Lot of people out here, Mike, but not seeing anybody matching that description. You think she's involved?"

"A violent crime in a friendly quiet neighborhood is a red flag. And she lives just a couple blocks over from the park." Maybe he was jumping the gun. Just because she lived walking distance from the crime didn't mean she was involved.

"If I see Julia Bagal, you want me to detain her?"

"Yeah. She could be in danger."

"10-4."

"Any sign of the Feds?"

"Not yet."

"If you see a male who limps and looks suspicious, I want him detained as a person of interest."

"Want me to hold his hands to see if they're rough?"

"Just work the crowd smart ass and find me a witness."

"Copy that."

There was a problem with this case, he thought. If they are related, why'd the killer delay blowing up the room at the motel. Why wait?

Kill cops?

Then why not blow up Chance Martin Stephens' car when the officers showed up? Blowing things up and killing cops was the MO for two different gangs in town. And neither gang's territory was near the crime scene. Maybe the perp wanted the cops to believe it was gangs fighting a turf war. Amber Bull had taught him the ABCs of a crime scene. Assume nothing. Believe nobody. Check everything.

Right now, he needed to find the guy with the limp.

† † †

When Julia walked up to the crime scene the crowd was being managed by uniformed cops securing the area. The thick throng of bystanders obstructed her view. Maybe Lester wasn't involved. Hopefully he heard sirens and left.

She pulled her phone out of her pocket and checked. No calls or messages from Lester or the Bridge Club.

Word rapidly spread through the crowd about what had happened. One woman bundled in what looked like a man's coat and wearing fuzzy bedroom slippers said she heard somebody was murdered.

"Do you know if it was an older man?" Julia asked.

"Oh dear." The woman's face contorted with pity when she saw Julia's face.

Julia's hand shot up to her eye. "Slipped and fell in my living room the other night. My roommate likes to rearrange furniture."

The woman's eyes said *I don't believe you,* but she didn't press the issue. "Does somebody you know live there, dear?"

"Yes. My uncle."

The woman's hand squeezed her arm. "Let's pray it wasn't him. Maybe it was somebody who doesn't even live in our neighborhood."

Annoyed, Julia pulled away and thanked the woman. She snaked her way through the crowd until she saw the car. Her heart stopped. She wanted to throw up.

Her hope that Lester wasn't involved vanished.

CHAPTER 45

L ester was dead.

    Julia had just met Lester earlier today. He was the man parked outside her home. The man from the Bridge Club. The one she asked to help her.

She heard the orders from the police to clear the area, but she wasn't ready to leave. On the other side of the crime scene, there was a uniformed officer talking into the radio mic attached to his vest. Next to him she spotted a young skinny man dressed in jeans, a dark windbreaker with long hair pulled back in a ponytail.

He wasn't leaving either.

He was doing the same thing she was doing, scanning the bystanders, many of them pressed against the barricades trying to capture the crime scene with their cellphones. Even though he wasn't in uniform, he was standing behind the crime scene tape by other policemen and talking to them. He had to be a plainclothes cop.

Instinctively, she drifted back behind a tall man to shield her from the young cop's view. Her eyes continued to travel across the remaining people, most of them slow to withdraw from all the excitement. They seemed the kind of neighbors who liked to gossip. Several were trying to get information from the uniformed officers.

She looked to the right of the plainclothes cop and saw a man who sent goosebumps racing up her arms. A tall man with dark eyes. He wore a dark fedora. A cigarette dangled from his large lips. Not only was he not moving away from the area, his eyes seemed to have settled on her. The hardened look on the man's face made her panic. Could he be the one who killed Lester? Pretty ballsy to stay at the crime scene. Unless.

Unless he was waiting for his real target.

Her.

Shoving her hand in her coat pocket, she wrapped her hand around the pistol grip. She shifted to the side of the tall man in order to see what the plainclothes cop was doing. He was walking away and headed in the same direction as another man. She had to elbow her way out of the crowd to see who the cop might be following. When she was able to get a better look, the plainclothes cop was already out of sight. She glanced back in the direction of the tall man wearing the fedora. He was gone.

Her muscles twitched uncontrollably. She began to shake. Where was he? She twisted around, making a 360-degree turn. He had vanished into the shadows of the night.

She spun on her heels. gripped the pistol tighter and started back the way she came. A few people tried to stop her to see if she knew what had happened. Their words didn't register, they sounded hollow. She picked up her pace.

She snagged her phone from her coat pocket and was going to call Laquita when it buzzed.

Assuming it was Laquita, she quickly answered, "Laquita, I'm almost…."

The voice on the other end cut in.

"Julia, this is the Bridge Club. We've lost contact with Lester. Where are you?"

"Lester's dead," her unsteady voice replied.

✝ ✝ ✝

Shockley thought he was taking the fastest route to the homicide scene, but soon realized traffic was a problem. Cars in front of him were pulling to the side, but the number of vehicles on the street was slowing him down.

He'd be there in five if the woman driver in front of him would look in her rear-view mirror. *Was she deaf?*

His cell began buzzing. Before he could identify himself, Hauser blurted out, "Does she have a black eye?"

The question caught him off guard. "Who?"

"Julia Bagal."

"Probably." The last time he saw her, her eye was swollen with purple yellow bruising. By now her eye probably looked like a black eye.

Hauser continued, "There's a shit load of old people limping around here. I followed the wrong guy. After I was threatened with 'I'll have your badge' from some old guy, who by the way is related to the Mayor, I had one of the uniforms tell me when I got back that a woman had told him some young girl with a black eye was asking about the crime scene. She'd never seen her in the neighborhood before and thought she might know the victim."

"Did the woman see which direction Julia came from?"

"Negative. Just stated she suspected there might be a connection. Said the young girl was acting weird. Like she'd seen a ghost or something."

"I want you to recruit eyes for the area. If it was Julia Bagal then her life's probably in danger."

"Already got officers checking the area."

"You search to the north and west around the playground. I'll take south and east. I should be there in 5." *If this damn woman would get out of my way.*

The woman driver in front finally looked in her rearview mirror. She stopped. Shockley slammed on the brakes, barely missing a rear end collision.

"Dammit." *She thinks I'm pulling her over and stops in the middle of the road.* He honked his horn several times. "Get out of my way or I'm gonna run your ass over," he yelled knowing the driver couldn't hear a word.

Slowly she eased her vehicle over allowing him enough room to go around. The old woman wasn't a woman. It was an elderly man who could barely see over the steering wheel.

He stomped the gas pedal, his car racing past the elderly driver. Just a couple more minutes and he'd be there. His adrenaline was pumping as he had one thought rolling in his head, don't let this bastard get away or harm Julia. He knew Hauser had it handled on his end.

When he was close to the crime scene, he turned east and headed south. He killed his siren and emergency lights so he wouldn't alert the perp.

The guy was still in the area.

He could feel it.

† † †

There was an extended pause on the line while Julia waited for a response from the Bridge Club. She was certain the woman on the phone was in shock about Lester's murder. She heard muffled voices in the background. Maybe they were trying to figure out what she should do.

Finally, it came. "Get back to your house. We'll be in touch soon." The woman clicked off.

That was it? That's all?

She wasn't even given a chance to tell the woman about the creepy man she saw at the crime scene. And that he might be involved. Or that he might have been waiting on her to meet with Lester. Maybe the club was going to notify Elke since she had refused to go to a safe house and now the man she was supposed to meet had been murdered? Right now, she wasn't sure how she felt about anything.

There were more porch and floodlights on than earlier as she hustled back in the direction she had just come from. The walk back felt like it was taking longer. Perhaps it was the dread of telling Laquita that everything had gone to shit, and a good man had paid the price trying to help them.

Looking ahead she saw no sign of Laquita at the entrance to Kathryn Lane. Maybe she was sitting down beside the shrubbery next to the alley. *How on earth could she see anything suspicious sitting on her butt.* Her irritation with Laquita grew.

She rounded the corner of the shrubs and stood idle in the lane.

Laquita wasn't here.

She crept into the darkness of the lane. She paused long enough to let her eyes adjust to the darkness.

She whispered, "Laquita, we need to get back to the house."

No response.

She descended deeper into the lane calling, "Laquita."

Silence.

Would Laquita have gone back to the house? She checked her phone log. Nothing. *Come on Laquita, where are you? At least call me.*

That was it. She needed to call Laquita. Lester's murder and the strange man wearing the fedora had distracted her focus. Just calm down and get a grip, she told herself. She pulled her phone and called Laquita.

A gust of cool wind tunneled down Kathryn Lane muting a sound she thought she heard in the distance. Tapping her foot, she pressed the phone harder against her ear. After what seemed like too many rings, Laquita's phone went to voice mail.

Her stomach lurched. This wasn't good. Laquita should have answered.

She eased the pistol out of her coat pocket. Crouching, she used a two-handed grip and aimed the barrel straight ahead.

In her peripheral she caught a streak of movement near the dead-end alley to her left. She caught her breath and proceeded forward. The streetlight casted eerie shadows across the alley entrance.

The open area was flanked by an oversized shed on one side. She shoved her back against the shed that extended into the alley. She kept low to make herself a smaller target. Her pistol trained in front of her. Her weapon and self-defense classes were like learning to ride a bicycle, you never forget how to do it.

Cautiously she eased along the side of the shed toward the back of row houses. This was the same place she and Laquita tried to cross earlier that evening but were blocked by backyard fences—the dead-end alley. Floodlights on several of the homes lit up their yards, but most of the space was dark.

She thought about calling out Laquita's name but decided against it. At the corner of the shed, she took a step away, pulled out the small mag light and shined across the area while keeping her pistol pointed straight ahead. She didn't see anything and decided to move back to the lane when she heard a high-pitched primeval shriek.

She jumped and lost her footing causing her to fall against the shed, her eyes stretched open. Breathing hard, she pointed the light and her weapon toward the sound. Fleeing past her was a large furry cat.

She stood still, her heart pounding. She blinked and slowly breathed deeply. After she caught her breath, she again attempted to call Laquita. The phone kept ringing. She started to pocket the phone when her eyes caught a glimpse of a light shining in a patch of grass near where she was standing.

The light disappeared. She immediately hit Laquita's number again and saw the light shine against the blades of grass. She raced over to the light.

It was Laquita's phone.

She raised her pistol and swept the area. There was no sign of Laquita. She had to act fast and smart.

Her friend's life was in danger.

CHAPTER 46

He needed a bit of luck right now. Hopefully this wouldn't end up being like other cases he'd been on where he felt he was near to closing in on the target, only to find out the perp had outsmarted him.

Shockley eased his car down the street craning his neck to check both sides of the street. He needed to find the man he believed was the killer and Julia. Hopefully not together.

The street was quiet. His thumbs tapped hard against the steering wheel as he cruised past small yards and inviting homes. A few of the homes emitted a glow from a TV set through open curtains. People sitting inside the safety of their home unaware of what was happening in their own neighborhood.

He'd never been on this street before. There were cars parked nose to tail along the curb on both sides of the narrow road. Right now, he had no clear idea of where to search. There were too many places a perp could disappear and lurk in the shadows. Hell, for all he knew, the perp could be hiding behind a bush right now watching him drive by.

In a perfect world he'd lock down the area and issue a BOLO for the man he believed to be the killer. Yet without a description, all he had was the guy smoked and limped. Without any hard evidence it wouldn't fly. This was like trying to fight a three-alarm fire with a squirt gun.

Most of the older two-story homes were attached. One of the homes was under construction. Looked like it was being gutted from the inside out. Transitional neighborhoods were what people liked to call it. In D.C. what that meant was there were nice homes mingled among dilapidated homes in desperate need of fixing up. Some of the homes had iron bars on the windows indicating that there was crime, even in this part of the city. Or at least used to be. Overall the street was deserted except for an occasional dog walker or runner.

His cell phone started chirping.

"I'm headed to check out the area to the west and north," said Hauser. "Several uniforms on foot are checking the south and east side around the crime scene area, and I've got a couple of guys trying to scrounge up witnesses around here."

"Is the crime scene locked down?"

"Barricades are up. Perimeter secure. Forensics is here and the crowd is slowly thinning out."

"Good. I've seen nothing suspicious. I'm gonna circle back around and check some of the alleyways I see on my GPS."

"10-4."

When Shockley rounded the corner onto the street which led toward the crime scene, he could see in the distance a host of cruisers, their red and blue lights whirling. This was a one-way street with a designated bike lane. Most of the neighborhood homes had their porch lights on, lighting up their yards and sidewalks. Even this far from the crime scene neighbors wanted to feel safe and a porch light was a good first line of defense.

There was an alleyway up ahead, a short distance on his left. He slowed to a stop and studied his GPS map which indicated the back alley snaked its way between and behind houses till it dumped onto a street at the far end of the park. It'd be a good escape route for the perp. He started to commit turning down the alley when he noticed a couple walking out of the corridor with a medium sized dog that at first glance resembled a German Shepherd.

He stepped out of the car with his badge in hand and carefully approached the couple. The dog sat down on a command from the woman.

"I'm Officer Mike Shockley. There's been a shooting near the park, and I was wondering if you've seen anybody suspicious?"

The young woman answered, "We just came from there Heard somebody was murdered inside a vehicle. Might be drug related. We're headed back home."

Shockley pointed behind them. "Did you see anyone in the alley? Pass anyone?"

They looked at each other and shook their heads in unison. The woman spoke up, "No, we were the only ones."

"Is there a problem with drugs in this area?" Shockley asked.

"Not really a problem, but I have heard of drugs being sold in the park. And some of the people at the crime were saying they thought that's what might have happened. A drug robbery."

"Did either of you see a man with a limp tonight?"

"No sir. Are we in danger?" The couple shared a concern look.

"I'd advise you head on home for now. I appreciate the information." He pulled out a card from his coat pocket and handed it to them. "Call if you notice any suspicious activity."

He had no need to check this alleyway. The couple said drugs were sold in the park. He wondered where in the city drugs weren't sold. He'd arrested a preacher using his church as a front to make drug deals.

He climbed back in his car and continued up the street. There was another road, Kathryn Lane, on his right. His GPS showed this one intersected a street he had not driven down. And if he continued across the street to the next alley it would take him to the street Julia lived on. Maybe Julia had been at the crime scene? And if she had, he wanted to find out if she had any connection to the victim?

One possibility was Julia could have taken this short cut over to the park to meet the victim. And she might have taken it back to get home. Hopefully the perp didn't follow her.

He turned into the lane, headlights breaking through the darkness. There were no oncoming vehicles which allowed him to continue down the narrow one-lane passage. In his peripheral he saw a porch door swing open. An elderly hunched woman with a plaid blanket draped over her shoulders and what resembled a fur trapper hat stepped out. She peered down the street toward the crime scene. He stopped, lowered his car window and yelled at the woman to get her attention.

"Ma'am." He shoved his badge out the window. "Officer Mike Shockley. Did you see anybody walk down this way tonight?"

She slowly turned and pulled the blanket tight against her chest. She stretched her neck forward struggling to see what he was holding. He thought he should get out when she cautiously ambled to the side of her porch. "You looking for that young policeman who knocked on my door?"

"Yes. Did he walk down this alleyway?"

She used one hand to push her glasses up on the bridge of her nose. Her thin, breathy voice said, "I told him to be careful."

"How long ago was that?"

"A little while ago."

"Did you see anybody else enter this alley tonight?"

She shook her head. "No. I haven't seen anybody but him, and now you."

"Thank you, ma'am. You better get back inside. Keep your doors locked.'

She nodded. "You be careful too," she warned.

He put his vehicle in gear and drove down the lane with his high beams illuminating the road ahead. He didn't see any sign of the uniform. Maybe the officer had already walked the entire alleyway and had exited onto the street.

He had an uneasy feeling.

Something was off.

CHAPTER 47

He blinked his eyes open and examined the dull sterile room. He felt an intense loss for his father. A feeling he thought was gone.

He had been in a room like this when he was thirteen. Only this time it was him lying in the hospital bed, not his father.

When he raised his hand to scratch his nose, the attached IV got caught on the bed railing. He remembered seeing his father attached to IV's, heart monitors and oxygen. Just like he was now.

His father had been getting ready for work when he had a massive heart attack. Wagner was picked up from school by a neighbor and taken to the hospital. His mother met him in the waiting room and told him his father had quadruple by-pass surgery. He recalled the fear and guilt he had when he was allowed to see his father after surgery. The night before, he and his father had gotten into a heated argument about something. Something he could no longer remember. There were lots of arguments with his parents during his teen years.

Closing his eyes, he tried to clear his mind and concentrate on his situation. Not on his health, but how he could get out of the mess he was in with Razor. If only Razor would die, he thought. All his problems would go away.

He'd have to figure out how to handle Megan. Did she really care for him? She called 9-1-1 and stayed with him at the hospital for hours until he finally ordered her to go home and get some rest.

He told himself she cared. He needed her to care. Right now, he had nobody.

"Alan, how are you doing?" A voice boomed from the door.

He was so deep in thought he didn't hear Dan Quatterman come in. This was the last person on earth he wanted to see right now.

"Megan told me what happened? Are you okay?"

"Yeah Dan, I'm fine." A strange thought popped in his head—*I'd be a lot better if you could arrange to kill somebody for me.* The idea made him smirk.

"Good to see you smile. What are the doctors saying?"

"Looks like I'll live. But they want to keep me here a couple of days for observation and run some more tests since I have a family history of heart disease."

"Thank goodness. I just couldn't believe it when I heard what happened. A lot of people are very concerned about you. You made the news."

"Well, I hope it was good press."

"Megan made sure of that. She really takes care of you. Wish I had an assistant like her."

I bet you do.

A light rap on the door right before a doctor pushed it open. Dr. King was an older woman. She wore a white lab coat over green scrubs. There were wrinkles etched in her forehead and around her eyes. Late fifties maybe. He had no skill at gauging a person's age. She wore her gray hair short above her ears. Her deep-set brown eyes serious but kind. A pair of reading glasses hung from a chain around her neck.

She addressed him first even though Quatterman moved

in an attempt to introduce himself.

"How are you feeling Mr. Wagner?"

"Great. You going to release me now?"

Quatterman couldn't stand being side-lined. Wedging himself between the hospital bed and the doctor, he shoved his meaty hand out. "Hello. I'm Congressman Dan Quatterman. Alan and I are close friends."

No, we're not, Wagner wanted to say. Instead he gave a weak smile and fought the urge to roll his eyes.

She extended her hand and shook Quatterman's hand. "Good to meet you. I'm Dr. Beth King, Speaker Wagner's attending physician."

Then she slid her hands in her white coat pocket and turned her attention to him. "Mr. Wagner, due to HIPPA compliance I have to ask if you want me discuss your medical condition with Congressman Quatterman present in the room?"

This was as good as any excuse to get rid of the man. "Dan, do you mind giving the doctor and me a few minutes?"

"No problem. I understand. I have to get back to the office anyway." Quatterman turned to the doctor and said, "It was nice meeting you. Take good care of our Speaker of the House."

Dr. King nodded.

After Quatterman left, the doctor continued, "The good news is your electrocardiogram was normal. I do want to run a few more tests since you have a family history of heart disease. The not so good news is we did find that you're severely dehydrated and you have high blood pressure." She pointed to the IV. "We're giving you fluids to rehydrate you. Your bloodwork reveals your blood sugar levels are higher than normal. This is probably a result of the dehydration. Therefore, I'd like to do more bloodwork after you've rehydrated. I think with some lifestyle changes, it's possible to control your high blood pressure."

He appreciated the fact that Dr. King communicated the results of his health in a calm and knowledgeable manner.

"What kind of lifestyle changes are we talking about?" he asked.

"Exercise regularly, eat a healthy diet, reduce the sodium in your diet, cut back on caffeine, and reduce your stress. Do you have any questions for me?"

"Yes. Do you have any idea when I'll be discharged?"

"In the next day or two. Depends on what the other tests show. Right now, you need to rest. I'm sure a lot of what brought you to us is stress related."

She has no idea.

He shot a glance at a man he recognized standing guard outside his hospital room. The thick neck man in uniform was talking to a young nurse.

The doctor noticed his interest and said, "He says he's your protection detail."

"That's correct. He's Capitol Police."

"Have you had threats on your life recently?"

"A third to half of my colleagues receive threats depending on what they're working on."

"Sounds like a dangerous and stressful job keeping our government running."

"Unfortunately, it can be at times." *And deadly,* he added to himself.

"I have rounds to make. If you don't have any other questions, I'll see you again tomorrow."

"None at this time. Thanks Dr. King."

The doctor turned toward the door, just as Megan entered.

"Good to see you again, Dr. King."

"Nice to see you." The doctor disappeared down the hall.

"You look much better today," Megan said with a smile stretched across her face. In her hands was a vase of colorful flowers with a balloon attached.

Trying hard not to be obvious, he noted that Megan looked especially attractive in the slim gray slacks, a leather jacket with a deep purple shirt underneath.

"You didn't need to get me flowers. I'll be out of here in another day or two."

"It was no problem. Have they set your discharge date?"

"More or less."

After she placed the vase on the windowsill, she walked over to his bedside, and placed a hand on the bedrail.

"You gave me quite a scare, Alan."

"I feel bad I got angry with you yesterday. The stress of the job and the investigation is getting to me. I was afraid I might have jeopardized the FBI's investigation by foolishly leaving that note on my desk. It's important we tread very cautiously right now."

"I'm sure nobody saw it besides me. You don't need to worry. I haven't told a soul." Her tongue wet her full lips.

Was she trying to be seductive or was she nervous? He wished he could read her. There was something she wasn't telling him. But, if she had told somebody about the note, like the authorities, he'd be handcuffed to his hospital bed.

Maybe he was over thinking this.

"Can I get you anything?"

He gestured toward the pitcher of water on the metal tray. "A drink of water would be nice. My throat's very dry."

She filled the cup with the pitcher of water, his eyes

catching her every move. He liked watching her.

When she handed him the Styrofoam cup, he made sure his hands touched her delicate fingers.

"Thank you." He took several sips and noticed her face had relaxed.

With his eyes boring into hers, he said, "I don't have any family still living. You being here means a lot to me."

She searched his eyes, her brows furrowed. "I thought you had an uncle who recently had a heart attack."

He tilted the cup draining the liquid while his mind struggled to devise a cover up lie. The problem with lying is you have to remember the lie for the next time you lie.

"I do have an uncle, but he's not a biological uncle. He was a very close family friend when I was growing up. As a little kid, my parents would call him Uncle Frank and it stuck. I was a teenager before I realized it was just a nickname. I care very much for him. It's just not the same as having family."

"Oh. I understand. I have friends that I'm super close to."

She held his gaze and then looked away. "I guess I better get back to the office." She pulled the well fitted leather jacket snug across her chest as if she suddenly felt self-conscious. "I'm sure you need your rest. Call me if you need to talk. Or if there's anything at the office I can help you with."

Need to talk? What did that mean?

"Thanks Megan. I feel good knowing you're holding down the fort."

She turned and left.

He mumbled as he watched her walk down the hall, "Loose ends."

CHAPTER 48

Shockley cruised down the narrow lane. If the uniformed officer had cut down this passageway, he should see him any minute now.

Sandwiched between the two-story buildings made him feel vulnerable. This cold-blooded killer was no amateur. He could be hiding behind a building, waiting for him to drive by. The element of surprise was an advantage.

Without his Glock in his hand, his reaction time would be slower. With a hand on the steering wheel, he used his other to unsnap his holster and withdraw his Glock. Fortunately, he wouldn't be between the tall buildings for much longer.

He didn't know the officer who was canvassing this area, but hoped he was a seasoned cop and not a rookie. A sense of dread ramped up his nerves. He didn't want another cop not reporting to duty tomorrow weighing on his conscience.

Halfway down the lane, he saw a glow from a tall metal streetlight partially illuminating the entrance to an alley on his left. Maybe the uniform had gone into that area to check it out and that's why he didn't see him in the lane. He edged the car to the opening and stopped. Peering out the driver's window, he didn't see any movement. He did see a lot of places where the perp could be hiding.

He got out with his Glock in hand and quietly closed the car door. A rush of night air brushed against his face. He stooped low, keeping his weapon aimed straight ahead and ready. With his senses on high alert he crept deeper into the dark alley.

After rounding a building that looked like an oversized storage shed, the light from the streetlamp diminished. A smattering of household floodlights was on, but he couldn't see shit in most of the surrounding area. He stepped back and removed his powerful Maglite from his jacket. With a hand on his weapon and the other on the Maglite, he swept the area from left to right. His light flickered on litter strewn across the ground. Car parts, a rusty bike, a washing machine and a pile of old tires had been dumped back here. All the back yards had wooden fences around them. He figured these homeowners didn't want to have a view of a mini landfill.

It looked like the only way to pass through here to the next street over was to jump fences and hope like hell there weren't any dogs in the backyards. He was sure it wouldn't be a choice unless it was the only choice.

Convinced nobody was hiding in the alley, he tried to size up the situation. Maybe the uniform had already cleared this alley, left the lane and was now checking the intersecting street.

Something felt wrong.

But there was nothing here.

He decided to head back to his car and continue his search out to the street.

After he holstered his Glock, he quickly turned and stumbled into a large object. He fell hard against a plastic trash can that toppled over causing the attached lid to flip open. A dog started barking and a backdoor light flickered on. A woman yelled, "Shut up Reggie. Be quiet." The dog continued to bark.

He stood and started to get the hell out of there when he saw what looked like a person that had unfolded out of the trash can. He angled his Maglite over the body that was half in and half out of the can. He squatted and quickly pressed his fingers to the uniform's neck.

The young police officer was dead.

† † †

E asing from Kathryn Lane onto the sidewalk, she felt a jolt of adrenaline that broke her whole body out in a sweat.

Down the street standing on the sidewalk near the corner was the man in the fedora.

And he had Laquita.

The man had his hand on Laquita's arm keeping her close to him as they walked down the street. Laquita looked back where Julia was standing. The man twisted in her direction.

"Run Julia," yelled Laquita.

She did. But not in the direction Laquita meant. Her legs took off before her brain caught up. Instead of taking cover, she was running down the sidewalk toward Laquita and her captor. In the open. She pulled up short from a streetlight, not wanting to be a more visible target. The man put Laquita in a choke hold. His other hand held a semi-automatic muzzle jammed against her temple.

She studied the man's features, unsure if he was the man she saw at the motel. She imagined the worst. If he kidnapped Laquita, Julia might never see her again. If she took a shot at the man, it'd have to be to the head. She didn't like her options.

The closer she got, the easier it would be for him to shoot her. *Focus.* What she needed was to buy some time. She could accurately hit a target, but this one had a human shield in front of it. Mark Miller, the guy who taught her how to shoot targets from every angle, even moving targets had never trained her on what to do in a hostage situation.

What Mark did teach her was never focus on the target's weapon. Only on the target.

She aimed her pistol at the man's head, sucked in several breaths and edged cautiously forward.

The cool breeze evaporated the beads of sweat on her forehead. She tightened her grip on the pistol keeping it aimed straight ahead.

"Close enough, Julia. Stop right there or I'll pull the trigger," he ordered. His voice chillier than the night air.

She stopped.

"The police will be here soon," she warned.

He let out a deep grunt. "Put the gun down. You don't want to be responsible for your friend being killed."

"What do you want?"

"I want you. And I want all the photos you took. It's just that simple."

"I don't know what you're talking about. You're mistaken."

"I don't have time for games. The old man told me everything. Not easily, but he finally talked."

"You can have them, but first let Laquita go."

"I give the orders, not you," barked the killer.

"I'm sure we can agree you want what I have, but I want Laquita freed first."

"My bargaining chip is better than yours. Mine has a heartbeat. At least for now."

Julia surprised the killer by taking a step forward.

He shoved the muzzle harder against Laquita's head. Her friend yelped. She stopped, keeping her weapon aimed at the man's head.

"You already got that nice 'ol man killed. How much blood do you want on your hands? Drop your weapon. The deal is you for your friend and, of course, the photos."

Another step forward.

"Julia don't do it," Laquita said with a panicky edge in her tone. "'Em photos is all that's keepin' us alive."

She could now see his burning eyes. The scar above his brow. The only facial feature she recognized was the man's full lips and slightly flared nostrils. He was right that he had the stronger bargaining chip, but if he killed Laquita, he was a dead man.

Even though the police weren't far away, she couldn't gamble on them arriving in time. This was bad at every level. If she got closer, her shot would be more accurate. This guy wasn't going to let Laquita walk away.

"I'll do what you want." She took another step. "You can have the photos, take me hostage, but first…"

"Another fucking step and she's dead."

Even after his warning, she knew what to do.

As if Laquita had read her mind, she yelled, "Julia. Don't shoot."

He tightened his grip around Laquita's throat causing her to gasp for air.

"Shut up," he ordered Laquita. "Or I'll pull the trigger and blow your brains out."

Laquita's hands futilely tugged on the arm wrapped around her neck. She gagged, desperately trying to breathe. Her eyes bulged wide.

The man was powerful and angry. *He's choking her.* She felt panic.

"Stop," she pleaded. "She can't breathe."

He kept his arm tight around Laquita's neck. Laquita gasping.

"You're gonna kill her," Julia yelled.

The corner of his mouth pulled up in mock amusement

The bastard is enjoying this.

Slowly he lightened his grip around Laquita's neck. She began coughing and gasping for air.

"You're smarter than I thought. But not smart enough. You made a bad decision."

He began to drag Laquita backwards toward a car parked by the curb. That's when she caught sight of movement out of the corner of her eye. Somebody was across the street. The shadow figure was using the parked cars for cover. She held her eyes on the man dragging Laquita.

She steadied her aim. Waiting for an opportunity.

Suddenly a sound sent Julia's heartbeat into a roaring frenzy.

CHAPTER 49

The skinny uniformed officer's neck had been snapped. His lifeless eyes open. His attacker was strong. Shockley knew it took violent force to kill a person this way.

The body dumped in the trash receptacle was still warm. The killer wasn't far from here. Shockley wanted to call it in, but the officer's radio was missing, so the killer now had ears. He wasn't about to alert him.

He drew his Glock and headed toward the passageway. In his other hand he thumbed Hauser's number on his cell.

After several rings the call went to voice mail. *Shit.* He must have it on silent.

Shockley left a brief message, filling Hauser in. A uniform DRT, officer's radio missing, maintain radio silence, he was in pursuit and gave his approximate location. Hopefully Hauser would discover the message and ride in with backup. But right now, he couldn't wait for the cavalry. Every second counted.

He was on his own.

He raced back to his car, jumped in and started the engine. The perp could still be in the passageway or on the street or worse, at Julia's house. A lot of ground to cover. He drove as slow as his adrenaline rush would allow, rubber necking back and forth as he continued down the alley.

Shockley slowed before he got to where the alley intersected the street and clicked on his low-beam lights.

What he saw when he eased out of the alley caused fear to

surge through him. "Things just got a lot more complicated," Shockley said aloud. There was nothing more difficult than a hostage situation.

Except when there was a hostage situation with a citizen in the line of fire of the suspect.

It had to be Julia Eagal he saw standing under the streetlight in a firing stance. Her weapon aimed at the man holding a gun muzzle against a Black woman's head.

There'd be no negotiation for the release of the hostage.

The suspect was approximately fifty yards down the street. The man was wearing a fedora. He was tall and bulky. Strong guy. A good thing the street was quiet at this hour of the evening.

His choices were limited.

Think.

Without slowing, he drove straight ahead, crossing the street and into the lane across the street. It didn't really matter if the perp noticed him. He had no choice. Hopefully, the perp was focused on Julia's weapon pointing at him and didn't pay much attention to his car.

Once he had his car out of sight, he killed the engine and jumped out. He lowered his Glock and peered around the corner of the building facing the street.

He had no backup, nobody watching his six. At this moment he could rely only on himself. He stayed low, kept his eyes alert and sprinted toward the parked car nearest him. Crouching on the sidewalk across the street from Julia and the target, he moved stealthily, using parked cars as cover.

He needed to position himself for the kill shot. A head shot, risky unless at close range. Normally he'd aim for the target's largest body mass, the torso, but the hostage was in front of him and a round to the target's back could exit and strike the hostage.

He wanted this guy alive, but tonight it wasn't going to happen. He was trained to only use lethal force when there was imminent threat of harm to himself or others. All boxes had been checked on that requirement. This suspect was armed and dangerous.

He was counting on the target being unaware of his presence. He needed a clean line of sight to deliver the kill shot to the target's head. In a gunfight his accuracy could be the difference between life or death for him, the hostage and Julia. He blew out a puff of air.

In several long quick strides, he closed enough distance to give him the advantage shot he needed.

The suspect was walking backwards dragging his hostage with him toward a car. The Black woman looked like Laquita which meant that was Julia. He had no way of knowing if Julia knew how to use the weapon she was holding, but from the way she held the pistol his bet was this wasn't the first time she had used a weapon.

He had to act fast. He repositioned himself beside a Honda Accord and squatted down.

Quickly he made sure there was a round in the chamber. Check.

He rose and used the hood of the car to steady his hands.

Across the street, the target's head was moving into his line of sight.

Then a familiar sound instantly distracted him.

† † †

Julia heard the noise before she saw the short heavy man standing on his porch holding what appeared to be a shotgun. He racked a shell into the chamber.

"Drop your weapon," the heavy-set man hollered at the man dragging Laquita. "I've called the cops. They're on their way."

The killer's attention turned toward the man on the porch.

A voice from across the street yelled, "Police, drop your weapon."

It happened fast. The killer's hand moved. She saw the muzzle flash as he fired a round at the man on his porch. The man grunted, pitched forward, then collapsed on the porch. A woman from inside rushed out screaming. The killer swung his weapon in the direction of the cop, firing in rapid succession while he continued to drag Laquita toward the car. Laquita stumbled. The killer grabbed her hair and pulled her up, shouting at her to get in the car.

Julia tightened her grip on the pistol, aimed and squeezed off two rounds at the killer's exposed chest.

Laquita screamed.

The killer's arm swung back in her direction. He fired several rounds at her.

One missed.

Another grazed her leg.

Julia discharged more rounds and immediately dove to the ground and stretched out flat.

She saw muzzle flashes from the direction where the cop yelled, but she couldn't see him.

A man yelled, "Get down, get down."

Her only protection was her backpack which was on the ground by her head.

She heard more shots.

The killer slid down to the sidewalk with his back against the parallel parked car. He pulled Laquita down beside him. His arm holding Laquita dropped. Now the cop across the street wouldn't be able to see the killer or provide her cover fire.

Julia was a smaller target flattened out in the grass next to the sidewalk. But still a target with no protection.

Her eyes scanned nearby for anything that would provide cover. A tree. She gauged the distance. Her options. Stay down or make a run for it.

The killer raised his arm, pointed his weapon in her direction.

She rolled to her right. A spray of bullets hit close but missed.

She made her decision.

Get up and run. She sprang to her feet and took off running like her life depended on it.

It did.

If the killer was a good shot, she'd never make it to the tree.

CHAPTER 50

There was an old saying in law enforcement—*better to be judged by twelve than carried by six.*

He knew the sound a pump-action shotgun made when a round was racked. What the hell was the man on the porch thinking? The heavy-set man just announced to the suspect his location standing in full view under a porch light.

The millisecond distraction was enough for Shockley to lose his angle for the kill shot. In a millisecond, the suspect moved, his arm swung toward the man on the porch. The hostage was now blocking his clear line of sight.

Shockley did what he didn't want to do. He alerted the suspect to his position on the other side of the street. Shockley wanted the shooter to twist toward him and away from the man on the porch.

"Police. Drop your weapon," he hollered.

The perp fired, dropping the man on the porch. His hand swung and he fired two more rounds in Shockley's direction. One shattered the car's passenger window he was behind sending shards of glass flying. He ducked just as the next blast blew past his right ear. With a surge of battle-fueled adrenaline, Shockley sucked in a deep breath. In a crouch he peeked around the front of the car. Shockley gripped hard, aimed and fired two rounds at the target, praying like hell he wouldn't hit the hostage. One round aimed at the head missed and the second he was sure hit since the target disappeared behind a parked vehicle pulling the hostage down with him.

In his peripheral Shockley saw people by their windows and a few out on their porches with cellphones taking pictures. He yelled, "Get down. Get down."

He saw Julia lying flat in the grass by the sidewalk, her backpack by her head. The target was no longer in sight. A loud pop. The gunman was still active. Julia was exposed. He knew if she stayed in the open or made a run for it, her odds were slim.

Julia went for it.

He jumped upward and bolted toward the car the shooter was hiding behind.

† † †

A bullet had pierced her left arm. Laquita winched in pain as she wrapped her fingers around her bleeding arm.

The killer had pulled Laquita down with him against the side of a car when he got hit in the chest. She was sure the cop across the street was the one who hit him. It sure wasn't Julia.

Sitting on the sidewalk with his back against the car, the killer released his hold on her. He was using one hand to apply pressure to the gunshot wound in his chest. Blood seeped through his coat and flowed across his hand. He told her if she moved an inch, he'd shoot her in the face.

She was scared and unsure what to do. It wasn't like she'd never heard gunfire. The neighborhood she grew up in had gang activity. She heard gunfire most nights. This was different. She'd never been *in* the line of fire.

Sitting beside the man shooting at Julia, Laquita felt helpless. Blood oozing from her arm had soaked the sleeve of her pink sweatshirt. It was warm and sticky. Staring at the blood unearthed a memory from long ago.

"I'm sorry Lance," Laquita cried.

Big G tried to keep her and her brothers safe. But her brother, Lance, got mixed up with some bad dudes. Laquita wanted Lance to take her to the market one afternoon so she could buy candy. She begged Big G to let them go. Big G finally relented. On the way home, a police car pulled up to the curb. Two cops, one white and one black got out. Lance took off running. They yelled for him to stop, pulled out their guns and fired. By the time Laquita got to him he was dead, and she had a scar on her forehead as a reminder. A bullet had ricochet off the sidewalk and grazed her.

Laquita wanted to do what she did when she was small. Close her eyes and pretend she was someplace else. Yet, she kept them wide open and silently prayed Julia would stay down. The killer next to her was getting weak, his aim not as good. Julia would stand a better chance to stay down, not run like her brother that day. A shaky breath escaped her lips.

Laquita had never been next to a man this violent. A man more violent than her own daddy. This killer's face was scary. He had a scar above his right eyebrow. Maybe he grew up in a bad neighborhood like she did. That's what made him like he was, a killer. Or maybe he was just born that way.

Laquita turned and a flash of fear flew across her face. Julia was getting up to run. She swung her attention toward the killer. He was taking aim at Julia.

It was her fault Lance got killed. She couldn't let this happen again.

She tightened her fist, cocked her arm and rammed her elbow into the killer's wound. He yelled—a mixture of pain and anger then dropped his hand holding his weapon. He swung his attention to Laquita. The killer raised his arm and pointed the gun.

The pungent smell from the muzzle filled her nose. She squeezed her eyes shut.

A loud pop echoed in her ears. Then another.

I'm dead, she thought.

† † †

Kneeling down he placed his hand on her trembling shoulder, his chest heaving in and out. "Laquita, you okay?" Shockley asked.

When her eyes popped open, it startled him. She took a hard look at the dead man lying next to her. Laquita's lower lip began to quiver.

"Wha–." She burst into tears.

"I figgered he's gonna kill me after I hit him with my elbow."

"That was very brave of you." Shockley looked at her bloody sleeve. "You've been wounded." He took her hand and pressed it against the wound. She cried out.

"Keep pressure on your arm.," instructed Shockley. "Help is on the way."

She slowly nodded. With tears streaming down her face she said, "Thanks for savin' my life."

He felt a hand tug on his arm. He turned and saw Julia breathing hard, her face pallid. She pushed around him.

"Laquita are you okay?"

"She's fine. Looks like she got…"

Laquita interrupted, "I can't believe ya shot me, Julia. I told ya not to shoot. Ya coulda killed me."

"I'm sorry Laquita. I had a clear shot, but you moved."

"For cryin' out loud. I said don't shoot. Ya shoulda listened. That crazy maniac was choking me, he's shootin', you shootin'. I'm smack dab in the middle. I can't believe ya shot me."

"I said I'm sorry."

"I'm gonna bleed to death."

"You're not going to bleed to death," Shockley reassured Laquita as he stood next to Julia. "Julia did the right thing. If he'd got you in his car, he would've killed you."

Shockley hated being in the crosshair of two women in such an emotional state. He continued, "Both of you were brave tonight. Julia stood up to the man holding you hostage and Laquita slugged the shooter so he couldn't take a shot at you, Julia."

"I wondered why he didn't fire when I ran. Thank you, Laquita."

Laquita softened and added, "I guess we both done good."

Julia dropped beside her friend and hugged her. Laquita winched. "Watch the arm. You gettin' blood on ya."

They hugged again. "You're going to be okay, Laquita. We're going to be okay." Tears rolled down her cheek.

When Julia straightened, her bright blue eyes stared into his. "Thank you, Detective. Your words are kind, but I'm responsible for the man murdered at the park. I was supposed to meet him tonight." Her face twisted in distress. There was a trace of pain in her deep blue eyes. "And I put my friend's life in danger."

He had a strong urge to draw her next to him. Wrap his arms around her and comfort her. He wished he could read her.

"You can't blame yourself for all of this. There were things you had no control over."

"Thanks again, Detective Shockley. If you still want the photos, they're in my backpack."

"Thanks. The photos might help us make a positive I.D. that this guy is the one responsible for the Willow Oaks murders."

The night air filled with sirens and strobes of flashing lights.

Blues were screeching to a stop all around them. Uniforms jumped out of their cruisers and started securing the scene. Shockley yelled for medical help. Two paramedics rushed over carrying their jump-bags.

"You okay?" asked a male responder to Julia.

"She's fine. I'm the one over here dyin'," moaned Laquita.

Shockley couldn't suppress the grin that spread across his face.

CHAPTER 51

Julia was instructed by the receptionist in the emergency waiting room to take a seat. The receptionist said she'd call her when Laquita was ready to be discharged or moved to a room. She found a chair in the overcrowded area sandwiched between a man who appeared to be asleep and a woman with a red nose clutching her purse and a box of Kleenex tissues in her lap.

The paramedic who examined Laquita at the crime scene told her she'd be okay. The bullet had exited her arm. He explained that after the E.R. doctor examined her they'd have more information.

Julia's thigh was sore from the bullet that grazed it. The medic at the scene cleaned the wound and put a sterile adhesive dressing on it. He told her she was lucky. It was a minor wound that wouldn't need any other treatment.

Julia glanced at her watch. It wasn't as late as she felt it should be. She still felt shaky. How could all this have happened in such a short amount of time? She replayed the shoot-out scene in her mind. She had told Laquita she had a clear shot of the shooter's chest, but did she? Everything happened so fast, it was a blur. Her foot began tapping the floor.

Seconds counted in a shoot-out. A single second could be the difference between living or going to the morgue. She hesitated once and somebody died. That person was the man whose business she now owned. Perhaps if she had acted faster, she could have saved his life. That's why she took the shot tonight at the man holding Laquita hostage. She had made a promise to herself never to hesitate again. And now her friend was angry with her. She dropped her face into her hands. The outcome could have been worse.

There was an orchestra of coughing, wheezing, and moaning sounds from the people waiting to be seen by doctors. She wasn't sure how long this was going to take, but by the tired weary look of the people surrounding her, she figured she'd be here a long time.

All her energy had drained, and she was no longer able to focus on what had happened.

Tomorrow morning she had to go to the police station and give a statement. But currently she was fighting to keep her eyes open. If she stayed seated much longer, she'd fall asleep. Maybe there was some place close by to get coffee.

She stood and walked over to the check-in counter. The receptionist on her cell phone glanced up. Dark circles under her eyes made her look the same as Julia felt. Exhausted. There was a large mug on the counter next to the woman. She could smell the aroma of coffee. It smelled good. Just what she needed.

"Excuse me, where could I get a cup of coffee?"

The petite Black woman pointed to a small table in the far corner. "Free coffee over there."

"Thank you. I could use a good cup of coffee."

"Then don't get it from over there. The stuff down here sucks. You can get the good stuff on the third floor of the hospital. There's a Starbucks that should be…" She checked her watch and continued, "open for thirty more minutes."

"Third floor in the main hospital?"

"Uh-huh. Go to the main lobby and take the elevator up."

"I'm here for Laquita Morrison. Would I have time to get something to drink before they call me?"

"Look around, honey. You got lots of time."

† † †

Julia pressed the *UP* button by the elevator door and waited. She glanced at the digital display above the door. The elevator was on the fifth floor and descending. A woman in scrubs walked up and stood next to her. They shared a polite smile and then the woman began double thumbing her cell phone.

Rocking from toe to heel she wondered if her blood sugar had dropped. She had a headache and her legs felt unsteady. A coffee fix was needed. Some food would be nice too.

A ding announced the elevator had arrived. *Thank goodness.* She couldn't get that cup of coffee soon enough. When the elevator door slowly slid open, she moved over to allow a woman to exit. She caught a glimpse of the attractive young Black woman who barged past her. The woman in scrubs stepped inside the elevator and Julia followed. The woman pressed the fourth-floor button and asked her what floor she was going to.

It was as if a lightning bolt struck her groggy head. She reached around the woman and frantically mashed the lobby button over and over to stop the closing door.

"Come on," she muttered, but it was too late. The elevator was headed to the next floor.

"Are you okay?" asked the woman in scrubs.

"No." She pressed the button for the second floor.

The elevator stopped on the second floor and before the door fully opened, she darted out. Her eyes searched for stairs. "Where are the stairs? I need to get to the lobby," she shouted to the woman in the elevator.

The woman in scrubs held the elevator door open, yelled at her and pointed to the left.

Down in the lobby she made a beeline past the elevators and out the main entrance doors. Her eyes searched the area desperate to see the woman she saw exit the elevator. There were plenty of lights illuminating the parking area. She saw a couple getting in their car and a SUV drive past. Suddenly, she saw a woman hurrying toward the far end of the lot. It had to be her.

She ran hard-and-fast toward her. The woman began running. The woman stopped next to a white car and opened the door.

Julia yelled, "Kat... Lejeune... stop." Lejeune turned and looked directly at her, then quickly jumped in the car.

Julia kept running. She heard the engine fire up and then screeching tires.

She stopped. She could see her breath in the cold air. Her chest was heaving. Standing there trying to catch her breath, she watched the taillights get dimmer and dimmer. Soon the car was out of sight.

She threw up her hands and stomped her foot against the pavement.

Kat Lejeune had gotten away.

CHAPTER 52

Shockley walked into the 24-hour mom and pop cafe. The first smell to hit him was the aroma of cinnamon and vanilla Near the door was a display case featuring an assortment of homemade breads, cakes and pastries that made his stomach growl just looking at them.

But tonight, that's not what brought him here. Chief Nowakowski called him before he left the crime scene and ordered him to meet here.

He spotted Wheels in the back corner. The man still had the look of a Ranger from the waist up. Always clean-shaven, and a gray high and tight haircut. He had a thick neck, strong arms and a broad chest. Years in a wheelchair had taken a toll on his leg muscles.

Glancing around he saw there weren't many people in the shop at this late hour. Good.

A medium built man with collar-length mousy hair stood at the front counter ordering some specialty drink to go. The young girl behind the counter looked like a college kid working to help pay for her education. There was a young couple at a table near the window. Hauser would call them hipsters.

He moved past the patrons to the back of the shop where Wheels was waiting.

"Chief." He didn't want to use his nickname. Not with that look on Wheels' face.

"Got you a coffee," said Wheels.

"Thanks." He pulled the chair out and sat wishing he had Wheels' oversized desk between them right now.

"You okay?" asked Wheels.

He shrugged, then answered, "Rough night."

Shockley wrapped a hand around the warm mug. He took a swallow. The warm liquid knocked the chill down. He kept the mug in his hand and took another long pull on his coffee.

After he sat the mug down, he released a sigh.

"We lost another Blue," was all he could manage to say. Wheels already knew that, but he needed to remind himself. This case was taking a toll on him.

"How bout you bring me up to speed." Wheels leaned back in his chair. His eyes narrowed as he stared at Shockley.

Wheels knew how to make anyone sweat.

Shockley read him in starting with the call he received of a probable homicide through the events leading up to him killing the man who had held Laquita hostage.

Wheels snapped, "You were told in no uncertain terms to stay away from Julia Bagal. What the fuck were you doing?

"I beg your pardon?" He cocked an eyebrow. His tone changed, not for the better. "Are we no longer allowed to investigate a homicide?"

Wheels tapped his finger on the table in front of Shockley. "I got my orders from the mayor who said I was to cooperate fully with the Feds, no questions asked. You were told to back off. What's wrong with you? You begging to get kicked off the force, along with shit-canning my career? Cause after that stunt you pulled tonight that's a real possibility."

"I saw a crime in progress near a homicide scene I was responding to and I took action. It was pure happenstance that it turned out to be Julia Bagal. We both know that what went down tonight has nothing to do with that National Security bullshit the Feds are feeding us."

"At this time, we don't know jack-shit. For all we know, that fucking cop killer could be a foreign government's hired assassin or some home-grown terrorist plotting the next 9/11. Maybe Julia Bagal was the best lead they had until you fucked it."

"The guy I killed tonight wasn't a national security threat."

"And exactly how would you know that?"

"Sooner or later this is gonna come back round to me."

"What boneheaded thing did you do?"

"Remember Amy Miller?"

"Sure I do. She died two years ago from breast cancer. She was a damn good cop."

"Amy was his T.O."

"Wha? Amy was his training officer? The same guy you just put a bullet in his skull? He's one of our own?"

"No. He *was* a cop. A bad cop" He took another swig of coffee and continued, "Amy and I were friends and she asked me for advice."

"What kind of advice?"

"After working with him, Amy sensed the guy had some serious mental issues and wanted him re-evaluated. He was getting more aggressive in their arrests. She asked my opinion and I agreed."

"Who is he?"

"Darius Johnson."

"Must have been before I became Chief." Wheels picked up his coffee mug and took a slug.

"He flunked his psych eval and was let go."

"And what? He had a hard-on for cops?"

"He was pissed and blamed some of us for what happened. He was involved in a case I worked afterwards. It was an altercation where he chased a couple of guys down in his car claiming they cut him off on the road. When I arrived on the scene, Darius had been shot in the leg. One of the two guys was down and later died at the hospital. Darius claimed self-defense and got off."

"And you were the arresting officer?"

"Yes."

"Shit."

"Chief, there's no way Darius Johnson was anything but a psychopath. He's not a terrorist."

Wheels looked away toward the large window in the shop and fidgeted with the spoon next to his mug.

When Wheels looked back, he asked, "Did Darius have a cell on him?"

"He did, but it's password protected."

"And just how does Julia Bagal fit into all of this?"

"Not sure. We have a probable I.D. on the female vic at the Willow Oaks Motel. Hauser and I worked a crime scene yesterday. A male vic. After running his tags, we learned he had driven from Nashville to check on his girlfriend whom he hadn't heard from in over a week. Turns out she was a freelance reporter working some big story."

"And you figure that's our Jane Doe?"

"Officer Bone told me Jane Doe didn't look like she belonged at the scene. Said his first impression when he saw her was that she was a reporter doing a story on drugs in our city."

"Wait a minute. Does Julia Bagal have this intel?"

"No. She was hired by somebody else to do surveillance

at Willow Oaks Motel. She was to get photos of the woman's husband cheating."

"And did the woman who hired Julia Bagal collaborate her story?"

"Julia believes the woman used an alias name. Kat Lejeune."

"How convenient. Not a very smart detective."

"She just bought the investigative business. This was her first big assignment."

"That's an understatement." Wheels leaned back against his wheelchair, crossed his arms letting them rest on his chest. He fixed his eyes on Shockley.

"In other words, Mike, all you got is speculation. You have no hard evidence? Am I clear on this?"

Shockley knew his boss was right. "From the beginning this case didn't make sense. If the Feds had coordinated with us on it, then maybe we wouldn't have two murders tonight."

"Where's Julia Bagal now?"

"She's at the hospital with her roommate, Laquita, who is being treated for her injury. It doesn't appear to be serious. Julia will give a statement tomorrow."

"And I better have my story straight for tomorrow. Special Agent Black will be in my office at eight sharp."

Shockley's phone buzzed inside his jacket. He slipped his hand inside his suit jacket to silence it when Wheels told him to go ahead and answer it.

"Shockley." He held it tight against his ear not wanting Wheels to hear the woman on the other line.

He thumbed it off. "That was my sister. She said our father has been admitted to the hospital with chest pains." Shockley lied. His father wasn't at the hospital. He was home, probably in bed. His father liked to get up early and go to bed early.

Wheels tipped his mug and drained it.

"Wouldn't happen to be the same hospital where Julia Bagal's roommate was admitted, would it?"

"Matter of fact, it is."

Wheels slapped a ten-dollar bill on the table. "I got this. You did a good job tonight, Mike."

"Thank you, sir. That means a lot."

As Shockley stood to leave, Wheels warned, "If you continue down this path, you know the consequences. Do the right thing Mike. You're a good cop."

"Yes sir."

"And give my best to your father." Wheels smiled.

"I will, thank you."

He walked out of the cafe wondering why Wheels hadn't made him turn in his shield.

CHAPTER 53

She couldn't believe what had just happened as she stood staring at the disappearing taillights. The last person on earth she expected to see tonight was Kat Lejeune.

It took a few seconds for her to realize that the black woman that got off the elevator was her. By the time it clicked, it was too late. Uncovering the real identity of Lejeune and whatever her connection was to the murders had just vanished.

What was Lejeune doing at the hospital? In order to find out she'd at least need to know her real identity. This was a big hospital.

She tried not to dwell on the fact that she might never know who Lejeune really was. Yet the worst thing about this was that Lejeune was the one who involved her in this nightmare. Tonight, innocent people died. Laquita could have died.

She had a sinking feeling that the death of the killer from the Willow Oaks Motel was not the end of her investigation. Two things stood out in her mind. Laquita was right. There was a connection between Lejeune and her. And second, the players interested in the motel murders, the Feds and Bridge Club had a common tie. Russian spies.

It had gotten colder outside. Her headache was now pounding. She checked the time. She still had a little more than twenty minutes before the Starbucks closed.

She wrapped her arms around herself and rushed back into the hospital.

On the third floor she was glad to see the Starbucks still

open. After purchasing a Café Mocha and a chocolate chip muffin, she rode the elevator back down to the main lobby. Standing beside her was a middle-aged woman who kept glancing in her direction. The woman dug in her purse, pulled out a business card and handed it to Julia.

"There's a 24-hour hotline on it," the woman said in a voice that sounded like a funeral director.

Puzzled she read the card.

GET HELP TODAY
We're here for you.

The card was for a National Domestic Violence hotline.

"Oh. No. I don't need this." She tried to hand back the card.

The woman pushed back on her hand. "Just keep it. You might need it one day."

Thank goodness the elevator stopped and the doors to the main lobby pulled apart.

Julia marched to the nearest trash can and threw the card away. No telling what that woman and everybody else in the hospital thought. The bruising around her eye was now a putrid yellow green color. She had dried blood on her sweater from where she had hugged Laquita. Good thing her sweater was black.

A sudden thought occurred to her. Detective Shockley had given her his card. It was in her crossover bag. She found the card and thumbed the number.

"Detective Shockley, this is Julia Bagal. I don't know if this is helpful, but I just saw the woman who hired me to do surveillance at Willow Oaks Motel."

"Yes. Thanks for letting me know. Are you still at the hospital?"

"I am, but she ran out the door of the main lobby and I lost her."

"I'll meet you in the lobby. I should be there in fifteen to twenty minutes."

She clicked off her cell and leaned against the wall. He didn't sound enthused. Why should he? She didn't give him anything to work with.

Finding a seat facing the elevators, she took a sip of her hot drink and gobbled her muffin. Feeling better from the caffeine and food, she watched the elevator doors opening and closing. Since it was late, not many people got on or off. Did she think if she stared long enough Kat Lejeune would magically reappear?

"I'm an idiot," she mumbled to herself.

Tipping her cup upward to get the last drop of caffeine, she happened to note the digital display above the elevator. The elevator was on the fifth floor. She watched it descend without stopping on any other floors till it got to the lobby. When the doors opened an Asian man and teenage boy exited.

She remembered the fifth floor was the floor Kat Lejeune had been on. With a surge of excitement, she darted inside the elevator and pressed floor three. The woman clerk was closing up the Starbucks. Julia was able to persuade her to let her buy all the muffins and pastries they had left. Then she got back on the elevator and headed to the fifth floor.

The fifth floor had several hallways with numbers and directional arrows printed on the slate gray wall. In one direction there was a large double metal door separating another area. She saw a young nurse in blue scrubs hit a round metal button on the wall with her elbow. The double doors opened slowly, one swinging outward and one swinging inward.

She followed the nurse into the area. This floor had a nurse's station circled by rooms. Maybe she'd get lucky and discover if Lejeune was on this floor visiting a patient.

She strolled over to the station where a woman with dyed blonde hair and dark roots was sitting. The woman was riffling through folders. She guessed the woman was her age.

"Hello. I'm sorry to bother you when I know you're busy."

"Are you okay?"

Julia touched her eye and replied, "I am. I was trying to do home repairs. It's tough when you live alone and have to do everything yourself."

"I know what you mean. I'm a single mom."

"Wow. That's tough. I guess I have no right to complain."

The nurse's name tag said Lisa.

Julia introduced herself saying, "My name is Sonja Hall. A non-profit my friend and I work for decided this month to show our gratitude to the nurses in our community."

Julia held up the large bag she had purchased from Starbucks letting the woman behind the station see it. A big smile swept across Lisa's face.

"That is very kind of you. What's the name of your non-profit organization?"

All the reasons why this was a bad idea flooded her mind. She didn't think about giving the non-profit a name.

A big-boned lady in scrubs sitting close to Lisa wheeled her chair around and exclaimed, "Let me guess. Are you that group called Communities Together? Cause I saw that on the TV last month. They were handing out baked goods to our firefighters."

"I saw that too, Monica," said Lisa to the large woman.

Julia drew a long breath and answered, "Yes. Communities Together."

Monica's face seemed pleased that she knew the answer. And Julia was relieved she let her off the hook.

"My friend Kat is supposed to bring more food and meet me here. Have you seen her? She's a young attractive Black woman who is wearing gray pants and a leather jacket. I'm late and I'm afraid she came up here, didn't see me and left."

Monica answered first, "There was a young woman like you described here earlier, but she left. She didn't say anything to us about being with Communities Together."

"Are you sure?"

"I'd remember if she brought me something good to eat," cackled Monica. "She visited Congressman Alan Wagner. I'm not sure, but I was told she was his assistant or something like that."

Julia put the bag on the counter, turned around and left.

CHAPTER 54

The large display on the digital clock glowed 6:10 A.M. She gently pulled back the covers and rolled out of bed. The room was dark. Using her hands, she fumbled around the floor until she found her sweater and pants. She couldn't locate her underwear. Holding her clothes tight against her chest, she tip-toed using her hands to guide her around furniture to the kitchen.

The kitchen door was closed. There was a sliver of light shining beneath the door. She scurried back to the bedroom, flipped on the light, located all her clothes and dressed. In the bathroom she washed her face and brushed her hair before heading back to the kitchen.

When she opened the kitchen door, Mike's head whipped around. "Good morning Julia." Mike was standing by the counter pouring coffee in a mug.

"I don't have any milk. I do have sugar," he apologized.

He looked good standing barefoot in his jeans and t-shirt. He was tall and had a lean athletic physique. She liked his thick tousled brown hair with gray temples and his unshaven face.

"Thanks. Just a little sugar. I thought you were still in bed. What time did you get up?"

"Not sure. Probably around five."

When he turned, he had a mug of coffee in each hand. His eyes smiled which ignited her pulse. She quickly averted her gaze. He put the mugs on the table and sat.

"Can I fix you some breakfast?"

She pulled a chair out and sat across from him.

"No thanks. I'm fine."

"I've been told you get hangry when you don't eat."

She hated people telling her that. Her response surprised her. "Thanks, some food would be great."

She arched back in her chair and stared at the empty wine bottles on the counter.

"About last night," she began, her voice soft.

He lifted an eyebrow and interjected, "You have regrets?"

"No. It's just that I usually get to know somebody before I sleep with them."

"I think we got to know each other pretty well last night. By the way, you did great detective work getting a lead in this case."

He smiled, exposing his dimples.

She felt the warmth from the flush on her face. "Thanks. I needed to hear that. Lately, I've questioned why I bought the business."

"I've never met anybody quite like you. You've got an interesting past." He moved to the refrigerator and started pulling food out and placing it on the counter.

"Did I talk too much?" she asked.

Mike waited too long to answer. She wished she'd shared less.

Finally, he turned his attention to her, winked and replied, "I hope I'll continue to learn more about you."

Sipping her coffee, she reflected on what had happened. After calling Mike, she went to the Emergency Room to check on Laquita's status. The receptionist told her Laquita would be released but wasn't sure how much longer it'd take. Julia left her phone number with the receptionist and then raced back to the lobby to meet Mike.

When he arrived, they found an area in the hospital lobby that offered privacy. She filled him in on what she had discovered about Kat Lejeune visiting Alan Wagner on the fifth floor.

While they sat in the lobby and talked, Adam West called. She let Adam know what had happened and that Laquita was at the hospital being treated. He wanted to pick both her and Laquita up and take them to a safe house. The Bridge Club suspected she might still be in danger.

She lied and told Adam she wasn't at the hospital, but with a friend. She told him he needed to take Laquita to the safe house and that she would be safe at her friend's place. Following a few combative exchanges, he relented if she'd agree to stay in touch.

After explaining to Mike who the Bridge Club was, he urged her to go with them. He suspected there was more to this case.

"No. I'm not going. This has my grandmother's name written all over it."

"Your grandmother?" he quizzed.

She gave him an abridged background on Elke and being raised by her after her parents died.

"Whoa. So, your grandma's a spy?" He sounded impressed.

She hated how everybody was always impressed with Elke. Maybe she was a little jealous too.

Mike didn't hesitate to offer for her to stay at his place and she didn't hesitate to accept. Their excuse was they could go over everything related to the case and try to figure out what was going on.

Her first impression of his condo was that he was a man who was satisfied with just the bare necessities in furnishings. No feminine touches.

Two hours later, after they had shared information about the case, themselves and two bottles of wine, they quit resisting and ended up in his bed. She didn't regret it. For the first time in her life, she had chosen not to be practical and just enjoy the moment.

"Is something burning?" she asked.

"Damn." He hustled over to the toaster oven and popped up the blackened muffins.

"Looks like it's just eggs and sausage. I'm afraid I suck at cooking. That's why I usually eat out."

"No problem." She grinned.

While they ate, she asked, "What do you think we've got?"

"A connection. And something tells me Kat Lejeune knows you and that's why she hired you to do the surveillance."

"Like I told you, I'd never seen her before she hired me."

"Perhaps she didn't know you personally, but through somebody. You told me that you met the Speaker when the President and he visited your grandmother in the hospital."

"And, the Speaker is recovering on the fifth floor of the hospital," she said finishing his thought. "Same floor Kat Lejeune was on."

"Yep. You were told that woman could be his assistant by the nurse on duty. That's a connection," he pointed out.

"It doesn't make sense. Why would Kat Lejeune or the Speaker want photos of a journalist and a drug dealer? And none of this explains why Darius Johnson was involved."

"That's where the water gets muddy. Maybe the Speaker had Lejeune hire you."

"That might be it," she agreed. "I remember the President telling Speaker Wagner to work with the FBI and help identify a suspected Russian spy who might have ties to our government. Maybe he found out the reporter had discovered something. And before he goes to the FBI, he wanted to find out who she was meeting and gets his assistant to hire me under false pretense. That way nobody would know what he was doing."

"Doesn't explain the drug dealer or Darius Johnson." Mike stroked his chin. "Unless. Somebody hired Darius to kill the reporter because she was zeroing in on the Russian spy."

"Wait a minute." Julia was taken aback. "Are you implying the Speaker or Kat Lejeune might be a Russian spy."

"No," said Shockley. "I don't know. Maybe. Remember I told you about Darius Johnson. He's a psychopath, not a national security threat or some kind of spy. What we do know is that the Bridge Club, your spy grandma, and the Feds are involved."

"And whenever my grandmother is involved," she added, "you can bet it has to do with Russians. But that theory still doesn't explain why a drug dealer was found dead in the same room as the reporter."

"There are times being a cop means I have to think like a criminal to catch the criminal. If I was going to kill somebody and needed to point the authorities in the wrong direction, then I'd make it look like something it wasn't."

"You're right. The location would make you think it was prostitution or drugs or both. Mike, I think you're on to something."

"Except for one problem."

"What?"

"They wanted you involved."

"But why?" Julia asked.

He shook his head. "Wish I knew."

"Do you think we should talk to the Speaker first and find out what he knows?" suggested Julia.

"No. Let's stick to our plan. Gather some hard evidence. If his receptionist is your Kat Lejeune, then we'll know our next move."

"And if she isn't?"

"Then we're back to square one. My boss is meeting with the Feds this morning. We don't have time on our side."

"Hauser will be at the hospital?"

"Yep. If Kat Lejeune ties Congressman Wagner to this murder which I suspect she will, then Hauser will arrest him before he's released."

"I hope our plan works."

"It will," he replied with confidence.

CHAPTER 55

Wagner thought about nothing else but Megan ever since she left yesterday.

She was a link that could blow his cover. Razor had taken care of all the other *loose lips* as he'd called them. The idea of her being hurt or worse, murdered, was inconceivable to him. There had to be other ways. He didn't have the stomach for this.

She told him last night if he needed to talk call her. Maybe she'd understand he was the victim. Surely, she'd believe that he had no idea Razor would handle things the way he did.

And yet, could he take that chance?

It was when Joe delivered his supper to him last night that he realized what had to be done. The man from Nigeria worked at the hospital delivering food to patients. He told him people in America could not pronounce his Nigerian name, Enakpodia. He decided it would be easier to call himself Joe.

Joe was a talkative man with a thick Nigerian accent. Wagner learned about his family, what brought him to America and his dream to be a doctor one day. Joe had heard from the nurses about a young woman who worked with a non-profit organization. This month they were showing appreciation for nurses. Since the nurses had more than they could eat they wanted to give one of the muffins to the Speaker. Joe said it was funny that the young woman thought his assistant was supposed to help her deliver the food.

Last night alone in his hospital room, he thumbed the

number on his cell. Not his personal phone on which numbers could be traced. He used the one provided to him by his handler.

He wanted to relax and believe everything would get back to normal. The clock on the wall said 8 a.m. He felt sick. Nothing would ever be normal for him. He grabbed the water pitcher, held it to his mouth and vomited.

† † †

"What friend is Julia staying with?" Elke demanded of the man on the other line.

"We don't know. She refused to say. When we contacted her, she instructed us to pick up her friend, Laquita, from the hospital and transport her to the safe house."

"Are you telling me that Julia is now giving the orders and not me?"

The man remained silent.

Finally, he spoke, "She's a carbon copy of you. You can't force her to do what she doesn't want to do. She agreed to check in. She's safe."

"What do the cameras show?"

"Julia went back home last night. She grabbed her to-go-bag and left the same way she came in, back door. Her vehicle is still parked out front."

"Was somebody with her?"

"No."

"No, there wasn't somebody with her or no, you don't know?"

"No, in that no other person was in the house or visible from outside."

"Damn, she's smart. Julia made sure the vehicle and whoever she was with, stayed out of view of the cameras."

"Did you get what you needed from your source in Ireland?" he asked.

"More or less. Things don't always go as planned. Looks like I might have to make a deal to get what we want."

"Is that wise?"

"The stakes are too high not to do this."

"We all do what we have to do to keep our country safe. Good luck."

"You know I never believe in luck."

A discernible chuckle was heard from the man. She added, "You and I have a busy morning. Don't let me down this time."

She clicked off.

Adam West was probably the best spook she had ever known. What made him so effective was he always got the job done even if he bent the rules to do it. That's why the agency let him go. That would have been her fate too, if she hadn't quit first.

Right away she needed to make a call and set up a meeting.

† † †

Shockley parked her car in a spot across the street from the Rayburn Building. The sun's rays streaming in through the windshield felt good washing across her face. The morning temperature, in the upper forties, was slowly rising. It was turning out to be a beautiful cloudless day.

Shockley raised his watch and tapped on the crystal.

"It's time," he instructed her. "You okay making the call?"

She nodded while she thumbed the number. Before the first ring, she sucked in a deep breath and blew it out to calm her nerves.

When the woman answered, she swung her head and gave Shockley a thumbs up.

"Hello. I'm trying to reach Speaker Wagner about a very urgent matter. Is he available?"

"No. Not at the moment. Can I take a message for him?"

"Are you his assistant?"

"I'm a staff assistant to the Speaker."

"If this is Kat Lejeune, do not hang up."

After a long hesitation, the woman said, "I think you've made a mistake. I have no clue what you're talking about." It was her, the woman who posed as Kat Lejeune. "I'm sorry but...."

Julia cut her off, saying, "I know who you are and what you did for your boss. If you don't want to be charged with accessory to murder, then I'd advise we meet."

Silence. After a few seconds, Julia cautioned, "Don't hang up on me. Be smart. We can help each other."

"What do you want from me? I can pay you the rest of the money I owe you."

"Meet me outside your office in ten minutes. I'm parked across the street."

"I can't. This matter is too serious for me to be seen with you. Alan, I mean Speaker Wagner didn't do anything wrong."

"I can go public with this."

"No. Please don't do that," she pleaded. "Give me twenty

minutes and I'll meet you at the cafe on 2nd Street. It's called The Split Bean Cafe."

"I'll be there," replied Julia. As soon as she swiped off, she exhaled with relief.

Facing Shockley, she explained, "She said to meet her in twenty minutes at a cafe called *The Split Bean Cafe* on 2nd Street."

He slid out his phone and used google map to locate the cafe. "It's less than a ten-minute walk from here. Let's leave the car and walk there."

She gathered her bag and started to open the door when he grabbed her arm, pulled her close, and kissed her. Her entire body tingled from the taste of his lips.

"You did a good job, detective Bagal," his voice deep and penetrating.

She stared into his brown eyes.

She hoped he was right.

CHAPTER 56

The Split Bean Cafe was an easy walk from where Shockley had parked. The sun was doing its best to warm the air, but the steady cool wind blowing against them was a reminder that winter was not far away.

As soon as they entered the cafe, an inviting aromatic smell filled her nostrils. Mike located a table next to the large picture window, giving her an unobstructed view of the direction from which Kat Lejeune should be walking. If Lejeune took the same route they had, she'd be able to spot her as soon as Lejeune turned south on 2nd Street.

She understood why Lejeune picked this place. Even though the cafe wasn't large, the small tables were spaced far enough apart to give customers privacy for conversations. The inside was inviting with colorful walls covered in quirky artwork.

"We're early." She tucked her hair behind her ears. "Would you mind getting me a hot tea while I keep a look-out?" she asked. She couldn't shake the chill she had.

"Sure. I could use some caffeine too. Anything fancy or just plain tea?"

"If they have it, a Chai Tea Latte, skim milk, hot."

She started to reach in her purse for her wallet, but he protested. "I got it." He rose from his chair and headed to the barista standing behind a counter.

She sat by the window keeping her eye trained in the direction Lejeune would be coming from. She still didn't know

Lejeune's real name.

There were steady streams of people walking in both directions. She only had to watch the pedestrians walking south and for a young Black woman. That eliminated many people hustling along the walkway.

Her thoughts drifted back to the day when Lejeune came into her office. It seemed like a long time ago when in reality it had only been a week. She traced the woman's features as best she could recall in her mind. It was hard to believe that one assignment could bring her to this point in her life.

Checking her watch, she saw they had at least five more minutes till she'd know Lejeune's real name and why she'd lied to her.

Mike set the hot cup of tea she wanted in front of her and took a seat on the other side of the table.

"You okay?" he asked.

"Yeah." She grabbed the handle and took a sip from the cup never taking her eyes off the people outside.

"Good. She'll be here soon."

"I hope she'll tell us the truth." She set her cup down, clasped her hands letting them rest on the table in front of her.

Out of the corner of her eye, she saw him reach across the table and wrap his warm hands around her tight fists. She noticed he had a reassuring smile on his face.

"She will. I think you scared her about being an accessory to murder. Which unfortunately she could be."

"Have you ever been wrong about a murder case?"

"I've made mistakes."

She returned her focus to the outside and thought, *so have I*. She withdrew her hands and took a sip of tea.

The table was small causing Mike's long legs to touch hers.

She adjusted her seat so she wouldn't be distracted by him.

A few times she thought she spotted Lejeune, only to realize it wasn't her. Every time it happened her heart began to race.

Mike must have gotten into her head. "Waiting is sometimes the hardest part of a case."

"Well, it definitely is now."

In the distance a young Black woman crossed the street and was now walking briskly in their direction. Julia squinted from the glare of the sun, raised a hand to protect her eyes. She strained a hard look wanting to be certain it was her.

"It's her," she exclaimed with a rise in her voice.

Shockley swiveled in the chair to look in the same direction she was looking. "You sure?"

"I'd bet my life on it."

He swiftly moved to her side of the table and sat next to her. "Which one's her?"

She pointed and said, "The Black woman wearing a beige knee length coat and low pumps. Her hair is short."

"Walking next to a man in a plaid parka and wool beanie?" he asked.

"No. Look to my right and behind that man. A woman and small child are near her left now."

"Got her."

They both kept their eyes locked on the woman moving toward the cafe. Julia squeezed Mike's arm. She was feeling confident it wouldn't be long before she'd learn the truth. *Why'd she hire me?*

"Whaa…" she stuttered as she stared in disbelief.

Mike turned his attention toward her. "What's wrong?"

Without a word, she pushed her chair out from the table,

stood and proceeded toward the cafe door. Mike was right behind her.

They walked slowly toward Lejeune who had stopped when she appeared to have recognized Julia. Julia's focus was now on the man behind Lejeune who was quickly closing the gap between Lejeune and himself.

It happened without warning. She saw an older man shoved into oncoming traffic. Mike took off running toward the man lying in the street. People nearby stopped and turned their attention to the horror about to unravel in front of them. A car was traveling in the direction of the fallen man. Honking. People screaming. Hard braking.

Chaos.

She saw Kat Lejeune shifting away from the crowd. A man in a long dark overcoat was walking right behind her with his hand shoved against the small of her back. Julia couldn't see what was in his hand, but she was certain it was a gun.

She raced toward them, but abruptly stopped, shocked to see a familiar man who had maneuvered behind the man in the dark overcoat.

It was Adam West.

He quickly closed the gap.

She saw the shiny silver blade in Adam's hand hanging close to his side. What was Adam doing? In a millisecond Adam raised the knife and slit the man's neck. The man with the weapon to Kat Lejeune's back dropped, his gun clattering against the pavement.

A woman spun around and screamed when she saw the blood pooling on the pavement beside the man's neck. The crowd panicked, more screamed and a few ducked and ran for cover.

Julia rushed forward, locked her arm around Lejeune's arm and tugged her away from the dead man. Lejeune stared at her. There was genuine fear in the young woman's eyes.

"He said he'd kill me if I didn't do as he said," her voice cracked.

"You're safe now. We'll protect you."

She scanned the crowd searching for Adam. The person she knew was responsible for the man's death. And keeping Lejeune safe.

Adam West was gone.

Vanished.

How was that possible?

Mike shouldered his way through the crowd to the man lying on the sidewalk. He pulled his badge and waved it to the onlookers.

"Police. Back up," ordered Shockley. He knelt down and checked for a pulse. Then Shockley reached inside the man's overcoat searching for what Julia figured was identification. Julia already knew he wouldn't find any. Shockley stood. His eyes found hers. He shook his head.

She put her arm around Lejeune's shoulders to comfort the frightened woman.

Mike began instructing the crowd to back up. A police cruiser with lights flashing and sirens blaring pulled up and two officers jumped out. Mike barked orders to the two cops as more police cruisers arrived. An ambulance rounded the corner.

Julia kept her arm tight around the frightened woman. She was impressed with the way Mike was handling the murder scene. Two medics were running with their bags to where she last saw the old man lying in the street.

She said to Lejeune, "We need to go now. You're not safe here."

After they were a distance from the crowd, Julia glanced back at Mike. He wasn't going to like what she had decided to do.

CHAPTER 57

"How about we start with your real name," she said to the frightened woman.

The home was located on the outskirts of the city. It looked like every other home in this middle-class neighborhood. Only behind these doors, the Bridge Club provided a secret haven to protect those inside.

On the drive to the safe house, Julia did her best to assure Lejeune that her friends knew how to keep people safe and that this was the right thing to do. She was honest with Lejeune for the most part, but not entirely. Her motivation was self-serving.

After a long silence, the woman answered.

"Megan," Lejeune's voice barely audible.

Perhaps there were too many strangers sitting around the oval dining table, hindering a conversation that sounded more like an interrogation.

"Yous got a last name?" asked Laquita.

"Megan Lipscomb."

Megan began nervously fiddling with the buttons on her shirt.

"Would you like something to drink, Megan? Tea, soft drink or water?" Julia offered.

"Yes please. Do you have a Coke?"

"Laquita, would you please get Megan a Coke?"

Laquita glared at Julia and replied, "Sure. I still got one good arm."

When Laquita sat back down, Julia said, "Now that we

know Megan's name, why don't we introduce ourselves to her. Starting with you Laquita."

"Laquita Morrison. I'm Julia's partner at the investigation business." Laquita shot Julia a smug smile and then turned her attention to the man on her right.

"Bai Lin," said the Asian looking man. I live in this home. I worked twenty years with the Central Intelligence Agency. I now work as an IT consultant."

The red-haired woman next to Lin smiled and announced, "Amy Lovelace, dear. I'm a good friend of Julia's grandmother. I'm an expert on collection and analysis of data for our security watch list."

Neither Lin nor Lovelace acknowledged that they now worked with the Bridge Club.

The introductions helped Megan relax a little. She nodded to everybody sitting around the table.

Julia, impatient to learn what Megan knew began, "Please tell me why you hired me to do surveillance on your husband at Willow Oaks Motel?

Megan asked, "First tell me who was that man who said he'd kill me if I didn't go with him?"

"We aren't sure. But if you can help us put together the missing pieces of the puzzle we'll find out. That's what we do for a living. We work with intelligence agencies on cases like this." Julia didn't discern anybody at the table including Laquita who wanted to challenge that lie.

"I don't know." Megan shook her head. Her eyes downcast.

"Megan," Julia began, her voice confident. "I know you're confused and scared. I didn't let them take you to the police station because we believe this crime has national security implications."

Megan's face bounced up. She asked, "Was that man going to kill me?"

"Yes, he was."

Megan's chest began heaving in and out in short rapid breaths. "The other man who saved my life, do you know him?"

"Yes. He works with an organization that is helping us," Julia said. She hoped Megan wouldn't ask other questions about Adam West or what organization she was referring to. At first, she considered Adam might show up at the safe house. It was smart not to test if Megan could recognize him. There were other safe houses in the city.

Megan began, "Speaker Wagner told me about you and your grandmother when the attempt on the President and Vice President's life was made. Later I learned you had bought an investigative service. We had never met." Her eyes focused on Julia. She continued, "I felt safe posing as a jealous wife when I came to your office. The Speaker never knew I had hired you."

"Then it wasn't his idea for you to hire me?"

"No. It was my idea," answered Megan.

"The reason you hired me wasn't to get photos of your cheating husband. Was it?"

"No. I'm not married."

"Tell us the real reason you hired me," said Julia.

"I don't snoop. Honest. But, one day I was putting some files on his desk and I inadvertently found a note about meeting a Charlotte at Willow Oaks Motel."

She blinked, fighting back tears. "I thought he was meeting another woman at that horrible place. It could ruin his career and I needed to know."

"You wanted to protect him," inferred Julia.

Megan nodded. "I care very deeply for him."

"But he never went to the motel, did he?" questioned Julia.

"No. But I didn't know that at first."

Julia had the photos she'd taken of the man at the hotel. The man who was killed when he tried to abduct Laquita. She slid the photo of the man in front of Megan.

"Do you recognize this man?"

Megan shook her head.

"Do you know the identities of the people who were murdered at the motel?" asked Lovelace.

Megan's attention shifted to Lovelace. She shook her head hard. "All I know is the name Charlotte from the note."

Lovelace turned to Lin and asked, "Do we have an autopsy report?"

Lin thumbed through papers in a file in front of him. He found one and removed it.

He said, "Joe was able to get a copy of the report." Lin's finger ran down the page till he found what he wanted.

Lin read, "Male identified as Mateo Martinez. 35 years old. Local gang drug runner. Female, twenty-six, free-lance reporter from Nashville. No known family. Name is Charlotte Bollinger."

Lovelace added, "That part of her story checks out."

"Megan, when did you know the Speaker was involved in a crime?" asked Julia.

"It happened gradually. I trusted him. One day I confessed to him that I saw the note on his desk. He got angry and then he told me he was working with the FBI to uncover the traitor in our government. He made me promise not to tell anybody."

"Did you?"

"No. He's a good man."

"But?" said Laquita. "You figgered out he lied to ya."

"I only suspected. I had no proof. I began paying attention to things he said. It was a lot of little things that didn't add up. He was leaving work during the day, told me his uncle had a heart attack and then told me he didn't have any family still living. He changed. But I didn't want to believe he was involved in anything bad or illegal."

"You're in love with him," stated Julia.

Megan let her face drop into her hands sobbing. "Yes. Yes, I am."

Laquita's phone began vibrating on the table in front of her. She picked it up, glanced at the screen and said, "I better see who this is."

She stood and moved to the kitchen.

Julia instructed Lovelace to check with the FBI and verify if they were working with the Speaker on an arranged meeting at Willow Oaks Motel.

"Julia, I need ya right now in the kitchen," yelled Laquita.

"Bai Lin, would you please take care of Megan?"

He nodded.

As soon as she put one foot in the kitchen, Laquita snatched her arm and pulled her to the far corner. Laquita frantically began whispering in her ear.

"Now what should we do?" asked Laquita.

"Keep this to yourself and tell him not to talk to anybody till he hears back from you and you only. Got that."

Laquita nodded. "Got it."

Julia walked out the kitchen door into the backyard. It wasn't her first choice, but she knew it had to be done.

She slipped her phone out of her jean pocket and made the call.

CHAPTER 58

L ater that day, Julia, Laquita and Megan were seated next to each other at a long table in the FBI's Washington Headquarters. She was glad she had been given an opportunity to change clothes before the meeting. Those in attendance were dressed to impress.

The only person she recognized when she entered the room was Detective Mike Shockley. His piercing stare made her look away. It made her uncomfortable which was exactly what he wanted. She knew he was mad she left the crime scene without telling him where she went.

There were eight other people in the room, men and women of influence and power. The Director of the FBI, the Assistant Director, the Director of National Intelligence, Senior Special Agent for the FBI, the Attorney General, Chief of the Metropolitan Police Department, Detective Shockley and a man who stood near the door and didn't introduce himself. He was an attractive older man. Average height, of slim build and thick silver hair. She guessed he was in his late fifties. He was dressed in a suit like most of the attendees except his features were stoic, unfazed by all the chatter in the room.

She hadn't arranged the meeting, however she was informed who would probably be attending. It wasn't going to be easy to get a room full of testosterone to listen when she needed to speak.

A man with thinning gray hair and wire rim glasses perched on his eagle-like nose was instructed to begin by the Director of the FBI.

"Miss Megan Lipscomb, we need your cooperation. Do you understand?" asked Agent Sid Black.

"Am I in trouble?"

"Just tell us what you told Miss Julia Bagal earlier today."

While interviewing Megan, her statements were electronically recorded. There were a few tense exchanges between Chief Nowakowski and Agent Black. The Assistant Director for the FBI kept reaching over and hitting the off button on the recorder, chastising the men for disrupting the meeting.

"Do you have the note you allege was on the Speaker's desk?" asked Agent Black.

"No. It was sitting on a stack of papers on the Speaker's desk. All I did was read it."

"Do you have anything else to connect the Speaker to this crime?"

"Just that he hasn't been himself and …"

Special Agent Black cut her off, "Miss Lipscomb, we're not talking about just anybody. This is a serious accusation levied against the Speaker of the House. We can't arrest him solely based on a note you claim to have seen."

"How would she know the name, Charlotte, if she didn't see that note?" demanded Shockley.

"The note alone isn't enough. I need hard evidence. Not the baseless claims of a jealous secretary."

"You prick." Shockley raised and locked eyes with Agent Black. Chief Nowakowski yanked Shockley's arm pulling him back in his seat.

Julia straightened in her chair, cleared her throat and spoke up, "This meeting was called because we have the evidence.

The note with the name hasn't been released to the public and yet Megan knew that name." She paused making sure all eyes were on her. Then she continued, "And we have a witness who helped the Speaker find the man who ultimately killed Charlotte Bollinger and another victim at the motel."

The group of men and women glanced at each other quizzically. All except the man standing. He just crossed his arms resting them against his chest.

"Where is this mystery man. Why didn't you bring him?" asked Agent Black, his arrogant tone taunting her.

"Because he's in jail," Julia replied curtly.

Agent Black's face turned as red as the shirt Laquita wore. She saw a grin slide across Shockley's face.

"He wants a plea bargain in exchange for his testimony," Julia declared.

The room erupted in people talking over each other. Julia stood to get their attention. Before they ended this meeting, she had a demand to make.

† † †

It took most of the day before the FBI sent two Special Agents to arrest Speaker Wagner in his hospital room. Laquita had been allowed to go to the jail and talk to Max before his confession was taken. Chief Nowakowski told her Max would be put in protective custody while the Speaker awaited trial. A gag order was placed on everyone in the room until the President was informed and released an official statement.

† † †

Shockley waved his badge at the men guarding the Speaker's hospital room as he escorted Julia inside. The Speaker, lying in bed cuffed to the rails, stared out the window.

"Mister Speaker, I'm Detective Mike Shockley. I worked the Willow Oaks Motel homicide case. This is Julia Bagal, a private investigator who helped us solve the case. I believe you two have already met."

The sunlight streaming through the window was fading fast.

Wagner took his time shifting his attention to her and Shockley.

"You just missed my lawyer. I have nothing to say."

Julia faced Mike. "Ten minutes is all I need."

He nodded, flashed a look at Wagner, opened the door and walked out.

"I guess you didn't hear me. I've got nothing to say. Especially to an investigator who is still wet behind the ears," he said angrily.

Julia moved next to the hospital bed and stared into the Speaker's eyes.

"I know who you really are."

Wagner grunted. "You should. I'm one of the most powerful men in Washington. Second in line to be President. Speaker of the House of Representatives. You can address me as Mister Speaker."

"Or why don't I call you Alan Bezrukov? Bezrukov was your parent's real name, before they stole the identity of two dead Americans. Isn't that correct?"

She had his attention. The astonished look on his face confirmed her source was right.

Julia kept talking, "I got suspicious when Charlotte

Bollinger's identity was discovered from her DNA. Same name your assistant, Megan, saw on a note on your desk. A meeting had been set up by the man you hired to kill her at Willow Oaks Motel. She was a freelance reporter that had been snooping around Capitol Hill. She was investigating a rumor that there was a White House mole. According to Megan, Charlotte was asking a lot of questions. Consequently, I asked myself, why would the Speaker be so worried about what Charlotte might discover that he'd have her murdered? This got me thinking about something my grandmother told me happened during the Cold War. A Russian defector gave her a list of the real identities of KGB Illegals planted in America. Sleepers. Your parents' true identities were on that list."

"I'm not a fucking sleeper."

"No, you're not. Your parents on the other hand were. They were never activated, but you were."

"You little know nothing prick investigator. You think you got me. You're naive. I'm not just some low-level peon working in our government. You're in way over your head."

"You're wrong. You'll be prosecuted for murder and treason."

"This is politics. This is a major failure of our intelligence community. I know people who'll never let the truth come out."

"Yeah. I know people too," Julia said sharply.

"If I were you, I'd watch my back," he threatened.

She was done talking.

Julia turned, stormed out of the hospital room, shaking from anger.

CHAPTER 59

The sun had been swallowed by the darkness of the evening. Hospital visitation hours had come to an end and most departments had moved to minimal staffing till morning.

There was a cacophony produced by nurses transferring patient information and handing off half-done tasks to the night shift coming onboard.

She already had her patient information. The older nurse dressed in blue scrubs checked her watch. It had been a long day, but she only had one patient to take care of and then she'd call it a day. Before she started down the hallway, she patted the pocket on her scrubs making sure she had everything she needed. A retractable ID badge was clipped on her upper chest pocket.

She began to push the vital sign cart along the polished linoleum floors, the wheels rolling smoothly. Not wanting to touch the metal button on the wall she used her elbow to press, causing the double doors to slowly open. She noticed a young woman dressed in scrubs sitting at the nurse's station with her head down. The young nurse was probably on her cell phone doing everything but her job, she thought.

Past the nurse's station, two men standing guard in front of a hospital room looked in her direction, neither made eye contact. Without slowing her stride, one of the men opened the door allowing her to enter the room.

"For God sakes, how many times do you need to take my blood pressure?" Wagner snapped.

He had his bed raised and was watching the news on a television set attached to the wall.

The nurse parked the vital sign cart, strolled over to his bedside and smiled. She checked the name on his hospital admission bracelet.

"This will be the last time it's necessary to check your vitals, Mr. Wagner." Her bright blue eyes sparkled as she gazed at him. Then she returned to the rolling cart, punching in information on a keyboard.

With her back to him, he said, "I wondered who would come. I assumed it would be the Russians. But I remember you."

The nurse turned and responded, "I hoped you would." She could not restrain a smile.

"You're the woman who was recovering in the hospital room where I met the President. He credited you and your granddaughter with helping to save him and the Vice President's life."

"Yes, that's right. And just like Robert Hanssen, also a traitor who was tasked to find the spy in the FBI ranks, you, Alan Bezrukov were tasked to help find a spy within our government. How ironic both of you were looking for yourselves."

"Just like I told your granddaughter earlier, you can't do anything to me. Do you understand the ramifications if any of this came out? Can you imagine the headlines? A Russian spy almost succeeded in becoming the Commander-In-Chief of the United States. Not only would this create fear in America, it would undermine the standing of the U.S. in the eyes of the world. Our government—our President—won't let this happen."

"Yes. Again you are right. We do have a dilemma. You, Mr. Bezrukov have put our country in a very difficult situation."

He glanced nervously when she snapped on latex gloves.

She continued, "And you have put Russia in a very dangerous position. They have denied any connection between their government and you. You're a liability to them."

"Please listen to me," he said, desperately pleading. "If I'm given protection and granted asylum I'll cooperate with the American authorities. I can give you the name of my handler and provide intelligence on Russia."

"Your handler is dead. The Russians are quickly cleaning up," she replied calmly.

Wagner was obviously shaken. His forehead glistened with beads of sweat. He frantically tried to reach for the nurse call button. He discovered it was out of reach of his cuffed wrist. She had moved the button box when she pretended to check his wristband.

She marched quickly to the side of the bed. "This is your best option. Your comrades won't be so humane."

"What are you going to do?" his voice quavering.

"You'll die of natural causes. You're going to have a heart attack."

"You can't get away with that. My assistant, Megan knows there's nothing wrong with my heart."

"You mean the assistant you tried to murder? I don't think she'll be a problem."

She slipped the syringe from her pocket and began to administer the drug through the needleless port on an existing IV line in his arm.

Within seconds his tears stopped as the color drained from his face and his hands twitched involuntarily.

She walked out of the room and disappeared down the hallway.

The overhead sound system paged Code Blue room 512.

† † †

As soon as Elke stepped outside the main hospital entrance, a car drove up and stopped.

Elke walked around the back of the car and got in the front passenger seat next to the driver.

"Is it done?" asked the driver.

"It is," replied Elke.

"Any problems?"

"None that I'm aware of," stated Elke.

"What does that mean?"

"It means what it sounds like. We'll know the success later."

"That doesn't sound very reassuring."

Elke leaned her head back against the headrest. "All of the Speaker's hospital records have been scrubbed. They've been replaced with new health records. The room was sanitized the moment I left. But there are always moving parts to missions like this. I think you should remember that."

"Do you think this was necessary? Could it have been handled differently?"

Elke's replied sarcastically, "A little late to be second guessing, don't you think?"

Except for the humming engine, there was silence inside the car.

Glancing at Elke the driver spoke, "Tell me. We are the

good guys, right?"

"That's what we tell ourselves. Alan Bezrukov did what he was trained to do. Just like I do."

The driver shot Elke a look. The silvery haired woman looked tired and closed her eyes.

Twenty minutes passed without a word exchanged.

Finally, Elke broke the silence, "It's not easy doing what I do."

"Then quit. You've sacrificed more than most people have for this country."

"Perhaps I will."

"Good."

"But, I'm so good at my job." Elke smirked.

"Would you like to stay at my place tonight?"

"I would," Elke said without hesitation. She paused and then continued, "The Director said you did a good job in the meeting today."

"Director of FBI?"

"No, but I'm sure he'd have agreed. Rick Piagno, Director of the CIA."

"That's the man who never identified himself in the meeting?"

"Yes. He told me you were to be commended for helping to discover the Russian mole."

"Wow. That's impressive to have the Director of the CIA say that about me." They exchanged a smile. "So, what will he give me? An award? A ceremony? A medal?"

"I'm proud of you Julia. As far as our government is concerned, what happened, didn't happen. This has already been buried. Our footprints erased."

"So, the CIA doesn't give out medals?"

"No."

"How about a gift card?"

Elke started laughing. "Julia you're going to be a great private investigator."

EPILOGUE

Three Weeks Later

Julia impatiently tapped her wristwatch. Fifteer. minutes till her appointment.

She glanced around the small waiting room. In the far corner, attached to the wall, was a rack full of neatly arranged magazines. The pale green walls had an odd assortment of pictures hanging on them. There was only one other person waiting. An average man sitting across from her with his head down, staring at the iPhone in his hands.

It had been a little over a month since she'd seen her therapist. She had a lot of baggage in her twenty-nine years of life.

She mused knowing she was older than twenty-nine. But that's what her birth certificate had recorded.

A short breath escaped her lips. She began to retrace what had happened in less than a month of time.

Mike Shockley was now living in a different time zone. He left the police force instead of being asked to resign. His boss, Chief Nowakowski went to bat for him with Internal Affairs, but this wasn't the first time he hadn't followed orders. The very next day, his father had a mild stroke in his home. Luckily, he was going to be okay. Mike made the decision to move with his father back to Texas and let his father live out his remaining years on the ranch he loved. He was unsuccessful trying to buy back the old ranch, but was able to find a smaller spread, as he called it, nearby. Actually, in the same town.

It was tempting when he asked her to pack up and come with them. They talked about it over dinner one evening. He told her about Terrance Bone, nicknamed T-Bone and Amber Bull. T-Bone was a good friend and a patrol officer. Bull worked as the Crime Scene Investigator and was also a friend. Both had been seriously injured the day the bomb went off at Willow Oaks Motel. T-Bone had been discharged and was on his way to making a full recovery. Bull was not as lucky. He broke down when he told her she had died. She knew he was hanging on to guilt and it drove his decision to move back to Texas.

She knew about guilt.

And its side effects.

She remembered that day in the park when Fly, a friend of Elke, was gunned down by somebody she thought was her friend. She killed the woman, but it was too late. Fly was dead. Guilt was the driving force when she purchased Fly's investigative business.

Perhaps it was Elke telling her she was going to be a great investigator that played a part in her declining Mike's offer to go with him. She had to respect his decision to leave. Before he left, he handed her an envelope with a ticket voucher inside.

Who knows? Long distance relationships were difficult and challenging but not impossible.

Maybe she'd go visit.

Maybe not.

What she did know was that life rarely turned out the way anyone expected it to.

Elke stayed almost a week with her. She wasn't surprised when she woke up one morning and found the note on the kitchen table.

> I had to leave for business. Be back when the job is done.
> Love Elke
> P.S. Don't ever look back.

Her grandmother was a restless soul. She was never going to stay with her for long. She was surprised she stayed as long as she did. The whole week Elke refused to talk about what happened. Julia had no idea if her grandmother felt remorse after administering the fatal dose to the Speaker of the House. Elke was a private person. She accepted that they were different.

The death of the Speaker of the House was all that dominated news channel for weeks. His funeral drew world leaders and powerful Americans along with hundreds of everyday people. There was one person close to Alan Wagner who did not attend, Megan Lipscomb. She had already left town and went home to Michigan to live with her mother.

Julia glanced at the receptionist, smiled and tapped her watch again. Five more minutes. The therapist was never on time.

She envisioned the tall fit therapist who looked like she was fifty, but she knew from her bio was closer to retirement age, sitting in a chair across from her. A laptop to one side of her on a portable stand. Her slim fingers typing away as they talked. The therapist's unknowing face would be relaxed when she asked what had happened since their last visit.

Julia imagined saying, "I know this doesn't sound like me, but I dressed up as a hooker and went to a strip joint where I got beat up. I did accidentally shoot my friend when she was taken hostage by a killer, which she still reminds me of on a daily basis. And the biggest news is that I was the get-a-way driver for my grandmother who murdered the Speaker of the House."

Besides the possibility of being committed, it would cost her $150 for that conversation.

She stood. The receptionist looked up.

"I'm sorry, but I have an emergency and must cancel today's appointment."

"Oh, I'm sorry. Can I go ahead and reschedule you?"

Julia shook her head. "No. Not at this time. Thanks."

Outside, she drew in a breath of cool morning air. The sun was shining. She smiled. Today she wasn't going to look back.

One hour later, Julia pulled up to her office.

Inside she admired the new paint job. The drab olive walls were repainted a light blue gray color to lighten the atmosphere. On order were two nice desks and two high-back leather chairs. There were live plants on the bookshelves, on her desk and spaced around the office.

She sat and opened the laptop on her desk.

She didn't miss her old life. There had been some press on her role in solving the Willow Oaks murders, which had given her business a boost.

The office door swung open.

"Julia, what ya doin' back so soon?" asked Laquita.

"My appointment got canceled," replied Julia.

"Too bad. I know you probably needed to talk to that shrink about shootin' your partner." Laquita winked.

"I'm not going to keep saying I'm sorry. And, you're an employee, not a partner."

"I got no hard feelin's." She pointed. "You ain't watering that plant in the corner enough." Laquita walked to her desk and sat. "Julia, I appreciate the car ya bought me. And the clothes. I was just wonderin' where ya got all that money. It's legal, ain't it?"

"Made it with my new side job as a hooker. You know, now that I have the right clothes and all."

Laquita stared at Julia, expressionless for a few seconds then smiled. "Not gonna tell me how you got that money, are ya?"

"Nope."

Elke was right, Julia wouldn't get any recognition for uncovering the mole inside the government. But somebody, and she had her suspicions who, had made a substantial deposit in her bank account.

A card came the day the deposit was made.

All it said was, "Medals are overrated."

ACKNOWLEDGEMENTS

First and foremost, I want to thank my husband, bestselling thriller writer Chuck Barrett, who is my editor, IT man and sounding board. You kept me as sane as possible during my writing meltdowns. Working together has enriched my novels and made them better. You are always honest and not afraid to point out issues with my story line. Which unfortunately are many. You are my rock.

To Kates, my daughter, whose enthusiasm and encouragement made me believe I could write a second novel.

Every manuscript evolves from a rough draft, a cycle of rewrites to the finished product. Chuck Barrett is the first set of eyes to review my story. After a rewrite, the manuscript is sent to beta readers who have agreed to dedicate their time and energy to review the manuscript and give honest, constructive feedback. They are essential in improving the overall structure of the story. A big thanks to my wonderful beta readers, Artie Lynnworth, Nancy Mace, Early McCall and Terrance Traut.

Special thanks to my readers. When I get an email telling me how they enjoyed my book, it means the world to me. I wanted this novel to be better than my first novel and I believe I accomplished my goal. Hopefully this story, full of intrigue, mystery and humor will give you a short break from reality.

A few facts

The location scene (Chapter 32) where Elke visits Adrik on Inishmore, one of Ireland's western Aran Island is factual. The cottage is fictional. In 2019 my husband and I, along with good friends toured Ireland. It was this visit that inspired me to include this location in the story. Dún Dúchathair, the Black Fort does exist. It's an arduous hike but well worth the effort. We also rode bikes to Dún Aonghasa and along the way spotted a seal colony. Like all fiction stories there is always some truth to what authors include.

I did a lot of research on Russian spies and the threat to the United States. My story is fiction, yet during my research I learned that Moscow for years has been cultivating well-placed contacts. Alan Wagner would have been a prize for them. Is it possible, if not probable, that a Soviet illegal could penetrate the U.S. government? What do you think?

The title Night Moves is from a Bob Seger song. Why did I use it? It's a good song and Laquita had fun with the lyrics. And I had a blast writing Laquita's character.

Enjoy.

www.ingramcontent.com/pod-product-compliance
Lightning Source LLC
Chambersburg PA
CBHW022241020726
47496CB00004B/1013